FROM THE TOWER WINDOW
of MY BOOKHOUSE

Edited by
Olive Beaupré Miller

CHICAGO
The BOOKHOUSE for CHILDREN
PUBLISHERS

LIST OF STORIES AND POEMS

LIST OF STORIES AND POEMS

LIST OF STORIES AND POEMS

LIST OF STORIES AND POEMS

The BUGLE SONG
Alfred Tennyson

The Splendour falls on Castle walls
And snowy Summits old in Story;
The long light shakes across the lakes,
And the wild Cataract leaps in glory.
Blow, bugle, blow, set the wild echoes flying,
Blow, bugle, answer, echoes, dying, dying, dying.

UNA AND THE RED CROSS KNIGHT
Retold from Book I of The Faerie Queene
Edmund Spenser

NOW Glo-ri-an'a was that greatest, most glorious Queen of Faeryland and she did keep her feast for twelve days every year, during which time, as the manner then was, she might not refuse to any man or woman what boon soever he desired of her. On a certain year it happened in the beginning of the feast that there presented himself before the throne of Gloriana a tall, clownish young man, who, falling before the Queen, made request that he might have the achievement of any adventure which during that feast should happen. That being granted, he rested him on the floor, unfit through his rusticity for a better place.

Soon after, entered a fair lady in mourning weeds, riding on a white ass, with a dwarf behind her leading a warlike steed and bearing the arms and spear of a knight. The Lady, falling before the Queen of Faeries, complained that her father and mother, an ancient King and Queen, had been by an huge dragon many years shut up in a brazen castle, who thence suffered them not to issue; and therefore besought the Faery Queen to assign her some one of her knights to take on him the deliverance of these twain. Presently that clownish person, upstarting, desired that adventure; whereat the Queen much wondering, and the Lady much gainsaying, yet he earnestly importuned his desire. In the end the Lady told him that unless that armor which she brought would serve him, he could not succeed in that enterprise; for that armor was of such a sort as would fit him only who had great courage and faith, great uprightness and truth; which armor being forthwith put upon the youth with due furnitures thereunto, he seemed the goodliest man in all that company and was well liked of the Lady.

And eftsoons, taking on him knighthood, and mounting on

that strange courser, he went forth with her on that adventure. Right faithful and true he proved, and on his breast and shield he wore a blood-red cross in dear remembrance of his dying Lord and to make known to all the world that he would give battle only in the cause of righteousness and truth.

Beside the Red Cross Knight, upon her snow white ass, Una, the lovely Lady, rode, her face well veiled from sight beneath her wimple, and over all her garments she wore a long black robe, as one who inwardly did mourn for thinking ever on that ancient King and Queen, her father and mother, shut up in prison by so foul a beast. After her, on a line, she led a snow-white lamb. As pure and innocent as that same lamb the Lady Una was and all her heart was full of virtue, loyalty and truth. Far away behind the Lady and the Knight the dwarf did lag, bearing fair Una's bag of needments at his back.

As they passed thus along the road the sky was sudden overcast and down upon the path there poured a hideous storm of rain. Enforced to seek some covert, they espied a grove not far away,

> *Whose lofty trees, yclad with summer's pride,*
> *Did spread so broad that heaven's light did hide,*
> *Not pierceable with power of any star.*
> *And all within were paths and alleys wide,*
> *With footing worn, and leading inward far;*
> *Fair harbor that them seems, so in they entered are.*

Safe enshrouded from the tempest beneath those sheltering boughs they journeyed forward, led on with pleasures, and joying to hear the sweet harmony of birds that sang within that wood as though no tempest raged without. Thus with delight they beguiled the way until the storm was overblown, when they weened to return out of that wood, and once more take the highway they late had quitted. But now when they looked about to find that path down which they had so carelessly strayed, lo! it was nowhere to be seen. So far within the wood they had pursued their way that they knew not how they might come out.

To and fro they wandered, but so many paths there were, so many turnings, that they were ever in doubt which one to take and found their wits grown quite confused. They only wandered round and round and deeper in. At last, resolved to fare straight forward along a certain road until at least it brought them somewhere, they chose the one that seemed beaten most bare by travellers' feet, and journeyed on.

But, though they knew it not, alas! this was the Wandering Wood, wherein many a traveller had lost himself and never found a way out more. For in a hollow cave amid the dismallest density of those dark trees, there lurked a monster vile, who was the sovereign of that whole domain and hated God and man. By wicked spells of that same evil creature, all who entered in that wood were made to take the false for true, the true for false, and so to wander in a circle hopelessly. Ever her joy was to bewilder men, mislead them into sore mistakes and errors grievous to be borne.

At length the Knight, with Una and the dwarf, came sudden on that hideous, darksome cave, which Una had no sooner seen, than she, whose clear vision ever grasped the truth, knew this for the Wandering Wood and that cave for the fearsome dwelling place of that foul breeder of bewilderment. Then, all too late, she would fain have had her Knight draw back and not rush forth to call the monster from its lair; and eke the dwarf, thrilled on a sudden with the weird unspoken horror of the place, quoth shrilly, "Fly! fly! This is no place for living men!"

But the youthful Knight, full of fire and hardihood, could not be stayed for aught. Dismounting from his horse, he hurried to the darksome entrance of that cave and looked within. His glistening armor made a little glooming light, by which he saw the ugly monster plain, half like a serpent, loathsome, filthy, foul. And as she lay upon the dirty ground, her huge tail overspreading all the den and pointed with a deadly sting, a thousand young ones all about her lay, of sundry shapes, each more

14

FROM THE TOWER WINDOW

ill-favored than the rest. No sooner did the light flash on them from the Knight's bright suit of mail than they in terror crept into their mother's mouth and sudden all were gone. Then that old serpent, hurling her hideous tail about, rushed forth out of her den afraid. There seeing one all armed in mail, she sought to turn back again, for creature, as she was, of foul deceits, deluding all, she ever hated light and lurked in darkness where none might see her plain. But when the valiant Knight perceived what she would do, he leapt fierce as a lion on his foe. With his stout blade he boldly stayed her from returning to the dark, forced her to face him squarely and do battle in the light. Lifting his powerful arm, he struck a stroke that glanced her head and spent its stunning weight upon her shoulder. Much daunted by the blow, she gathered herself around, reared fiercely up and leapt upon his shield, winding her tail all suddenly about his body round and round, till hand and foot she had him so embound he could not move a muscle, even as when, once yielded to her deceits, she wraps a man in endless train of errors and mistakes and holds him altogether in power of her delusions.

The Lady Una, seeing her Knight in so sore strait, cried out:

"Now, now, Sir Knight, show what ye be,
Add faith unto your force and be not faint;
Strangle her, else she sure will strangle thee!"

In answer to her bidding, the Knight knit all his force together, got one hand free and seized the monster's throat with grip so strong that soon she was constrained to loose her wicked bands. Therewith she spewed out of her filthy mouth a flood of poison, horrible and black, filled full of frogs and toads and serpents small, her loathly offspring, foul and blind and black as ink. These, swarming all about, climbed up the good Knight's legs and sore encumbered him, but had no power to do him harm. Thus, ill-bestead, he suddenly resolved to win, and struck at the serpent with such force as one would never dream was possible to man, so that he clove her hateful head from off her body. A stream of coal black blood gushed forth, whereon the serpent's scattered brood, finding no more their wonted refuge in her mouth, plunged in that coal black stream and perished all. Thus the good Knight's evil foes did slay themselves.

His lady, seeing from afar all that was come to pass, rode up in haste to greet the victor with rejoicings of his victory. Then he mounted once again upon his steed, and with his lady and the dwarf, chose that path leading from the hateful place which was beaten most plain. Nor would he again let aught tempt him to turn aside into a byway. That one path he followed steadfastly until it brought him well without the Wandering Wood.

Now as they three journeyed forward once more in search of adventure, it chanced at length that they came upon an aged man in long black robes, with bare feet and a beard all hoary gray. Sober he seemed, and simple, wise and good, and ever as he walked he bent his eyes full humbly on the ground, and seemed to pray. The Red Cross Knight saluted him and asked him if he knew of any strange exploit that needed to be done. The old man answered that he knew little of such matters, so far did he live in his quiet cell away from all worldly cares and strife. Yet had he heard of a strange wild man that wasted all the countryside and never had been mastered and he could lead the Knight to him if sobeit he desired. Then did Una in her simple wisdom show her Knight 'twere wiser that he rest that night after his sore affray and seek new adventure with the morrow. The Hermit bade them pass the night with him and so in his company they rode on to his home.

A little, lowly Hermitage it was,
Down in a dale, hard by a forest's side,
Far from resort of people that did pass
In travel to and fro.   A little wide
There was an holy Chapel edified,
Wherein the Hermit duly wont to say
His holy things each morn and eventide.
Thereby a crystal stream did gently play,
Which from a sacred fountain wellèd forth alway.

In this simple, rustic retreat Una and the Knight found no great entertainment, but rest was their feast and the evening passed in fair discourse, for that old man had store of pleasing words as smooth as glass. But when the drooping night came creeping on them fast, and weariness weighed down their lids, the Hermit led his guests each unto his several lodging and bestowed them there to sleep. Then to his study and magic books he went and sudden threw aside the holy Hermit's guise. For this old man, enwrapped in false hypocrisy and well appearing words, was none other than Ar-chi-ma'go, a magician foul, enemy to Gloriana, Queen of Faeryland, and foe of all things good. He knew full well upon what worthy quest the Red Cross Knight was bound, and hating above all things else to see good accomplished in the world, was well resolved to bring that quest to naught by means of wicked spells and foul enchantments that he knew. So long as all true holiness within the heart of that good knight in closest union stood with that sage wisdom and straightforward truth that shone from Una, none could withstand these two. Together they were invincible; apart, each could but wander uselessly without the other, and so Archimago was resolved first in his wicked plan to separate the two.

From out his book he chose a few most horrible words, whereof

17

he framed weird verses dread that spoke reproachful shame of highest God, the Lord of life and light. With these and other devilish spells, like terrible, he called out of the darkness legions of wicked sprites, the which like little flies fluttered about his head, waiting to do what service he should bid. Of these he chose the falsest two, those fittest for to forge true-seeming lies.

One he sent to Mor'pheus, god of sleep, to fetch an evil dream. The other with charms and hidden arts he made into a lady fair, most like to lovely Una. The first wicked sprite returned from the bowels of the earth where Morpheus dwelt and brought the evil dream. Coming where the Knight in slumber lay, he placed the dream upon his hardy head, and straightway the Knight did dream that Una, whom he loved and honored above all maids of earth and whose true love for him he trusted quite, was false to him, left to him the dangers of her quest, yet loved another in secret. Still was the Red Cross Knight too true and brave a man to let himself be troubled by a dream. Again and once again that troublous dream essayed to make him rise and leave the lovely maid. He held his ground and nought could make him disbelieve the pure and loyal faith of Una. When Archimago saw this labor all in vain, he took that same wicked sprite who brought the dream from Morpheus, and made him by his arts appear a knight. To him he brought the sprite whom he had cloaked with Una's form. Then with well feigned faithfulness, he ran and woke his guest and bade him rise and come to see his lady Una holding secret converse in the darkness with another knight. All in amaze the Red Cross Knight sprang up and, sword in hand, went with the aged man. When he beheld those sprites—one so like to Una—in close and hidden com-

FROM THE TOWER WINDOW

munion with a stranger knight, then indeed at last he held her truth for false and held the false for true. Within himself he struggled long until the evening star had spent its lamp in highest sky. Then, sore tormented, he donned his armor to ride away, and that long-faithful dwarf, hearing his tale, deemed also that his mistress must be false, and so these two fled from the Hermitage, and left fair Una deserted and alone.

Now when the rosy fingered morning rose from her saffron bed to spread her purple robe through dewy air, and the rising sun touched the high hills with light, then Una rose from the couch where she had slept and sought her Knight and dwarf. Alas! She found them gone, herself deserted quite, and knew no reason why she should thus have been left in such a woful case. Weeping full sore, she set forth from the Hermitage alone upon her snow-white ass and rode after the Red Cross Knight with all the speed that her slow beast could make. All was in vain. The Knight's light-footed steed, pricked by his master's wrath, had borne him so far away that following him was fruitless. Yet would faithful Una never rest. Every hill and dale, each wood and plain she searched, sore grieved that he whom she loved best had left her so ungently all alone.

Meantime the Red Cross Knight pursued his way, flying before his thoughts and led astray by grief. And so it chanced he met at last a faithless Saracen, all armed, and bearing a great shield whereon in gayest letters was writ his name, *Sansfoy.* He was a man full large of limb and by his bearing it was easy to be seen he had no care for God or man. Beside him a fair companion rode, a goodly lady clad in scarlet cloth embroidered with gold and pearls. Upon her head she wore a splendid headdress and her palfrey was all decked with tinsel, while her bridle rang with little golden bells.

When this lady saw the Red Cross Knight advance, she bade her companion address him to the fray. Forward the faithless Sansfoy sprang. The other couched his spear and rode likewise forward. Soon they two met in furious shock; the horses staggered and gave back a pace. Then both knights seized their swords and fell upon each other furiously so that the flashing fire flew from their stricken shields as from an anvil beat with hammers.

"Curse on that cross," quoth then the Saracen, "that keeps thee from all harm!" Therewith he smote a blow so fearful on his enemy's crest that in the breast of that good Knight the natural courage awoke, and such a blow he struck upon the Saracen's helmet in return, it cut clean through the steel and clove his head.

The lady, seeing her champion fall dead like the old ruins of a broken tower, fled from the place in fright, but the good Red Cross Knight rode after her, bidding the dwarf to come behind and bear the Saracen's shield as sign of victory. When the lady saw the victor-knight close on her heels, she turned and cried as though in great humility, "Mercy! Have mercy, Sir!" The humbleness of one clad in such rich garments did much enmove the stout heroic heart of that good Red Cross Knight. He gently bade the dame put fear away and tell him who she was, and who he was that had been her champion. Melting in tears the wretched woman told a tale all false, how that she was Fi-des'sa, the faithful maid, much wronged by fortune and fallen by force into the hands of the proud Sans-foy', one of three wicked brothers that were called Sans-foy', the faithless, Sans-loy' the lawless, and Sans-joy', the joyless. The Red Cross Knight, deceived by her beauty and her simple dainty ways, held all her words for true, and bade her rest assured and journey on with him protected by his care. Yet every word she spoke was false. Not Fidessa, the faithful maid, was she, but Du-es'sa, false, a vile enchantress, ever arrayed against all good. She had not been stolen by Sansfoy, for he, the faithless man, was chosen knight of her, the faithless dame. Yet now, that all too easily the Red Cross Knight had believed the evil spoken of his innocent Una and parted from her, fair falsehood stepped into true Una's place to work the Knight much woe.

They two journeyed on together until at last, wearied of the way, they came upon a spot

> *Where grew two goodly trees, that fair did spread*
> *Their arms abroad with gray moss overcast;*
> *And their green leaves, trembling with every blast,*
> *Made a calm shadow far in compass round.*

Yet, beautiful though the spot appeared, there lurked a something sinister in the air about, so that the fearful shepherds never sate beneath those boughs, but shunned the place and never there did sound their merry oaten pipes. The good Knight, howsoever, soon as he spied the trees, thought only of the cool shade they offered, for golden Phoebus had now mounted in the heavens so high that the beams hurled from the fiery wheels of his fair chariot were scorching hot, and the Knight's new dame might not abide them. They therefore alighted from their steeds and sate them down beneath the trees, and the Red Cross Knight, now altogether deceived by this false dame, thought her the fairest he had ever seen. To make a garland for her dainty head, he plucked a bough from one of those two trees, whereon there trickled from the wound small drops of blood, and from the tree a human voice

cried piteously, "O spare to tear my tender side! And fly, Sir Knight! Fly far from hence, lest that befall you here that here befell to me." The good Knight's hair stood up in horror on his head at hearing words like these from out a tree and he made loud demand to know who thus addressed him in so strange a way. Then, groaning deep, the voice cried out that he was once a man, Fradubio, now a tree, and she who was to blame for his sad fate was one Duessa, a false dame. It happened in his youthful days he loved a fair and lovely maid, Fraelissa, yet fell in on his travels by chance with that Duessa, who by her wiles beguiled him so he grew confused and knew not which was fairer, she or his own maid. His own dear dame was fair as fair might be, yet ever false Duessa seemed as fair, till at the last, bewildered quite by her enchantments, he saw his true and faithful dame as foul and ugly and herself, Duessa, alone as fair. Then he in anger cast his true-love off and chose Duessa for his dame and she, Duessa, turned Fraelissa to a tree. With her, the witch, he journeyed on, beguiled by her appearance of fair innocence, until the year turned round to that one day when witches must appear in their true guise. Then did it chance Fradubio came all unexpectedly upon Duessa bathing in a stream and saw her for what she was, a filthy, foul, old hag, misshapen, monstrous and more hideous than man could have believed. Awakened thus to see the truth, he secretly resolved to free himself from her foul snares, but she, perceiving how his thought toward her had changed, through charms and magic changed him also to a tree to stand there by his true-love's side.

The Red Cross Knight was much enmoved by this unhappy tale and with fresh clay he closed the wound that he had made, yet was he blind as ever to the truth that this dame, here with him, who called herself Fidessa, was none other but that same false witch. Well she pretended that fear and sorrow and pity at this tale had made her swoon, and so drew his attention to her need, that he could think of none but her. At length he brought her to herself again, set her upon her steed and they fared forth, forgetting Fradubio and his dame.

Long they two journeyed till at last they saw rising before them a splendid castle, toward which a smooth broad highway led, whereon great troops of people travelled thitherward, yet ever those returning from the place seemed only wretched beggars that sank beside the road and lay in misery beneath the hedges.

A stately palace built of squarèd brick,
Which cunningly was without mortar laid,
Whose walls were high but nothing strong or thick,
And golden foil all over them displayed,
That purest sky with brightness they dismayed.
High lifted up were many lofty towers
And goodly galleries far overlaid,
Full of fair windows and delightful bowers,
And on the top a dial told the timely hours.
It was a goodly heap for to behold,
And spoke the praises of the workman's wit;
But full great pity that so fair a mould
Did on so weak foundation ever sit;
For on a sandy hill, that still did flit
And fall away, it mounted was full high,
That every breath of heaven shakèd it.
And all the hinder parts, that few could spy,
Were ruinous and old, but painted cunningly.

Thither Duessa bade her knight to bend his way. The gate stood open wide to all; they entered in and sought the hall where dwelt the proud, disdainful lady of the place. On every side were wondrous rich array and many people clad in splendor. High above all upon a cloth of state there rose a rich and shining throne, whereon in gorgeous royal robes that shone with gold and precious jewels, sat the fair maiden queen. So proud she was, she kept her eyes raised high as though disdaining to look so low as on the humble earth, and in her hand she held a mirror, wherein she often viewed her face, taking delight in naught so much as in gazing on her own self-loved semblance. Proud Lu-ci-fer'a men called this queen, and she had usurped her throne with tyranny and wrong, for she had no rightful kingdom at all. Nor did she rule her realm with laws, but by changing policies and evil advisements of six old wizards.

An usher, full of pompous vanities, led Duessa and the Knight before proud Lucifera's feet to do her reverence, but she looked down upon them haughtily as though loath to cast her eyes so low and greeted them disdainfully, scarce bidding them to rise, nor did she vouchsafe them any other favor as a worthy Princess would have done. The knight and ladies received Duessa and her champion well, for in that court Duessa was well known, yet the stout-hearted Red Cross Knight in spite of this display, thought all this glory empty and most vain and that great Princess too exceeding proud.

On a sudden the royal dame rose up from her throne and called for her coach. Then she sallied forth, her brightness all ablaze with glorious glitter, and climbed into her coach that was adorned with gold and hung with gayest garlands. But lo! what strange steeds bore that splendid chariot—six strange beasts on each of which rode one of those six evil counsellors that had governance of the realm. First rode a sluggish, lazy, idle wight in a black monk's robe, astride a slothful ass, and even as he led the way, his head was nodding and he drowsed in sleep,—an evil one to guide the van, who knew not whether he went right or wrong.

Beside this idle counsellor there rode a loathsome gluttonous fellow upon a filthy swine. His belly was swollen with fat, his eyes deep sunk in rolls of fat, but his neck was long like any crane's, that he might swallow up excessive food. In green vine leaves he was clad; he wore an ivy garland on his head and ever as he rode he ate and drank—not fit to be the counsellor of a queen, whose mind was drowned in meat and drink.

The third counsellor in a fair green gown, rode upon a bearded goat, and man and beast were both wall-eyed, a sign of raging jealousy. The fourth, thin, spare and clad in threadbare coat, a greedy miser was, who sate astride a camel loaded down with gold. Two iron coffers hung on either side, full of precious metal, and in his lap an heap of coins he counted over. Of his ill-gotten treasure he made a god and unto hell had sold himself for money, so that he knew not right from wrong. Through daily care to get and nightly fear to lose what he had got, he led a wretched life, nor had of his possessions any joy at all.

Next him the fifth counsellor found place, an envious man and

full of malice, upon a ravenous wolf. His kirtle of discolored cloth was painted full of eyes and in his bosom secretly he bore a hateful snake with mortal sting. Still as he went he gnashed his teeth to see those heaps of treasure his companion bore.

Last of all, the sixth counsellor, a fierce and vengeful wight, rode on a wrathful lion. His eyes were stern and pale as ashes, yet hurled forth now and then most fiery sparks. One hand was ever on his dagger, trembling with hasty rage, the other brandished high aloft a burning brand, and all his clothes were torn to rags as though he had been oft in furious frays.

Such were proud Lucifera's counsellors, all impotent and eaten with disease, and on the wagon beam rode Satan with a smarting whip, lashing on the lazy team. So they marched forth in goodly sort to take solace of the open air and in fresh flowery fields to sport, but ever about them a foggy mist hung over all the land, and here and there beneath their feet lay skulls and bones of men that in that land had come to grief. Next to the Queen herself Duessa rode, but that good Knight would not ride so nigh, withdrawing himself from their vain joy, whose fellowship seemed all unfit for such as he.

So, having solaced themselves a space with pleasaunce of the

FROM THE TOWER WINDOW

fields, they returned to that proud palace and there found a knight arrived, bearing a heathenish shield whereon in scarlet letters was writ *Sansjoy*. When this knight espied the shield of his slain brother, Sansfoy, borne by the dwarf, page to the Red Cross Knight, he leapt upon that dwarf, desiring vengeance for his brother's death and snatched away the shield. But the Red Cross Knight, disdaining to have torn from him that which he had won in fair and open fight, fiercely encountered Sansjoy and rescued what the Paynim stole. Thereon they began to clash their arms in furious battle till the queen commanded them to refrain and on the following day contend in equal lists that one should by his skill defeat the other and there prove his right to the disputed shield.

That night was passed by all in joy and jollity, feasting and courting both in bower and hall. But when the darksome night had drawn her coal black curtain over brightest sky and all were gone to rest, up rose Duessa from her couch and secretly sought out Sansjoy to tell him how she sorrowed for Sansfoy, and hoped that he, Sansjoy, would overthrow the Red Cross Knight and take her for his dame, since next to his dear brother, Sansfoy, she loved Sansjoy—

"Wherever yet I be," she cried, "my secret aid shall follow you."

At last the golden oriental gate
Of greatest heaven gan to open fair,
And Phoebus, fresh as bridegroom to his mate,
Came dancing forth, shaking his dewy hair,
And hurled his glistening beams through gloomy air.

Which when the wakeful Knight perceived, he started up and donned his sun-bright arms and went forth to the affray.

With royal pomp and majesty Queen Lucifera was brought unto the lists and placed under a stately canopy. Opposite, Duessa sat, and on a tree the shield was hung.

A shrilling trumpet sounded from on high and bade the knights address themselves to battle. The Saracen was stout and wondrous strong and his blows fell like iron hammers. Yet was it true that after blood and vengeance the Saracen did strive, while he, the Red Cross Knight, fought not for vengeance but for honor only. So the one strove for wrong, the other for the right. At length Sansjoy struck the Knight so hard a blow upon his crest he reeled as if to fall, and false Duessa cried in joy, "Thine are the shield, Sansjoy, the shield and I and all!"

But when the Knight heard his lady's voice, he woke from his swooning dream, and with quickening faith, struck Sansjoy such a stroke as forced him to his knees, and had he not so stooped, he would have been cloven in twain. But when the goodly Knight raised up his sword to strike again, lo! a darksome cloud fell as by magic over that vile Paynim and hid him from his foe, so that the Red Cross Knight struck out for him in vain. Then Duessa, pretending joy that he had conquered, came swiftly to him and begged him as in all good faith to seek no further vengeance on his fallen foe, but spare his life.

Thereat the trumpets sounded victory, and heralds, running, brought unto the Red Cross Knight the shield. But all in secret, Duessa wept until the eventide. When the shining lamps were lit in the high heavens, she rose and went unto that wounded

28

heathen knight, and ministered unto him and bore him off to safety. Returning thence unto the Palace of Pride, she found the Red Cross Knight had fled away, for on a day his wary dwarf had come upon a dungeon in that proud palace where wretched creatures languished, who had come unto the place in haughty hopes to share the pride of that proud princess, yet were by her cast off at last into such sad misery; and the Knight, learning thereof, and in no mind to be in peril of like fate, took his flight ere dawn by a secret little postern gate, that he might be safe from power of such a tyrant.

Finding him gone, Duessa, loath to let so good a knight escape from out her clutches, made after him without delay.

All this long time, fair Una, pure and full of guileless truth, still wandered solitary o'er the earth, deserted and alone. Through woods and wastes, riding her slow-moving ass, she sought her knight in vain. At last one day, quite wearied out, she alighted from her beast and laid her dainty limbs to rest in secret shadow, far from all men's sight.

> *Her angel face*
> *As the great eye of heaven shinèd bright,*
> *And made a sunshine in the shady place.*

It chanced as she lay thus at rest, a ramping lion rushed forth from out the thickest wood. As soon as ever he spied that tender maid, he bore down upon her greedily with gaping mouth in search of prey. But when he was drawn nigh, and couched to spring, all suddenly he stayed himself.

> *"O, how can beauty master the most strong,*
> *And simple truth subdue avenging wrong!"*

Dazzled by such fair loveliness and pure innocence, he quite forgot his furious rage, fell at the maiden's feet and licked her lily hands with fawning tongue. When Una marked how this great, raging beast, Lord of all the forest, yielded up his pride before her seeming weakness in proud submission to her woman-

hood, her heart gan melt in great compassion, and with pure tenderness she stroked his shaggy hide. So when she sate her snowy palfrey once again and sorrowfully set forth upon her search, the lion would not leave her desolate, but journeyed by her side, as a strong guard and faithful comrade. Whene'er she slept, he kept both watch and ward, and when she waked, he waited diligently to do her will with humble service. From her fair eyes he took commandment and ever by her looks guessed her desires. So, long she travelled thus through deserts wide, and aye in weal or woe, in good or ill, the lion was her comrade, fending off from her full many an ugly foe,—bold courage guarding gentle innocence and truth.

At length it chanced the wicked Archimago, having by his arts taken upon himself the form and outward appearance of the Red Cross Knight, set out to seek fair Una and once more have power of her. He came upon her as she journeyed with the lion, but so well he had disguised himself that she mistook him for her long lost knight and joyed full innocently to find him once again. With fair words and good reasons for his desertion, he set her thoughts at rest and so they journeyed on together, in gladsome talk one to another.

But as they journeyed, there bore down on them in sudden charge, Sansloy, third brother of Sansfoy, who seeing here the arms of that same Red Cross Knight who slew Sansfoy, thought to take vengeance for the deed. Full loath was Archimago, faint with fear, to meet the charge, yet by presence of the lady, he was pricked thereto and in battle array did meet Sansloy, the lawless one, only to fall sore wounded by the Paynim's spear. Then had

FROM THE TOWER WINDOW

that been the end of Archimago had not Sansloy unlaced his helmet and to his surprise disclosed to Una and himself that here was no good Red Cross Knight, but that hoary-headed miscreant, Archimago, whom he knew right well. Leaving the foul enchanter on the ground, he turned him then to seize fair Una, plucking her full rudely from her ass. Seeing his sovereign dame so roughly handled, that true and loyal servant, her lion, sprang fiercely on Sansloy. Alas! strong as he was, he could not stand against the Paynim's sword. The Saracen with lifted blade pierced through that brave and faithful heart. The lion fell. Then Sansloy seized the helpless maid, and bore her, will or nill, away upon his courser, her prayers availing naught. So was poor Una, of every aid bereft, helpless in the power of that wild, lawless knight.

Naught could she do but scream full piteously. What wit of mortal wight could now devise to save a maid in such a case? But eternal Providence, far passing thought, can make a way where none appears. A wondrous way it wrought to save this lady true.

Far away within the wood a troop of Fauns and Sa'tyrs were

dancing in a round, while old Syl-va'nus, who was their king, slept in a shady arbor. Gay, rustic, wild-wood folk were these, with horns upon their foreheads and shaggy legs of goats. It chanced that in their sylvan games they heard the maiden's piteous shrieks. In haste they forsook their rural merriment and ran towards the spot whence came that cry. And when the raging Saracen, Sansloy, beheld that rude, misshapen, monstrous rabble rushing toward him, whose like he never saw before, he durst not bide, but got upon his ready steed and flew away.

Then Fauns and Satyrs all stood still, astonished at the beauty and the woful plight of Una, who still afrighted at their appearance, dared neither speak nor move. Perceiving her fear, those rustic folk, moved with pity of her helpless state and wonder at her beauty, gan first to smile in gentleness, and then fell prostrate at her feet. She, guessing thus their friendly, humble hearts, felt reassured and let them lead her thence. Joyous as birds they went, dancing, shouting, singing, strewing her way with green branches and crowning her with garlands.

> *And all the way their merry pipes they sound,*
> *That all the woods with doubled echo ring;*
> *And with their hornèd feet do wear the ground,*
> *Leaping like wanton kids in pleasant Spring.*
> *So towards old Syl-va'nus they her bring.*

An old man was Sylvanus, girdled with ivy leaves, and leaning on a cypress staff. When he beheld that lady Una, the flower of faith and beauty, he scarce could think her mortal, but deemed she must be some goddess. Then came the wood-nymphs, too, fair Ham-a-dry'ads, to behold her grace, and from the brooks and streams, the Nai'ads, water nymphs. Henceforth the Satyrs thought none but Una fair, and, wondering at her beauty, ere long they fell upon their knees and worshipped her as Goddess of the Wood. So was fair Una safe among that kindly savage race, yet could she take no joy at finding herself the image of idolatries, but plied her gentle wit to teach those simple creatures truth and show them how vain it was to look on her as source of sovereign power divine. Her words were useless. When she did at last restrain their bootless zeal from worshipping her, they only bowed before her ass and made of it a God.

Now while she stayed among these friendly folk, fair Una's wits were ever at work devising how she might escape and once more set forth to seek the Red Cross Knight. It fortuned at length a noble, warlike knight, Sir Satyrane by name, came to that wood, for he was kin to those strange woodland creatures. Won by her heavenly wisdom and fair beauty, he, on a day when all the Satyrs were gone to do their service to Sylvanus, helped her, once more mounted on her ass, to make her way beyond the forest and to the highway once again. Yet they were but a short way on their journey when once more they came upon Sansloy, and Sir Satyrane at once fell into combat with that Paynim. Full furiously they fought, but when Sansloy perceived the lovely Una whom he late had in his power, he left the conflict to pursue her. Sir Satyrane stayed his flight and drew him once more into conflict, but Una, sore afraid of that unruly Saracen, fled far away.

Meantime the Red Cross Knight fleeing from the Palace of Pride had been once more overtaken by Duessa false, still calling herself Fidessa, faithful and true. She found him dismounted in a green and shady glade beside a bubbling fountain.

He feeds upon the cooling shade and bayes
His sweaty forehead in the breathing wind,
Which through the trembling leaves full gently plays,
Wherein the cheerful birds of sundry kind,
Do chant sweet music to delight his mind,
The witch approaching gan him fairly greet,
And with reproach of carelessness unkind,
Upbraid, for leaving her in place unmeet,
With foul words tempering fair, sour gall with honey sweet.

And so once more deluded and deceived, that foolish Red Cross Knight did take her as his lady true. Together they

lingered in that pleasant spot and dallied slothfully. But alas! as false Duessa knew full well, the fountain by which they sat, that tempted them thus to slothful dalliance, was enchanted with a spell, so that whoever drank thereof lost all his strength and manly force. And yet she never stayed the Knight with telling what she knew when he lay down upon the brink and drank of that clear, crystal stream.

Eftsoons his manly force began to fail and he grew weak as water. Yet still he gave no hint of what he felt but paid his foolish idle court to false Duessa. At length he heard loud bellowing through the wood, a fearful sound, and ere he could don his armor or seize his shield, a monstrous enemy came stalking in his sight, a hideous giant, horrible, and so high, he seemed to threat the very skies. Beneath his feet the ground did groan for dread and in his hand he bore as weapon a shaggy oak, torn by its root, from out the earth. Or-go'gli-o was the giant's name. His mother was the earth, his father Ae'o-lus, that blustering God of Wind, and all puffed up with blustering boastfulness he seemed.

When he espied the Knight he gan advance with dreadful fury and huge force, who, hopeless, hapless, sought to array himself to battle; yet all disarmed and eke so faint he was, he scarce could stand. The Giant's stroke fell merciless and had the Knight not leapt aside, he had been surely slain, but though he was not stricken of the blow, yet did the very wind it raised have power to overthrow the Knight and hurl him senseless to the ground. There he did lie at mercy of the giant, but false Duessa begged Orgoglio that he spare his enemy's life, make him his slave, and take her for his dame. Orgoglio, thereunto agreeing, took up the senseless Knight, bore him to his castle and cast him into

FROM THE TOWER WINDOW

his deepest dungeon. Duessa, he took, even as she begged, to be his dame. He gave her gold and purple to wear and for to make her more dreaded of men, he gave her as steed to ride upon a monstrous beast with seven great heads, its scales of iron and brass and its foul tail so long that it could reach the very stars, cast those sacred things to earth and trample them beneath its feet.

The woful dwarf when thus he saw his master fall, took up his arms, his silver shield and spear, and fled away. He had not travelled far when he did come at last on Una, fleeing from the lawless Sansloy's clutch. Much it rued the dwarf to tell his mistress all the tale of what had chanced to her dear knight, and much it rued fair Una to hear, yet still she was resolved never to stay from going forward and, alive or dead, to find her knight.

High over hills and low adown the dale,
She wandered many a wood and measured many a vale.

At last she chanced to meet a goodly knight marching by the way, together with his squire. His glittering armor shone from far and across his breast he wore a baldric shining with precious stones. His sword was buckled with a golden thong, its sheath of ivory curiously carved, its hilt of burnished gold, its handle bright with mother-of-pearl. His golden helmet was surmounted by a dragon with golden wings and over all waved high a bunch of vari-colored hairs, sprinkled with pearls and gold. His warlike shield was closely covered from sight, and might never be seen of mortal eyes, for it was made of diamond, dazzling, pure, and clean, and eke so hard that no spear point could ever pierce it. No magic arts against that shield had any power, but all that was not truly as it seemed to sight, faded and fell before it.

Whenas this knight, by name Prince Arthur, drew near to Una, he greeted her full courteously, but from her answers loath, he saw some secret sorrow troubled her. Thus with kind words and gentle he won her to tell him all her woful tale, and

35

hearing how her knight lay languishing in a dungeon in power of that huge giant, Orgoglio, he bade her be of cheer, and vowed he would not forsake her in her need until he had acquitted her captive knight. Thus they two fared forth together with the dwarf, their guide, and so they came unto Orgoglio's castle. There the noble Knight alighted from his steed and bade the lady stay to see what fortune should befall him in the fight. So with his squire he marched forward to the castle wall. But the gates they found fast shut and no warder there to guard the same, nor was there any answer to their calls. Then the squire took up a little horn that hung at his side by a rope of twisted gold with gayest tassels. It was a wondrous horn—for three miles round its blast was heard, and no enchantments or deceits could stand before it. No gate was so strong, no lock so firm and fast, but that before that piercing noise it flew wide open. Before the Giant's gate Prince Arthur's squire now blew that horn. All the castle quaked upon the ground and every door sprang open. The Giant himself, dallying with Duessa in a flowery bower, was sore dismayed, and came rushing forth, Duessa following, high mounted on her beast, whose every head did flame with fiery tongue.

When the Knight beheld Orgoglio approach, he flew fiercely toward him. Orgoglio, lifting up his dreadful club all armed with ragged snubs and knots, thought to have slain him with a single blow. But wary Arthur leapt aside, so that the mighty mace, missing its mark, embedded itself within the earth, and while the giant bending, struggled to free the encumbered club, Prince Arthur with his shining blade, clove off his left arm, so that the Giant roared and bellowed with rage and pain. Then came Duessa rushing with her beast to the defence of Orgoglio. Ramping and threatening, all his heads like flaming brands, he came, but Arthur's squire did meet him with his single sword, and like a bulwark stood, fending that beast from off his lord. Then false Duessa, full of wrath, took from a golden cup which she still bore for working magic arts, a secret poison that she sprinkled on the squire, so that his strength and courage fled and he fell helpless to the ground. When the good Knight saw his beloved squire fallen at mercy of that cruel beast, he left Orgoglio and turned to save the squire. With his stout blade he smote one of the monster's heads and clove it to the teeth. Thereat the creature ramped and scourged the empty air with his long tail, and would have cast his rider from his back, had not the Giant come to succor her. With all the force of his two arms now joined in one, he raised his club and smote Prince Arthur on the shield, so that he hurled him to the ground. Yet in his fall the veil that covered his blazing shield was rent asunder and lo! such dazzling brightness smote the Giant's eyes, he let his arm fall down that he had raised to slay the Knight, and likewise that foul beast was blinded by the light and tumbled to the earth to yield him conquered. In answer to Duessa's screams, Orgoglio sought once more to raise his mace. It was in vain. In the flashing beams of that bright shield he had no power to strike nor to defend. And so Prince Arthur slew him. But when the breath was gone from out that blustering, boastful Giant, his huge great body shrunk and shrivelled up and vanished quite and of that monstrous mass was nothing left, save like an empty bladder.

When false Duessa saw her champion fall, she sought to flee away, but that light-footed squire gave chase and brought her back as prisoner to his lord. The lovely Una, having seen all this from far, came hurrying up to greet the victor. Then Prince Arthur entered without delay into the castle. None but a doting old porter, most ignorant and infirm, stood there to bar his passage; and so he passed him by and made his way through all the length and breadth of that rich castle. Nowhere did he find the Red Cross Knight until he came at last unto a fast locked door, wherein there was a little grate. Through this, he called to know if there was any living wight within. Therewith a hollow, dreary voice made answer with a piteous plaint. Then, filled with pity and with horror, the champion rent asunder the iron door with furious force. He entered in, but found no floor beneath his feet. Instead, he dimly saw a deep descent as dark as hell, from whence a baneful smell breathed forth. But neither darkness, filthy bands, nor noisome smells could withhold Arthur from his purpose pure. With constant zeal and boldest courage, he found the means to lift the prisoner up, although the thighs of that good Red Cross Knight had grown so feeble from long durance in that hole, that he could little help himself. His sad, dull eyes, deep sunk in hollow pits, could scarce endure the light. His cheeks were thin and bare, his arms rawboned, that once had been so strong. Yet when his lady saw him once again, whom she had sought so long, despite his dolorous look, she flew to him with hasty joy and cried: "Welcome, my lord, in weal or woe!" Then Arthur showed him where his foe lay dead and that false dame stood conquered, who had been the root of all his woes.

"Now is it in your power," quoth he, "to let her live or die."

"It were a shame," quoth Una, "to avenge ourselves on one so weak. Slay her not, but despoil her of her robe and let her fly."

So they stripped the witch of all her royal robes and ornaments and jewels and when she stood despoiled of all this outward show, their eyes beheld her truly as she was, a loathly, wrinkled hag, ill-favored, fearsome, old, her gums all toothless and her head quite bald. She had a fox's tail and monstrous feet, one like an eagle's claw, one like a bear.

> *"Such then," said Una, "as she seemeth here,*
> *Such is the face of falsehood; such the sight*
> *Of foul Duessa, when her borrowed light*
> *Is laid away, and counterfeiting known."*

Thus unmasked, and knowing all men saw her as she was, the false witch fled to the wilderness to hide her shame in rocks and caves. But Una and the two knights abode for a space within the castle to rest themselves. Then those two knights swore true friendship to one another, and parted to go their several ways.

Una and her knight set forth once more to rescue Una's parents from the dragon. Yet soon adown the long, white road they saw come galloping toward them fast, a knight, disheveled, pale, his hair on end for horror. About his neck he wore a hempen rope and seemed to flee as if in terror of some fearsome thing. Scarce could the Red Cross Knight prevail on him to stay and tell his tale. He fled, he said, from an old man who had met him and a friend of his returning from a quest whereon they had not met success, and that old man had spoken first with honey words, but later subtly, cunningly. He argued that they two were good for naught, could never be happy, nor honorable, nor good, could never achieve aught great or useful in the world and so might better die. Ere they knew it, the wily words of that old man had filled their souls with such despair, that one of these poor knights had seized a knife and slain himself, while he, who fled with staring eyes, had even had the rope about his neck to hang himself, when from the evil enchantment of those words he broke away and fled.

When the Red Cross Knight heard this, he cried that he would meet this sorcerer that gave out poison of despair. Ere long they came upon a dark and doleful cave beneath a craggy cliff, whereon there sat a ghastly owl. All about stood sticks and stumps of trees without a single leaf, whereon many a man had hanged himself for sheer despair. Within the cave they found a cursed man in rags, sitting upon the ground full sadly musing. His long gray locks hung all disordered over his rounded shoulders and hid his face, but through that

wild entanglement, his eyes shown deadly dull. Beside him lay the knight who had slain himself with a knife for hearkening to the old man's words. The Red Cross Knight rushed forward full of zeal to do that old man punishment for such a deed, but, or ever he laid his hand upon him, the old man began to speak. With evil charmed words he brought before the Knight all the evils of this mortal life, fear, sickness, death, old age, loss, labor, sorrow, strife, pain, hunger, cold, till one had thought his deed was good to lead the knight now dead to take a way out of such miseries. Subtly, too, he began to mind the Red Cross Knight of all the sins that he himself had done, how he had deserted his faithful dame for a false witch, and lived in pride and sloth, all barren of deeds of good, and to suggest that he who had wandered so far from righteousness could never find the Way of Right again, nor ever dare to hope for aught but everlasting wrath from God. So might he better die, far better die. Ere he knew it, those poisoned words of despair took full possession of the Knight's bewildered mind. He saw himself hopeless altogether and worthy of naught but everlasting punishment by righteous sentence of the Almighty's law. So when that hideous old man made offer to him of a dagger, he seized it from him and lifted his hand to plunge it in his breast. But Una, clear-eyed and undeceived, snatched from his hand the dagger. "Fie, fie, faint-hearted Knight!" she cried. "Is this the way thou doest battle with the dragon, and savest my imprisoned parents? Let not vain words and devilish thought dismay thy constant spirit! Why shouldst thou despair, who can most confidently expect a share in heavenly mercies? Though God be just, yet eke with Him is grace to save men from their wickedness. Arise, Sir Knight! Arise and leave this cursed place."

So up he rose and straightway mounted on his steed and rode away, leaving that old man so enraged by his escape, he took a rope and hanged himself. But, alas! Many a man that boasts of mighty prowess and strength of arms, and many victories in battle

40

fields, all so soon as he doth come to fight against spiritual foes, doth yield and like a coward fly. So this Red Cross Knight, who stood against the fiercest outward foes, but lamely fought despair within his heart, and Una, perceiving this, how weak in body and soul he was, led him to an ancient house not far away, that there he might recover, through companionship and aid of those pure men and women who dwelt therein. The home was governed by wisdom of a matron named Dame Celia, whose only joy was doing deeds of good, and she had three most lovely daughters, Fi-del'i-a, Sper-an'za, and Cha-ris'sa.

Arrived at her door, Una and her knight found it fast locked, but they had no sooner knocked than it was opened and with all due gentleness and humility a porter bade them enter. Low they had to bend their heads to pass, for straight and narrow was the way which he did show, but when they had once entered through the narrow gate, they saw a broad and spacious court, plain and yet pleasant to be walked in. A squire of rare courtesy, yet simple and sincere withal, led them to the lady of the place. She had been at her prayers, but rose and greeted Una joyously, for well she knew the true and faithful maid. Then in her modest guise she bade the Red Cross Knight warm welcome, and entertained them both with all sweet courtesies, so that nought was wanting to show her bounteous and wise.

Thus as they began to talk together, lo! two most goodly virgins came into the hall, linked arm in arm in lovely wise, and walking with even steps at equal pace. Their countenances were demure and full of modest grace. The eldest of these, Fidelia, was arrayed all in lily white, and her face like crystal shone with sunny beams, while all about her head gleamed rays of light. In her right hand she bore a golden cup filled to the brim with water and wine, and in her left hand she held a book both signed and sealed with blood. Her younger sister, Speranza, was clad in blue, and on her arm a silver anchor lay, whereon she leaned, and her steadfast glance was ever upward nor swerved any other way.

These greeted Una and her knight full kindly, and when their weary limbs had been that night refreshed with kindly sleep, Una besought Fidelia to teach the Red Cross Knight her heavenly wisdom that she might save him from his dark despair. And so the shining maid opened his dull eyes that he might see and understand, and disclosed unto him every whit that in her sacred book was writ with words of blood, which none could read except she taught them. She taught him of God, of grace, of justice, of free will, and how by faith men find the power to move great mountains from their places and eke the power to part the mighty floods in twain and walk dry-shod through midst of seas.

In little space the Knight was much improved through teaching of that maid of light, yet by her very light did he see but more clearly all the wickedness of his past ways, which grieved him still so sore he wished to die. Then came Speranza with her steadfast upward gaze, and gave him hope, sweet hope and firm assurance that it was not even now too late to redeem the evil he had done with works of good. Yet must he, ere his heart could quite be purged and healed, repent in sackcloth and in ashes for his sins. But when through repentance, prayer and patience, he was once more whole, and ready to go forth into the world again, fair Una led him to Dame Celia's third and loveliest daughter, Charissa, a woman in her freshest age, of wondrous beauty and rare bounty, whose like it was not easy to find on earth. Upon her head she wore a tire of gold adorned with richest gems, and she was sitting in an ivory chair, a pair of turtle doves perched by her side. About her arms, her breast, her chair there hung a multitude of babes, playing their sports that filled her full of joy to see, and ever she fed these little ones while they were weak and young and cared for them in tenderest wise till they were of an age to keep themselves, when then she thrust them forth. This bounteous, tender-beaming dame the Knight and Una greeted, and bade her

FROM THE TOWER WINDOW

joy of all her happy brood.

Then Una besought the fair Charissa to school her Knight in those sweet virtues she knew best. Charissa was right joyous of this request and in her gracious tender way made known unto the Knight the joys of heavenly charity and all things good.

Of love, and righteousness and well to done,
And wrath and hatred warily to shun.

And when she had filled that good knight full of love, benevolence and good will, she called to her an aged Dame, known for her great mercy unto men, and bade her guide his weak and faltering steps along the straight and narrow path that leads to heaven. The goodly matron bore him by the hand along a way made rough by thorns and ragged briars, but ever she removed obstructions from his path that nothing might stay his advance, and ever, that he might not go astray, she held him fast and bore him up as firmly as a careful nurse her child. They rested at the Hospice of the Seven good Bead-men on their journey, that gave loving aid to all in need, and of their goodness gained much inspiration. And so they came at last to a high, high hill, both steep and eke surpassing high, atop of which a sacred Chapel stood and near thereto a little hermitage, wherein an aged man did dwell that had retired from worldly cares and spent his days and nights in devotion and deep and holy contemplation.

Of God and goodness was his meditation.

43

Hardly up to his great height could the Red Cross Knight have climbed, had not that Dame of Mercy upborne his steps and helped him on.

There they do find that goodly aged sire,
With snowy locks adown his shoulders shed;
As hoary frost with spangles doth attire
The mossy branches of an oak half dead.

Little that old man cared for meat and drink, whose mind was full of spiritual repast, and when first the Knight and dame interrupted his meditations, he was scarce willing to lay his heavenly thoughts aside, but learning from the dame how they had clomb that tedious height that he might show this knight the way to heaven, which he alone could do, he made promise to reveal that wondrous path that never leads the travellers astray, but brings them after their long labor joyous rest and endless bliss.

"First for a season, fast and pray," he said, "to purify thy spirit."

And when the Knight had fasted well and prayed, the old man led him to the highest pinnacle of his high mount of meditation.

From thence, far off, he unto him did show
A little path that was both steep and long,
Which to a goodly city led his view,
Whose walls and towers were builded high and strong,
Of pearl and precious stone, that earthly tongue
Cannot describe, nor wit of man can tell;
Too high a ditty for my simple song,
The City of the Great King, hight it well
Wherein eternal peace and happiness doth dwell.

New Jerusalem, the old man called the city's name, which God hath built for those to dwell in that are purged of sin. Which, when he saw how beautiful it was and full of light and joy, the Knight cried out, "O let me not again turn back unto the world, whose joys are all so fruitless. Let me go straight unto that city and rest there forever in peace!"

The old man shook his head, and thus addressed the Knight.

FROM THE TOWER WINDOW

"Not yet may that be. First thou must do thy work on earth. Here canst thou but have the vision of the place. Go— slay the dragon, set the maiden's parents free, and lo! men shall call thee for thy deed a Saint, St. George. When thou hast steadfastly performed all thy labors upon earth, then and not until then, doth that city there await thee. Go!"

Dazzled by the light of all that heavenly glory, the Red Cross Knight could see the earthly things but dark and dim below. Yet did he find his way back to the faithful Una. And now, well purged of sin, his heart rejoicing, full of faith and hope, of charity and mercy, and in his thoughts high visions of that life of joy to win, that life that man can never see but from the highest mount of contemplation, he bade farewell to Celia and her daughters and with Una fared forth upon his way once more.

Eftsoons they came upon the brazen tower where that old king and queen were held in durance by the dragon, and all at once they heard a hideous roaring sound and on the sunny side of a great hill they saw the monster. When the dreadful beast espied the gleam of armor, half flying and half footing, he drew near, his largeness casting much wide shadow under his huge wings. He reared his monstrous body swollen with wrath and armed with brazen scales. His long tail, wound in hundred folds, overspread his back and at its point it bore two deadly stings. His cruel jaws were sharp, exceeding steel, his horrible wide gaping jaws had three rows of iron teeth, and from his gorge came issuing a cloud of smothering smoke. His blazing eyes, like two bright shining shields, burned with wrath and sparkled living fire. The Knight couched his spear and made at him fiercely, but no lance could pierce that brazen hide. The beast turned swift about and with his tail swept horse and rider to the ground. Both lightly rose again and the Knight rained such good blows upon those brazen scales, that though no stroke could pierce, they so enraged the beast, he mounted in the air and stooping low, snatched up both horse and rider in his talons. Yet that strong knight so struggled in his grasp, he was constrained at last to drop him to the ground, where, laying three men's strength unto the stroke, the Knight then struck a blow that glanced his scaly neck but made a piercing wound beneath his wing. As raging seas are wont to roar beneath the wintry storms, so roared the monster. Flames of fire he threw forth from his nostrils. Blow after blow the good Knight dealt him, but those flames of fire piercing the good Knight's armor, singed his flesh, and in such heat, faint and full weary, worn out with toil and wounds, he could not hold his own, but was by that foul dragon's tail hurled deep into a well that lay behind his back.

Then, truly the dragon deemed the victory won, and with expanded breast and mighty clapping of his iron wings, proclaimed himself the victor. Yet all night long the faithful Una watched and prayed, and when the morning came, behold! the Red Cross Knight sprang from that well with strength renewed, for that was none other than the well of life with wondrous virtue to recover health and strength.

Amazed at sight of him, his foe, whom he had thought quite vanquished, the dragon stood in doubt. The Knight then dealt his crest so sore a blow it cleft the skull. Loud yelling, the beast

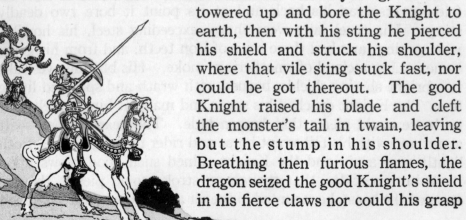

towered up and bore the Knight to earth, then with his sting he pierced his shield and struck his shoulder, where that vile sting stuck fast, nor could be got thereout. The good Knight raised his blade and cleft the monster's tail in twain, leaving but the stump in his shoulder. Breathing then furious flames, the dragon seized the good Knight's shield in his fierce claws nor could his grasp

DONN P. CRANE

46

DONN P. CRANE

be loosened, till the Knight rained on him such a storm of blows, that he loosed one claw to defend himself, when the Knight, smiting with might and main, clean hewed off the other claw. Then such a storm of fire the beast sent forth, he made the Knight retire, and wearied with the fray, the good Knight lost his footing in the mire and fell again. Thus as before the dragon left the fray deeming himself the victor. And thus as before the gentle Una spent the night in prayer.

But the Knight had fallen now beside a tree whence flowed a trickling stream of balm that gave him life and strength as had the well of life and when the morning came, once more he rose and addressed him to the battle. When a second time the dragon saw him appear whom he thought dead, he waxed dismayed. Yet still he advanced with wonted rage, opening wide his jaws to swallow him at once. Adown that gaping mouth the good Knight plunged his sword and pierced his throat, and then at last, the dragon fell. Like some huge cliff whose false foundations have been washed away by waves, he fell. He fell down dead and all the earth did groan for shock of his great fall.

Then Una came, praised God, and thanked her faithful Knight for his great victory. And from the walls of that old castle, the watchman who had seen the dragon's fall, ran to proclaim the news unto his lord, and that old King in joy, bade open wide the Castle gate which had been shut so long, and proclaimed joy and peace throughout the land. Then triumphant trumpets sounded the victory and all the people flocked to meet the victor and to do him honor. Forth came the ancient King and Queen, arrayed in antique robes and sober garments, amid a noble crowd of sages and of peers. Before them all, there marched a band of tall young men with laurel boughs; and in their wake, all dancing in a row, a crew of comely virgins came with garlands of fresh flowers and tinkling timbrels in their hands, while little children, making wanton sport with childish mirth, sang to the music of the timbrels and made music all the way. Last after all there ran in disarray the rude and rascal rabblement. So they crowned fair Una with a garland and laid their laurel boughs at the good Knight's feet, the whiles that hoary King greeted his savior with a thousand thanks and princely gifts of ivory and of gold. And after he and his good queen had held their daughter in a warm embrace, they led the two into their palace with sweet music of shawms and trumpets and of clarions, while all the people strewed the streets before them with costly robes and richest garments in their joy.

What needs it to tell more of the goodly feast that followed, in which was nothing riotous or vain? At length that good old King, when he had heard the story of the Red Cross Knight, declared that he should have his only daughter, Una, for his dame, and that fair lady who had retired into her chamber came forth again into the hall, her mourning weeds all laid away, that she had worn so long. Bright as the morning star she beamed, as fair and fresh as freshest flower in May, and she was clad in lily white, that seemed like silk and silver woven into one. And so the King gave Una to her Knight and thus in happiness did end that long and toilsome quest.

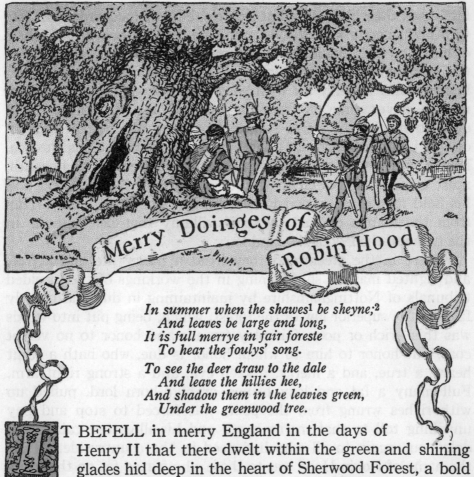

Ye Merry Doinges of Robin Hood

In summer when the shawes[1] be sheyne;[2]
And leaves be large and long,
It is full merrye in fair foreste
To hear the foulys' song.

To see the deer draw to the dale
And leave the hillies hee,
And shadow them in the leavies green,
Under the greenwood tree.

IT BEFELL in merry England in the days of Henry II that there dwelt within the green and shining glades hid deep in the heart of Sherwood Forest, a bold and sturdy outlaw of the name of Robin Hood, and with him sevenscore merry men. Strong of limb and stout of heart was Robin, and man more just and true where it deemed him truth and justice had been earned ne'er dwelt by dale or down.

Now it was full pity in those days that Justice abode not in courts of law, neither in officers of the Crown; for barons oppressed the poor, the clergy did likewise, and judges and sheriffs of the

[1]*woods.*   [2]*beautiful.*

land used their high office but as a cloak for their corruptions. He who had naught was everywhere ground down beneath the heel of him who had; Justice went limping, blind, and halt, throughout the land, and the King himself in far-off London-town, though he had many a merry tilt with barons and clergy too on this very matter, never came off from the wordy frays with the prize of even so much as a single statute to protect the sturdy yeomen of good old England in their sovereign rights. Thus Justice, beaten out as with cudgels from courts and churches and castles, must e'en go and dwell in the stout hearts of Robin Hood and his bold men of Sherwood Forest, brave yeomen all, each driven from the haunts of men by some villainy that befell them in the name of the law of the land.

There in the greenwood they lived a merry life and a free, and righted many a shortcoming in the workings of the lopsided tribunals of Nottinghamshire by maintaining in due and orderly fashion the superior law of the forest, which, being put into words was this—rich or poor, fair play for all; and honor to no velvet coat, but honor to him to whom honor is due, who hath a stout heart, a true, and a merry, a keen eye, and a strong right arm. Full many a fat and lazy bishop or high-born lord, puffed up with riches wrung from the poor, was forced to stop and pay unwilling toll to that merry band, and his ill-gotten gains were doled out again to all who had need in the countryside. Thus the name of Robin Hood was to those who waxed fat on the fruits of other men's labors a name of terror, but in every humble and honest home throughout the whole North Country a word of household blessing.

Now it chanced at this time that there dwelt in Nottingham the most inveterate, most obdurate, most stubborn enemy of Robin and his men, the right worshipful, right powerful, right proud and haughty Lord High Sheriff of Nottingham. Many a time had good Robin put a spoke in the Sheriff's wheel when he or his

FROM THE TOWER WINDOW

friends sought to fleece some innocent squire or yeoman of his goods under fair pretense of right and proper process of law, and many a merry prank had Robin and his men played on that same most worshipful Lord High Sheriff. So had the Sheriff vowed a vow by this and that and all he held most holy to catch bold Robin, have him in chains, and punished with such dire punishment as was meet for a thief and a robber. Yet in all Nottinghamshire could he find not a single man to serve his warrant of arrest on Robin. Too dearly the yeomen and hus-bandmen loved him, and a certain good tinker who but lately set forth to Sherwood Forest to obey the Sheriff's commandment, had fallen, instead, for love of the greenwood and its chief, and joined the band, alack! in place of serving his warrant, whereof that most worshipful Lord High Sheriff had suffered much scorn and laughter of men, and vowed a still more awful vow to have bold Robin Hood yet in irons!

On a bright morn in early spring up rose Robin Hood from his couch of grass and moss beneath the broad-spreading branches of an age-old oak, and plunged his hands and face in the swift-running brook that chattered in saucy ripples over the pebbles. The sun was up and came glimpsing, glancing down through the tangle of leaves overhead, flooding all the velvety greensward with sheen, and waking the cowslips and pink-tipped daisies to laugh back a morning greeting. All the air was fragrant with perfume, and merry with little birds' singing—the lark and the mavis, the cuckoo and throstle. Here a pheasant, his tail feathers tipped with gold, strutted warily down a woodland path; there, a graceful doe and a spotted fawn sprang lightly bounding into the thicket, and everywhere in that deep hidden glade, fringed round about with majestic old oaks, was the stirring joy of the new-risen day. Bold Robin, as he scoured face and neck to a dusky red, caroled lustily a gladsome matin-song.

Soon, stretching and yawning, up rose Robin Hood's men and

came likewise to make themselves clean at the brook. Ere you could say "Jack Robinson," fires were burning away in the wood, flames leaping and crackling in jolly sort, and black kettles boiling and bubbling with savory odor of breakfast a-cooking. In short order the board was spread and sevenscore men all in Lincoln green, with jaunty cock's feathers in their caps, sat merrily down to eat of venison pasty and good white bread in the free and open out-of-doors, with never a wall to shut them in and never a roof save the bright blue sky. There were that huge yokel, Little John, and George-a-green, and Will Stutely, and Gil o'the White Hand, and jolly Friar Tuck and Much, the Miller's son, and Arthur-a-bland, and that sweet singer of ballads, Allen-a-dale, and the dainty dandy, Will Scarlet, who came first to Sherwood Forest clad in scarlet and dallying with a rose, yet had such strength he could tear up a sapling by the roots, and many another right merry fellow, whose courage and mettle Robin had made occasion to prove ere ever he was in-vited to join that doughty band. One and all, those sturdy followers rendered unto Robin Hood and the just and equable law of the greenwood full and implicit obedience.

Breakfast over and done, up rose Robin Hood and quoth:

"Lith and listen, my merry men all. Today is the fair in Nottingham-town and the proud Sheriff holdeth there a splendid shooting match. Far and wide through the countryside his messengers have gone to proclaim the contest and thither will go all the best archers of the North Country. He that shooteth the best of all shall win as prize a silver arrow with head and feathers of gold. Now where be archers of greater skill than we of Sherwood Forest? To the shooting match we must go to compete for the prize."

Scarce had Robin Hood finished speaking when up rose that lumbering fellow, Little John, of all the band best loved of Robin, and second to him in command.

FROM THE TOWER WINDOW

Though he was called little, his limbs they were
*   large,*
*   And his stature was seven foot high;*
Wherever he came, men quaked at his name,
*   For soon he would make them to fly.*
With a hey down derry, derry down,
*   And a hey down, down and a down!*

"Good master," quoth Little John, "I was yestere'en at the
Blue Boar Inn on Nottingham Road and thither came a stupid
oaf, an archer of the Sheriff's, who being over full of the landlord's best home-brewed ale, made bold to whisper in mine ear
that the Sheriff laughs in his beard and saith to himself, 'Though
I get no man to go to Sherwood Forest and serve my warrant
on Robin Hood, yet by means of my shooting match will I entice
him and his men, and corner them all as easily as foxes in a hencoop.'"

"Ho! Ho!" laughed Robin Hood. "Now buske[1] ye, bowne[2] ye, my merry men all. If such be our friend the Sheriff's intent, we must then more surely than ever hie us to Nottingham-town!"

When the sun was well up in the sky, lo! sevenscore men, their Lincoln green hid beneath sundry disguises, some clad as poor peasants, some as curtal friars, some as tinkers, some as beggars, made off for Nottingham-town. By deep-hidden, tangled wild-wood paths, 'neath lofty green arches of the dusky forest, and over the stile to the highway they went; then down the long, dusty, white road edged with trim, green hedgerows and flowery meadows whence the lark soared singing into the sky; through villages with little thatched cottages, where merry lassies peeped out from the casements, up hill and down dale, till they saw looming up before them and glistening in the sun, the battlements and spires of old Nottingham-town. Here they fell in with a goodly crowd, all going in the same direction, common people afoot, knights and squires on horseback, their ladies in little carts or on gaily curvetting palfries adorned with rich trappings and merry tinkling bells. In the midst of this jolly company, Robin Hood and his men passed on into the town. Here all was hubbub and merriment. On every side were gay booths of colored canvas with floating flags and streamers, wherein cakes and barley sugar and many another good thing were for sale. Tumblers were tumbling on the green, bag-pipes screeching, lads and lassies dancing, and within a ring in the town square a wrestling match was toward. But Robin and his good fellows lingered nowhere. They pressed on out the further gate of the town to the place reserved for the archery contest.

On a green meadow before the old gray wall the range had been set, sevenscore yards and ten in length, and the rows of benches, one above another, that ran along the wall, were filled with all the gaily dressed folk of rank and wealth from the country round about, while opposite them a railing kept back the poor rabble, who

[1]prepare.   [2]make ready.

54

FROM THE TOWER WINDOW

might only stand to look on. At one end of the range, near the great target with its bull's eye and vari-colored circles, rose a lofty seat beneath a splendid canopy, where the Sheriff and his lady were to sit. Robin and his men repaired to a great tent with fluttering banners and there joined the other archers who were gathering to make ready for the contest.

At last and at last, to a mighty fanfare of trumpets that drew all eyes to the town-gate, came issuing forth the proud Sheriff and his lady, all splendidly mounted on horseback and surrounded by a bodyguard of soldiers. They bore themselves right haughtily, and both were clad in marvelous silks and velvets, ermines and swansdown, with chains of gold a-glitter with jewels. No sooner had they taken their seats than a herald sounded three blasts on his silver horn, in answer to which the archers sprang lightly forth to the range mid loud shouts of acclaim from the people.

Such shooting as was done that day had never been seen in the whole North Country before. Now the while William O'Leslie, the Sheriff's head archer, was sending his arrows into the very blue circle that surrounded the bull's eye, and leading all the rest, the Sheriff himself peered squinting about for sight of a single gleam of Lincoln green amongst the archers.

"Ho!" says he, swaggering to his lady. "Methinks that thief, Robin Hood, hath not dared to put his head into my noose. My good William O'Leslie, belike, will win the prize and throughout the countryside men shall proclaim the head archer of the Sheriff of Nottingham to be the best marksman in all the land."

Just then stepped up to the mark where the archers stood when shooting, a ragged beggar with dirty brown hair and a patch over one eye.

"Ho!" says the Sheriff's lady, "Yon rogue is as broad and sturdy as Robin Hood. Look to him well, my love."

"Now, now!" says the Sheriff in scorn, "A lady's fancy doth run away with her like a skittish mare a-start at a shadow. Canst

55

thou not see yon fellow's beard is brown where Robin's is yellow and he hath but one eye. Know well that no man could befool the Sheriff of Nottingham. Were Robin here in this crowd my sharp eye would surely find him."

The stranger took his place, fixed his gray goose shaft in his stout yew bow, took careful aim and twanged the string. Straight flew the arrow to its mark, striking the bull's eye in the very centre. A shout went up from the people, but the Sheriff himself called out in some heat: "Now to it, William O'Leslie. Split the beg- gar's shaft with as good a shot. No better archers live than serve the Sheriff of Notting-ham."

But the gray-haired old archer shook his head and flung his quiver back on his shoulder with a mighty rattling of arrows.

"Nay," quoth he. "Against such a marksman I will not shoot. I did not ween in all England there dwelt such an one save only Robin Hood of Sherwood Forest."

"Now, Robin Hood, Robin Hood, Robin Hood," quoth the Sheriff in hot anger. "Who says to me always Robin Hood? There be plenty of better marksmen than he, and the cowardly knave hath not even dared show his face here in my presence this day! Come hither, fellow." The ragged beggar approached to the foot of the Sheriff's splendid seat. "Here take the prize. Thou hast won it fairly enough," and he handed to him the gold and silver arrow. "Now hark! I bid thee join my service. With me thou shalt be well paid and thou shalt eat and drink of the best. There is no good man in any line but I call to my standard, and since thou hast defeated William O'Leslie, thou must be my man. Marry, I rejoice that thou art a better marks-man than that coward Robin Hood, and one day we will show him full fair the worth of the Sheriff of Nottingham's men!"

The beggar looked up with a twinkle in his one sorry eye.

"I will serve thee, O Sheriff, as thou deservest!" said he.

"Here, fellow," the Sheriff turned to a huge lumbering rogue dressed in the uniform of his guards, who had appeared suddenly beside the beggar. "Take this man off to the barracks for my archers. Henceforth he shall dwell midst the very best marksmen in all Nottinghamshire."

The great lumbering fellow looked up not only with a twinkle but with a prodigious wink of one jolly eye.

"Aye, aye," says he, "I will take him off to the spot where dwell the very best marksmen in all Nottinghamshire!" And he put his huge hand on the beggar's shoulder and the two disappeared in the crowd.

At sunset in the depths of Sherwood Forest, Robin Hood emerged amidst much laugher from the tatters of the beggar, while Little John cast off the garments of the soldier.

"Now, now," says Little John, "I have kept my promise and brought thee where dwell the best marksmen in Nottinghamshire."

"Aye," quoth Robin, "but I have still to keep my promise of serving that rascally Sheriff as he hath deserved. I like not that he called Robin a coward for fearing to come to the match!"

That night the Sheriff sat dining in the great hall of his house in Nottingham-town, with gay candles a-flicker on the long table before him, sending dancing shadows to play hide and seek over the splendid dishes and adown the long rows of men-at-arms and household servants that sat below the Sheriff and his lady at meat. All men talked of the shooting.

"By my troth!" cried the Sheriff. "I did not reckon that knave Robin so great a coward as to fear to come to the contest. Let that good fellow who won the prize come hither to me."

But lo! as men looked among the archers at the foot of the table, the prize-winner was nowhere to be seen, nor neither that huge lumbering fellow in the uniform of the guard who had led him from the field. And even as the Sheriff's attendants sought for the two, hiss! a gray goose shaft shot in at the window, just missing the Sheriff's nose and so startling him that he came near tumbling out of his chair. Recovering himself with much dignity, the Sheriff picked up the arrow from among the dishes before him. Tied to it was a little scroll. Unrolling the same, he read:

> *May heaven bless thy grace this day,*
> *Say all in sweet Sherwood;*
> *For thou didst give the prize away*
> *To merry Robin Hood.*

With an angry snarl the Sheriff crushed the scroll in his hand.

II

Now of a moonlight night soon after this Robin Hood and his men sat about in a circle in their greenwood glade, and out from a lodge built of rustic boughs in a fragrant bower on the edge of the wood came the minstrel Allen-a-dale with his fair bride Ellen, whom Robin and his men had saved of late from being by her father wedded perforce to a rich and rascally baron. And Allen and Ellen took their seats on the soft grass in the circle and Allen sang to his silver-toned harp, plaintiff, mournful, sweet old ballads of England. *"There lived a lass in yonder dale, and down in yonder glen, O!"* and many another such. Then rose Robin Hood from the circle and wandered away alone down a moonlit trail through the wildwood. It was a fairy night of witching elfin splendor; the glistening silver moonbeams went coquetting with the shadows, peeping from a thicket saucily but to flit away upon the instant as if in dainty mischief, calling delicately to mind sweet fancies of the Fairy Queen, Titania, and Oberon, the Elfin King, and jolly Robin Goodfellow, and all those other sprightly elfin folk who once danced their merry round within the moonlit greenwood. All the beauty of the night went warm to Robin's heart, but ah! good Robin was lonely. He, too, loved a lassie, a bonny, bonny lassie, yet would he never coax her from her safe and sheltered home to share his wild life in the forest. Thinking on his dear Maid Marian, he strode slowly down the path.

So he came at last to a narrow little bridge over a babbling brook where he had first met Little John and made occasion to challenge him months agone to a contest. There Little John had proved himself so skillful at play of quarter staves as to pitch bold Robin into the brook, wherefore bold Robin had invited him to join his band and ever after dearly loved him. As he stood by this memorable spot, he saw come tripping down the very same road over which Little John had come, a jaunty page with a feather in his cap.

"Now, by my faith," said Robin to himself, "though I see yon fellow none too clearly, his look speaks overmuch of courts and baron's halls to be to my liking. Still he hath broad shoulders and a confident gait. I will e'en try his mettle. He cannot seem more lackadaisical than did Will Scarlet, when first I tested him, yet is no better man in all my band. The youth looks worth a trial of his courage."

So saying, he tied a kerchief over his face below his eyes and stepped out roughly on the bridge.

"Ho, fellow!" he cried in a hoarse threatening voice. "Stop! Thou hast gone far enough over this road! None passes here save as I will! Face thee round about and march whence thou didst come, or marry! I have here by my side a jolly good blade that plays a right merry tune!"

"Nay now, good sir," quoth the page full courteously. "I mean mischief to no man, but I have business beyond. Pray let me pass."

"Pass thou shalt not, saving it be that I pass thee over my head on the point of my sword!"

"Pass then I will," cried the page. "My humor is to do no man harm, yet in sooth my business lieth across this bridge!" And he drew his sword and came forward right sturdily. Now it was a merry sight to see how that sweet youth fell to with his blade, how bold were the strokes he struck, and how stoutly he stood to his own defence. It was click and clack and thwack and whack, and a scratch here for Robin and a scratch there for the page, nor had either one whit the better of the other, till at last good Robin dropped his rough and threatening voice and cried once more in his own fair tone: "Enough, courteous stranger! Put up thy sword. I have tried thee and found thee, in spite of thy clothes, a right sturdy fellow. Come, join my band and range the greenwood with me. 'Tis Robin Hood bids thee!" And he pulled the kerchief from off his face. Then Lauk-a-mercy-on-us! the youth dropped his sword and crumpled up in a heap on the ground at Robin Hood's feet, and all his bold strength was vanished and he began to cry in a weak, little voice:

"O Robin, my Robin, so near had I wounded thee. Dost thou not know me—thine own Maid Marian? I ran away from the town where the scoundrel Sheriff sought to force me to wed his cross-eyed son and am come all the way to the greenwood just to seek thee, my Robin, O!"

"Marian! My lassie!" Good Robin could scarce believe his ears and he raised up the maiden and held her face to the moonlight, and there sure enough, but with hair cut short like a boy's, was his own dear lassie. "Marian, mine only dear!"

"Come to dwell with thee, Robin, in the greenwood forever!"

Then Robin's heart leaped like a doe for joy and he took his true-love by the hand and led her back to fair Ellen's bower in the greenwood glade, and fair Ellen received Maid Marian with gladness and gave her shelter for the night. When the morrow was come, Maid Marian and Robin were wedded by Friar Tuck in the great cathedral of the arching wildwood, and lo! what a day it was for joy. For of all merry days in the forest, it was the first of May, the festival of the coming of Spring, when lads and

lassies from the villages came out a-maying, and burst from the woodland paths into the greenwood glade, their arms filled with flowers, their heads decked with wreaths and over all the fragrance of the white hawthorn bloom. And they romped singing and laughing about Maid Marian and made her Queen of the May. They set her up high on a throne of green boughs and crowned her with garlands. Then Robin Hood's men cut down the tallest and straightest birch tree in the wood and set it up for a Maypole in the centre of the glade, while the maidens wreathed it about with flowers, and the lads fastened to its top long streamers of gay-colored ribbons with little tinkling bells. When all was done, came merry dancers, some in rag-tags of costumes, some in simple clothes of the countryside, and lads and lassies each seized a ribbon and fell a-dancing—twisting, turning, weaving gracefully in and out, singing a merry song, and plaiting the long colored ribbons. With quips and sports and pranks the day was filled. There were contests at quarter-staves and wrestling, and Robin Hood's men set up the willow wands hung with garlands that served them for targets, and held a shooting match, the victor being crowned with a wreath by Maid Marian, Queen of the May. A stately feast closed the gladsome day, then lads and lassies went back once more to the little thatched cots in the villages. But Maid Marian was come in sooth to stay in the greenwood, and Robin Hood built for her a lodge in a flowery bower, and there, sharing Robin's life, she continued to dwell.

III

It happened all on a Summer's day that Robin Hood leaned him against a tree and said to Little John: "Today is a fair day, Little John, and I make mine avow that I will not dine till thou hast brought me here some bold baron, knight or squire to be my guest. Take then thy good bow in thine hand and let Much and Will Scarlet wend with thee up to Watling Street to fetch me a guest. See ye do no party any harm that hath a woman in it, nor no husbandman, nor no yeoman, nor no knight nor squire that will be a good fellow, but, purse-proud baron or pompous earl, bring willy-nilly to me. If my guest be over-rich he shall pay for the feast; if poor, I will share my goods with him."

"Marry, good Master," quoth Little John, "Right glad I am to obey." And off he went with Much and Will Scarlet, till through highways and byways they came out at last on that fine old road that was builded in days long gone by the Romans and hight Watling Street. They looked east, they looked west and no man did they see, but by and by came a knight a-riding past, all dreary of semblance and poorly clad, one foot hanging carelessly out of his stirrup.

Little John advanced full courteously and fell upon his knee.

"Welcome to the greenwood, gentle Knight," said he. "My master hath waited fasting these three long hours to dine with thee."

"Who is thy master?" quoth then the knight.

"My master is Robin Hood."

"Ah, a good yeoman," said the knight. "Of him I have heard much good and so doth it please me to dine with him."

Yet ever as they went their way, the tears rolled down the good Knight's cheeks, and a sorry man he seemed. Unto Robin Hood's lodge they led him and Robin right courteously bade him welcome. Then fairly answered the gentle Knight:

"God save thee, good Robin, and all thy fair many. I am called Sir Richard of the Lea, and right gladly will be thy guest at meat."

So the board was laid on the trestles and the cloth was spread. Robin and his guest washed together and wiped together and sat them down with Maid Marian and the rest to a sumptuous wildwood dinner.

"Such a dinner have I not had in many a year," quoth the Knight, when he had eaten his fill.

"If it hath pleased thee, sir Knight," said Robin Hood, "then

I prithee pay for the feast ere thou takest leave. Surely thou knowest it was never the custom that a yeoman should pay for a knight."

"I take thy meaning," said the Knight gravely, "yet have I naught in my coffers to offer thee."

"Nay now," quoth Robin Hood, "too many of thine order these days keep no troth with Truth. Speak honestly."

"I have no more but ten shillings," said the Knight full sorrowfully, "for sooth as I you say!"

"If that be true," cried Robin, "then I will not have of thee one penny. And if thou have need of any more, more shall I lend thee."

The good Knight opened his purse and shook out ten shillings.

"Alack! the more pity," quoth Robin Hood. "But how didst thou come in so sorry a case? Thou must have been a poor husbandman and let thy lands go to rack and ruin if thou hast no more but ten shillings to thy name."

"Nay, by my faith," cried Sir Richard. "No such fault is mine. My son, for that there are those who hate him high in favor at court, was cast into prison on a paltry charge, and to get him free I must e'en pay a ransom of four hundred pounds. 'Twas more ready money than I had on the spot, nor would those friends who supped of my best in happier days give me aid of any kind or sort. So was there naught for me to do but go to the rich Lord of Ely for aid. A wicked hard bargain the baron drove with my need. For the loan of four hundred pounds I must pledge him all my fair lands and castle worth three score times the same, nor would he leave me the money to work my land and earn once more wherewithal to repay him. Now the day of settlement is come and here am I on my way to tell him I cannot pay him a penny. What will he do but seize my castle and lands from me. O, alas and alack! I grieve not so much for myself but for my dear wife and tender babes that will have nowhere to lay their heads."

Now for ruth of this sad tale wept Maid Marian and Little John and Will Scarlet, and many another stout fellow there. And Maid Marian whispered somewhat in Robin Hood's ear. Then cried Robin Hood loudly: "Sir Richard of the Lea, if no other man be thy friend in need, then is Robin Hood that man." And he rose up from the board. "Little John, go to my treasure and tell me out four hundred pounds. Will Scarlet, measure me three yards each of our stoutest green and scarlet cloth, and bring all here to me."

Off went Little John and Will Scarlet, but that large hearted fellow, Little John, made such pretense of stupidity at counting, that for four hundred pounds he told out eight and twenty score, while Will Scarlet boldly measured yards by his good six-foot bow.

"If our measure be over-full," said Little John, "yet what better alms can there be than to help a poor gentle knight that is fallen in poverty?"

So they bore all back to Robin Hood, who gave it unto Sir Richard upon the spot, and the good Knight wept for thanksgiving and joy.

"And when shall I come to repay thee?" said he.

"This day twelvemonth," said Robin, "here under this trystel tree."

Meantime in the dining hall of Ely Castle, where blue and crimson light from the high arched windows streamed over the richly spread table, sat the baron at meat, and with him, all in splendid robes, his friend, the Lord High Sheriff of Nottingham.

"Now, friend Sheriff," says the baron in the Sheriff's ear,

"but an Sir Richard come this very day to pay me, he shall be dispossessed and all his fair lands fall to me. A good bargain I made—to purchase for four hundred pounds an estate that will yield me full four hundred pounds every year. Now, remember, I paid thee thy good fat fee to see that the case proceeds all in fair process of law. I count on thee to uphold me."

"Aye," said the Sheriff. "But I prithee do not forget when betwixt us both Sir Richard is fleeced in due and proper fashion, that thou owest me still another fat fee, for my services at the shearing."

Now even as they spoke, Sir Richard was announced and, clad in his poor sorry garments, into the great room he came.

"Do gladly, my lord," says he. "I am come to keep my day."

The only greeting the baron gave, was, "Hast thou brought my pay?"

"Never a penny," said the knight and the baron's eyes sparkled full covetously. "For now," thought he, "those fair lands must surely be mine."

"Then why didst thou come if not to pay?" cried he hoarsely.

"My lord, to beg thee that thou give me longer time."

"Not a single day more," quoth the baron. "Forfeit be all thy lands, this hour."

"Now, good Sheriff," cried Sir Richard, turning him to that proud and haughty officer of the law. "I beg thee be my friend and declare my lands may not be forfeit for a paltry four hundred pounds."

"Nay," quoth the Sheriff sternly. "I hold with my Lord of Ely. Thy lands are forfeit this day and hour."

"But my fair wife and tender babes, where shall they lay their heads?"

"That concerns us not," cried the Sheriff. "Thy wife is *thy* wife. Do thou find where she may lay her head. My lord, what wilt thou give this fellow if he signs the release at once?"

"A hundred pound," said the baron, "and not a penny more."

"Take then the hundred pounds, Sir Knight, if thou hast any wits to thine own advantage," quoth the Sheriff, "and let the matter end."

"Nay, now!" cried the Knight, on a sudden loosing all the bold spirit pent within. "Though ye gave me a thousand pounds, yet would I never sign the release!" He strode to a round table standing hard by, and shook out of a bag that he held in his hand an even four hundred pound. "Have here thy gold, my lord!" he cried, "which that thou lentest me! Hadst thou been courteous at my coming, I should have rewarded thee. But thou hast bespoke me villainously, so shalt thou have not a penny more but thy four hundred pound. Now have I repaid thy loan on the very day and shall have my lands again for aught that thou canst do!" And off he strode, merrily whistling, to tell his fair lady at home how their castle and lands were free.

But that purse-proud baron he left behind had no more stomach for bite or sup, for all his royal fare.

"Give me back my gold that I paid thee in fee to get me these lands," he began to roar in the Sheriff's ear.

"Never a penny will I give back! Thou wert at fault to bring a fox instead of a sheep to the shearing!"

And so they fell to at quarrel and squabble and snitch and snatch, but in such worthy care of their skins as to have naught more sharp than their tongues for weapons.

It chanced on a day soon after that Robin sent Little John and Much, the Miller's son, and Will Scarlet once again to Watling Street to bring back a guest for dinner, and whom do they see come ambling down the long white road but a pompous baron, splendidly clad, and that right worshipful Sir, The Lord High Sheriff himself, and with them two and fifty wight young men for guard.

"Now, my Lord of Ely," the Sheriff was saying, "thou doest

well to go to London and start proceedings at law against that same fellow, Sir Richard, that of late rode his high horse with thee. I ween thou wilt still find some legal means to strip him of his lands, and in London the name of the Sheriff of Nottingham is well known at court. Thou wilt still find it to thy vantage to have such an one to thy friend."

"So, so," growled the Lord of Ely, "little hast thou vantaged me thus far!"

Even at that moment, stepped forth Little John, Much, and Will Scarlet, stopped the cavalcade, and said right courteously:

"Worshipful sirs, our master bids thee dine with him."

"Master! Who may thy master be?" quoth the Lord of Ely.

"My master is Robin Hood," saith Little John so gently as once he spake to Sir Richard.

"Robin Hood!" cried the Sheriff. "He is a thief and a robber!"

"Robin Hood!" cried the Lord of Ely. "Of him heard I never good!" and the two started up their horses and bade their young men ride on. Then blew Little John a blast on his silver horn, and all the wood along the road seemed alive with men in Lincoln green, with bows strung and arrows aimed at the cavalcade. Went up a cry from the two and fifty wight young men that guarded the baron and sheriff, and marry! they all turned tail and fled, leaving their masters a-snivelling and cursing fast in Little John's hands. So Little John and his men blindfolded the two and led them off to Robin Hood's lodge.

"Do gladly, right worshipful sirs," says Robin Hood full courteously, "I bid you welcome to dinner!"

"Do gladly, right worshipful sir," stammered the Sheriff. "We thank thee but are not an-hungered!"

Yet was there naught for the Sheriff and baron to do but wash with Robin and wipe with Robin and set themselves down with him to the board, while their knees knocked together for fear. Right sumptuous was the dinner, but little stomach to food had the guests, and when the Sheriff saw at head of the table as Robin's own lady that same bonny lass, Maid Marian, whom, willy nilly, he had meant to wed to his son, he choked on a bitter mouthful and must e'en be pounded well on the back or ever he found his breath once more. Dinner over and done, quoth Robin in courteous wise, "Now, worshipful sirs, that you have dined of our best, I pray you pay for the feast!"

Whined the Lord of Ely, "But twenty marks have I with me!"

"And naught but two pounds with me," quoth the Sheriff.

"If this be true, good sirs," said Robin, "and you are in such poor wise, then will I take from you not one penny, for never I rob no poor man; but if you have lied, then, by my faith, will I take all you have."

And he bade Little John turn out the contents of the two men's saddle bags. Little John spread out his mantle, and from the Lord of Ely's bag poured out chinking eight hundred pounds in gold, "Wherewith he was on his way to start proceedings in London to fleece Sir Richard!" cried Little John. And from the Sheriff's bag rolled two hundred pounds, the amount of the fee in full wherewith the baron had bribed him to sanction his fleecing of Sir Richard.

"Now," quoth Robin. "Here is the quickest payment that ever yet saw I me. Look where in three days is settlement made of Sir Richard's debt to me!" And he took the money and bade Little John lead the howling Lord of Ely back once more to the road. "But thou, Sir Sheriff," says he, "hast so long been our friend that we cannot so quickly part with thee. Thou shalt stay for a twelvemonth with us in the greenwood—an outlaw we'll make of thee!"

"O, heaven have mercy," cried the Sheriff. "Now let me go, I pray!"

But they took off his satins and velvets and linens and wrapped him in Lincoln green, and there 'neath the greenwood by night he must sleep on the hard, hard ground, and by day dress the King's deer, that the outlaws shot, and scrape vegetables, and wash kettles and pots, and serve as a common scullion. At the end of a fortnight's time a sorrier man than that Sheriff ne'er dwelt by dale or down.

"Ere I lie another night here," cried he, "now, Robin, I pray thee, smite off mine head and I will forgive it thee."

"Ah," laughed bold Robin. "We aim but to teach thee to be a good outlaw."

"Now for Saint Charity," cried the Sheriff, "let me go, and I will be the best friend that ever you had."

"Then," quoth Robin sternly, "by my bright sword thou shalt swear never more to do harm to my men nor me, nor to those poor folk in the countryside whom I make it mine affair to aid."

And that Sheriff he swore him a mighty oath, never more to harm Robin nor his men nor those poor folk of the countryside. Then he took his satins and velvets and home he went, nor journeyed abroad in the greenwood again for many a long day to come.

So the year rolled round; passed the time for gathering the harvest home, when reapers sang 'neath the harvest moon, passed the time of snow-laden forest trees with crackling of fires in the greenwood huts, and roasting of crabs, and ballad and song. Came the springtime once more with singing of birds, and Sir Richard all in fine array to pay his debt 'neath the greenwood tree.

"For that I have my lands once more, thank I God, and thee," quoth he to good Robin. "This year have I prospered, and here have I brought the four hundred pounds to repay thee, and some little gifts of good bows and arrows beside."

But Robin embraced and welcomed him well and told him how that in sound justice he was already repaid on the third day after the borrowing, and that settlement being far and away above the amount of the debt, he gave good Sir Richard thereof four hundred pounds more to build up his lands and once more work them to good advantage. So Robin holp Richard of all his cares and ever they two were fast friends henceforth.

IV

Now when the King in London-town heard all that went forward in Sherwood Forest, how that there a bold outlaw dwelt who killed the King's deer that none but the King might shoot, and defied the officers of the crown and never could be captured, "By my kingdom," quoth he, "I'll take him myself!" and away with a mighty many he rode to far-off Nottingham-town. But though, day after day he lingered there in company of the Sheriff, and scoured the countryside with his men, never a sign of Robin did he see. Said an old forester then: "Liege Lord, take five of thy men alone, dress thyself up as an abbot, thy men as monks Then roam at large in the greenwood and I'll warrant thou wilt soon fall in with Robin Hood."

The King made no delay at carrying out of the plan. All in the greenwood he wandered in the garb of an abbot, with his five stout knights clad as monks. And in sooth he had not gone far when out stepped bold Robin and after his manner bade him stay and come with him to dine. And Robin blindfolded the good King and his men and led them away to the greenwood glade, in thought to relieve them there, as often he did others, of any over-abundance of this world's goods.

But the King, when he reached the greenwood glade, showed Robin a ring that bore the seal of the King himself. "I am a messenger come from the King," quoth he, "to bid thee, bold Robin, come to Nottingham to be his guest both at meat and meal."

Then cried Robin, "If such thou art, in sooth not a penny will I take from thee, for I love no man in all the world as I love my good liege lord, that doth ever tilt with barons and clergy to win fair justice for yeomanry, and for his sake, welcome art thou to the greenwood."

"If thou lovest thy liege," said the King, "methinks thou shootest a many of his deer."

"Aye, but," says Robin, "the deer in truth belong to him not—all the game of the forest should be free, free to the people who need it, and not to serve but as sport to him who needs it not. By the law of the greenwood all men have equal rights and if the King's law agree not, then must it give place to the better law of the greenwood."

Now the King said to himself that Robin's words rang true, though never would it do to admit the same. So they washed together and wiped together and dined full well, and Robin he talked of this and Robin he talked of that, and ever the good King saw how his deeds were done to right the scales of justice. When they had left the board, good Robin cried, "Now, Sir Abbot, ere thou wendest thy way, thou shalt see what life we lead in the greenwood." And he blew a blast on his silver horn and seven-score men sprang at once to his bidding.

"A seemly sight," quoth the King to himself. "By my faith, his men are more at his bidding than my men are at mine!"

They set up the willow wands hung with garlands for targets at a range of six score paces.

"By fifty paces," said the King, "that range is too far away."

"Whoso faileth to hit the rose garland," cried Robin Hood, "shall get a good buffet on his head!"

Twice Robin shot and ever he cleft the wand, and so did Gil o' the White Hand, best archer of them all, but when Little John's arrow went astray and Will Stutely's too, then Robin bade stout Will Scarlet smite them each a buffet, and such a buffet he smote that they both fell to the ground. But at the last shot, what should chance but Robin himself failed of the garland by three fingers' width and more.

"Ha! Ha!" laughed Gilbert o' the White hand. "Master, thou hast lost. Now like thy men stand forth and take thy pay."

"So must it be," quoth Robin, shamefaced, "what is good for a man is good for the master. Sir Abbot, I deliver thee mine arrow and since I have failed of my mark, I pray thee smite me well."

"I like not to smite a good yeoman," said the King, "lest I grieve him, for sorely can I smite."

"Smite on boldly," said Robin, "I give thee large leave!"

Anon, at that word, the King he folded up his sleeve and gave such a buffet to Robin that he sprawled his full length on the ground. Now Robin was sore astounded that a monk should have such an arm.

"I make mine avow to God," says he, "thou art a stalwart friar."

But as he spoke the monk's cowl fell back from the good King's head and Robin saw full in his face. Then sudden he fell on his knee. "My lord, the King of England!" he cried. "Now I know thee well." And down on their knees fell all Robin Hood's men. "Mercy then, Robin," said the King, "We are in thy power, my knights and me." "Fear naught from me," quoth Robin, "for my men and I must crave mercy, my lord, from thee."

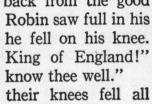

"Mercy, good Robin, shalt thou have," cried the King, full heartily. "For well have I seen 'tis sheriffs and such as they that in this day true outlaws be, and here in the heart of the greenwood dwelleth freedom and true justice. Come thou and thy men to my service, for much have I need of stout arms like thine, and stout hearts like thine and true, to do battle with such outlawry as dwelleth in the hearts of the rich and powerful. Come thou and thy men and I pledge thee my word I shall not rest till outlawed Justice shall find once more her seat in the common courts of the land!"

"I make mine avow to God," says Robin. "Thou speakest nobly. I am right glad to serve so stout a lord." And all the sevenscore men in Lincoln green hurled up their caps in air and shouted too:

"We are right glad to serve so stout a lord."

And so it befell when that the King went back to Nottingham-town, went Robin and all his men and Maid Marian and fair Ellen in his good company.

"Hast captured the outlaw then?" quoth the Sheriff in glee.

"Nay," the King made answer. "The outlaw hath captured me! At least he hath captured mine heart, and for love of his hardihood have I made him Captain of my guard. His very first duty, Sir Sheriff, shall be to take thee his prisoner and bring thee in chains to London, there to answer to me for the felonies thou hast committed in the name of the law of the land."

It was a goodly many save for the poor, sorry Sheriff that set off for London-town all on a summer's day. But as they journeyed, Robin Hood whispered in bonny Maid Marian's ear:

"Belike our life will be busy in service of the King, sweetheart; yet sometimes we will slip away for a little breathing space and hie us once more to the greenwood on a merry morn in May, there to see the deer draw to the dale and hear the small birds singing."

Under the Greenwood Tree

William Shakespeare

Under the greenwood tree,
Who loves to lie with me,
And tune his merry note
Unto the sweet bird's throat,
Come hither, come hither, come hither!
Here shall he see
No enemy
But winter and rough weather.

FROM THE TOWER WINDOW

THE EMPEROR'S NEW CLOTHES
Hans Christian Andersen

MANY years ago there was an Emperor who was so excessively fond of new clothes that he spent all his money on them. He cared nothing about his soldiers, nor for the theatre, nor for driving in the woods except for the sake of showing off his new clothes. He had a costume for every hour in the day, and instead of saying as one does about any other King or Emperor, "He is in his council chamber," here one always said, "The Emperor is in his dressing-room."

Life was very gay in the great town where he lived; hosts of strangers came to visit it every day, and among them one day two swindlers. They gave themselves out as weavers, and said that they knew how to weave the most beautiful stuffs imaginable. Not only were the colours and patterns unusually fine, but the clothes that were made of these stuffs had the peculiar quality of becoming invisible to every person who was not fit for the office he held, or if he was impossibly dull.

"Those must be splendid clothes," thought the Emperor. "By wearing them I should be able to discover which men in my kingdom are unfitted for their posts. I shall distinguish the wise men from the fools. Yes, I certainly must order some of that stuff to be woven for me."

He paid the two swindlers a lot of money in advance so that they might begin their work at once.

They did put up two looms and pretended to weave, but they had nothing whatever upon their shuttles. At the outset they asked for a quantity of the finest silk and the purest gold thread, all of which they put into their own bags while they worked away at the empty looms far into the night.

"I should like to know how those weavers are getting on with the stuff," thought the Emperor; but he felt a little queer when he reflected that anyone who was stupid or unfit for his

75

post would not be able to see it. He certainly thought that he need have no fears for himself, but still he decided he would send somebody else first to see how it was getting on. Everybody in the town knew what wonderful power the stuff possessed, and everyone was anxious to see how stupid his neighbour was.

"I will send my faithful old minister to the weavers," thought the Emperor. "He will be best able to see how the stuff looks, for he is a clever man and no one fulfills his duties better than he!"

So the good old minister went into the room where the two swindlers sat working at the empty loom.

"Heaven preserve us!" thought the old minister, opening his eyes very wide. "Why, I can't see a thing!" But he took care not to say so. Both the swindlers begged him to be good enough to step a little nearer, and asked if he did not think it a good pattern and beautiful colouring. They pointed to the empty loom, and the poor old minister stared as hard as he could but he could not see anything, for of course there was nothing to see.

"Good heavens!" thought he, "is it possible that I am a fool? I have never thought so and nobody must know it. Am I not fit for my post? It will never do to say that I cannot see the stuffs."

"Well, sir, you don't say anything about the stuff," said the one who was pretending to weave.

"Oh, it is beautiful! quite charming!" said the old minister looking through his spectacles; "this pattern and these colours! I will certainly tell the Emperor that the stuff pleases me greatly."

"We are delighted to hear you say so," said the swindlers, and then they named all the colours and described the peculiar pattern. The old minister paid great attention to what they said, so as to be able to repeat it when he got home to the Emperor.

Then the swindlers went on to demand more money, more silk, and more gold, to be able to proceed with the weaving; but they put it all into their own pockets—not a single strand was ever put into the loom, though they went on weaving as before.

The Emperor soon sent another faithful official to see how the stuff was getting on and if it would soon be ready. The same thing happened to him as to the minister; he looked and looked, but as there was only the empty loom, he could see nothing.

"Is not this a beautiful piece of stuff?" said both the swindlers, explaining the beautiful pattern which was not there to be seen.

"I know I am not a fool!" thought the man, "so it must be that I am unfit for my good post! However one must not let it appear!" So he praised the stuff he did not see, and assured them of his delight in the beautiful colours and the originality of the design. "It is absolutely charming!" he said to the Emperor. Everybody in the town was talking about the splendid stuff.

Now the Emperor thought he would like to see it while it was still on the loom. So, accompanied by a number of selected courtiers, among whom were the two faithful officials who had already seen the imaginary stuff, he went to visit the crafty impostors, who were working as hard as ever at the empty loom.

"It is magnificent!" said both the honest officials. "Only see, your Majesty, what a design! What colours!" And they pointed to the empty loom, for they thought that no doubt the others could see the stuff.

"What!" thought the Emperor; "I see nothing at all! This is terrible! Am I a fool? Am I not fit to be Emperor? Why, nothing worse could happen to me!"

"Oh, it is beautiful!" said the Emperor. "It has my highest approval!" and he nodded his satisfaction as he gazed at the empty loom. Nothing would induce him to say that he could not see anything. The whole suite gazed and gazed, but saw nothing more than all the others. However, they all exclaimed with his Majesty, "It is very beautiful!" and they advised him to wear a suit made of this wonderful cloth on the occasion of a great procession which was just about to take place.

"It is magnificent! gorgeous! excellent!" went from mouth to mouth; they were all equally delighted with it. The Emperor gave each of the rogues an order of knighthood to be worn in their buttonholes and the title of "Gentlemen weavers."

The swindlers sat up the whole night before the day on which the procession was to take place, burning sixteen candles, so that people might see how anxious they were to get the Emperor's new clothes ready. They pretended to take the stuff off the loom. They cut it out in the air with a huge pair of scissors, and they stitched away with needles without any thread in them. At last they said: "Now the Emperor's new clothes are ready!"

The Emperor, with his grandest courtiers, went to them himself, and each of the swindlers raised one arm in the air, as if he were holding something, and said: "See, these are the trousers, this is the coat, here is the mantle!"  and so on. "It is as light as a spider's web. One might think one had nothing on, but that is the very beauty of it!"

"Yes!" said all the courtiers, but they could not see anything, for there was nothing to see. "Will your imperial majesty be graciously pleased to take off your clothes," said the impostors, "so that we may put on the new ones, along here before the great mirror."

The Emperor took off all his clothes, and the impostors pretended to give him one article of dress after the other, of the new ones which they had pretended to make. They pretended to fasten something round his waist and to tie on the train, and the Emperor turned round and round in front of the mirror.

"How well his Majesty looks in the new clothes! How becoming they are!" cried all the people round. "What a design, and what colours! They are most gorgeous robes!"

"The canopy is waiting outside which is to be carried over your majesty in the procession," said the master of the ceremonies.

"Well, I am quite ready," said the Emperor. "Don't the clothes fit well?" and then he turned round again in front of the mirror, so that he should seem to be looking at his grand things.

The chamberlains who were to carry the train stooped and pretended to lift it from the ground with both hands, and they walked along with their hands in the air. They dared not let it appear that they could not see anything.

Then the Emperor walked along in the procession under the gorgeous canopy, and everybody in the streets and at the windows exclaimed, "How beautiful the Emperor's new clothes are! What a splendid train! And they fit to perfection!" Nobody would let it appear that he could see nothing, for then he would not be fit for his post, or else he was a fool.

None of the Emperor's clothes had been so successful before.

"But he has got nothing on," said a little child.

"Oh, listen to the innocent," said its father; and one person whispered to the other what the child had said. "He has nothing on. A child says he has nothing on!"

"But he has nothing on!" at last cried all the people.

The emperor writhed, for he knew it was true, but he thought, "The procession must go on now," so he held himself stiffer than ever, and the chamberlains held up the invisible train.

THE STORY OF ALFRED, THE SAXON

IN THE ninth century when England had long been split up into numerous petty Saxon kingdoms usually at war with one another, there suddenly came plundering her out of the North, piratical bands of Norsemen whom the English called Danes. These were a fierce and warlike people, pagans still, worshiping Woden in the fastnesses of the North-land, and they bore down upon the English coasts in long narrow ships with rows of shields along their sides and high curved prows carved like beasts. Ravens, dragons, dolphins, eagles, ploughed through the foaming waves and boldly poked their beaks up on the gleaming sands of Britain. Then swarms of barbarians sprang to the shore, in their savage headdresses bristling with horns, and they burned and plundered and pillaged, while the Saxons fled terror-stricken before them. At first the Danes came but to steal and made off once more when sated with spoils, but, as time passed, they began to stay and settle in various parts of England. Then the Saxons, forced by the power of their savage foes to drop their own paltry differences and unite in one body for defence, acknowledged, one and all, Ethelred, King of the West Saxons, as their over-lord. Ethelred fought right nobly against the Danes, yet even so, the wild Danish chiefs, Ing'war and Hub'ba, sons of Rag'nar Lod'brok, that gigantic scourge of the North, took Edmund, King of East England, prisoner, demanded of him that he forsake Christianity and bow his neck to their yoke, and when Edmund stoutly refused, they bound him to a tree, taunted him with cruel jests, shot at him with arrows, and finally cut off his head. Against marauders of such a sort England had need of a real hero, and as Ethelred, shortly after this event, in the year 871, died of wounds received in battle, it was well that there came to the throne in his stead, the best and wisest King who ever ruled over England—Alfred the Saxon, called Alfred the Great.

Now Alfred from a child had been a remarkable boy, sturdy, vigorous, intelligent. When he was but four years old, his father had intended making a journey to Italy, to visit the Bishop of Rome, but, being at the last moment prevented from going himself, whom did he choose from amongst all his sons, (one of whom was a young man grown) to go to the Bishop in his stead, but Alfred, the youngest, a mere babe! And off went the little fellow with a mighty escort of nurses, servants and churchmen, over the sea to Flanders in an open boat rowed by oarsmen. From Flanders he proceeded on horseback, or else perhaps swung in a pannier at the side of a horse, through the heart of Old Gaul, stopping now at some warrior noble's castle, now at a convent, now in a walled town, lingering for a time at the splendid court of Charles the Bald, King of the Western Franks, and thence on over the towering, snow-capped Alps, by the Pass of St. Bernard, into Italy. Northern Italy at that time was a place of most unsavory repute by reason of the number of bandit nobles who infested it, but straight through their midst by some means or other, went the child and his attendants, and came marching at length in safety beneath the great gates of Rome. Thus before he was five years old, Alfred had made a journey tremendously long and difficult even for men in such wild days as these.

But when this much travelled youngster was once more at home in England, in the low, rambling, draughty building where his father held court, though he knew a vast deal of the world, he was still unable to read. This fact was perhaps not remarkable in one so young, but what is truly remarkable, his older brothers, well grown youths, were likewise unacquainted with letters, so little was learning cared for in those early days in England. But it chanced one day that Alfred and his brothers came strolling together into their good mother's room, a handsome chamber with rush-strewn floor, and walls hung with splendid tapestries. Os-bur'ga, in a long, loose robe, with full, flowing sleeves, sat in a cushioned chair, with lions' heads at the arms and lions' claws at its feet. On her lap she held a volume of Saxon poetry, and her sons in boyish tenderness came crowding up around her. Since printing was as yet unknown, the book was hand-illumined; that is, richly painted with bright and beautiful letters. All the brothers cried out with admiration of the volume, and the good mother, hearing their words of praise, said smilingly, "This book is truly a treasure. I will give it to that one among you who first learns to read." Thus spurred on, little Alfred sought out a tutor without delay, and applied himself so diligently and persistently to conning of letters that he won the volume.

FROM THE TOWER WINDOW

Now when Alfred's father died, the boy, at that time grown a youth, served under his older brothers right loyally for all his superior talents, faithfully rendering unto them so long as they lived implicit obedience; but he was only three and twenty years of age, when the death of Ethelred left him King. The country at that time was well nigh panic stricken for fear of the Danes, many a Saxon thegn having deserted his home and fled over-seas to escape them, and those who were left behind were far too disorganized to offer solid resistance. Yet the courage and energy of the young King lent spirit to the disheartened people and soon he was administering many a sound rapping to the marauders. But the Danes under their fierce leader, Guth'rum, were never to be relied on. No matter how faithfully in some hour of defeat, they might swear a mighty oath never to plunder or pillage again, they broke their promise as soon as it suited their purpose. After one most signal defeat, they swore by the sacred bracelets they wore, supposedly a most binding oath to their pagan hearts, but in no time at all there they were at their old tricks as before. During this period Alfred fought not only on land, but he defeated the Danish host also in a mighty battle at sea, the first naval engagement ever won by the English, who have since made so much of their fleet.

Thus matters went till it came to the year 878, the saddest and yet most glorious of all Alfred's reign, when the Danes swarmed into Wessex in such multitudes that, as the old Saxon Chronicle says, "Mickle of the folk over sea they drove, and of the others the most deal they rode over; all but the King Alfred. He with a little band hardly fared after the woods and on the moor-fastnesses." With but a slender band of faithful followers, the young King found himself almost deserted, hiding in the marshes and wild bogs of Somersetshire. Yet as he was never puffed up or over-confident in victory, so was he never cast down in defeat, but surely, persistently, steadfastly as ever, laid his plans to drive

the foes from the land; and this from no paltry motives of personal ambition, but to save and succor the people over whom he felt that God had called him to rule, thereby entrusting to him a mission from which he could never turn. It was during this period, that he wandered one day alone to a cowherd's lonely hut, and there sought for shelter. The cowherd's wife, not knowing who he was, but taking him for a common vagabond, admitted him to a place by her hearth, whereon she was baking some little cakes. Being soon after called out of the hut on some errand or other, she roughly bade her guest watch her cakes and see that they did not burn. The King smilingly undertook to obey her, but he was working at repairing a bow and arrow, and his thoughts soon travelled far away to his harried people and their mighty need. When the cowherd's wife returned the cakes were burned to a cinder.

"Now, now, idle dog," scolded the woman, never dreaming she was scolding her liege lord and king, "couldst thou not even watch the cakes? Thou wouldst have been glad enough to *eat* them!"

Soon after this the great Danish Yarl, Hubba, appeared in Devonshire with his wonderful raven banner, that had been woven by the three daughters of Ragnar Lodbrog in a single afternoon and was believed to be enchanted. The great raven, it was said, rose up and flapped his wings before every battle wherein the Danes were to be victorious. Yet the men of Devonshire, meeting Hubba right stoutly, administered to him a sore defeat, and took from him the raven banner. The loss of this standard greatly discouraged the Danes, and news of the victory was a source of much comfort to Alfred in his hiding place.

DONN P. CRANE

About Easter time Alfred had gathered together a sufficient number of men to build a fortress of wood and earthworks on a little hillock or island in the midst of the marshes. The place was called Athelney and from here he could attack such foraging parties of Danes as roved the countryside. From here also he secretly issued forth by night in the guise of a minstrel or glee-man, and entered all alone into the camp of the enemy to learn how numerous they were, how they were armed, and what was the true temper of their leader. He was received as a strolling glee-man and ordered to sing while the Danes caroused in the very tent of Guthrum himself. There he sat alert, with eyes wide open, stoutly singing to the music of his harp, surrounded

85

by those who, had they but dreamed who he was, would have had his head on the instant.

Now when Alfred knew himself strong enough to attack the enemy, he caused a huge bonfire to be built on a hill near Athelney, where the red flames streaking the sky could be seen throughout the three lower counties, wherein dwelt the English, but were hidden by rising ground from the camp of the Danes. To him then gathered all his men, not many in numbers, but deeply devoted and determined in spirit. At Ethandun they fought a mighty battle with the Danes, putting their foes to flight and pursuing them hot on their heels to their fortress. There they maintained a siege for fourteen long days, at the end of which time, the Danes were forced to surrender. Alfred had his enemies now entirely at his mercy and might have repaid Guthrum's frequent treacheries with like cruelty, but in Alfred's heart was blent ever the most steadfast firmness with a broad mercy and tolerant charity. Preferring to win his enemy rather than annihilate him, he stipulated that he give hostages and become a Christian, whereby he had hopes that the Dane might be led more faithfully to keep the covenant which now he made, than when all the surety he gave was merely pagan oaths. Three weeks later came Guthrum with thirty men that in his host were worthiest, to Wedmore, near Athelney, where Alfred had a house. There beneath a huge wide-spreading oak, the savage, stern, old pagan and his thirty bearded warriors, all boasting descent from Woden, knelt before the cross and were baptised in the name of Jesus Christ and all the ideals for which Christianity stands, and it is evident that this act in truth wrought some change in the heart and spirit of Guthrum, since he appears never again to have broken the covenant, whereby he promised to remain within that territory allotted him in North England and forever to leave off harrying Wessex.

Now for twelve splendid years, England saw peace. The

FROM THE TOWER WINDOW

King, so bold and courageous a warrior, was anxious to lay aside the sword, and it is remarkable that one so able in war fought never a battle of conquest, but always solely in defense. And now that he had saved England from her foes, he began organizing the various activities of the land, bringing order out of chaos, and proving himself greater even in peace than in war. He had a definite system of laws worked out where no system had been before, and himself saw that these laws were administered, thus converting a country recently overrun by bandits, into one so safe and secure, that the saying was, "Treasures of gold and silver might be left lying on the streets and no man would dare to touch them." He rebuilt fortifications, monasteries, churches, and above all else, he was so interested in the advancement of education in a land where before had been naught but the darkest ignorance, that he invited to England the greatest scholars of the age and established a school in his court for the sons of Saxon nobles. He himself spent every spare moment studying and translating books from Latin into the Anglo-Saxon, thereby laying the first foundations of a real English literature. His broad and active interest in greater knowledge prompted him to send Saxon monks to the far-off Christians of India and a Saxon whaler to explore all the Northern Countries. He gave too the greatest encouragement to artisans, goldsmiths, jewelers, and the like. Recently there was found near Athelney, a beautiful jewel—the figure of a man holding a flower in each hand, wrought in colored enamel on gold under a plate of rock crystal, and on the rim are the words "Alfred mee heht gewyrcan," that is to say, "Alfred had me worked."

The keynote to all the King's unselfish persistence in doing good was his simple, sincere, devout Christianity. Always the thought of God stirred him to noble deeds and his days were filled with the joyous intelligent activity of one whose whole life was consecrated to the highest ideals of Christianity. In the service of his people, in devotion to all that was fine, he wasted never an hour. The better to gauge how time passed in a day when as yet there were no clocks, he had candles made each to burn four hours, and notched with four notches at regular intervals. Thus six of these candles told off for him the twenty-four hours of the day. And as he found his candles often flickering and burning unevenly in the draughty rooms, he next contrived a little case of wood or horn in which they could be set, which is said to have been the origin of the first lanterns.

In the last years of Alfred's reign, the Danish pirate Hastings sought to harry the land once more, but now so well ordered and strong had the Saxons grown, that Hastings was defeated with little difficulty. In the struggle with him, Alfred showed the same wonderful depth of charity that had characterized him before. Once the King captured a stronghold wherein he found the wife and children of Hastings, but he did them no harm whatever, letting them go again in safety.

In 901 Alfred died, leaving the England he had found in such panic, well organized, strong and free. Never before had the world seen a ruler who lived solely for the good of his people. Practical, energetic, patient as he was, always just and temperate, always genial and lovable, always deeply religious and profoundly intelligent, Alfred embodied as no other man has ever done, all that is best and most lovable in the English character. And so is King Alfred rightfully called Alfred the Saxon and Alfred the Great.

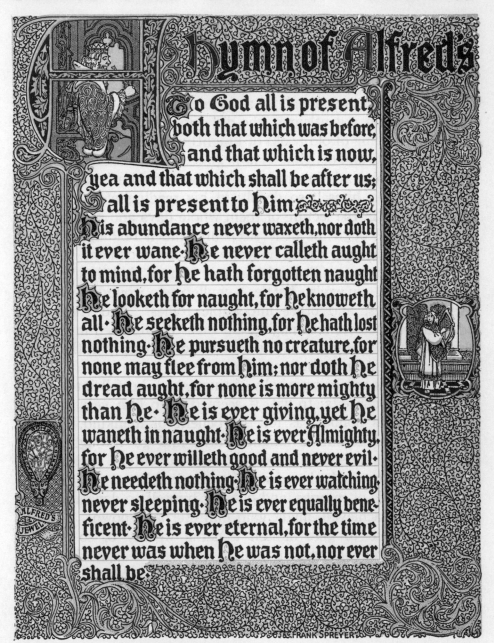

Hymn of Alfred's

To God all is present, both that which was before, and that which is now, yea and that which shall be after us; all is present to him. His abundance never waxeth, nor doth it ever wane. He never calleth aught to mind, for he hath forgotten naught. He looketh for naught, for he knoweth all. He seeketh nothing, for he hath lost nothing. He pursueth no creature, for none may flee from him; nor doth he dread aught, for none is more mighty than he. He is ever giving, yet he waneth in naught. He is ever Almighty, for he ever willeth good and never evil. He needeth nothing. He is ever watching, never sleeping. He is ever equally beneficent. He is ever eternal, for the time never was when He was not, nor ever shall be.

C. J. FRANK SPREYER

THE SURPRISING ADVENTURES OF
DON QUIXOTE OF LA MANCHA
Miguel De Cervantes
Edited by Frances Jenkins Olcott

THERE once lived, in a certain village of La Mancha in Spain, a gentleman who did apply himself wholly to the reading of old books of knighthood. And that with such gusts and delights, as he neglected the exercise of hunting; yea and the very administration of his household affairs.

He plunged himself so deeply in his reading of these books that he spent in the lecture of them whole days and nights. And in the end, through his little sleep and much reading, he dried up his brains in such sort as he lost wholly his judgment.

His fantasy was filled with those things that he read, of enchantments, quarrels, battles, challenges, wounds, wooings, loves, tempests, and other impossible follies. And these toys did so firmly possess his imagination that the dreamed inventions which he read were true, that he accounted no history in the world to be so certain and sincere as they were.

Finally, his wit being wholly extinguished, he fell into one of the strangest conceits; to wit, it seemed unto him very needful, as well for his honour, as for the benefit of mankind, that he himself should become a knight-errant, and go throughout the world, with his horse and armour, to seek adventure, and practice in person all that he had read was done by knights of yore, revenging of all kinds of injuries, and offering himself to dangers, which once happily achieved, might gain him eternal renown.

He resolved to give himself a name worthy of so great a knight as himself, and in that thought he laboured eight days; and in conclusion called himself Don Quixote of La Mancha. Then he donned certain old armour that had belonged to his great-grandfather, mounted his old lean horse, Rozinante, and sallied forth into the world to seek adventure.

FROM THE TOWER WINDOW

With him rode as his squire, one Sancho Panza, a labourer, and an honest man, but one of very shallow wit. Don Quixote had said so much to him, had persuaded him so earnestly, and had made him so large promises, that the poor fellow determined to go away with the knight, and serve him as his squire. Don Quixote bade him to dispose himself willingly, for now and then such an adventure might present itself, that in as short space as one would take up a couple of straws, an island might be won, and Sancho be left as governor thereof.

This same squire, Sancho Panza, did ride upon an ass. About the ass Don Quixote had stood a while pensive, calling to mind whether ever he had read that any knight-errant carried his squire assishly mounted; but he could not remember any authority for it. Yet, notwithstanding, he had resolved that Sancho might bring his beast, intending to dismount the first discourteous knight they met from his horse, and give it to his squire.

Don Quixote bethought himself that now he wanted nothing but a lady on whom he might bestow his service, and affection. For a knight-errant that is loveless resembles a tree that wants leaves and fruit, or a body without a soul. He bethought him of a damsel who dwelt in the next village to his manor, a young handsome wench with whom he had been some time in love, although she never knew or took notice thereof. Her he chose as the Lady of his thoughts, she being ignorant of it, and he called her Dulcinea of Toboso.

Things being thus ordered, Don Quixote and his squire rode forth into the world, and had, with some good success, many ridiculous and rare adventures, as well as some that were dreadful and never-imagined—all worthy to be recorded. All these adventures may be read in that strange book, The History of the Valorous and Witty Knight-Errant, Don Quixote of La Mancha.

Herein will be related three of his adventures, to wit: The Dreadful and Never-Imagined Adventure of the Windmills; How

Don Quixote Fought with Two Armies of Sheep and The High
Adventure and Rich Winning of the Helmet of Mambrino.

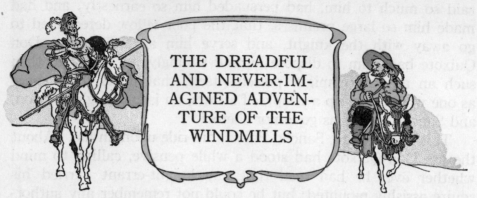

THE DREADFUL AND NEVER-IM-AGINED ADVEN-TURE OF THE WINDMILLS

THE first day that Don Quixote and his squire, Sancho Panza,
sallied forth to seek adventure, they travelled almost all day
without encountering anything worthy the recital, which made
Don Quixote fret for anger. For he desired to encounter presently some one upon whom he might make trial of his invincible
strength. Riding thus, toward evening they discovered some
thirty or forty windmills, that were in a field. And as soon as
Don Quixote espied them he said to his squire:

"Fortune doth address our affairs better than we ourselves
could desire. For behold there, friend Sancho Panza, how there
appear thirty or forty monstrous giants, with whom I mean to
fight, and deprive them of their lives, with whose spoils we will
begin to be rich. For this is a good war, and a great service unto
God, to take away so bad a seed from the face of the earth."

"What giants?" quoth Sancho Panza.

"Those that thou seest there," quoth his lord, "with the long
arms. And some there are of that race whose arms are almost
two leagues long."

"I pray you understand," quoth Sancho Panza, "that those
which appear there are no giants, but windmills. And that

which seems in them to be arms, are their sails, that, swung about by the wind, do also make the mill go."

"It seems well," quoth Don Quixote, "that thou art not yet acquainted with the matter of adventures. They are giants. And, if thou beest afraid, go aside and pray, whilst I enter into cruel and unequal battle with them."

And, saying so, he spurred his horse Rozinante, without taking heed to his Squire Sancho's cries, who called out that they were windmills that he did assault and no giants. But Don Quixote went so fully persuaded that they were giants that he neither heard his squire's outcries, nor did discern what the windmills really were, although he drew very near to them.

Then he called out to them as loud as he could:

"Fly not, ye cowards and vile creatures! for it is only one knight that assaults you."

With this the wind increased, and the mill sails began to turn about; which Don Quixote espying, said:

"Although thou movest more arms than the giant Briareus, yet thou shalt stoop to me."

And, after saying this, desiring Lady Dulcinea to succour him, he covered himself well with his buckler, and set his lance on his rest. Then he spurred on Rozinante and encountered with the first mill that was before him. As he struck his lance into the sail, the wind swung it about with such fury, that it broke his lance into shivers, carrying him and his horse after it, and finally tumbling him a good way off from it on the field in very evil plight.

Sancho Panza repaired presently to succour him as fast as his ass could drive. And when he arrived, he found his lord not able to stir, he had gotten such a crush with Rozinante.

"By my beard!" quoth Sancho, "did I not foretell unto you that you should look well what you did, for they were none other than windmills? Nor could any think otherwise, unless he had also windmills in his brains."

FROM THE TOWER WINDOW

"Peace, Sancho," quoth Don Quixote; "for matters of war are more subject than any other thing to continual change; how much more, seeing that some magician—such is the enmity he bears towards me—hath transformed these giants into mills to deprive me of the glory of the victory. But yet, in fine all his bad arts shall but little prevail against the goodness of my sword."

"God grant it as He may!" said Sancho Panza, and then he helped his master arise; and presently he mounted him on Rozinante, who was half shoulder-pitched by the rough encounter. And thus discoursing upon the adventure they followed on the way which guided towards a passage through the mountains. For there, as Don Quixote avouched, it was not possible but to find many adventures because it was a thoroughfare much frequented.

HOW DON QUIXOTE FOUGHT WITH
TWO ARMIES OF SHEEP

ONE day Don Quixote and his squire while they rode, perceived a great and thick dust to arise in the way wherein they travelled. Turning to Sancho, Don Quixote said, "This is, Sancho, the day wherein shall be manifest the good which fortune hath reserved for me. This is the day wherein the force of mine arm must be shown as much as in any other whatsoever; and in it I will do such feats as shall forever remain recorded in the books of fame. Dost thou see, Sancho, the dust which ariseth there? Know that it is caused by a mighty army and sundry and innumerable nations, which come marching there."

"If that be so," quoth Sancho, "then must there be two armies; for on this other side is raised as great a dust."

Don Quixote turned back to behold it, and seeing it was so indeed, he was marvellous glad, thinking that they were doubtless two armies, which came to fight one with another in the midst of that spacious plain.

The dust which he had seen, however, was raised by two great flocks of sheep, that came through the same field by two differ-

95

ent ways, and could not be discerned, by reason of the dust, until they were very near. Yet Don Quixote did affirm that they were two armies so earnestly that Sancho believed it, and demanded of him, "Sir, what then shall we two do?"

"What shall we do," quoth Don Quixote, "but assist the needful and weaker side? For thou shalt know, Sancho, that he who comes towards us is the great Emperor Alifamfaron, lord of the great island of Trapobana; the other, who marcheth at our back, is his enemy, the King of the Garamantes, Pentapolin of the naked arm, so called because he still entereth in battle with his right arm naked."

"I pray you, good sir," quoth Sancho, "to tell me why these two Princes hate one another so much?"

"They are enemies," replied Don Quixote, "because that this Alifamfaron is a furious pagan, and is enamoured of Pentapolin's daughter, who is a very beautiful and gracious Princess, and, moreover, a Christian. Her father refuseth to give her to the pagan King, until first he abandon Mahomet's false sect, and become a Christian Knight."

"By my beard," quoth Sancho, "Pentapolin hath reason, and I will help him all that I may."

"By doing so," quoth Don Quixote, "thou performest thy duty; for it is not requisite that one be a knight to enter into such battles."

"I do know that myself," quoth Sancho, "very well; but where shall we leave this ass in the meantime, that we may be sure to find him again after the conflict?—For I think it is not the custom to enter into battle mounted on such a beast."

"It is true," quoth Don Quixote; "that which thou mayest do is to leave him to his adventures, and care not whether he be lost or found; for we shall have so many horses, after coming out of this battle victors, that very Rozinante himself is in danger to be changed to another. But be attentive; for I mean to describe unto thee the principal knights of both the armies; and to the end thou mayest the better see and note all things, let us retire ourselves there to that little hillock, from whence both armies may easily be de- 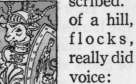 scribed."

They did so; and, standing on the top of a hill, from whence they might have seen both the flocks, Don Quixote, seeing in fancy that which he really did not see at all, began to say, with a loud voice:

"That knight which thou seest there with the yellow armour, who bears in his shield a lion, crowned, crouching at a damsel's feet, is the valorous Laurcalio, lord of the silver bridge. The other, limbed like a giant, that standeth at his right hand, is the undaunted Brandabarbaray of Boliche, lord of the three Arabias, and comes armed with a serpent's skin, bearing for his shield, as is reported, one of the gates of the temple which Samson over-threw to be revenged on his enemies.

"But turn thine eyes to this other side, and thou shalt see first of all, and in the front of this other army, the ever victor and never vanquished Timonel of Carcajona, Prince of New Biscay, who comes armed with arms parted into blue, green, white, and yellow quarters, and bears in his shield, in a field of tawny, a cat of gold, with a letter that says Miau, which is the beginning of his lady's name, which is, as the report runs, the peerless Miaulina, daughter of Duke Alfeniquen of Algarve."

And thus Don Quixote proceeded forward, naming many knights of the one and the other squadron, even as he had imagined them. And he attributed to each knight his arms, his colours, and mottoes, for he was suddenly borne away by the imagination of his wonderful distraction.

Sancho Panza stood suspended at his master's speech, and spoke not a word, but only would now and then turn his head, to see whether he could mark those knights and giants which his lord had named; and, by reason he could not discover any, he said:

"Sir, I give to the devil any man, giant, or knight, of all those you said did appear; at least I cannot discern them. Perhaps all is but enchantment, like that of the ghosts of yester-night."

"How sayst thou so?" quoth Don Quixote. "Dost not thou hear the horses neigh, the trumpets sound, and the noise of the drums?"

"I hear nothing else," said Sancho, "but the great bleating of many sheep."

And so it was, indeed; for by this time the two flocks did approach them very near.

"The fear that thou conceivest, Sancho," quoth Don Quixote, "makest thee that thou canst neither hear nor see aright; for one of the effects of fear is to trouble the senses, and make things appear otherwise than they are. And, seeing thou fearest so much, retire thyself out of the way; for I alone am sufficient to give the victory to that army which I shall assist."

And, having ended his speech, he set spurs to Rozinante, and, setting his lance in the rest, he flung down from the hillock like a thunderbolt.

Sancho cried to him as loud as he could, saying, "Return, good sir Don Quixote! for I vow unto God, that all those which you go to charge are but sheep and muttons; return, I say. Alas, that ever I was born! what madness is this? Look; for there is neither giant, nor knight, nor cats, nor arms, nor shields parted nor whole, nor pure azures nor devilish. What is it you do? Wretch that I am!"

For all this Don Quixote did not return, but rather rode, saying with a loud voice, "On, on, knights! all you that serve and march under the banners of the valorous Emperor Pentapolin of the naked arm; follow me, all of you, and you shall see how easily I will revenge him on his enemy, Alifamfaron of Trapobana."

And saying so, he entered into the midst of the flock of sheep, and began to lance them with such courage and fury as if he did in good earnest encounter his mortal enemies.

The shepherds that came with the flock cried to him to leave off; but, seeing their words took no effect, they unloosed their slings, and began to salute his pate with stones as great as one's fist. But Don Quixote made no account of their stones, and did fling up and down among the sheep, saying:

"Where art thou, proud Alifamfaron? Where art thou? Come to me; for I am but one knight alone, who desires to prove my force with thee man to man, and deprive thee of thy life, in pain of the wrong thou dost to the valiant Pentapolin."

At that instant a stone gave him such a blow on one of his sides, as did bury two of his ribs in his body. He beholding himself so ill dight, did presently believe that he was either slain

or sorely wounded. And, remembering himself of his oil-pot, which he thought to contain some magic healing liquor, set it to his mouth to drink. But ere he could take as much as he thought requisite to cure his hurts, there cometh another stone, which struck him so full upon the hand and oil-pot, as it broke it into pieces, and carried away with it besides three or four of his cheek teeth, and did moreover bruise two of his fingers.

Such was the first and the second blow, as the poor knight was constrained to fall down off his horse. And the shepherds arriving, did verily believe they had slain him; and therefore, gathering their flocks together with all speed, and carrying away their dead muttons, which were more than seven, they went away without verifying the matter any further.

Sancho remained all this while on the height, beholding his master's follies, pulling the hairs of his beard for very despair; and he cursed the hour and the moment wherein he first knew him. But seeing him overthrown to the earth, and the shepherds fled away, he came down to him, and found him in very bad plight, yet had the knight not quite lost the use of his senses.

"Sir Knight," quote Sancho, "did not I bid you return, and tell you that you went not to invade an army of men, but a flock of sheep?"

"That thief, the magician who is mine adversary," quoth Don Quixote, "can counterfeit and make men to seem such, or vanish away, as he pleaseth; for, Sancho, thou oughtest to know that it is a very easy thing for men of that kind to make us seem what they please; and this magician that persecuteth me, envying the glory which he saw I was like to acquire in this battle, hath converted the enemy's squadrons into sheep. If thou wilt not believe me, Sancho, yet do one thing for my sake, that thou mayest remove thine error, and perceive the truth which I affirm. Ride ahead on thine ass, and follow the armies fair and softly aloof, and then thou shalt see that, as soon as they are parted any distance from hence, they will turn to their first form, and, leaving to be sheep, will become men, as right and straight as I painted to thee at first. But go not now, for I have need of thy help and assistance. I pray thee, give me thy hand, and feel how many cheek teeth, or others, I lack in this right side of the upper jaw."

Sancho put in his finger, and whilst he felt him, demanded, "How many cheek teeth were you accustomed to have on this side?"

"Four," quoth he, "besides the hindermost; all of them very whole and sound."

"See well what you say, sir," quoth Sancho.

"I say four," quoth Don Quixote, "if they were not five; for I never in my life drew or lost any tooth."

"Well, then," quoth Sancho, "you have in this lower part but two teeth and a half; and in the upper neither a half, nor any; for all there is as plain as the palm of my hand."

"Unfortunate I!" quoth Don Quixote, hearing the sorrowful news that his squire told him, "for I had rather lose one of my arms, so it were not that of my sword; for, Sancho, thou must know, that a mouth without cheek teeth is like a mill without a mill-stone; and a tooth is much more to be esteemed than a diamond. But we knights-errant which profess the rigorous laws of arms are subject to all these disasters; wherefore, give the way, gentle friend; for I will follow thee what pace thou pleasest."

Talking thus they rode on their way where they thought they might find lodging, and about nightfall they perceived an inn near unto the highway wherein they travelled, which was as welcome a sight to Don Quixote as if he had seen a star that did guide him to the porch, if not to the palace, of his redemption.

OF THE HIGH ADVENTURE AND RICH WINNING
OF THE HELMET OF MAMBRINO

THE next morning as Don Quixote and his squire were riding over the plains it began to rain, and Sancho would fain have sought shelter in some near-by mill, but Don Quixote would in no wise come near one. But, turning his way on the right hand, he fell into a highway, as much beaten as that wherein they rode the day before.

Within a while after, Don Quixote espied one a-horseback, that bore on his head something that glistered like gold. And scarce had he seen him, when he turned to Sancho, and said:

"Methinks, Sancho, that there's no proverb that is not true; for they are all sentences taken out of experience itself, which is the universal mother of sciences; and especially that proverb that says: 'Where one door is shut another is opened.' I say this because, if fortune did shut yesterday the door that we searched, deceiving us in the adventure of the armies, it lays for us now wide open the door that may lead us to a better and more certain adventure, whereon, if I cannot make a good entry, the fall shall be mine. If I be not deceived, there comes one towards us that wears on his head the helmet of Mambrino, which I have made an oath to win."

"See well what you say, sir, and better what you do," quoth Sancho; "for I would not wish that this were new shepherds to batter you."

"The devil take thee for a man!" replied Don Quixote; "what difference is there betwixt a helmet and shepherds?"

"I know not," quoth Sancho, "but if I could speak as much now as I was wont, perhaps I would give you such reasons as you yourself should see how much you are deceived in that you speak."

FROM THE TOWER WINDOW

"How may I be deceived in that I say, scrupulous traitor?" demanded Don Quixote. "Tell me, seest thou not the knight which comes riding towards us on a dapple-grey horse, with a helmet of gold on his head?"

"That which I see and find out to be so," answered Sancho, "is none other than a man on a grey ass like mine own, and brings on his head something that shines."

"Why, that is Mambrino's helmet," quoth Don Quixote. "Stand aside, and leave me alone with him. Thou shalt see how, without speech to cut off delays, I will conclude this adventure, and remain with the helmet as mine own which I have so much desired."

"I will have care to stand off. But I turn again to say, that I pray God that it be a purchase of gold, and not flocks of sheep."

"I have already said unto thee not to make any more mention, no, not in thought, of sheep. For if thou dost," said Don Quixote, "I vow, I say no more, that I will batter thy soul."

Here Sancho, fearing lest his master would accomplish the vow which he had thrown out as round as a bowl, held his peace.

This, therefore, is the truth of the history of the helmet, horse and knight, which Don Quixote saw. There were near this spot two villages, the one so little as it had neither shop nor barber, but the greater was furnished with one. This barber did therefore serve the little village when they had any occasion, as it now befell. For which reason he came bringing with him a brazen basin.

And as he travelled, it by chance began to rain, so he clapped his basin on his head to save his hat from staining, because it belike was a new one. And the basin being clean scoured, glistered half a league off.

He rode on a grey ass, as Sancho said, which Don Quixote mistook for a dapple-grey steed, and the barber for a knight, and the basin for a helmet of gold. For Don Quixote did, with all his facility, apply everything which he saw to his raving

chivalry and ill-errant thoughts. And when he saw that the poor barber drew near, without settling himself to talk with him, he inrested his javelin low on the thigh, and ran with all the force Rozinante might, thinking to strike him through and through. And, drawing near unto him, without stopping his horse, he cried:

"Defend thyself, caitiff! or else render unto me willingly that which is my due by all reason."

The barber, who without fearing or surmising any such thing, saw that knight come suddenly upon him, had no other remedy, to avoid the blow of the lance, but to fall off his ass to the ground. And scarce had he touched the earth, when rising up again as light as a deer, he ran away so swiftly through the plain as the wind could scarce overtake him, leaving his basin behind him on the ground.

Don Quixote rested content, and commanded Sancho to take up the helmet; who lifting it, said:

"The basin is a good one."

Then he gave it to his lord, who presently set it on his head, turning it about every way to see whether he could get the beaver. And seeing he could not find it, he said:

"The pagan for whom this famous helmet was first forged had doubtlessly a very great head. And that which grieves me most is that this helmet lacks the beaver."

When Sancho heard him call the basin a helmet, he could not contain his laughter; but presently remembering his master's anger, he checked himself in the midst.

"Why dost thou laugh, Sancho?" demanded Don Quixote.

"I laugh," said he, "to think on the great head the pagan owner of this helmet had; for it is for all the world like a barber's basin."

FROM THE TOWER WINDOW

"Know, Sancho," quoth Don Quixote, "that this enchanted helmet did fall, by some strange accident, into some one's hands that knew not the worth thereof, who seeing it was of pure gold, without realizing what he did, melted the half, to profit himself therewithal. Then he made of the other half this, which seems a barber's basin, as thou sayest. But be it what it list, to me who knows well what it is, its change makes no matter, for I will dress it in the first town where I shall find a smith. And in the meanwhile I will wear it as I may, for something is better than nothing; seeing it may defend me from the blow of a stone."

"That's true," quoth Sancho, "if the stone be not thrown out of a sling, such as that of the battle of the two armies, when they blessed your worship's cheek teeth, and broke the bottle wherein you carried the most blessed healing potion."

"I do not much care for the loss of it, Sancho," quoth Don Quixote; "for as thou knowest, I have the recipe in memory."

"So have I likewise," quoth Sancho,—bethinking him of the night he had been made ill by it, "but if ever I make it or taste it again in my life, I pray God that here may be mine end. And

more, I never mean to thrust myself into any occasion wherein I should have need of it. For I mean, with all my five senses, to keep myself from hurting any, or being hurt.

"But, leaving this apart, what shall we do with this dapple-grey steed, that looks so like a grey ass? This beast which that barber whom you overthrew left behind? For I think the man is minded not to come back for him again, since he laid feet on the dust and made haste. But, by my beard, the grey beast is a good one!"

"I am not accustomed," quoth Don Quixote, "to ransack and spoil those whom I overcome. Nor is it the practice of chivalry to take their horses and let them go afoot; unless it befall the victor to lose in the conflict against his own; for in such a case it is lawful to take that of the vanquished as won in fair war. So, Sancho, leave that horse, or ass, or what else thou pleasest to call it; when his owner sees us departed, he will return for it."

"Truly," said Sancho, "the laws of knighthood are strait, since they extend not themselves to license the exchange of one ass for another. And I would know whether they permit at least to exchange the one harness for another?"

"In that I am not very sure," quoth Don Quixote; "and as a case of doubt (until I be better informed), I say that thou exchange them, if by chance thy need be extreme."

"So extreme," quoth Sancho, "that if they were for mine own very person, I could not need them more."

And presently, enabled by his master's license, he made the change, and set forth his beast with the harness of the barber's ass.

This being done, they broke their fast, and drank from a near-by stream. And, having by their repast cut away all melancholy, they followed on the way which Rozinante pleased to lead them, who was the depository of his master's will, and also of the ass's, who followed him always wheresoever he went, in good amity and company. Thus they returned to the highway, wherein they travelled at random, seeking new adventures.

FROM THE TOWER WINDOW

WOLFERT WEBBER, OR GOLDEN DREAMS

 *A Tale of Old New York*
Washington Irving

N THE year of grace one thousand seven hundred and blank, for I do not remember the precise date; however, it was somewhere in the early part of last century, there lived in the ancient city of the Manhattoes a worthy burgher, Wolfert Webber by name. He was descended from old Cobus Webber of the Brill in Holland, one of the original settlers, famous for introducing the cultivation of cabbages, and who came over to the province during the protectorship of Oloffe Van Kortlandt, otherwise called the Dreamer.

The field in which Cobus Webber first planted himself and his cabbages had remained ever since in the family, who continued in the same line of husbandry, with that praiseworthy perseverance for which our Dutch burghers are noted. The whole family genius, during several generations, was devoted to the study and development of this one noble vegetable; and had the portraits of this line of tranquil potentates been taken, they would have presented a row of heads marvellously resembling in shape and magnitude the vegetables over which they reigned.

The seat of government continued unchanged in the family mansion:—a Dutch-built house, with a front, or rather gable end of yellow brick, tapering to a point, with the customary iron weather-cock at the top. Everything about the building bore the air of long-settled ease and security. Flights of martins peopled the little coops nailed against its walls, and swallows built their nests under the eaves. In a bright morning in early summer, it was delectable to hear their cheerful notes, as they sported about in the pure sweet air, chirping forth, as it were, the greatness and prosperity of the Webbers.

Thus quietly and comfortably did this excellent family vegetate under the shade of a mighty button-wood tree. The city gradually spread its suburbs round their domain. Houses sprang up to interrupt their prospects. The rural lanes in the vicinity began to grow into the bustle and populousness of streets; in short, with all the habits of rustic life they began to find themselves the inhabitants of a city. Still, however, they maintained their hereditary character, and hereditary possessions, with all the tenacity of petty German princes in the midst of the empire. Wolfert was the last of the line, and succeeded to the patriarchal bench at the door, under the family tree, and swayed the sceptre of his fathers, a kind of rural potentate in the midst of the metropolis.

To share the cares and sweets of sovereignty, he had taken unto himself a helpmate, one of those notable little housewives who are always busy where there is nothing to do. Her activity, however, took one particular direction: her whole life seemed devoted to intense knitting; whether at home or abroad, walking or sitting, her needles were continually in motion. This worthy couple were blessed with one daughter, who was brought up with great tenderness and care; uncommon pains had been taken with her education, so that she could stitch in every variety of way; make all kinds of pickles and preserves, and mark her own name on a sampler. The influence of her taste was seen also in the family garden, where the ornamental began to mingle with the useful; whole rows of fiery marigolds and splendid hollyhocks bordered the cabbage-beds; and gigantic sunflowers lolled their broad jolly faces over the fences.

Thus reigned and vegetated Wolfert Webber over his paternal acres, peacefully and contentedly. Not but that, like all other sovereigns, he had his occasional cares and vexations. The growth of his native city sometimes caused him annoyance. His little territory gradually became hemmed in by streets and houses, which intercepted air and sunshine. The expenses of living doubled and trebled; but he could not double and treble the mag-

nitude of his cabbages; and the number of competitors prevented the increase of price; thus, therefore, while every one around him grew richer, Wolfert grew poorer, and he could not, for the life of him, perceive how the evil was to be remedied.

This growing care, which increased from day to day, had its gradual effect upon our worthy burgher; insomuch, that it at length implanted two or three wrinkles in his brow; things unknown before in the family of the Webbers.

Perhaps even this would not have materially disturbed the serenity of his mind, had he had only himself and his wife to care for; but there was his daughter gradually growing to maturity. How her blue eyes grew deeper and deeper, and her cherry lips redder and redder! Ah, well-a-day! could I but show her as she was then, tricked out on a Sunday morning, in the hereditary finery of the old Dutch clothes-press, of which her mother had confided to her the key. The wedding-dress of her grandmother, modernized for use, with sundry ornaments, handed down as heirlooms in the family. Her pale brown hair smoothed with buttermilk in flat waving lines on each side of her fair forehead, the chain of yellow virgin gold, that encircled her neck. Suffice it to say, Amy had attained her seventeenth year.

At this period a new visitor began to make his appearance under the roof of Wolfert Webber. This was Dirk Waldron, the only son of a poor widow, a fresh bucksome youth. This young-ster gradually became an intimate visitor of the family. He talked little, but he sat long. He filled the father's pipe when it was empty, gathered up the mother's knitting-needle, or ball of worsted when it fell to the ground; stroked the sleek coat of the tortoise-shell cat, and replenished the tea-pot for the daughter from the bright copper kettle that sang before the fire. All these quiet little offices may seem of trifling import; but they were not lost upon the Webber family. The winning youngster found marvellous favor in the eyes of the mother, and if the glances of the daughter might be rightly read, as she sat bridling and dimp-ling, and sewing by her mother's side, she was not a whit behind Dame Webber in good-will.

Here arose new cares for Wolfert. He was a kind father, but he was a prudent man. The young man was a lively, stirring lad; but then he had neither money nor land. Wolfert's ideas all ran in one channel; and he saw no alternative in case of a marriage but to portion off the young couple with a corner of his cabbage-garden, the whole of which was barely sufficient for the support of his family.

Like a prudent father, therefore, he forbade the youngster the house; though sorely did it go against his fatherly heart, and many a silent tear did it cause in the bright eye of his daughter.

FROM THE TOWER WINDOW

She showed herself, however, a pattern of filial piety and obedience. She never pouted and sulked. On the contrary she acquiesced like an obedient daughter, shut the street-door in her lover's face, and if ever she did grant him an interview, it was either out of the kitchen-window, or over the garden-fence.

Wolfert was deeply cogitating these matters in his mind, and his brow wrinkled with unusual care, as he wended his way on Saturday afternoon to the rural inn, about two miles from the city. It was a favorite resort of the Dutch part of the community, from being always held by a Dutch line of landlords, and retaining an air and relish of the good old times. It was a Dutch-built house, that had probably been a country seat of some opulent burgher in the early time of the settlement. It stood near a point of land called Corlear's Hook, which stretches out into the Sound. The venerable and somewhat crazy mansion was distinguished from afar by a grove of elms and sycamores that seemed to wave a hospitable invitation, while a few weeping willows, with their dank, drooping foliage, resembling falling waters, gave an idea of coolness, that rendered it an attractive spot during the heat of summer.

Here, therefore, as I said, resorted many of the old inhabitants of the Manhattoes, where, while some played at shuffleboard and quoits and ninepins, others smoked a deliberate pipe, and talked over public affairs.

It was on a blustering autumnal afternoon that Wolfert made his visit to the inn. The grove of elms and willows was stripped of its leaves, which whirled in rustling eddies about the fields. The ninepin alley was deserted, for the premature chilliness of the day had driven the company within doors. As it was Saturday afternoon, the habitual club was in session, composed principally of regular Dutch burghers, though mingled occasionally with persons of various character and country, as is natural in a place of such motley population.

Beside the fireplace, in a huge leather-bottomed armchair, sat

the dictator of this little world, the venerable Rem, or, as it was pronounced, Ramm Rapelye. He was a man of Walloon race, and illustrious for the antiquity of his line; his great-grandmother having been the first white child born in the province. But he was still more illustrious for his wealth and dignity; he had long filled the noble office of alderman, and was a man to whom the governor himself took off his hat. He had maintained possession of the leather-bottomed chair from time immemorial; and had gradually waxed in bulk as he sat in his seat of government, until in the course of years he filled its whole magnitude.

"This will be a rough night for the money-diggers," said mine host, as a gust of wind howled round the house.

"What! are they at their works again?" said an English half-pay captain, with one eye, who was a very frequent attendant at the inn.

"Aye, are they," said the landlord, "and well may they be. They've had luck of late. They say a great pot of money has been dug up in the fields, just behind Stuyvesant's orchard. Folks think it must have been buried there in old times, by Peter Stuyvesant, the Dutch governor."

"Fudge!" said the one-eyed man of war.

"Well, you may believe it or not, as you please," said mine host, somewhat nettled; "but everybody knows that the old governor buried a great deal of his money at the time of the Dutch troubles, when the English red-coats seized on the province. They say, too, the old gentleman walks; aye, and in the very same dress that he wears in the picture that hangs up in the family house."

"Fudge!" said the half-pay officer.

"Fudge, if you please!—But didn't Corney Van Zandt see him at midnight, stalking about in the meadow with his wooden leg, and a drawn sword in his hand, that flashed like fire? And what can he be walking for, but because people have been troubling the place where he buried his money in old times?"

Here the landlord was interrupted by several gutteral sounds from Ramm Rapelye, betokening that he was laboring with the unusual production of an idea. As he was too great a man to be slighted by a prudent publican, mine host respectfully paused until he should deliver himself. The corpulent frame of this mighty burgher now gave all the symptoms of a volcanic mountain on the point of an eruption. First, there was a certain heaving of the abdomen, not unlike an earthquake; then was emitted a cloud of tobacco-smoke from that crater, his mouth; then there was a kind of rattle in the throat; at length his voice forced its way into a slow, but absolute tone of a man who feels the weight of his purse, if not of his ideas; every portion of his speech being marked by a testy puff of tobacco-smoke.

"Who talks of old Peter Stuyvesant's walking?—puff—Have people no respect for persons?—puff—puff—Peter Stuyvesant knew better what to do with his money than to bury it—puff—I know the Stuyvesant family —puff—every one of them—puff—not a more respectable family in the province—puff—puff —Don't talk to me of Peter Stuyvesant's walking—puff—puff—puff."

Here the redoubtable Ramm redoubled his smoking with such vehemence, that the cloudy volume soon wreathed round his head, as the smoke envelops the awful summit of Mount Aetna.

A general silence followed the sudden rebuke of this very rich man. The subject, however, was too interesting to be readily abandoned. The conversation soon broke forth again from the lips of Peechy Prauw Van Hook. Peechy could, at any time, tell as many stories in an evening as his hearers could digest in a month. He now resumed the conversation, by affirming that, to his knowledge, money had, at different times, been digged up in various parts of the island. The lucky persons who had discovered them had always dreamt of them three times beforehand, and what was worthy of remark, those treasures had never been found but by some descendant of the good old Dutch families, which clearly proved that they had been buried by Dutchmen in the olden time.

"Fiddlestick with your Dutchmen!" cried the half-pay officer. "The Dutch had nothing to do with them. They were all buried by Kidd the pirate, and his crew."

Here a key-note was touched that roused the whole company. The name of Captain Kidd was like a talisman in those times, and was associated with a thousand marvellous stories.

The half-pay officer took the lead. He was a man of great weight among the peaceable members of the club, by reason of his warlike character and gunpowder tales. All his golden stories of Kidd, however, and of the booty he had buried, were obstinately rivalled by the tales of Peechy Prauw, who rather than suffer his Dutch progenitors to be eclipsed by a foreign freebooter, enriched every field and shore in the neighborhood with the hidden wealth of Peter Stuyvesant and his contemporaries.

Not a word of this conversation was lost upon Wolfert Webber. He returned pensively home, full of magnificent ideas. The soil of his native island seemed to be turned into gold dust; and every field to teem with treasure. His head almost reeled at the thought

FROM THE TOWER WINDOW

how often he must have heedlessly rambled over places where countless sums lay, scarcely covered by the turf beneath his feet. His mind was in an uproar with this whirl of new ideas. As he came in sight of the venerable mansion of his forefathers, and the little realm where the Webbers had so long, and so contentedly flourished, his gorge rose at the narrowness of his destiny.

"Unlucky Wolfert!" exclaimed he; "others can go to bed and dream themselves into whole mines of wealth; they have but to seize a spade in the morning, and turn up doubloons like potatoes; but thou must dream of hardships, and rise to poverty—must dig the field from year's end to year's end, and yet raise nothing but cabbages!"

Wolfert Webber went to bed with a heavy heart; and it was long before the golden visions that disturbed his brain permitted him to sink into repose. The same visions, however, extended into his sleeping thoughts, and assumed a more definite form. He dreamt that he had discovered an immense treasure in the centre of his garden. At every stroke of the spade he laid bare a golden ingot; diamond crosses sparkled out of the dust; bags of money turned up their bellies, corpulent with pieces-of-eight, or venerable doubloons; and chests, wedged close with moidores, ducats, and pistareens, yawned before his ravished eyes, and vomited forth their glittering contents.

Wolfert awoke a poorer man than ever. He had no heart to go about his daily concerns, which appeared so paltry and profitless; but sat all day long in the chimney-corner, picturing to himself ingots and heaps of gold in the fire. The next night his dream was repeated. There was something very singular in this repetition. He passed another day of reverie, and though it was cleaning-day, and the house, as usual in Dutch households, completely topsy-turvy, yet he sat unmoved amidst the general uproar.

The third night he went to bed with a palpitating heart. He put on his red night-cap wrongside outwards, for good luck.

Again the golden dream was repeated, and again he saw his garden teeming with ingots and money-bags.

Wolfert rose the next morning in complete bewilderment. A dream, three times repeated, was never known to lie; and if so, his fortune was made. In his agitation he put on his waistcoat with the hind part before, and this was a corroboration of good luck. He no longer doubted that a huge store of money lay buried somewhere in his cabbage-field, coyly waiting to be sought for; and he repined at having so long been scratching about the surface of the soil instead of digging to the centre.

He took his seat at the breakfast-table full of these speculations; asked his daughter to put a lump of gold into his tea, and on handing his wife a plate of slapjacks, begged her to help herself to a doubloon.

His grand care now was how to secure this immense treasure without its being known. Instead of his working regularly in his grounds in the daytime, he now stole from his bed at night, and with spade and pickaxe went to work to rip up and dig about his paternal acres, from one end to the other. In a little time the whole garden, which had presented such a goodly and regular appearance, with its phalanx of cabbages, like a vegetable army in battle array, was reduced to a scene of devastation; while the relentless Wolfert, with night-cap on head, and lantern and spade in hand, stalked through the slaughtered ranks, the destroying angel of his own vegetable world.

Every morning bore testimony to the ravages of the preceding night in cabbages of all ages and conditions, from the tender sprout to the full-grown head, piteously rooted from their quiet beds like worthless weeds, and left to wither in the sunshine. In vain Wolfert's wife remonstrated; in vain his darling daughter wept over the destruction of some favorite marigold. "Thou shalt have gold of another sort," he would cry, chucking her under the chin; "thou shalt have a string of crooked ducats for thy

wedding necklace, my child." His family began really to fear for the poor man's wits. He muttered in his sleep at night about mines of wealth, about pearls and diamonds, and bars of gold. In the daytime he was moody and abstracted, and walked about as if in a trance. Dame Webber held frequent councils with all the old women of the neighborhood; scarce an hour in the day but a knot of them might be seen wagging their white caps together round her door, while the poor woman made some piteous recital.

In the meantime Wolfert went on digging and digging; but the field was extensive, and as his dream had indicated no precise spot, he had to dig at random. The winter set in before one-tenth of the scene of promise had been explored. The ground became frozen hard, and the nights too cold for the labors of the spade.

No sooner, however, did the returning warmth of spring loosen the soil, and the small frogs begin to pipe in the meadows, but Wolfert resumed his labors with renovated zeal. Still, however, the hours of industry were reversed. Instead of working cheerily all day, planting and setting out his vegetables, he remained thoughtfully idle, until the shades of night summoned him to his secret labors. In this way he continued to dig from night to night, and week to week, and month to month, but not a stiver did he find. On the contrary, the more he digged, the poorer he grew. The rich soil of his garden was digged away, and the sand and gravel from beneath was thrown to the surface, until the whole field presented an aspect of sandy barrenness.

In the meantime, the seasons gradually rolled on. The little frogs which had piped in the meadows in early spring, croaked as bull-frogs during the summer heats, and then sank into silence. The peach-tree budded, blossomed, and bore its fruit. The swallows and martins came, twitted about the roof, built their nests, reared their young, held their congress along the eaves, and then winged their flight in search of another spring; and finally the leaves of the button-wood tree turned yellow, then brown, then rustled one by one to the ground, and whirling about in little eddies of wind and dust, whispered that winter was at hand.

Wolfert gradually woke from his dream of wealth as the year declined. He had reared no crop for the supply of his household during the sterility of winter. The season was long and severe, and for the first time the family was really straitened in its comforts. By degrees a revulsion of thought took place in Wolfert's mind. The idea gradually stole upon him that he should come to want. Haggard care gathered about his brow; he went about with a money-seeking air, his eyes bent downwards into the dust. He could not even pass the city almshouse without giving it a rueful glance, as if destined to be his future abode.

The strangeness of his conduct and of his looks occasioned much speculation and remark. For a long time he was suspected of being crazy; and then everybody pitied him; and at length it began to be suspected that he was poor, and then everybody avoided him. Thus everybody deserted the Webber mansion, everybody but honest Dirk Waldron, who indeed seemed to wax more affectionate as the fortunes of his mistress were in the wane.

Many months had elapsed since Wolfert had frequented his old resort, the rural inn. He was taking a long lonely walk one Saturday afternoon, musing over his wants and disappointments, when his feet took instinctively their wonted direction, and on awaking out of a reverie, he found himself before the door of the inn.

Wolfert found several of the old frequenters of the inn at their usual posts, and seated in their usual places; but one was missing, the great Ramm Rapelye, who for many years had filled the leather-bottomed chair of state. His place was supplied by a stranger, who seemed, however, completely at home in the chair and the tavern. He was rather under size, but deep-chested, square and muscular. His broad shoulders, double joints, and bow knees, gave tokens of prodigious strength. His face was dark and weatherbeaten; a deep scar, as if from the slash of a cutlass, had almost divided his nose, and made a gash in his upper lip, through which his teeth shone like a bull-dog's. A mop of iron-gray hair gave a grisly finish to this hard-favored visage. He wore an old hat edged with tarnished lace, and cocked in martial style, on one side of his head; a rusty blue military coat with brass buttons, and a wide pair of short petti-coat trousers, or rather breeches, for they were gathered up at the knees. He ordered everybody about him with an authoritative air; talking in a brattling voice, that sounded like the crackling of thorns under a pot; d—d the landlord and servants with perfect impunity, and was waited upon with greater obsequiousness than had ever been shown to the mighty Ramm himself.

Wolfert's curiosity was awakened to know who and what was this stranger who had thus usurped absolute sway in this ancient domain. Peechy Prauw took him aside, into a remote corner of the hall, and there, in an under voice, and with great caution, imparted to him all that he knew on the subject. The inn had been aroused several months before, on a dark stormy night, by repeated long shouts, that seemed like the howlings of a wolf. They came from the water-side, and at length were distinguished to be hailing the house in the sea-faring manner, "House-a-hoy!" The landlord turned out with his head waiter, tapster, hostler, and errand-boy—that is to say, with his old negro Cuff. On approaching the place whence the voice proceeded, they found this amphibious-looking personage at the water's edge, quite alone, and seated on a great oaken sea-chest. How he came there, whether he had been set on shore from some boat, or had

floated to land on his chest, nobody could tell, for he did not seem
disposed to answer questions; and there was something in his
looks and manners that put a stop to all questioning. Suffice it
to say, he took possession of a corner-room of the inn, to which
his chest was removed with great difficulty. Here he had remained ever since, keeping about the inn and its vicinity. Sometimes, it is true, he disappeared for one, two, or three days at a
time, going and returning without giving any notice or account
of his movements. He always appeared to have plenty of money,
though often of very strange outlandish coinage; and he regularly
paid his bill every evening before turning in.

He had fitted up his room to his own fancy, having slung a
hammock from the ceiling instead of a bed, and decorated the walls
with rusty pistols and cutlasses of foreign workmanship. A
greater part of his time was passed in this room, seated by the

window, which commanded a wide view of the Sound, a short old-fashioned pipe in his mouth, a glass of rum-toddy at his elbow, and a pocket-telescope in his hand, with which he reconnoitered every boat that moved upon the water.

All this might have passed without much notice, for in those times the province was so much the resort of adventurers of all characters and climes, that any oddity in dress or behavior attracted but small attention. In a little while, however, this strange sea-monster, thus strangely cast upon dry land, began to encroach upon the long-established customs and customers of the place and to interfere in a dictatorial manner in the affairs of the ninepin alley and the bar-room, until in the end he usurped an absolute command over the whole inn. It was all in vain to attempt to withstand his authority. He was not exactly quarrelsome, but boisterous and peremptory, like one accustomed to tyrannize on a quarterdeck; and there was a dare-devil air about everything he said and did, that inspired wariness in all bystanders. Even the half-pay officer, so long the hero of the club, was soon silenced by him; and the burghers stared with wonder at seeing their inflammable man of war so readily and quietly extinguished.

And then the tales that he would tell were enough to make a peaceable man's hair stand on end. There was not a sea-fight, nor marauding, nor freebooting adventure that had happened within the last twenty years, but he seemed perfectly versed in it. He delighted to talk of the exploits of the buccaneers in the West Indies, and on the Spanish Main. How his eyes would glisten as he described the waylaying of treasure-ships, the desperate fights, yard-arm and yard-arm—broadside and broadside—the boarding and capturing huge Spanish galleons! All this would be told with infinite glee, as if he considered it an excellent joke; and then he would give such a tyrannical leer in the face of his next neighbor, that the poor man would be fain to laugh out of sheer faintheartedness. If any one, however, pretended to contradict him in any of his stories, he was on fire in an instant. His very cocked hat assumed a momentary fierceness, and seemed to resent the contradiction, and he would at the same time let slip a broadside of thundering oaths and tremendous sea-phrases, such as had never been heard before within those peaceful walls.

Indeed, the worthy burghers began to surmise that he knew more of those stories than mere hearsay. Day after day their conjectures concerning him grew more and more wild and fearful. The strangeness of his arrival, the strangeness of his manners, the mystery that surrounded him, all made him something incomprehensible in their eyes. He was a kind of monster of the deep to them—he was a merman—he was a behemoth—he was a leviathan—in short, they knew not what he was.

The domineering spirit of this boisterous sea-urchin at length grew quite intolerable. He was no respecter of persons; he contradicted the richest burghers without hesitation; he took possession of the sacred elbow-chair, which, time out of mind, had been the seat of sovereignty of the illustrious Ramm Rapelye. Nay, he even went so far, in one of his rough jocular moods, as to slap that mighty burgher on the back, and wink in his face, a thing scarcely to be believed. From this time Ramm Rapelye appeared no more at the inn; and his example was followed by several of the most eminent customers. The landlord was almost in despair; but he knew not how to get rid of this sea-monster.

Such was the account whispered cautiously in Wolfert's ear by Peechy Prauw as he held him by a button in the corner of the hall, casting a wary glance now and then towards the door of the bar-room, lest he should be overheard by the terrible hero of his tale. Wolfert took his seat in a remote part of the room in silence; impressed with profound awe of this unknown.

The stranger was on this evening in a more than usually communicative mood, and was narrating a number of astounding stories of plunderings and burnings on the high seas. He dwelt upon them with peculiar relish, heightening the frightful particulars in proportion to their effect on his peaceful audience. The honest burghers cast fearful glances at the deep scar slashed across the visage of the stranger, and moved their chairs a little farther off.

The half-pay officer now tried to match the gunpowder tales of the stranger by others equally tremendous. Kidd, as usual, was his hero. The seaman had always evinced a settled pique against the one-eyed warrior. On this occasion he listened with peculiar impatience. He sat with one arm akimbo, the other elbow on the table, the hand holding on to the small pipe he was pettishly puffing; his legs crossed; drumming with one foot on the ground, and casting every now and then the side-glance of a basilisk at the prosing captain. At length the latter spoke of Kidd's having ascended the Hudson with some of his crew to land his plunder in secrecy.

"Kidd up the Hudson!" burst forth the seaman, with a tremendous oath.—"Kidd never was up the Hudson! What a plague do you know of Kidd and his haunts?"

The half-pay officer was silenced; but Peechy Prauw, who never could remain silent, observed that the gentleman certainly was in the right. Kidd never did bury money up the Hudson, nor indeed in any of those parts, though many affirmed such to be the fact. It was Bradish and others of the buccaneers who had buried money; some said in Turtle Bay, others on Long Island, others in the neighborhood of Hell-gate. "Indeed," added he, "I recollect an adventure of Sam, the negro fisherman, many years ago, which some think had something to do with the buccaneers.

"Upon a dark night many years ago, as Black Sam was returning from fishing in Hell-gate"—

Here the story was nipped in the bud by a sudden movement from the unknown, who laying his iron fist on the table, knuckles

downward, with a quiet force that indented the very boards, and looking grimly over his shoulder, with the grin of an angry bear,—"Heark'ee, neighbor," said he, with significant nodding of the head, "you'd better let the buccaneers and their money alone,—they're not for old men and old women to meddle with. They fought hard for their money; they gave body and soul for it; and wherever it lies buried, depend upon it, he must have a tug with the devil who gets it!"

This sudden explosion was succeeded by a blank silence throughout the room. Peechy Prauw shrunk within himself, and even the one-eyed officer turned pale. Wolfert, who from a dark corner of the room had listened with intense eagerness to all this talk about buried treasure, looked with mingled awe and reverence at this bold buccaneer; for such he really suspected him to be. Wolfert would have given anything for the rummaging of the ponderous sea-chest, which his imagination crammed full of golden chalices, crucifixes, and jolly round bags of doubloons.

The dead stillness that had fallen upon the company was at length interrupted by the stranger, who pulled out a prodigious watch of curious and ancient workmanship, and which in Wolfert's eyes had a decidedly Spanish look. On touching a spring it struck ten o'clock; upon which the sailor called for his reckoning, and having paid it out of a handful of outlandish coin, without taking leave of any one, he rolled out of the room, muttering to himself, as he stamped upstairs to his chamber.

It was some time before the company could recover from the silence into which they had been thrown. The very footsteps of the stranger, which were heard now and then as he traversed his chamber, inspired awe.

Still the conversation in which they had been engaged was

too interesting not to be resumed. A heavy thunder-gust had gathered up unnoticed, while they were lost in talk, and the torrents of rain that fell forbade all thoughts of setting off for home until the storm should subside. They drew nearer together, therefore, and entreated the worthy Peechy Prauw to continue the tale which had been interrupted. He readily complied, whispering, however, in a tone scarcely above his breath, and drowned occasionally by the rolling of the thunder; and he would pause every now and then, and listen with evident awe, as he heard the heavy footsteps of the stranger pacing overhead.

ADVENTURE OF THE BLACK FISHERMAN

Everybody knows Black Sam, the old negro fisherman, or, as he is commonly called, Mud Sam, who has fished about the Sound for the last half century. It is now many years since Sam, having finished his day's work at an early hour, was fishing, one still summer evening, just about the neighborhood of Hell-gate.

He was in a light skiff; and being well acquainted with the currents and eddies, had shifted his station according to the shifting of the tide; but in the eagerness of his sport he did not see that the tide was rapidly ebbing until the roaring of the whirl-pools and eddies warned him of his danger; and he had some difficulty in shooting his skiff from among the rocks and breakers, and getting to the point of Blackwell's Island. Here he cast anchor for some time, waiting the turn of the tide to enable him to return homewards. As the night set in, it grew blustering and gusty. Dark clouds came bundling up in the west; and now and then a growl of thunder or a flash of lightning told that a summer storm was at hand. Sam pulled over, therefore, under the lee of Manhattan Island, and coasting along, came to a snug nook, just under a steep beetling rock, where he fastened his skiff to the root of a tree that shot out from a cleft, and spread its broad branches like a canopy over the water. The gust came scouring along; the wind threw up the river in white surges; the rain rattled among the leaves; the thunder bellowed worse than that which is now bellowing; the lightning seemed to lick up the surges of the stream; but Sam, snugly sheltered under rock and tree, lay crouching in his skiff, rocking upon the billows until he fell asleep. When he woke all was quiet. The gust had passed away, and only now and then a faint gleam of lightning in the east showed which way it had gone. The night was dark and moonless; and from the state of the tide Sam concluded it was near midnight. He was on the point of making loose his skiff to return homewards, when he saw a light gleaming along the water from a distance, which seemed rapidly approaching. As it drew near he perceived it came from a lantern in the bow of a boat gliding along under shadow of the land. It pulled up in a small cove, close to where he was. A man jumped on shore, and searching about with the lantern, exclaimed, "This is the place—here's the iron ring!" The boat was then made fast, and the man returning on board, assisted his comrades in conveying something heavy on shore. As the light gleamed among them, Sam saw that they were five stout desperate-looking fellows, in red woolen caps, with a leader in a three-cornered hat, and that some of them were armed with dirks, or long knives, and pistols. They talked low to one another in some outlandish tongue which he could not understand.

On landing they made their way among the bushes, taking turns to relieve each other in lugging their burden up the rocky bank. Sam's curiosity was now fully aroused; so leaving his skiff he clambered silently up a ridge that overlooked their path. They had stopped to rest for a moment, and the leader was looking about among the bushes with his lantern. "Have you brought the spades?" said one. "They are here," replied another, who had them on his shoulder. "We must dig deep, where there will be no risk of discovery," said a third.

FROM THE TOWER WINDOW

A cold chill ran through Sam's veins. He fancied he saw before him a gang of murderers, about to bury their victim. His knees smote together. In his agitation he shook the branch of a tree with which he was supporting himself as he looked over the edge of the cliff.

"What's that?" cried one of the gang.—"Some one stirs among the bushes!" The lantern was held up in the direction of the noise. One of the red-caps cocked a pistol, and pointed it towards the very place where Sam was standing. He stood motionless—breathless! Fortunately his dingy complexion was in his favor, and made no glare among the leaves.

"'Tis no one," said the man with the lantern. "What a plague! you would not fire off your pistol and alarm the country!"

The pistol was uncocked; the burden was resumed, and the party slowly toiled along the bank. Sam watched them as they went; the light sending back fitful gleams through the dripping bushes, and it was not till they were fairly out of sight that he ventured to draw breath freely. He now thought of getting back to his boat, and making his escape out of the reach of such dangerous neighbors; but curiosity was all-powerful. He hesitated and lingered and listened. By and by he heard the strokes of spades,—"they are digging a grave!" said he to himself; and the cold sweat started upon his forehead. Every stroke of a spade, as it sounded through the silent groves, went to his heart; it was evident there was as little noise made as possible; everything had an air of terrible mystery and secrecy. Sam could not resist an impulse, in spite of every danger, to steal nearer to the scene of mystery, and overlook the midnight fellows at their work. He crawled along cautiously, therefore, inch by inch; stepping with the utmost care among the dry leaves, lest their rustling should betray him. He came at length to where a steep rock intervened between him and the gang; for he saw the light of their lantern shining up against the branches of the trees on the other side.

Sam slowly and silently clambered up the surface of the rock, and raising his head above its naked edge, beheld the villains immediately below him, and so near, that though he dreaded discovery, he dared not withdraw lest the least movement should be heard. In this way he remained, with his round black face peering above the edge of the rock, like the sun just emerging above the horizon, or the round-cheeked moon on the dial of a clock.

The red-caps had nearly finished their work; the grave was filled up, and they were carefully replacing the turf. This done, they scattered dry leaves over the place. "And now," said the leader, "I defy the devil himself to find it out."

"The murderers!" exclaimed Sam, involuntarily.

The whole gang started, and looking up, beheld the round black head of Sam just above them. His white eyes strained half out of their orbits; his white teeth chattering, and his whole visage shining with cold perspiration.

"We're discovered!" cried one.

"Down with him!" cried another.

Sam heard the cocking of a pistol, but did not pause for the report. He scrambled over rock and stone, through brush and brier; rolled down banks like a hedgehog; scrambled up others like a catamount. In every direction he heard some one or other of the gang hemming him in. At length he reached the rocky ridge along the river; one of the red-caps was hard behind him. A steep rock like a wall rose directly in his way; it seemed to cut off all retreat, when fortunately he espied the strong cord-like branch of a grape-vine reaching half way down it. He sprang at it with the force of a desperate man, seized it with both hands, and being young and agile, succeeded in swinging himself to the summit of the cliff. Here he stood in full relief against the sky, when the red-cap cocked his pistol and fired. The ball whistled by Sam's head. With the lucky thought of a man in an emergency, he uttered a yell, fell to the ground, and detached at the same time a fragment of the rock, which tumbled with a loud splash into the river.

"I've done his business," said the red-cap to one or two of his comrades as they arrived panting. "He'll tell no tales, except to the fishes in the river."

His pursuers now turned to meet their companions. Sam, sliding silently down the surface of the rock, let himself quietly into his skiff, cast loose the fastening, and abandoned himself to the rapid current, which in that place runs like a mill-stream, and soon swept him off from the neighborhood. It was not, however, until he had drifted a great distance that he ventured to ply his oars, when he made his skiff dart like an arrow through the strait of Hell-gate, nor did he feel himself thoroughly secure until safely nestled in bed in the cockloft of the ancient house of the Suydams.

Here the worthy Peechy Prauw paused to take breath. His auditors remained with open mouths and outstretched necks.

"And did Sam never find out what was buried by the red-caps?" said Wolfert, eagerly, whose mind was haunted by nothing but ingots and doubloons.

"Not that I know of," said Peechy; "he had no time to spare from his work, and, to tell the truth, he did not like to run the risk of another race among the rocks. But have none of you heard of father Red-cap who haunts the old burnt farmhouse in the

woods, on the border of the Sound, near Hell-gate?"

"Oh, to be sure, I've heard tell of something of the kind, but then I took it for some old wives' fable."

"Old wives' fable or not," said Peechy Prauw, "that farm-house stands hard by the very spot. It's been unoccupied time out of mind, and stands in a lonely part of the coast; but those who fish in the neighborhood have often heard strange noises there; and lights have been seen about the wood at night; and an old fellow in a red cap has been seen at the windows more than once, which people take to be the ghost of the body buried there. Once upon a time three soldiers took shelter in the building for the night, and rummaged it from top to bottom, when they found old father Red-cap astride of a cider-barrel in the cellar, with a jug in one hand and a goblet in the other. He offered them a drink out of his goblet, but just as one of the soldiers was putting it to his mouth—whew! a flash of fire blazed through the cellar, blinded every mother's son of them for several minutes, and when they recovered their eye-sight, jug, goblet, and Red-cap had vanished, and nothing but the empty cider-barrel remained."

The deep interest taken in this conversation by the company had made them unconscious of the uproar abroad among the elements, when suddenly they were electrified by a tremendous clap of thunder. A lumbering crash followed instantaneously, shaking the building to its very foundation. All started from their seats, imagining it the shock of an earthquake, or that old father Red-cap was coming among them in all his terrors. They listened for a moment, but only heard the rain pelting against the windows, and the wind howling among the trees.

A sullen pause of the storm, which now rose and sank in

gusts, produced a momentary stillness. In this interval the report of a musket was heard, and a long shout, almost like a yell, resounded from the shore. Every one crowded to the window; another musket-shot was heard, and another long shout, mingled wildly with a rising blast of wind. It seemed as if the cry came up from the bosom of the waters; for though incessant flashes of lightning spread a light about the shore, no one was to be seen.

Suddenly the window of the room overhead was opened, and a loud halloo uttered by the mysterious stranger. Several hailings passed from one party to the other, but in a language which none of the company in the bar-room could understand; and presently they heard the window closed, and a great noise overhead, as if all the furniture were pulled and hauled about the room. The negro servant was summoned, and shortly afterwards was seen assisting the veteran to lug the ponderous sea-chest down-stairs.

The landlord was in amazement. "What, you are not going on the water in such a storm?"

"Storm!" said the other, scornfully, "do you call such a sputter of weather a storm?"

"You'll get drenched to the skin," said Peechy Prauw.

"Thunder and lightning!" exclaimed the veteran, "don't preach about weather to a man that has cruised in whirlwinds and tornadoes."

The obsequious Peechy was again struck dumb. The voice from the water was heard once more in a tone of impatience; the by-standers stared with redoubled awe at this man of storms, who seemed to have come up out of the deep, and to be summoned back to it again. As, with the assistance of the negro, he slowly bore his ponderous sea-chest towards the shore, they eyed it with a superstitious feeling,—half doubting whether he were not really about to embark upon it and launch forth upon the wild waves. They followed him at a distance with a lantern.

"Dowse the light!" roared the hoarse voice from the water. "No one wants light here!"

"Thunder and lightning!" exclaimed the veteran, turning short upon them; "back to the house with you!"

Wolfert and his companions shrunk back in dismay. Still their curiosity would not allow them entirely to withdraw. A long sheet of lightning now flickered across the waves, and discovered a boat, filled with men, just under a rocky point, rising and sinking with the heaving surges, and swashing the waters at every heave. It was with difficulty held to the rocks by a boathook, for the current rushed furiously round the point. The veteran hoisted one end of the lumbering sea-chest on the gunwale of the boat, and seized the handle at the other end to lift it in, when the motion propelled the boat from the shore; the chest slipped off from the gunwale, and, sinking into the waves, pulled the veteran headlong after it. A loud shriek was uttered by all on shore, and a volley of execrations by those on board; but boat and man were hurried away by the rushing swiftness of the tide. A pitchy darkness succeeded; Wolfert Webber indeed fancied that he distinguished a cry for help, and that he beheld the drowning man beckoning for assistance; but when the lightning again gleamed along the water, all was void; neither man nor boat was to be seen; nothing but the dashing and weltering of the waves as they hurried past.

FROM THE TOWER WINDOW

The company returned to the tavern to await the subsiding of the storm. They resumed their seats, and gazed on each other with dismay. The whole transaction had not occupied five minutes, and not a dozen words had been spoken.

"He came," said the landlord, "in a storm, and he went in a storm; he came in the night, and he went in the night; he came nobody knows whence, and he has gone nobody knows where. For aught I know he has gone to sea once more on his chest, and may land to bother some people on the other side of the world."

The thunder-gust which had hitherto detained the company came at length to an end. The cuckoo clock in the hall told midnight; every one pressed to depart, for seldom was such a late hour of the night trespassed on by these quiet burghers. As they sallied forth, they found the heavens once more serene. The storm which had lately obscured them had rolled away, and lay piled up in fleecy masses on the horizon, lighted up by the bright crescent of the moon, which looked like a little silver lamp hung up in a palace of clouds.

Wolfert Webber had now carried home a fresh stock of stories and notions to ruminate upon. These accounts of pots of money and Spanish treasures, buried here and there and everywhere, about the rocks and bays of these wild shores, made him almost dizzy. As he turned over in his thoughts all that had been told of the singular adventure of the negro fisherman, his imagination gave a totally different complexion to the tale. He saw in the gang of red-caps nothing but a crew of pirates burying their spoils, and his cupidity was once more awakened by the possibility of at length getting on the traces of some of this lurking wealth. Indeed, his infected fancy tinged everything with gold. Caskets of buried jewels, chests of ingots, and barrels of outlandish coins, seemed to court him from their concealments, and supplicate him to relieve them from their untimely graves.

On making private inquiries about the grounds said to be

haunted by Father Red-cap, he was more and more confirmed in his surmise. He learned that the place had several times been visited by experienced money-diggers, who had heard black Sam's story, though none of them had met with success.

Wolfert Webber was now in a worry of trepidation and impatience; fearful lest some rival adventurer should get a scent of the buried gold. He determined privately to seek out the black fisherman, and get him to serve as guide to the place where he had witnessed the mysterious scene of interment. Sam was easily found. Wolfert found him at his cabin, which was not much larger than a tolerable dog-house. It was rudely constructed of fragments of wrecks and drift-wood, and built on the rocky shore, at the foot of the old fort, just about what at present forms the point of the Battery.

Many years had passed away since the time of Sam's youthful adventure, and the snows of many a winter had grizzled the knotty wool upon his head. He perfectly recollected the circumstances, however, for he had often been called upon to relate them. Wolfert's only wish was to secure the old fisherman as a pilot to the spot; and this was readily effected. The long time that had intervened since his nocturnal adventure had effaced all Sam's awe of the place.

The tide was adverse to making the expedition by water, and Wolfert was too impatient to get to the land of promise, to wait for its turning; they set off, therefore, by land. A walk of four or five miles brought them to the edge of a wood, which at that time covered the greater part of the eastern side of the island. Here they struck into a long lane, straggling among trees and bushes, very much overgrown with weeds and mullein-stalks, as if but seldom used, and so completely overshadowed as to enjoy but a kind of twilight. Wild vines entangled the trees and flaunted in their faces; brambles and briers caught their clothes as they passed; the garter-snake glided across their path;

the spotted toad hopped and waddled before them, and the restless catbird mewed at them from every thicket. Had Wolfert Webber been deeply read in romantic legend, he might have fancied himself entering upon forbidden, enchanted ground; or that these were some of the guardians set to keep watch upon buried treasure. As it was, the loneliness of the place, and the wild stories connected with it, had their effect upon his mind.

On reaching the lower end of the lane, they found themselves near the shore of the Sound in a kind of amphitheatre, surrounded by forest-trees. The area had once been a grass-plot, but was now shagged with briers and rank weeds. At one end, and just on the river bank, was a ruined building, little better than a heap of rubbish, with a stack of chimneys rising like a solitary tower out of the centre.

Wolfert had not a doubt that this was the haunted house of Father Red-cap, and called to mind the story of Peechy Prauw. The evening was approaching, and the light falling dubiously among the woody places, gave a melancholy tone to the scene. The nighthawk, wheeling about in the highest regions of the air, emitted his peevish, boding cry. The woodpecker gave a lonely tap now and then on some hollow tree, and the fire-bird streamed by them with his deep-red plumage.

They now came to an enclosure that had once been a garden. It extended along the foot of a rocky ridge, but was little better than a wilderness of weeds, with here and there a matted rose-bush, or a peach or plum tree grown wild and ragged and covered with moss. At the lower end of the garden they passed a kind of vault in the side of a bank, facing the water. It had the look of a root-house. The door, though decayed, was still strong, and appeared to have been recently patched up. Wolfert pushed it open. It gave a harsh grating upon its hinges, and striking against something like a box, a rattling sound ensued. Wolfert drew back shuddering, but was reassured on being informed by the negro that this was a family vault, belonging to one of the old Dutch families that owned this estate; an assertion corroborated by the sight of coffins of various sizes piled within. Sam had been familiar with all these scenes when a boy, and now knew that he could not be far from the place of which they were in quest.

They now made their way to the water's edge, scrambling along ledges of rocks that overhung the waves, and obliged often to hold by shrubs and grape-vines to avoid slipping into the deep and hurried stream. At length they came to a small cove, or rather indent of the shore. It was protected by steep rocks, and overshadowed by a thick copse of oaks and chestnuts, so as to be sheltered and almost concealed. The negro paused; raised his remnant of a hat, and scratched his grizzled poll for a moment, as he regarded this nook; then suddenly clapping his hands, he stepped exultingly forward, and pointed to a large iron ring, stapled firmly in the rock, just where a broad shelf of stone furnished a commodious landing place. It was the very spot where the red-caps had landed. Years had changed the more perishable features of the scene; but rock and iron yield slowly to the influence of time. On looking more closely, Wolfert remarked three crosses cut in the rock just above the ring, which had no doubt some mysterious signification. Old Sam now readily recognized the overhanging rock under which his skiff had been sheltered during the thunder-gust. To follow up the course which the midnight gang had taken, however, was a harder task. His mind had been so much taken up on that eventful occasion by the persons of the drama, as to pay but little attention to the scenes; and these places look so different by night and day. After wandering about for some time, however, they came to an opening among the trees which Sam thought resembled the place. There was a ledge of rock of moderate height like a wall on one side, which he thought might be the very ridge whence he had overlooked the diggers. Wolfert examined it narrowly, and at length discovered three crosses similar to those on the above ring, cut deeply into the face of the rock, but nearly obliterated by moss that had grown over them. His heart leaped with joy, for he doubted not they were the private marks of the buccaneers. All now that remained was to ascertain the precise spot where the treasure lay buried; for otherwise he might dig at random in the neighborhood of the crosses without coming upon the spoils, and he had already had enough of such profitless labor. Here, however, the old negro was perfectly at a loss, and indeed perplexed him by a variety of opinions; for his recollections were all confused. Sometimes he declared it must have been at the foot of a mulberry tree hard by; then beside a great white stone; then under a small green knoll, a short distance from the ledge; until at length Wolfert became as bewildered as himself.

The shadows of evening were now spreading themselves over the woods, and rock and tree began to mingle together. It was evidently too late to attempt anything farther at present; and, indeed, Wolfert had come unprovided with implements to prosecute his researches. Satisfied, therefore, with having ascertained the place, he took note of all its landmarks, that he might recognize it again, and set out on his return homewards, resolved to prosecute this golden enterprise without delay.

The leading anxiety which had hitherto absorbed every feeling, being now in some measure appeased, fancy began to wander,

and to conjure up a thousand shapes and chimeras as he returned through this haunted region. Pirates hanging in chains seemed to swing from every tree.

Their way back lay through the desolate garden, and Wolfert's nerves had arrived at so sensitive a state that the flitting of a bird, the rustling of a leaf, or the falling of a nut, was enough to startle him. As they entered the confines of the garden, they caught sight of a figure at a distance advancing slowly up one of the walks, and bending under the weight of a burden. They paused and regarded him attentively. He wore what appeared to be a woolen cap, and, still more alarming, of a most sanguinary red.

The figure moved slowly on, ascended the bank, and stopped at the very door of the sepulchral vault. Just before entering it he looked around. What was the affright of Wolfert when he recognized the grisly visage of the drowned buccaneer! He uttered an ejaculation of horror. The figure slowly raised his iron fist, and shook it with a terrible menace. Wolfert did not pause to see any more, but hurried off as fast as his legs could carry him, nor was Sam slow in following at his heels. Away, then, did they scramble through bush and brake, nor did they pause to breathe, until they had blundered their way through this perilous wood, and fairly reached the high road to the city.

Several days elapsed before Wolfert could summon courage enough to prosecute the enterprise, so much had he been dismayed by the apparition, whether living or dead, of the grisly buccaneer. In the meantime, what a conflict of mind did he suffer! He neglected all his concerns, wandered in his thoughts and words, and committed a thousand blunders. He babbled about incalculable sums; fancied himself engaged in money-digging; threw the bedclothes right and left, in the idea that he was shovelling away the dirt; groped under the bed in quest of the treasure, and lugged forth, as he supposed an inestimable pot of gold.

Dame Webber and her daughter were in despair at what they conceived a returning touch of insanity. There are two family oracles, one or other of which Dutch house-wives consult in all cases of great doubt and perplexity—the dominie and the doctor. In the present instance they repaired to the doctor. There was at that time a little dark mouldy man of medicine, famous among the old wives of the Manhattoes for his skill, not only in the healing art, but in all matters of strange and mysterious nature. His name was Dr. Knipperhausen, but he was more commonly known by the appellation of the High-German Doctor. To him did the poor women repair for counsel and assistance touching the mental vagaries of Wolfert Webber.

They found the doctor seated in his little study, clad in his dark camlet robe of knowledge, with his black velvet cap; a pair of green spectacles set in black horn upon his clubbed nose, and poring over a German folio that reflected back the darkness of his physiognomy. The doctor listened to their statement of the symptoms of Wolfert's malady with profound attention; but when they came to mention his raving about buried money, the little man pricked up his ears. Alas, poor women! they little knew the aid they had called in.

Dr. Knipperhausen had been half his life engaged in seeking the short cuts to fortune, in quest of which so many a long life-time is wasted. His mind therefore had become stored with all kinds of mystic lore; he had dabbled a little in astrology, alchemy, divination; knew how to detect stolen money, and to tell where springs of water lay hidden; in a word, by the dark nature of his knowledge he had acquired the name of the High-German Doctor, which is pretty nearly equivalent to that of necromancer. The doctor had often heard rumors of treasure being buried in various parts of the island, and had long been anxious to get on the traces of it. So far from curing, the doctor caught the malady from his patient. The circumstances unfolded to him awakened all his cupidity; he had not a doubt of money being buried somewhere in the neighborhood of the mysterious crosses, and offered to join Wolfert in the search. He informed him that much secrecy and caution must be observed in enterprises of the kind; that money is only to be digged for at night; with certain forms and ceremonies, and burning of drugs; the repeating of mystic words, and, above all, that the seekers must first be provided with a divining rod, which had the wonderful property of pointing to the very spot in the surface of the earth under which treasure lay hidden. As the doctor had given much of his mind to these matters, he charged himself with all the necessary preparations, and, as the quarter of the moon was propitious, he undertook to have the divining rod ready by a certain night. Wolfert's heart leaped with joy at having met with so able a coadjutor. Everything went on secretly, but swimmingly; and the black fisherman was engaged to take them in his skiff to the scene of enterprise.

At length the appointed night arrived for this perilous undertaking. Before Wolfert left his home he counselled his wife and daughter to go to bed, and feel no alarm if he should not return during the night. Like reasonable women, on being told not to feel alarm they fell immediately into a panic. They saw at once by his manner that something unusual was in agitation; all their fears about the unsettled state of his mind were revived with ten-fold force; they hung about him, entreating him not to expose himself to the night air, but all in vain. When once Wolfert

FROM THE TOWER WINDOW

was mounted on his hobby, it was no easy matter to get him out of the saddle. It was a clear starlight night, when he issued out of the portal of the Webber palace. He wore a large flapped hat tied under the chin with a handkerchief of his daughter's, to secure him from the night damp, while Dame Webber threw her long red cloak about his shoulders, and fastened it round his neck.

The doctor had been no less carefully armed and accoutred, and sallied forth, a thick clasped book under his arm, a basket of drugs and dried herbs in one hand, and in the other the miraculous rod of divination.

The great church-clock struck ten as Wolfert and the doctor passed by the church-yard, and the watchman bawled in hoarse voice a long and doleful "All's well!" A deep sleep had already fallen upon this primitive little burgh, nothing disturbed this awful silence, excepting now and then the bark of some profligate night-walking dog, or the serenade of some romantic cat. It is true, Wolfert fancied more than once that he heard the sound of a stealthy footfall at a distance behind them; but it might have been merely the echo of their own steps along the quiet streets. He thought also at one time that he saw a tall figure skulking after them—stopping when they stopped, and moving on as they proceeded; but the dim and uncertain lamp-light threw such vague gleams and shadows, that this might all have been mere fancy.

They found the old fisherman waiting for them, smoking his pipe in the stern of the skiff, which was moored just in front of his little cabin. A pickaxe and spade were lying in the bottom of the boat, with a dark lantern.

Thus then did these three worthies embark in their cockle-shell of a skiff upon this nocturnal expedition, with a wisdom and valor equalled only by the three wise men of Gotham, who adventured to sea in a bowl. The tide was rising and running rapidly up the Sound. The current bore them along, almost without the aid of an oar. The profile of the town lay all in shadow. Here and there a light feebly glimmered from some sick-chamber, or from the cabin-window of some vessel at anchor in the stream. Not a cloud obscured the deep starry firmament, the lights of which wavered on the surface of the placid river; and a shooting meteor, streaking its pale course in the very direction they were taking, was interpreted by the doctor into a most propitious omen.

In a little while they glided by the point of Corlaer's Hook with the rural inn which had been the scene of such night adventures. Wolfert felt a chill pass over him as they passed the point where the buccaneer had disappeared. He pointed it out to Dr. Knipperhausen. While regarding it, they thought they saw a boat actually lurking at the very place; but the shore cast such a shadow over the border of the water that they could discern nothing distinctly. They had not proceeded far when they heard the low sounds of distant oars, as if cautiously pulled. Sam plied his oars with redoubled vigor, and knowing all the eddies and currents of the stream, soon left their followers, if such they were, far astern. In a little while they stretched across Turtle Bay and Kip's Bay, then shrouded themselves in the deep shadows of the Manhattan shore, and glided swiftly along, secure from observation. At length the negro shot his skiff into a little cove, darkly embowered by trees, and made it fast to the well-known iron ring. They now landed, and lighting the lantern, gathered their various implements and proceeded slowly through the bushes. Every sound startled them, even that of their own footsteps among the dry leaves; and the hooting of a screech owl, from the shattered chimney of the neighboring ruin, made their blood run cold.

In spite of all Wolfert's caution in taking note of the landmarks, it was some time before they could find the open place among the trees, where the treasure was supposed to be buried. At length they came to the ledge of rock; and on examining its surface by the aid of the lantern, Wolfert recognized the three mystic crosses. Their hearts beat quick, for the momentous trial was at hand that was to determine their hopes.

The lantern was now held by Wolfert Webber, while the doctor produced the divining rod. It was a forked twig, one end of which was grasped firmly in each hand, while the centre, forming the stem, pointed perpendicularly upwards. The doctor moved his wand about, within a certain distance of the earth, from place to place, but for some time without any effect, while Wolfert kept the light of the lantern turned full upon it, and watched it with the most breathless interest. At length the rod began slowly to turn. The doctor grasped it with greater earnestness, his hands trembling with the agitation of his mind. The wand continued to turn gradually, until at length the stem had reversed its position, and pointed perpendicularly downward, and remained pointing to one spot as fixedly as the needle to the pole.

"This is the spot!" said the doctor, in an almost inaudible tone. Wolfert's heart was in his throat.

"Shall I dig?" said the negro, grasping the spade.

"*Pots tausend, no!*" replied the little doctor, hastily. He now ordered his companions to keep close by him, and to maintain the most inflexible silence. That certain precautions must be taken and ceremonies used to prevent the evil spirits which kept about buried treasure from doing them any harm. He then drew a circle about the place, enough to include the whole party. He next gathered dry twigs and leaves and made a fire, upon which he threw certain drugs and dried herbs which he had brought in his basket. A thick smoke arose, diffusing a potent odor, savoring marvellously of brimstone and assafoetida, which, however grateful it might be to the olfactory nerves of spirits, nearly strangled poor Wolfert, and produced a fit of coughing and wheezing that made the whole grove resound. Dr. Knipperhausen then unclasped the volume which he had brought under his arm, which was printed in red and black characters in German text. While Wolfert held the lantern, the doctor, by the aid of his spectacles, read off several forms of conjuration in Latin and German. He then ordered Sam to seize the pickaxe and proceed to work. The close-bound soil gave obstinate signs of not having been disturbed for many a year. After having picked his way through the surface, Sam came to a bed of sand and gravel, which he threw briskly to right and left with the spade.

"Hark!" said Wolfert, who fancied he heard a trampling among the dry leaves, and a rustling through the bushes. Sam paused for a moment, and they listened. No footstep was near. The bat flitted by them in silence; a bird, roused from its roost by the light which glared up among the trees, flew circling about the flame. In the profound stillness of the woodland, they could distinguish the current rippling along the rocky shore, and the distant murmuring and roaring of Hell-gate.

The negro continued his labors, and had already digged a considerable hole. The doctor stood on the edge, reading formulae every now and then from his black-letter volume, or throwing more drugs and herbs upon the fire; while Wolfert bent anxiously over the pit, watching every stroke of the spade. Any one witnessing the scene thus lighted up by fire, lantern, and the reflection of Wolfert's red mantle might have mistaken the little doctor for some magician busied in his incantations, and the grizzly-headed negro for some swart goblin, obedient to his commands.

FROM THE TOWER WINDOW

At length the spade of the fisherman struck upon something that sounded hollow. The sound vibrated to Wolfert's heart. He struck his spade again.

" 'Tis a chest," said Sam.

"Full of gold, I'll warrant it!" cried Wolfert, clasping his hands with rapture.

Scarcely had he uttered the words when a sound from above caught his ear. He cast up his eyes, and lo! by the expiring light of the fire he beheld, just above the disk of the rock, what appeared to be the grim visage of the drowned buccaneer, grinning hideously down upon him.

Wolfert gave a loud cry, and let fall the lantern. His panic communicated itself to his companions. The negro leaped out of the hole; the doctor dropped his book and basket, and began to pray in German. All was horror and confusion. The fire was scattered about, the lantern extinguished. In their hurry-scurry they ran against and confounded one another. They fancied a legion of hobgoblins let loose upon them, and that they saw, by the fitful gleams of the scattered embers, strange figures, in red caps, gibbering and ramping around them. The doctor ran one way, the negro another, and Wolfert made for the water side. As he plunged struggling onwards through brush and brake, he heard the tread of some one in pursuit. He scrambled frantically forward. The footsteps gained upon him. He felt himself grasped by his cloak, when suddenly his pursuer was attacked in turn. A fierce fight and struggle ensued—a pistol was discharged that lit up rock and bush for a second, and showed two figures grappling together—all was then darker than ever. The contest continued —the combatants clinched each other, and panted, and groaned, and rolled among the rocks. There was snarling and growling as of a cur, mingled with curses, in which Wolfert fancied he could recognize the voice of the buccaneer. He would fain have fled, but he was on the brink of a precipice, and could go no further.

Again the parties were on their feet; again there was a tugging and struggling, as if strength alone could decide the combat, until one was precipitated from the brow of the cliff, and sent headlong into the deep stream that whirled below. Wolfert heard the plunge, and a kind of bubbling murmur, but the darkness of the night hid everything from him, and the swiftness of the current swept everything instantly out of hearing. One of the combatants was disposed of, but whether friend or foe, Wolfert could not tell, nor whether they might not both be foes. He heard the survivor approach, and his terror revived. He saw, where the profile of the rocks rose against the horizon, a human form advancing. He could not be mistaken! it must be the buccaneer. Whither should he fly!—a precipice was on one side—a murderer on the other. The enemy approached—he was close at hand. Wolfert attempted to let himself down the face of the cliff. His cloak caught in a thorn that grew on the edge. He was jerked from off his feet, and held dangling in the air, half choked by the string with which his careful wife had fastened the garment around his neck. Wolfert thought his last moment had arrived; when the string broke, and he tumbled down the bank, bumping from rock to rock, and bush to bush, and leaving the red cloak fluttering like a banner in the air.

It was a long while before Wolfert came to himself. When he opened his eyes, the ruddy streaks of morning were already shooting up the sky. He found himself grievously battered, and lying in the bottom of a boat. He attempted to sit up, but was too sore and stiff to move. A voice requested him in friendly accents to lie still. He turned his eyes towards the speaker; it was Dirk Waldron. He had dogged the party, at the earnest request of Dame Webber and her daughter. Dirk had been completely distanced in following the light skiff of the fisherman, and had just come in to rescue the poor money-digger from his pursuer.

Thus ended this perilous enterprise. The doctor and Black Sam severally found their way back to the Manhattoes, each having some dreadful tale of peril to relate. As to poor Wolfert, instead of returning in triumph laden with bags of gold, he was borne home on a shutter, followed by a rabble-rout of curious urchins. His wife and daughter saw the dismal pageant from a distance, and alarmed the neighborhood with their cries. The whole town was in a buzz with the story of the money-diggers. Many repaired to the scene of the previous night's adventures; but though they found the very place of the digging, they discovered nothing that compensated them for their trouble. Some say they found the fragments of an oaken chest, and an iron pot-lid, which savored strongly of hidden money; and that in the old family vault there were traces of bales and boxes; but this is all very dubious.

In fact, the secret of all this story has never to this day been discovered; whether any treasure were ever actually buried at that place; whether, if so, it were carried off at night by those who had buried it; or whether it still remains there under the guardianship of gnomes and spirits until it shall be properly sought for, is all matter of conjecture.

There were many conjectures formed, also, as to who and what was the strange man of the seas who had domineered over the little fraternity at Corlaer's Hook for a time; disappeared so strangely, and reappeared so fearfully. Some supposed him a smuggler stationed at that place to assist his comrades in landing their goods among the rocky coves of the island. Others, that he was one of the ancient comrades of Kidd or Bradish, returned to convey away treasures formerly hidden in the vicinity. The only circumstance that throws anything like a vague light on this mysterious matter, is a report which prevailed of a strange foreign-built shallop, with much the look of a picaroon,

having been seen hovering about the Sound for several days without landing or reporting herself, though boats were seen going to and from her at night; and that she was seen standing out of the mouth of the harbor, in the gray of the dawn, after the catastrophe of the money-diggers. I must not omit to mention another report, also, of the buccaneer, who was supposed to have been drowned, being seen before daybreak with a lantern in his hand, seated astride of his great sea-chest, and sailing through Hell-gate, which just then began to roar and bellow with redoubled fury.

While all the gossip world was thus filled with talk and rumor, poor Wolfert lay sick and sorrowfully in his bed, bruised in body and sorely beaten down in mind. His wife and daughter did all they could to bind up his wounds, both corporal and spiritual. The good old dame never stirred from his bedside, where she sat knitting from morning till night; while his daughter busied herself about him with the fondest care. It was a moving sight to behold him wasting away day by day; growing thinner and thinner, and ghastlier and ghastlier.

Dirk Waldron was the only being that seemed to shed a ray of sunshine into this house of mourning. He came in with cheery look and manly spirit, and tried to reanimate the expiring heart of the poor money-digger, but it was all in vain. Wolfert was completely done over. If anything was wanting to complete his despair, it was a notice served upon him in the midst of his distress, that the corporation were about to run a new street through the very centre of his cabbage-garden. He now saw nothing before him but poverty and ruin. His last reliance, the garden of his forefathers, was to be laid waste, and what then was to become of his poor wife and child?

His eyes filled with tears as they followed the dutiful Amy out of the room one morning. Dirk Waldron was seated beside him; Wolfert grasped his hand, pointed after his daughter, and for the first time since his illness, broke the silence he had maintained.

FROM THE TOWER WINDOW

"I am going!" said he, shaking his head feebly, "and when I am gone—my poor daughter—."

"Leave her to me, father!" said Dirk, manfully—"I'll take care of her!"

Wolfert looked up in the face of the cheery, strapping youngster, and saw there was none better able to take care of a woman.

"Enough," said he, "she is yours!—and now fetch me a lawyer and let me make my will and die."

The lawyer was brought—a dapper, bustling, round-headed little man, Roorback (or Rollebuck as it was pronounced) by name. At the sight of him the women broke into loud lamentations. Wolfert made a feeble motion for them to be silent. Poor Amy buried her face and her grief in the bed-curtain. Dame Webber resumed her knitting to hide her distress, which betrayed itself however in a pellucid tear, which trickled silently down, and hung at the end of her peaked nose; while the cat, the only unconcerned member of the family, played with the good dame's ball of worsted, as it rolled about the floor.

Wolfert lay on his back, his night-cap drawn over his forehead; his eyes closed; his whole visage the picture of death. He begged the lawyer to be brief, for he felt his end approaching, and that he had no time to lose. The lawyer nibbed his pen, spread out his paper, and prepared to write.

" I give and bequeath," said Wolfert, faintly, "my small farm"–

"What—all!" exclaimed the lawyer.

Wolfert half opened his eyes and looked upon the lawyer.

"Yes—all," said he.

"What! all the great patch of land with cabbages and sunflowers, which the corporation is just going to run a main street through?"

"The same," said Wolfert, with a heavy sigh, and sinking back upon his pillow.

"I wish him joy that inherits it!" said the little lawyer, chuckling, and rubbing his hands involuntarily.

"What do you mean?" said Wolfert, again opening his eyes.

"That he'll be one of the richest men in the place!" cried little Rollebuck.

The expiring Wolfert seemed to step back from the threshold of existence; his eyes again lighted up; he raised himself in his bed, shoved back his red worsted night-cap, and stared broadly at the lawyer.

"You don't say so!" exclaimed he.

"Faith, but I do!" rejoined the other.—"Why, when that great field and that huge meadow come to be laid out in streets, and cut up into snug building lots—why, whoever owns it need not pull off his hat to the patroon!"

"Say you so?" cried Wolfert, half thrusting one leg out of bed, "why, then I think I'll not make my will yet!"

To the surprise of everybody the dying man actually recovered. The vital spark, which had glimmered faintly in the socket, received fresh fuel from the oil of gladness, which the little lawyer poured into his soul. It once more burnt up into a flame.

Give physic to the heart, ye who would revive the body of a spirit-broken man! In a few days Wolfert left his room; in a few days more his table was covered with deeds, plans of streets, and building-lots. Little Rollebuck was constantly with him, his right hand man and adviser and instead of making his will, assisted in the more agreeable task of making his fortune. In fact Wolfert Webber was one of those worthy Dutch burghers of the Man-hattoes whose fortunes have been made, in a manner, in spite of themselves; who have tenaciously held on to their hereditary acres, raising turnips and cabbages about the skirts of the city, hardly able to make both ends meet, until the corporation has cruelly driven streets through their abodes, and they have suddenly awakened out of their lethargy, and, to their astonishment, found themselves rich men.

Before many months had elapsed, a great bustling street

passed through the very center of the Webber garden, just where Wolfert had dreamed of finding a treasure. His golden dream was accomplished; he did indeed find an unlooked-for source of wealth; for, when his paternal lands were distributed into building lots, and rented out to safe tenants, instead of producing a paltry crop of cabbages, they returned him an abundant crop of rent; insomuch that on quarter-day it was a goodly sight to see his tenants knocking at the door, from morning till night, each with a little round-bellied bag of money, a golden produce of the soil.

The ancient mansion of his forefathers was still kept up; but instead of being a little yellow-fronted Dutch house in a garden, it now stood boldly in the midst of a street, the grand home of the neighborhood; for Wolfert enlarged it with a wing on each side, and cupola or tea-room on top, where he might climb up and smoke.

As Wolfert waxed old, and rich, and corpulent, he also set up a great gingerbread-colored carriage, drawn by a pair of black Flanders mares with tails that swept the ground; and to commemorate the origin of his greatness, he had for his crest a full-blown cabbage painted on the panels, with the pithy motto ALLES KOPF, that is to say, ALL HEAD; meaning thereby that he had risen by sheer headwork.

To fill the measure of his greatness, in the fullness of time the renowned Ramm Rapelye slept with his fathers and Wolfert Webber succeeded to the leather-bottomed arm-chair, in the inn-parlor at Corlaer's Hook; where he long reigned greatly honored and respected, insomuch that he was never known to tell a story without its being believed, nor to utter a joke without its being laughed at.

—*Abridged*

Alles Kopf

MY BOOK HOUSE

THE TWO PILGRIMS*
Leo N. Tolstoy

Jesus saith unto her, Woman, believe me, the hour cometh when ye shall neither in this mountain, nor yet at Jerusalem, worship the Father.

But the hour cometh, and now is, when the true worshippers shall worship the Father in spirit and in truth: for the Father seeketh such to worship him.—John IV, 21, 23.

TWO old men once resolved to go on a pilgrimage to worship God in ancient Jerusalem. One was a rich peasant named E'fim Shev'e-lef. The other was not so well off—E-li'sha Bo'drof.

Efim was very sedate. He never drank vodka, never smoked tobacco, never took snuff. In all his life he had never used a bad word, and he was always strict and upright. His family was large,—two sons and a married grandson,—and all lived together. As for himself, he was hale, long-bearded, erect, and though he was nearly seventy, his beard was only beginning to grow gray.

Elisha was a little old man, neither rich nor poor. In former times he had gone about doing odd jobs in carpentry; but now as he grew older, he began to stay at home and raise bees. One of his sons had gone away to work, the other was at home. Elisha was good-natured and jolly. It is true he sometimes drank vodka, he sometimes took snuff and he liked to sing songs; but he was a peaceable man and lived on the friendliest terms with his family and neighbors.

Now the old men had taken a vow long ago to go to Jerusalem together, but Efim had never found the leisure,—his engagements had never come to an end. As soon as one was through with, another began. First he had to arrange his grandson's marriage; then to wait for his youngest son's return from the army; and then again, he planned to build a new out-building.

One holiday the old men met and were sitting in the sun. "Well," said Elisha, "when shall we set out to fulfil our vow?"

* Used by permission of the publishers, Thomas Y. Crowell Company.

152

FROM THE TOWER WINDOW

Efim knit his brow. "We must wait a while," says he. "This year it'll come hard for me. I am engaged in putting up this building. You see that'll take till summer. In the summer, God willing, we will go without fail."

"It seems to me," says Elisha, "we ought not to put it off. We ought to go today. It's the very time—spring."

"The time's right enough, but what about my building? How can I leave that. It's a great responsibility."

"Eh, friend, we can never get through all we have to do. The other day the women-folk at home were washing and cleaning house, fixing up for Easter. Here something needed doing, there something else, and they could not get everything done. So my eldest daughter who's a sensible woman, says: 'We may be thankful the holiday comes without waiting for us, or, however hard we worked, we should never be ready for it.'"

Efim grew thoughtful. "I've spent a lot of money on this building," he said, "and we can't start on our journey with empty pockets. We shall want a hundred roubles apiece,— and that's no small sum."

Elisha laughed out. "Come, come, old friend," says he, "you are ten times as well off as I, and yet you talk about money! Only say when we are to start, and though I have nothing now, I shall have enough by then."

Efim also smiled. "Dear me! Where will you get it all from?"

"I can scrape some together at home, and if that's not enough, I'll sell half a score of hives to my neighbor."

"If they swarm well this year you'll lose by it. You'll regret it!"

"Regret it! Not I, neighbor! I never regretted anything in my life except my sins! We took the vows, so let us go. Now seriously, let us go."

So Elisha succeeded in persuading his comrade.

At the end of a week the old men had made their preparations. Efim had money enough at hand. He took a hundred roubles himself and left two hundred for his wife. Elisha too got ready. He sold ten hives to his neighbor, and received from him, all told, seventy roubles. The rest of the hundred roubles he scraped together from the members of his household, fairly cleaning them all out. His old woman and his daughter-in-law gave him all their savings. Efim gave his eldest son definite commands about everything,—what meadows to rent out, where to put manure, and how to finish and roof in the out-building. He gave anxious thought to everything; he fore-ordered everything. But Elisha only directed his old woman to hive the young swarm of bees he had sold, and given them to his neighbor without trickery. About household affairs he did not have a word to say. "If anything comes up, you will know what to do when the time comes. You people at home do just as you think best."

The old men were now ready. Their wives baked a lot of flat cakes, made them some travelling bags, and cut them new leg wrappers. Then the men put on new boots, took some extra shoes of platted bark, and set forth. The folks kept them company as far as the common pasture.

Elisha set out in good spirits; and as soon as he left the village he forgot all about his cares. His only thoughts were how to please his companion, how not to say a single churlish word to anyone, and how to go in peace and love to the Holy Place. He walked along the road, always whispering a prayer or calling to memory some saint's life. And if he met any one on the road or came to a halting place, he made himself useful and as agreeable as possible, and even said a word in God's service. So he went his way rejoicing. One thing only Elisha could not do. He intended to give up snuff-taking and left his snuff-box at home, but a man on the road gave him some of the stuff, and now and again, he dropped behind his companion so as not to lead him into temptation, and took a pinch.

Efim also got along well. He did nothing wicked, and said

nothing churlish, but he was not easy in his mind. He could not help always thinking of his household affairs. He kept worrying about what was going on at home. Had he remembered to give his son this order or that? And was his son doing as he had been told? Efim was almost ready to turn round and go back to see for himself how things were going.

Five weeks the old men journeyed, till they came to the land of the Top-Knots (Little Russia). From the time that they left home they had been obliged to pay for lodging and meals, but now that they had come among the Top-Knots the people began to vie with each other in asking them into their huts. They gave them shelter and fed them and would not take money from them, but even put bread and flat cakes into their bags for them to eat on the journey. Thus the old men traveled nearly seven hundred versts. But when they passed through this province they came to a place where the harvest had failed. Here the people received them kindly and gave them free lodging at night but they could no longer feed them without pay. Sometimes the two pilgrims could not even get bread when they offered to pay for it, for there was none to be had. Those who were rich in the district had been ruined; those who lived in medium style had come down to nothing; but the poor had almost perished in their homes. All winter they had been living on husks and pig-weed.

One time the old men reached a little river. They sat down, filled their cups with water, ate a little bread, and changed their shoes. As they sat there resting, Elisha took out his snuff-box. Efim shook his head at him in reproof.

"Why," says he, "don't you throw away that nasty stuff?"

Elisha wrung his hands. "It is an evil habit. Please God, I may some day overcome it."

Soon they came to a great village. It had grown hot and Elisha was ready to drop with fatigue. He wanted to rest and have a drink, but Efim would not halt. Efim was the stronger in walking and it was hard for Elisha to keep up with him.

"I'd like a drink," says he.

"All right. Get a drink. I don't want any."

Elisha stopped.

"Don't wait," says he. "I'm only going to run in at this hut for a minute and get a drink. I'll overtake you in a jiffy."

So Efim proceeded on his way alone, and Elisha turned back.

The hut was small and plastered with mud, black below, whitewashed above. It was in bad condition, and apparently had not been kept up in a long time. In one place the thatch on the roof was quite broken through. Elisha went into the yard. There on a pile of earth, lay a thin, beardless man in shirt and drawers. Evidently he had lain down when it was cool, but now the sun beat straight upon him. Yet he lay there still, and was not asleep. Elisha shouted and asked him for a drink. The man made no reply.

"Either he's sick or he's ugly," thought Elisha and he went to the door. Inside, he heard children crying. He took hold of the ring that served as a door handle and rapped with it.

"Hey, masters!" he called. There was no reply. Again he rapped with his staff and called. No one answered. Elisha was about to proceed on his way when Hark! he thought he heard some one groaning behind the door.

FROM THE TOWER WINDOW

"Can some misfortune have befallen these people?" he thought. "I must look and see."

And Elisha went into the dwelling room. To the left he saw a brick oven, in front against the wall, an icon-stand with a table before it. By the table on a bench sat an old woman with dishevelled hair, wearing only a single shirt. She was resting her head on the table, and at her elbow stood an emaciated little boy, pale as wax, with distended belly. He was tugging at her sleeve, and screaming at the top of his voice begging for something.

In the hut the air was stifling. Elisha looked around and saw a woman lying on the floor behind the oven. She lay on her back and did not look up. Only sometimes she moaned. Evidently she could do nothing for herself and no one had been attending to her needs. The old woman raised her head.

"What do you want?" says she. "We hain't got nothing for you."

"I am a servant of God," says Elisha. "I came to get a drink."

"Hain't got any. Hain't got nothing to fetch it in. Go away."

Elisha began to question her. "Tell me, isn't there any one of you well enough to take care of the woman?"

"No, no one. My son is dying outside and we are dying in here."

The boy had ceased crying when he saw the stranger; but when the old woman spoke he began to tug again at her sleeve.

"Bread, granny, bread!" he screamed.

Elisha was going to ask more questions of the old woman, when the peasant came stumbling into the hut. He went along the wall and was going to sit on the bench but failed of it and fell into the corner at the threshold. He did not try to get up, but he did manage to speak. One word he speaks—then breaks off,—is out of breath,—speaks another:—

"Starving,—" says he, "he — is — dying — starvation." He motioned toward the boy and burst into tears.

Elisha shook off his sack from his shoulders, then lifted it to the bench and began to undo it. He took out a loaf of bread, cut off a slice with his knife and gave it to the man. The peasant would not take it, but pointed to the boy and to a girl crouching behind the oven as much as to say, "Give it to them, please."

Elisha held the bread out to the boy. The boy smelt it, stretched himself up, seized the slice with both hands and buried his nose in it. Then the little girl came out from behind the oven, staring at the loaf. Elisha gave her some also, and still another chunk he cut off for the old woman.

"Would you bring some water?" said the old woman, "their mouths are parched. I tried to get some, yesterday or today,— I don't remember which—I fell, couldn't get there. The bucket is where I dropped it unless some one has stolen it."

Elisha went and found the bucket, brought water, and gave the people a drink. The children and the old woman ate the bread with the water, but the man would not eat.

"I cannot eat," he said.

All this time the younger woman did not show any signs of consciousness but continued to toss about.

Elisha went to the village, bought at the shop some millet, salt, flour, butter. He found an axe, split some wood, and made a fire. The little girl began to help him. Then he boiled some soup and gave the starving people a meal.

The peasant and the old woman ate only a little, but the girl and boy licked the bowl clean, and lay down to sleep locked in each other's arms. Then the man and the old woman began to relate how all this had come upon them.

"We weren't rich even before this," said the peasant, "but when nothing grew we had to give all we had for food last autumn. Then we had to go begging among our neighbors and kind people. At first they gave to us, but then they sent us away because they had nothing. Yes, and we were ashamed to beg. We got in debt to everyone. I tried to get work, but there was no work to be had. The old woman and the little girl had to go a long way off begging. Not much was given them. No one had any bread to spare. And so we lived, hoping we'd get on somehow till new crops came. Then people stopped giving at all and we began to starve. We had nothing to eat but herbs. So my wife became sick and I haven't any strength left."

"I was the only one," says the old woman, "who kept up. But without eating I lost my strength too, and the little girl got puny. We tried to send her to the neighbor's but she would not go. She crept into a corner and wouldn't come out. Day before yesterday a neighbor came round and saw that we were starving, but her husband had left her and she hadn't anything to feed her own little children with. So she turned round and went off. And we lay here waiting for death."

Elisha listened to their talk, changed his mind about going to rejoin his companion that day and spent the night there.

In the morning he got up and did the chores as though he were master of the house. He and the old woman kneaded the bread, and he kindled the fire. Then he went with the little girl to the neighbor's to get what was needed, for there was nothing at all in the hut,—cooking utensils, clothing and all had been given for bread. Elisha began to lay in a supply of the most necessary things. Some he made and some he bought. Thus he spent one day, spent a second, spent also a third.

The little boy got better, began to climb up on the bench and caress Elisha. And the little girl became perfectly gay and began to help in all things. She kept running after Elisha crying, "Granddad, dear little granddaddy!" The old woman also got up and went among the neighbors, and the man began to walk, supporting himself by the wall. Only the wife could not get up. But on the third day she began to ask for something to eat.

"Well," thinks Elisha. "I didn't expect to spend so much time. Now I'll be going."

On the fourth day meat-eating was allowed for the first time after the fast, and Elisha thought, "Come, now, I will buy these people something for their feast, and toward evening I will go."

So he went to the village again, bought milk, white flour, lard, and he and the old woman boiled and baked. On this day the wife also got up and began to creep about. And the peasant shaved, put on a clean shirt,—the old woman had washed it out— and went to the village to ask mercy of a rich peasant to whom his plough-land and meadow were mortgaged. He went to beg the rich peasant to grant him the use of the meadow and field until after the harvest. Towards evening he came back, gloomy and in tears. The rich peasant would not have mercy on him. He said, "Bring your money."

Again Elisha fell into thought.

"How are they to live now?" thinks he. "Others will go hay-making, but there will be nothing for these people to mow. Their rye is ripening, but the rich peasant has the use of their field. If I go away, they'll all drift back into the same state I found them in."

Elisha was much troubled by these thoughts. At last he decided not to leave that evening but to wait until morning. He went into the yard to sleep, said his prayers and lay down. But he could not sleep.

"I must go," he kept saying to himself. "Here I've been spending so much time and money—but I'm sorry for these people. I meant to give them some water and a slice of bread, and just see where it has landed me. Now it's a case of redeeming their meadow and their field. And when that's done, I shall have to buy a cow for the children, and a horse to cart the man's sheaves. Here you are in a pretty pickle, brother Elisha! You're anchored here and you don't get off so easy!"

He lay and lay and the cocks were already crowing when he finally fell into a doze. Suddenly something seemed to wake him up. He saw himself, as it were, all dressed to go, with his sack and his staff; and the gate stood ajar so that he could just squeeze through. He was about to pass out when his sack caught against the fence on one side. He tried to free it, when lo! his leg-band caught on the other side and came undone. He pulled at the sack, and then he saw that it was not caught on the fence,— the little girl was holding it and crying, "Granddad, dear little granddaddy, bread!" He looked down at his leg, and the little boy was clinging to his leg-wrapper. The old woman and the man were gazing from the window.

Elisha woke up and said to himself aloud, "Tomorrow I will redeem the field and the meadow. I will buy a horse and a cow, and flour enough to last till the new crop comes. A man may go across the sea to find Christ, and lose him in his own soul. I must set these people right."

Early in the morning Elisha went to the rich peasant and redeemed the rye field and the meadow-land. Then he bought a scythe, brought it back with him and sent the man out to the field to mow. Hearing that the inn-keeper had a horse and cart for sale, he struck a bargain with him and bought them. He bought also a sack of flour, put it in the cart and started on to see about a cow. But as he jogged along he overtook two women talking. Elisha made out that they were speaking of him.

"Heavens! That is no ordinary man. He stopped to get a drink and then he stayed. Just think of all he has done for them! Whatever they needed, he bought! I myself saw him this very day buy a nag and a cart of the tavern keeper. There are not many such men in the world."

Elisha understood that they were making much of what he had done. So he did not go on to buy the cow but turned back and drove with the wheat to the hut. As he reined in at the gate, and dismounted from the telyega, everybody in the house saw the horse and was astonished. It came to them that he had bought the horse for them, but they dared not say so.

"Where did you get the nag, grandpa?" says the man.

"O, I bought her," says Elisha, "She was going cheap. Put a little grass in the stall for her, please. Yes, and lug in the bag."

The man unharnessed the horse, lugged the bag into the house, and put a lot of grass in the stall. Then everybody went to bed. But Elisha lay down out of doors. When all the folks were asleep, he got up, fastened his boots, put on his kaftan, and started on his way after Efim.

By-and-by it began to grow light. He sat down under a tree, opened his sack and counted his money. There were only seventeen roubles, twenty kopeks left.

"Well," thinks he, "with this I'll never get across the sea. But Friend Efim will get to Jerusalem and set a candle at the shrines in my name. As for me, I shall have to go back home. It looks as though I should never fulfill my vow in this life. Thank the Lord, the Master is kind. He will have patience."

Elisha got up, lifted his sack upon his shoulders, and started for home. Only he went out of his way to pass around the village instead of going through it, so that the people might not see him and praise him again for what he had done. And Elisha reached home quickly. In coming, the way had often seemed hard to him, and it had been almost beyond his strength to keep up with Efim, but going back God gave him such strength that he walked along gaily, swinging his staff, making his seventy versts a day, and knowing no fatigue.

When Elisha returned, the fields had already been harvested. The folks were delighted to see their old man. They began to ask him questions,—how and what and why he had left his companion and come home. Elisha only answered, "I spent my money on the road and got behind Efim. May God forgive me!"

And he handed his old woman his remaining money. Then he inquired about the domestic affairs. Everything was just as it should be. There had been nothing left undone in the farmwork and all were living in peace and harmony. On this very same day Efim's people heard that Elisha had returned, and came round to ask after their old man. Elisha told them the same thing.

"Your old man went on sturdily. I meant to catch up with him, but then I spent my money and, as I couldn't go on with what I had, I came back."

People wondered how such a sensible man could have done so foolishly,—start out, only waste his money and come home. They wondered and forgot. And Elisha forgot, too. He began to do the chores again, helped his son chop wood against the winter, threshed the corn with the women, rethatched the shed, and arranged about the bees. Then he settled himself down for the winter to plat shoes of bark and chisel out logs for bee-hives.

All that day while Elisha stopped behind in the sick people's hut, Efim waited for his companion. He went a little way and sat down. He waited, waited,—went to sleep, woke up,—still sat there,—no companion! He looked around with all his eyes. Already the sun had sunk behind the trees. No Elisha!

"Perhaps he has passed me," thought Efim. "If I should go back, we might miss each other. I will go on. Without doubt we will meet at our lodging."

So he went on to the next village, and asked the village policeman to send such and such an old man if he came along to yonder hut where he intended to lodge. But Elisha did not come.

As Efim went further, he asked everybody if they had seen a little, bald old man. No one had. Efim wondered and went on alone. By-and-by he met a pilgrim who was going to Jerusalem for the second time. He wore a skull-cap and cassock, and had very long hair. They got into conversation and went on together. At Odessa they waited thrice twenty-four hours for a ship. Here, many pilgrims were waiting from different lands, and again Efim made inquiries about Elisha. No one had seen him.

So Efim bought his ticket, also some bread and herring for the voyage, and the pilgrims embarked. At evening a wind sprang up, it began to get rough, and the waves dashed over the ship. People were thrown about, women began to scream, and the weaker among the men rushed around trying to find a safe place. Fear fell upon Efim also, but he did not show it. Exactly where he had sat down on coming aboard, near some old men from Tambof, there he kept sitting all night, and all the next day until it cleared off. The vessel stopped at Tsar-grad, at Smyrna, and Alexandria, and at last reached happily, the city of Jaffa, whence it was seventy versts on foot to Jerusalem. Here, all the pilgrims disembarked, and they were panic stricken again at landing. The ship was high, and they had to jump from the deck down into little boats. The boats rocked so much that one might easily miss them and fall into the water. Two men did get drenched, but at last all were safely landed.

They started off on foot, and on the third day after landing, reached Jerusalem. Here they established themselves at the Russian Hostelry. After dinner they went with the pilgrims to visit the Holy Places,—first to the Patriarchal Monastery where all the pilgrims assembled. The women were sitting in one place, the men in another and all were bidden to take off their shoes. Then a monk came in with a towel and began to wash their feet. Efim stood through vesper and matin services, prayed and placed candles at the shrines.

Next morning they visited the cell of Mary of Egypt, and then went on to Abraham's Monastery, to see the place where Abraham was going to sacrifice his son. They visited the spot where Christ appeared to Mary Magdalene, and also the church of James, the brother of the Lord. The pilgrim showed Efim all these sights and always told him just how much money he should give at each place.

They returned for dinner to the hostelry, and after dinner, just as they were getting ready to lie down and rest, the pilgrim began to say *Akh!* to shake his clothes, to search. "I have been robbed of my purse and all my money," he cried. And he mourned and mourned, but there was nothing to be done.

Efim lay down to sleep, but as he did so temptation fell upon him. He kept thinking, "The pilgrim's money was not stolen. He never had any. He told me where to give my money, but he never gave any himself. Yes, and he borrowed a rouble of me. It's all a trick!"

Then Efim began to scold himself, "What right have I to judge a man? It is a sin. I must not think about it."

But still he could not keep his thoughts from condemning the pilgrim.

Next morning they got up and went to early mass in the great Church of the Resurrection. The pilgrim would not leave Efim. He stuck tight to him wherever he went. A great crowd of pilgrims were collected in the church, Russians, Greeks, Armenians, Turks, Syrians, and all peoples. A monk led the crowd

through the sacred gates, past Turkish guards, to the place where the Savior was taken from the cross and anointed,—where the nine great candlesticks now are burning. Here Efim too placed a candle. The monk pointed out everything and told them everything. Then Efim was led to the right, up a little flight of steps to Golgotha, where the cross stood. Here he said a prayer, and saw the hole where the earth opened when it was shaken to its nethermost depths at the crucifixion. He saw too, the spot where they fastened the hands and feet of Jesus to the cross, the stone on which he sat when they put upon his head the crown of thorns, the pillar to which they bound him when they scourged him. The monk was going to show the pilgrims something more but the crowd was in a hurry. They all rushed to the very grotto of the Lord's sepulchre, and Efim went along with the throng.

He was anxious to get rid of the pilgrim, for in his thoughts he was continually judging the man instead of thinking on holy things. But the pilgrim would not be got rid of. In he went with Efim to mass at the Lord's sepulchre. They tried to get a place at the front, but were too late. The people were wedged so closely together that there was no moving either backwards or forwards. Efim stood looking toward the holy place and praying, but it was of no use. Every now and then he must feel whether his purse was still in its place. He was of two minds, wishing to pray and yet thinking, "Either the pilgrim deceived me, or if he was really robbed, why the same thing might happen to me."

Thus Efim stood, looking toward the chapel where the sepulchre was, with the thirty-six lamps burning beside it. He was peering over the heads of the people, when what a marvel! Just beneath the lamps where the blessed fire burns, in the very foremost place, he saw a little old man in a coarse kaftan, with a bald spot over his whole head,—for all the world like Elisha Bodroff.

"It's Elisha," he thinks. "Yet no! It can't be! He can't have got here before me. The ship before ours started a week sooner. He could not possibly have caught that. And he was not on our boat for I saw all the pilgrims."

While Efim was thus reasoning, the little old man bent to pray. As he did so, Efim recognized him. It was Elisha himself.

Efim was filled with joy and wondered how Elisha could have got there ahead of him. "Well done, Elisha!" he thought. "See how he has pushed ahead. He must have come across someone who showed him how to do it. Let me just meet him when he goes out, I'll get rid of this pilgrim fellow and go with him. Perhaps he will get me a front place too!"

All the time Efim kept his eyes on Elisha, so as not to miss him. Now the mass was over and the crowd reeled and struggled, in trying to make their way out. Efim was pushed to one side. Again the fear came upon him that some one would steal his money. Clutching his purse, he managed to break through the crowd into an open space, but now he had lost Elisha.

In the cloisters of the church he saw many people. Some were eating and drinking; some were sleeping and reading. But there was no Elisha anywhere. Efim returned to the hostelry and this evening the pilgrim failed to return. He disappeared and never gave back Efim's rouble. So Efim was left alone.

On the next day Efim went once more to the Lord's sepulchre. He wanted to get to the front as before, but was crowded back so he could only stand by a pillar and pray. But there again, under the lamps, in the very foremost place by the sepulchre of the Lord, stood Elisha with his arms spread out like a priest at the altar, and the light shining all over his bald head.

"Well," thinks Efim, "now I'll surely not miss him."

He tried to push through to the front. But when he succeeded, no Elisha! Vanished just as before!

On the third day Efim looked again toward the Lord's sepulchre; again he saw Elisha in the same place with the same aspect, his arms outspread, and the light shining all over his head.

"This time," thinks Efim, "I'll go and stand at the door. There we can't miss each other."

Half a day he stood by the door. All the people passed out, but there was no Elisha among them.

Efim spent six weeks in Jerusalem, and visited everything. He went to Bethlehem too, and Bethany, and the Jordan. He had a seal stamped on a new shirt at the Lord's sepulchre that he might be buried in it, and he took a bottle of water from the Jordan, and some holy earth, and bought candles that had been lit at the sacred flame. So he spent all his money except enough to get him home, and then started out on the return journey.

Efim walked alone over the same road as before. But again the worriment came over him as to how the folks at home had got on without him, and whether his son had conducted affairs

FROM THE TOWER WINDOW

so there would be no loss. Thus Efim reached that place where a year before he had parted from Elisha. It was impossible to recognize the people. Before they were so wretchedly poor, now there had been good crops and all lived in sufficiency and comfort. At evening, Efim reached the very village where the year before Elisha had stopped. He had hardly entered it when a little girl in a white smock, sprang out from behind a hut.

"Grandpa! Dear Grandpa! Come into our house!"

Efim was inclined to go on, but the little girl would not allow him. She seized him by the skirts, pulled him along into the hut and laughed. From the doorstep a woman with a little boy also beckoned to him. "Come in, please, grand-sire,—and take supper and spend the night with us."

Efim went in.

"I may as well ask about Elisha," he thought. "No doubt this is the very hut where he stopped to get a drink."

The woman took Efim's sack, gave him a chance to wash, and set him at the table. She put on milk, curd-cakes, and porridge. Efim thanked and praised her for being so hospitable to pilgrims. The woman shook her head.

"We have good reason to be hospitable to pilgrims," she said. "For we owe our lives to a pilgrim. Last summer things went so badly with us that we were all starving,—had nothing to eat and should have died, but that God sent such a nice old man to help us. He came in just at noon to get a drink. But when he saw us, he was sorry for us, and staid on with us. He gave us something to drink, fed us and put us on our legs. And beside all that, he bought back our land and gave us a horse and telyega."

Here the old woman came into the hut and interrupted the younger one. "And we don't know at all," says she, "whether it was a man or an angel of God. He loved us all and pitied us all, and went away without even telling us his name."

At nightfall came the peasant himself on horseback. He also

169

began to tell about Elisha and what he had done for them.

"If he had not come to us," says he, "we should all have died in our sins. We were perishing in despair. We murmured against God and against men. But he set us on our feet. Through him we learned to know God, and came to believe that there is good in man. Christ bless him! Before, we lived like cattle. He made us men."

The people fed Efim, and fixed him up for the night, then they themselves lay down to sleep. But Efim was unable to sleep. He kept thinking how he had seen Elisha in Jerusalem three times in the foremost place.

"That's how he got there before me," he thinks. "God may or may not have accepted my pilgrimage, but He has certainly accepted his."

Next morning Efim bade farewell to the people, they put some patties in his sack, and he continued his journey.

Efim had been away just a year, and it was spring when he reached home again. His son was not at the house. He had gone to the tavern. When he returned he was tipsy. Efim began to question him. He found that the young man had got into bad ways during his absence, had spent all the money foolishly and neglected everything. At this the father grew angry and beat his son. In the morning he went to the village elder to complain of the lad. On the way he passed Elisha's house. Elisha's old woman was standing on the doorstep. "How's your health, neighbor," says she. "Did you have a good pilgrimage?"

"Glory to God," says Efim. "Yes, I have been to Jerusalem. I lost your old man, but I hear he got home safely."

"Yes, he got back," the old woman began to prattle. "And glad enough we were that God brought him. It was lonesome for us without him. And how glad our lad was to see him. 'Without father,' says he, 'is like being without sunlight.' We love him and we missed him so."

FROM THE TOWER WINDOW

"Well, is he at home now?"

"Yes, friend, he's with the bees, hiving the new swarms. Such splendid swarms, he says, God never gave us before."

Efim passed on to the apiary where Elisha was. There he stood in his gray kaftan, under a little birch tree, without a face-net or gloves to protect him, looking upwards, his arms stretched out, and his bald head shining, just as Efim had seen him in Jerusalem at the Lord's sepulchre. And just as the sacred fire had burned above him in Jerusalem, so now the sunlight came sifting down through the birch-tree, and shone all over his head, the golden bees flew about like a halo, and never stung him.

Elisha's old woman called to her husband. "Our neighbor's come!"

Elisha was delighted, and came to meet his comrade, calmly detaching the bees from his beard.

"How are you, comrade?" he cries. "Did you have a good journey? Did you get to Jerusalem safely?"

Efim was silent for a moment, then he answered:

"My feet walked there, and I have brought you back some water from the river Jordan. But whether the Lord accepted my pilgrimage,—whether it was my soul or another's that has been there more truly,—"

"That is God's affair, comrade, God's affair," interrupted Elisha.

"On my way back I stopped also at the hut where you—"

Elisha became confused. He hastened to repeat:

"That is God's affair, comrade, God's affair. Come on into the house and I will give you some honey." So Elisha changed the conversation.

Efim sighed and did not again remind Elisha of the people in the hut nor speak of how he had seen him in Jerusalem. But he now understood that the best way to serve God is to have a heart full of love and to do good deeds.

—*Abridged*

THE NEW COLOSSUS*
Emma Lazarus

Not like the brazen giant of Greek fame,
With conquering limbs astride from land to
     land;
Here at our sea-washed, sunset gates shall
     stand
A mighty woman with a torch, whose flame
Is the imprisoned lightning, and her name
Mother of Exiles. From her beacon-hand
Glows world-wide welcome; her mild eyes command
The air-bridged harbor that twin cities frame.

"Keep, ancient lands, your storied pomp!" cries she
With silent lips. "Give me your tired, your poor,
Your huddled masses yearning to breathe free,
The wretched refuse of your teeming shore.
Send these, the homeless, tempest-tost to me,
I lift my lamp beside the golden door!"

* From *Poems*. Used by permission of Houghton Mifflin Company.

FROM THE TOWER WINDOW

THE MELTING POT*
Israel Zangwill

ON one of the giant ocean liners that ploughed its way through the broad Atlantic from Europe towards America, there crossed once a young Jewish lad from Russia. With hundreds of other Europeans, poor peasants mostly, in every sort of odd European costume and speaking every variety of odd European tongue, he was close packed in the rocking steerage of the boat. The berth in which he slept was scarcely wider than his fiddle case and it hung near the kitchen, where the hot rancid smell of food and the oil of the machinery made offensive odors all day long and all night long. But in spite of this, David Quixano was happy. He was going to America—America, the land of all his hopes! His whole life long he had dreamed of going to America. Everybody in Kishineff, the Russian city where he lived, had friends there, or got money orders from there, and the very earliest game he could ever remember playing was selling off his toy furniture and setting up in America.

If the journey sometimes seemed hard and long, he had only to pretend that he had been shipwrecked and that after clinging to a plank five days on the lonely Atlantic, his frozen form had been picked up by this great safe steamer, and then his poor little berth seemed delightful and the rancid food delicious. Some-

*Retold from the Play by permission of The Macmillan Company.

times too he got out his beloved little old fiddle and played and played till he drew crowds of friendly faces about him. Somehow faces that turned towards David were always friendly, for there was that in the sunny warmth of his smile that left no room for aught but friendliness to answer it.

"A sunbeam took human shape when he was born," his uncle once had said.

And yet back in Russia David had left blackest memories. In the crowded Russian pale at Kishineff, wherein alone the Russian government permitted the Jews to dwell, he had once been the wonder-child who learned to play on the violin none knew how, out of his own heart, out of his own soul, with no other master; and old and young, rich and poor among the Jews had loved him. There dwelt his mother, too, and his father, and his sisters and his brothers, all happy together in the simple life of their little home. Then one day came into Kishineff a mysterious colonel in the uniform of the Tsar, and from him there began to ooze out into the city a secret poison of hatred against the Jews. Hatred and prejudice, calling itself religion, stirring the ugliest passions of men—first rumbling faintly like thunder in the distance, then swelling and roaring and gathering momentum till at last it burst in a hideous storm. Men and women in mobs, the scum of the town population, bore down on the unoffending dwellers in the pale, shouting, "Bey Zhida!" that is to say, "Kill the Jews!" Hither and thither they ran like tigers, looting, trampling peaceful men and women under foot, pitching children out of windows, stealing money, gold, silver, jewels, while the police and military officials lifted not a finger to protect the helpless or to stay the dastardly crime. Before David's very eyes father, mother, sisters, brothers fell, down to the youngest babe, while that mysterious colonel in the uniform of the Tsar stood by with cold aloofness, giving orders and looking on. David himself but escaped with his life because he was shot in the shoulder and fell to the ground unconscious, so the murderers left him for dead.

Ah! David was a sunny lad indeed, but when he thought back on what had happened to him in Russia, all the world for him was twisted out of shape; he saw it all through a fiery red mist; grief and anger filled his soul and he shrieked out against that butcher's face, shrieked out as though in all his life was but one wish—to find the owner of that face and make him pay the penalty for his crime. At such times he would get down his beloved fiddle and play and play and play. At first his violin would send forth crashing discords like the discord in his soul, but always at last his music fell into the sweet concord of perfect harmony with all the notes blending in unison. Then gradually the red mist would disappear and David be himself again.

At length the great steamer drew into New York Harbor. A little tug came out to meet it, leaving behind a smudgy trail of smoke, and as the small boat bobbed up and down on the choppy waves just beside the great one, a pilot made a perilous ascent by a swinging ladder up the side of the liner to the deck. All round about were hundreds of other tugs and launches, great boats and little boats from every quarter of the world, with funnels painted all different colors and flags of every nation fluttering in the breeze. But best of all to David, as he stood close to the rail looking out on it all with a fast-beating heart, were the American flags he saw everywhere—the stars and stripes, emblem of the America of his dreams, the America where were forever impossible the horrors of Kishineff.

Soon the shore-line of lower New York appeared, its giant sky-scrapers at tremendous heights cleaving the blue of the sky, but as the sea-weary passengers crowded to the rail, that which beckoned them first, that which bade them tenderly welcome as to a land of promise, was the colossal Statue of Liberty rising out of the harbor. In the midst of Jew and Gentile, Russian and Pole, Greek and Italian, Armenian and Turk, German and

Hungarian, Norwegian and Swede, there stood David, and before these wanderers from Europe who had turned their backs on the old world and their faces toward the new, loomed up out of the shining blue waters, that great gilded statue, lifting high her torch to lighten all the world.

Some among those immigrants tossed their caps in the air and cheered, some laughed and sang, some turned soon to other things, but some, like David, kept their eyes fixed in that one direction, moved almost to tears. Back of them lay who knew what of suffering, injustice and crushing poverty, but before them lay the land of hope, of equal rights and opportunities. To David that gigantic torch lifted high above the world a great ideal of liberty and justice, equal rights for Jew and Gentile, rich and poor, black and white, an ideal which should some day draw all men up to it in one grand brotherhood. That was the dream that had led him there, led him forth out of blood-soaked Kishineff to the shores of the Land of Promise. And so, clasping tight in his arms his beloved fiddle in its shabby case, he watched with solemn joy.

His joyousness did not desert him even during the trying time when, like herded cattle, he and the other immigrants were put off at Ellis Island and marshalled and driven through all the series of rigid examinations with which our United States welcomes newcomers to her shores. No, David had no complaints to make. He loved it all. He could not even speak the language of America and yet he was not lonely; the language of its spirit spoke surely to his heart and made him feel at home.

At length the day came when there he was in New York itself, and there was his good uncle, Mendel Quixano, to meet him, and his dear old grandmother too, a venerable figure in the prescribed black wig of the orthodox Jewess, clasping him in her arms and half sobbing his name in Yiddish, "Dovidel! Dovidel! Dovidel!"

Ah! but the home where his uncle and grandmother lived in New York seemed fine to him after the garret from which he had come in Russia and his tiny cramped quarters on the boat. It was an old house having a veranda with pillars in the colonial style, and on the door was carefully nailed a Mezuzah, a tiny metal case containing a passage from the Bible which every good Jew was commanded to have fastened to his doorpost. In the comfortable living room cheap chairs stood next a grand piano piled with music; huge mouldering old Hebrew tomes assorted with modern English books; and on the walls pictures of Wagner, Columbus, Washington, and Lincoln had to make themselves at home beside the Mizrach, or sacred Jewish picture hanging ever on the east wall toward Jerusalem. The whole effect was a curious blend of shabbiness, Americanism, Jewishness and music, all four of which seemed combined in the figure of Mendel Quixano, an elderly music master with a fine Jewish face pathetically furrowed by misfortune and graced by a short grizzled beard.

"A shabby place enough," Mendel would often say, looking discontentedly about. But David always made answer, "What's the matter with this room? It's princely. If it were only on board a boat not the richest man in America could afford such a magnificent cabin!"

In truth Mendel Quixano had been somewhat soured by misfortunes and disappointments, and he had by no means the sunny nature of David. With big hopes of becoming a great musician he had come to America, only to find that in order to pay the rent and support himself and his mother he must give music lessons every day in the week to little "brainless, earless, thumb-fingered Gentiles!" When his whole soul longed for the best in music, he must play cheap waltzes and rag-time for dances, at theatres, and in music halls.

"Ach Gott! What a life! What a life!" he would often sigh.

Mendel did not see in America what David did. He saw that there was still much prejudice here against his race, still much injustice, greed and inequality among men. His thoughts were only half turned forward toward the new world; half they were still turned back towards the past, toward the sad history of the Jews and the wrongs they had suffered at the hands of the Gentiles all down through the ages. And the old grandmother who loved David so dearly, she who had lost her whole family save David and Mendel in Europe, she was wrapped up in thinking of the past, in observing the rites and ceremonies of her religion as her father had done and her father's father before her. Life was sad and lonely for her in America where she had no friends and understood nothing of the language, for never in all the ten years since Mendel had brought her there, had she dropped her Yiddish or learned to speak a single word of English.

Loving and considerate of the dear old grandmother was David, patient with all her little peculiarities and demands, affectionate and obedient to his uncle Mendel, yet his own face was always turned with joyous confidence toward the present and the future, away from the dead and vanished past. True, as time went on, he, too, perceived that in America men were greedy still, dishonest, selfish, unjust, that thither came many a one who thought that liberty meant the freedom to do as he chose, instead of the freedom to do as he ought. Yet in spite of it all, he kept his faith firm and strong in the America of his dreams— that America which he came to see existed yet as an idea only, but an idea that would surely compel men into line with it, one day govern them wholly, and so reveal itself as the only true America there ever was or ever could be.

With this unseen yet real America David kept his faith and he gradually came to express all that he thought and felt about it in a great piece of music, his American symphony. Yet he was only a poor musician playing as Mendel did, in theatres and cheap dance halls. How was he ever to get his symphony, into which he had put his whole heart and soul, played by a great orchestra before the public? It was the dream of his life to hear it actually coming out of violins and cellos, drums and trumpets, thundering its message to America and all the world. But how was he to get it done,—how? Mendel did not understand the symphony and only half believed it to be great. It must, he was sure, be full of faults, since David was so young, so inexperienced, and had never had a teacher for even the simplest rules of harmony. Yet Mendel was proud of his nephew and he believed that if only David could be sent to Germany to study, he might perhaps really produce something great. But how was even this to be accomplished when they were so poor and scarcely now made both ends meet?

One day David played, as he often did, without pay, at a charitable entertainment in a great Settlement house that lent its aid to hundreds of immigrants just such as he had once been. Thither came Dutchmen and Frenchmen, Italians and Greeks, Norwegians and Swedes, still in outlandish garments, still jabbering in outlandish tongues, with little, round, brown-eyed children and little, round, blue-eyed children, all meeting together on the grounds of a few broken words of English. And how they listened and soaked in David's music! How they cheered and whistled and applauded! At the Settlement David met Miss Vera Revendal, who was one of the workers there. Vera loved music as dearly as David and was interested at once in his playing.

Though David never dreamed it, Vera was Russian and had been born in that same Kishineff so connected for him with hideous memories overtopped by the "butcher's face." Her father was a member of the nobility and a faithful follower of the Tsar, sharing all the contempt of the Russian aristocrats for the lower classes and their hatred and prejudice against the Jews. Yet Vera even as a little school girl, had seen with a heart overflowing with compassion, what misery and poverty was wrought among the Russian people by the tyranny of the Tsar. What rights to liberty and happiness had the lower classes in Russia? None! None! None! All Russia existed for the pleasure of the nobles and the Tsar. With a fearless, uncompromising childish demand for justice Vera refused all respect or reverence for the Tsar. Once when she was in attendance at the Imperial High School, the Tsar had come thither to pay an annual visit. As was his custom he tasted the food that was served the children, and the high and mighty honor of finishing what he left was reserved for the show pupil from among all the classes. On Vera this honor fell, but when the plate of mutton, sanctified by the royal touch, was set before her, she horrified all the expectant circle about by passionately pushing it from her and passing it off to be consumed by the poorest among the servants! That was the sort of girl young Vera was, and though she had loved her father dearly, the Baron Revendal, honest but bigoted, clung obstinately to his class and the service of the Tsar.

So when Vera was arrested as a revolutionist, attempting to overthrow the government of tyranny in Russia, he had turned his back on his motherless daughter. Vera was sentenced to exile in desolate Siberia and thither she would have been sent had she not escaped from her gaolers and made her way to America where she found her life work among the poor in the Settlements of New York.

Of all this David knew nothing, and no more did Vera know or dream that David was a Jew. The two found simple pleasure in their mutual love of music. A short time after David's first appearance at the Settlement an invitation was sent him to play for them once more, and Vera went herself one bright winter's afternoon to seek him out and get his consent in person.

On that particular day David was from home, and Mendel Quixano, in a seedy velvet jacket and red carpet-slippers, had just given some little careless Johnny his music lesson. Suddenly from the kitchen came the noise of an irate Irish voice and the shrill Yiddish of an angry Frau Quixano.

"Divil take the butther!" cried Kathleen, the Irish servant. "I wouldn't put up wid yez, not for a hundred dollars a week!"

"*Wos shreist du?*" shrilled Frau Quixano. "*Gott in Himmel! dieses Amerika.*" Mendel heaved a deep sigh. "Ach! Mother and Kathleen at it again!" he muttered. It seemed to him that one's very servants in America hated the Jews.

"Pots and pans and plates and knives!" went on Kathleen still in the kitchen. "Sure, 'tis enough to make a saint chrazy!" And she burst into the living room clutching a white table cloth. "Bad luck to me if iver I take sarvice again with haythen Jews!" Just then she perceived Mendel huddled up in the arm chair by the fire, and gave a little scream. "Och! I thought ye was out!"

Mendel rose. "And so you dared to be rude to my mother!"

"She said I put mate on a butther plate," Kathleen angrily protested.

"Well," answered Mendel, "you know that's against her religion."

"But I didn't do nothing of the sort! I only put butther on a mate plate."

"That's just as bad. The Bible forbids both butter and meat—"

"Sure! who can rimimber all that?" Kathleen began venting her spite on the litter of things she was vigorously clearing off the table. "Why don't ye have a sinsible religion?"

"You are impertinent!" Mendel seated himself at the piano and began to play softly. "Attend to your work."

"And isn't it layin' the Sabbath cloth I am?"

"Don't answer me back!"

"Faith! I must answer *somebody* back and sorra a word of English *she* understands. I might as well talk to a tree! What way can I be understandin' her jabberin' and jibberin'? I'm not a monkey. Why don't she talk English like a Christian?"

"You are not paid to talk but work!" said Mendel.

"And who *can* work wid an ould woman nagglin' and grizzlin'

and faultin' me? Mate plates, butther plates, *kosher*, *trepha!*
Sure, I've smashed up folks' crockery and they makin' less fuss
about it!"

Mendel stopped playing. "Breaking crockery is one thing and
breaking a religion another," said he. "Didn't you tell me when
I engaged you that you had lived in other Jewish families?"

"And is it a liar ye'd make me out now?" cried Kathleen
angrily. "I've lived wid clothiers and pawnbrokers and vaude-
ville actors, but I niver shtruck a house where mate and butther
couldn't be as paceable on the same plate as eggs and bacon!
Faith, ye can keep yer dirthy wages. I give ye notice! I'll
quit off this blissid minute!"

And she dumped down a silver candlestick and rushed hys-
terically off to her room. Just then there came a rat-a-tat-tat at
the street door.

"Kathleen!" Mendel hurried to the door of the irate maiden's
room. "There's a visitor!"

"I'm not here," called Kathleen angrily from within.

"So long as you are in this house, you must do your work,"
ordered Mendel.

"I tould ye I was lavin' at once. Let ye open the door yerself."

"But I'm not dressed to receive visitors. It may be a new
pupil." And off went Mendel, leaving Kathleen naught to do
but obey.

"The divil fly away wid me if iver from this hour I set foot
again among haythen furriners," muttered Kathleen emerging
from her stronghold and crossing unwillingly to the door. As
she opened it Vera appeared in the vestibule, her beautiful face
glowing forth from a setting of snowy furs.

"Is Mr. Quixano at home?" asked Vera.

"Which Mr. Quixano?" queried Kathleen sulkily.

"The one who plays," answered Vera.

"There isn't a 'one' who plays." Kathleen's voice

was fairly snappy. "Yer wrong entirely. They both plays."

"Oh dear," smiled Vera. "Then it's the one who plays the violin—Mr. David—I want to see."

"He's out!" Kathleen made a move to slam the door.

"Don't shut the door," cried Vera. "I want to leave a message."

"Then why don't ye come inside? It's freezin' me ye are!" And Kathleen sneezed a loud and accusing "Atchoo!"

"I'm sorry," Vera entered the room. "Will you please tell Mr. Quixano that Miss Revendal called from the Settlement and—"

"What way will I be tellin' him all that?" bridled Kathleen. "I'm not here!"

"What!" cried Vera. "Not here!"

"I'm lavin' as soon as I've me thrunk packed."

"Then may I write the message at this desk?"

"If the ould woman don't come in and sphy you!"

"What old woman?" asked Vera.

"Ould Mr. Quixano's mother. She wears a black wig, she's that houly."

Vera was bewildered. "But why should she mind my writing?"

"Look at the clock," Kathleen drew her face into an expression of comical solemnity. "If ye're not quick, it'll be *Shabbos* and Lord forbid any work should be done in this house on *Shabbos*."

"Be what?" cried Vera.

Kathleen held up her hands in horror. "Ye don't know what *Shabbos* is? A Jewess not know her own Sunday!"

Vera froze on the instant. After all, the prejudice of the most aristocratic blood in Russia was not wholly blotted out in her. She felt outraged that anyone should mistake her for a Jewess.

"I a Jewess! How dare you!" she cried. "I am a Russian!" Then she added slowly, as if half dazed, "Do I understand that Mr. Quixano is a Jew?"

"Two Jews, Miss," answered Kathleen, "both of 'em."

"Oh, but it is impossible," murmured Vera. "He had such charming manners. Are you sure Mr. Quixano is not Spanish?"

"Shpanish!" Kathleen picked up an old Hebrew book on the arm chair. "Look at the ould lady's book. Is that Shpanish?" And she pointed to the Mizrach on the wall. "And that houly picture, is that Shpanish?"

Convinced against her will that David was a Jew, Vera suddenly changed her mind about leaving him a message. "Don't say I called at all," said she. But just at that moment Mendel Quixano appeared in the room, completely transformed in his neat Prince Albert coat, and Vera could not escape. When he learned it was David whom she had come to see, he invited her in so gentlemanly a manner to wait that she struggled with her prejudice, overcame it, and sat down.

"That wonderful boy a Jew," she kept saying to herself. "But then so was David the shepherd youth with his harp and his psalms, the sweet singer in Israel."

While she waited conversing with Mendel, Frau Quixano came into the room with excited gesticulations, chattering in Yiddish angry complaints against Kathleen. Perceiving her precious Hebrew book on the floor where Kathleen had dropped it, she cried out in horror, picked it up and kissed it piously.

"*Ruhig, Mutter, ruhig!*" Mendel pressed her soothingly into her fireside chair, then he added to Vera. "She understands barely a word of English."

Frau Quixano eyed the newcomer suspiciously.

"Tell her I hope she is well," said Vera.

Mendel translated the young woman's words into Yiddish but Frau Quixano only shrugged her shoulders and said in despairing astonishment. "*Gut? Un' wie soll es gut gehen—in Amerika?*"

"She asks how can anything possibly go well in America." Mendel explained.

"Ah!" said Vera, "then your mother does not like America!"

Mendel half smiled. "Her favorite exclamation is '*A Klog zu Columbussen!*' that is, 'Cursed be Columbus!' "

Vera laughed as the old woman settled herself to read. "But your nephew, he does not curse America?" she said.

"David—ah, no! He is crazy about America. My mother came here with her life behind her, David with his life before him!" Mendel paused for a moment, then he went on gloomily, "But what is there here for him, poor boy? Only a terrible struggle for existence—music halls and dance halls, beer halls and weddings. Every hope and ambition will be ground out of him and he will die obscure and unknown." The musician's head sank sadly on his breast and Frau Quixano began to sob faintly over her book.

"There," said Vera, "you have made your mother cry."

"Oh, no," said Mendel, "she understood nothing. She always cries on the eve of Sabbath. She knows that in this great grinding America David and I must go out to work and earn our bread on Sabbath as on week days. She never says a word to us but her heart is full of tears."

"Poor old woman," said Vera.

For a time nothing was heard in the room save the low sobbing of Frau Quixano and the roar of the wind. With the slowly gathering dusk there seemed to droop over all a lurking pall of sadness. Then suddenly a happy voice was heard outside singing:

> *"My country 'tis of thee,*
> *Sweet land of liberty,*
> *Of thee I sing."*

Frau Quixano pricked up her ears. "Do ist Dovidel!" she cried.

The whole atmosphere seemed changed at once from grief to joy as David opened the door and appeared on the threshold, a buoyant, snow covered figure carrying a violin case and clad in a cloak and a broad-brimmed hat.

"Isn't it a beautiful world, uncle," he cried, "snow, the divine white snow!" Then perceiving the visitor, he removed his hat and looked at her with boyish reverence and wonder.

"Miss Revendal here!" he cried. "If I had only known you were waiting."

"Don't look so surprised," said Vera, smiling. "I haven't fallen from heaven like the snow. I'm glad you didn't know I was waiting. Your uncle told me you were playing at the Crippled Children's Home. I wouldn't have cheated those little ones of a moment of your music."

"Ah! it was bully! You should have seen the cripples waltzing with their crutches! Even the paralyzed danced. If they hadn't the use of their legs, their arms danced on the counterpane! If their arms couldn't dance, their hands danced, if their hands couldn't dance their heads danced, if their heads couldn't dance—why, their eyes danced! Dear little cripples! I felt as though I could play them all straight again with the love and joy jumping out of this old fiddle! *Es war grossartig*, Granny!" And David moved toward the old grandmother by the fire, patting her cheek in greeting while she responded with a loving smile ere she settled herself to slumber contentedly over her book. When David learned that Vera had come to ask him to play once more at the Settlement he was overjoyed.

"But we can't offer you a fee," said Vera.

"A fee!" cried David. "I'd pay a fee to see all those happy immigrants you gather together. It's almost as good as going to Ellis Island."

"What a strange taste." Vera smiled. "Who on earth wants to go to Ellis Island?"

"Oh," David's face beamed, "I love going to Ellis Island to watch the ships coming in from Europe and to think that all those weary, sea tossed wanderers are feeling what I felt when America first stretched out her great mother-hand to *me*."

"You were very happy?" asked Vera softly.

"Happy? It was heaven. You must remember that all my life America was waiting for me, beckoning, shining—the place where God would wipe away tears from off all faces." His voice ended with a queer little catch in his breath that always proclaimed his thoughts had gone back to Kishineff. Mendel rose and went to him half frightened.

"Now, now, David, don't get excited," he said. But David paid no heed.

"To think that the same great torch of liberty which threw its light across all the broad seas and lands into my little garret in Russia, is shining also for all those other weeping millions of Europe, shining wherever men hunger and are oppressed."

"Yes, yes, David." Mendel laid his hand soothingly on his shoulder. "Now sit down and—"

"Shining over the starving villages of Italy and Ireland, over the swarming stony cities of Poland and Galicia, over the ruined farms of Roumania, over the shambles of Russia. Oh, Miss Revendal,—" David's voice was choking now with the depths of his feeling, "when I look at our statue of liberty I just seem to hear the voice of America crying: 'Come unto me, all ye that labor and are heavy laden, and I will give you rest—rest—'"

"Don't talk any more now, David." Mendel's voice had taken a tone of command. "You can express all this that you feel in your American Symphony."

"Ah, you compose music," cried Vera eagerly, for it was the first time she had known that David did more than play. "And you find inspiration for your composing in America?"

"Yes," David grew calm again. "I find inspiration in the seething of the crucible."

"The crucible!" cried Vera. "I do not understand."

"Not understand,—you the spirit of the Settlement! Not understand that America is God's crucible, the great Melting Pot, where all the races of Europe are melting and re-forming.

188

Here you stand, good folk, think I, when I see them at Ellis Island, in your fifty groups with your fifty blood hatreds and rivalries. But you won't be long like that, brothers, for these are the fires of God you've come to—these are the fires of God. A fig for your feuds and vendettas! Germans and Frenchmen, Irishmen and Englishmen, Jews and Russians, into the crucible with you all! God is making the American!"

"I should have thought the American was made already," said Mendel, "eighty millions of him."

"Eighty millions," cried David in good humored derision. "No, uncle, the real American has not yet arrived. He is only in the crucible, I tell you—he will be the fusion of all races, perhaps the coming superman! Ah! what a glorious ending for my symphony if I can only write it!"

Somehow Vera understood David better than his uncle or anyone else had ever done—David knew it; he felt it. Those others saw America as a certain wide stretch of land bounded by the Atlantic and Pacific; they saw the American as the man whom they daily met in the streets with his good points and his bad.

But Vera understood David's vision of America as a great ideal of liberty, humanity, and justice, and the real American as he who should some day express that ideal, representing in himself the melting together of all that was best and highest in the races of the world, purified from their old differences, their old false systems, their old hatreds and prejudices, their old suspicions and deceits.

"Won't you give a bit of your symphony at our concert?" asked Vera eagerly.

"Oh, it needs an orchestra!" David was once again boyishly shy.

"But you at the violin and I at the piano."

"Ah, you didn't tell me you played, Miss Revendal," interrupted Mendel.

"I told you less commonplace things," smiled Vera. "Yes, I studied at Petersburg. There wasn't much music at Kishineff—"

"Kishineff!" On the instant David was trembling.

"Yes," said Vera, "my birthplace!"

"So," David shuddered violently. "You are a Russian."

"Calm yourself, David." Mendel came protectingly toward him.

"Not much music at Kishineff!" David laughed strangely. "No! only the Death March. Mother! Father! Ah! cowards, murderers! And you!" He shook his fist in the air. "You looking on with your cold butcher's face! O God! O God!" And he ran shamefacedly out of the room.

"What have I done?" cried Vera.

Frau Quixano, who had fallen asleep over her book, awoke suddenly as if with a sense of horror and gazed dazedly about.

"*Dovidel! Wu ist Dovidel? Mir dacht sach—*"

Mendel pressed her back to her slumbers.

"*Du träumst, Mutter! Schlaf!*"

"His father and mother were massacred?" whispered Vera hoarsely.

"Yes! Before his very eyes," answered Mendel, sadly. "Terrible!" cried Vera, "Terrible."

Mendel shrugged his shoulders hopelessly. "It is only Jewish history."

Gone now was Vera's prejudice against David. On the contrary, her interest in the young musician had increased to such an extent that she offered to do her best to interest someone in him, someone rich enough to send him to Germany to study, and Mendel who would have been too proud to accept from a Gentile aught for himself, was grateful, almost ready to beg such a favor for David. Scarcely had she left the house when David came back into the room, once more composed, though somewhat dazed.

"She is gone?" he asked. "Oh, but I have driven her away by my craziness. But she understood, uncle. She understood my crucible of God. You don't know what it means to me to have someone who understands. Even you have never understood—"

"Nonsense." Mendel was wounded. "How can Miss Revendal understand you better than your own uncle? What true understanding can there ever be between a Russian Jew and a Russian Christian?"

"What understanding?" cried David. "Why, aren't we both Americans?"

Mendel shrugged his shoulders drily as he went out through the street door.

Once left to himself David set eagerly to work writing down on his musical manuscript all that had come to him as he talked with Vera, but he had worked only a few moments when Frau Quixano yawned, awakened and stretched herself, then looked at the clock.

"*Shabbos!*" she said and, rising, she lit the candlesticks on the table with a muttered Hebrew benediction. Crossing over to David, as he sat absorbed in his work, she touched him on the shoulder to remind him that he must stop his writing on *Shabbos*.

"Dovidel," he looked up dazedly while she pointed to the candles. "*Shabbos!*"

A sweet smile came over David's face. To him religion meant less a matter of rites and ceremonies than of a pure and contrite heart, nevertheless he threw the quill resignedly away and submitted his head to her hands and her ancient Hebrew blessing. As she left the room, she shook her finger at him warningly lest he should go back to work again. "*Gut Shabbos,*" she said. David smiled after her. "*Gut Shabbos!*" he answered.

A moment later he was ready in his coat and hat to go out and give a music lesson. He was almost at the door when Kathleen came bustling into the room, fully dressed in outdoor garments and laden with an umbrella and a large brown paper parcel.

"Why Kathleen, you're not going out this bitter weather," said David.

"And who's to shtay me?" bridled Kathleen, sharply fending him off with her umbrella as he offered to relieve her of her parcel.

"Oh, but you mustn't! I'll do your errand for you. What is it?"

"Errand is it indeed!" cried Kathleen indignantly. "I'm not here!"

"Not here?" questioned David in surprise.

"I'm lavin'. They'll come for me thrunk."

"But who's sending you away?"

"It's sending meself I am. Yer houly grandmother has me disthroyed intirely."

"Why, what has the poor old lady—"

"I don't be saltin' the mate and I do be mixin' the crockery—"

"I know, I know," David spoke gently, "but Kathleen, remember, she was brought up to these things from her childhood. And her father was a Rabbi."

"What's that?" demanded Kathleen, "a priest?"

"A sort of a priest. In Russia he was a great man. Her husband too was a mighty scholar and to give him time to study holy books, she had to do chores all day for him and the children. But he died and the children left her—went to America and other far-off places or to heaven, and she was left penniless and alone."

"Poor ould lady!"

"Not so old yet! She was married at fifteen!"

"Poor young craythur!"

"But she was still the good angel of the congregation, sat up with the sick and watched over the dead."

"Saints alive!"

"And then one day my uncle sent the old lady a ticket to come to America. But it is not so happy for her here, because you see my uncle has to be near his theatre and can't live in the Jewish quarter, and so nobody understands her, and she sits all day alone, alone with her books and her religion and her memories."

"Oh, Mr. David!" Kathleen was breaking down.

"And now all this long, cold, snowy evening she'll sit by the fire alone thinking of her dead, and the fire will sink lower and lower, and she won't be able to touch it because it's the holy Sabbath, and there'll be no kind Kathleen to brighten up the grey ashes. And then at last, sad and shivering, she'll creep up to her room, and there in the dark and the cold—"

Kathleen burst into tears, dropped her parcel on the floor and tore her bonnet strings open.

"Oh, Mr. David, I won't mix the crockery. I won't!"

"Of course you won't," David spoke heartily. "Good night!" And off he went while Kathleen fell down before the fire and began to poke it strenuously, all the best in her heart called forth by David's appeal to her sympathies. Jew or Gentile, what mattered it? Here in America all old-time enemies met, looked into each other's hearts and understood one another on the grounds of a common humanity.

Vera was as good as her word in seeking out someone who might be persuaded to send David to Europe, but among all her acquaintances the only one of great wealth in whom she could arouse the smallest interest was a certain young Quincy Davenport, and he was interested in David solely because he loved Vera and wished most particularly to please her. Quincy was one of those young Americans who had never done any useful work in all his life, but spent his days finding new and exciting ways in which to spend the enormous income that came to him from his father. The greater part of his time he passed in Europe and the rest in trying to ape European manners and customs and introduce them into America. Lazy, idle, pretentious, he saw in America only a crude sort of place, good for nothing much except as a spot where his father could make heaps of American dollars for his son to spend on thrilling amusements and pleasures.

Scarcely a month after Vera had first promised Mendel to find someone to help David, she sent him word that she was bringing Mr. Davenport and Herr Pappelmeister, the conductor of Mr. Davenport's private orchestra, to see the young man, and that if Herr Pappelmeister found in the music he had written any evidence of genius, the symphony would be produced in Mr. Davenport's wonderful marble music hall before five hundred of the most fashionable folk in America, and David would be sent to Europe. Mendel was aglow with hope. How much it meant—this coming of Quincy Davenport, yet he could hardly interest David at all in the matter. The young man scarcely even listened to his uncle's information. His head was full of the great ending he was writing to his symphony. He had just seen a thousand little foreign born children saluting the Stars and Stripes, and the sight had filled his soul with all he wanted to finish his work.

"Just fancy it, uncle!" he cried. "The Stars and Stripes unfurled, and a thousand childish voices, piping and foreign, fresh from the lands of oppression, hailing its fluttering folds.

FROM THE TOWER WINDOW

Ah! but if you had heard them—'Flag of our Great Republic'—the words have gone singing at my heart ever since—'Flag of our Great Republic, Guardian of our homes, whose stars and stripes stand for Bravery, Purity, Truth and Union, we salute thee. We, the natives of distant lands who find rest under thy folds, do pledge our hearts, our lives, our sacred honor, to love and protect thee, our Country, and the liberty of the American people forever.'"

"Quite right," said Mendel, who had been vainly trying to turn David's thoughts toward his own life and the great chance now before him. "But you needn't get so excited over it."

"Not get excited when one hears the roaring of the fires of God? When one sees souls melting in the Crucible? Uncle, all those little immigrants will grow up Americans!"

"But, David," cried Mendel. "Surely some day you'd like your music produced—you'd like it to go all over the world?"

"Wouldn't it be glorious—all over the world and all down the ages!"

"But don't you see that unless you go and study seriously in Germany?—" Just at that moment in came Kathleen from the kitchen, carrying a tea tray with ear-shaped cakes and bread and butter for the expected guests, and wearing a grotesque false nose.

"Kathleen!" cried Mendel in amaze, but David burst out into boyish laughter.

"Sure, what's the matter?" cried Kathleen standing still with her tray.

"Look in the glass!" laughed David.

Kathleen crossed to the mantel. "Houly Moses." She dropped the tray so quickly as she snatched off the false nose that it would all have gone to smash had not Mendel, fortunately, caught it. "Och, I forgot to take it off—'twas the misthress gave it me—I put it on to cheer her up."

"Is she so miserable then, the grandmother?" asked David.

"Terrible low, Mr. David, today bein' Purim."

Kathleen's voice was as sympathetic as though she had never been otherwise than most kindly disposed toward her mistress.

"But Purim is a merry time for us, Kathleen, like your carnival," said David.

"That's what the misthress is so miserable about. Ye don't *keep* carnival. There's noses for both of ye in the kitchen— didn't I go with her to Hester Street to buy 'em?—but ye don't be axin for 'em. And to see your noses layin' around so solemn and neglected, faith, it nearly makes me chry meself."

"Who can remember about Purim in America?" said Mendel bitterly, but David only smiled. "Poor granny, tell her to come in and I'll play her a Purim jig."

"No, no, David," interrupted Mendel hastily. "Not here— the visitors!"

"Visitors!" cried David. "What visitors?"

Mendel grew impatient. "That's just what I've been trying to explain."

"Well, I can play in the kitchen, then!" And off went David with his violin while Mendel shrugged his shoulders hopelessly at the boy's perversity. Soon from the kitchen was heard the sound of a merry Slavic jig with Frau Quixano laughing and calling Kathleen to join in the fun. Even Mendel's feet began to keep time to the music, when the hoot of an automobile and the rattling of a car warned him that the guests were come. In another moment Vera and Quincy appeared in the room. Quincy was adorned with an orchid and an eye-glass and was quite evidently a dude. It was equally evident, too, that he deeply admired Miss Revendal. There followed soon after them Herr Pappelmeister, a burly German with a leonine head, enormous spectacles, and a mane of white hair. He appeared very grave and silent and clutched a bunchy umbrella of which he never let go. Herr

FROM THE TOWER WINDOW

Pappelmeister was a famous musical conductor, who enjoyed a salary of twenty thousand dollars a year conducting Quincy's private orchestra for the amusement of Quincy's friends. Quincy himself had no knowledge of music, but he had brought Herr Pappelmeister to discover if David had any real genius.

"I'm so sorry," said Mendel to Vera. "I can't get David to come into the room. He's terrible shy."

"Won't face the music, eh?" sniggered Quincy.

"Did you tell him *I* was here?" questioned Vera, disappointed.

"Of course!" answered Mendel. "He will not come. But I've persuaded him to let me show you his manuscript." Then he turned anxiously to Pappelmeister. "You must remember his youth and his lack of musical education—" he said with an air of apology.

"Blease, the manusgribt," said Pappelmeister.

Mendel moved David's music stand into the center of the room and Pappelmeister put the manuscript on it. "So!" All eyes centered eagerly on him. With irritating elaborateness he polished his glasses and then read in silence.

"But!" cried Quincy, bored by the silence. "Won't you play it for us?"

"Blay it?" cried Pappelmeister. "Am I an orgestra? I blay it in my brain." And he went on reading, ruffling his hair unconsciously,—"So!"

"You don't seem to like it," said Vera anxiously.

"I do not comprehend it."

"I knew it was crazy," said Mendel. "It is supposed to be about America or a crucible or something. And of course there are heaps of mistakes."

Pappelmeister became absorbed again in the music, sublimely unconscious of all about him. "Ach, so—so,—So! Dot is somedings different!" He began to beat time with his ridiculous bunchy umbrella, moving more and more vigorously till at last he was conducting elaborately as if a whole orchestra sat before him, stretching out his left palm for pianissimo passages and raising it vigorously for forte with every now and then an exclamation. *"Wunderschön!* Now the flutes! Clarinets! Ach *ergötzlich*—bassoons and drums. *Kolossal! Kolossal!"*

"Bravo! Bravo!" Vera clapped her hands. "I'm so excited."

"Then it isn't bad, Poppy?" yawned Quincy.

But Pappelmeister went on not even listening. "Sh! Sh! Piano!"

"Don't say Sh! to me!" cried Quincy outraged. "Look here, Poppy," and he seized the wildly waving umbrella. "We can't be here all day."

With a blank stare Pappelmeister returned to himself.

"Ach! What it is?" he cried.

"What it is!—we've had enough!" said Quincy.

"Enough? Of such a beaudiful symphony?"

"It may be beautiful to you," said Quincy. "But it's blamed stupid for us! See here, Poppy, if you're satisfied that the young fellow has sufficient talent to be sent to study in Germany—"

"Germany!" interrupted Herr Pappelmeister. "Germany has nodings to teach him. He has to teach Germany."

"Bravo!" cried Vera again.

"I always said he was a genius!" said Mendel.

"Then you can put his stuff on one of my programs?" inquired Quincy.

"I should be broud to indroduce it to de vorld."

At that joyous news Mendel hastened to the kitchen and fairly dragged David into the room.

"Oh, Mr. Quixano, I'm so glad," cried Vera. "Mr. Davenport is going to produce your symphony in his wonderful marble music room."

"Yes, young man," said Quincy, "I'm going to give you the

most fashionable audience in America, and if Poppy is right, you are just going to rake in the dollars."

For one long moment David spoke not a word in answer to this magnificent offer. Was he trying to realize the good fortune that lay at his feet? All at once he drew himself up in a peculiar manner, then he turned to Vera and said: "I can never be grateful enough to you, and I can never be grateful enough to Herr Pappel-meister. It is an honor even to meet him."

"Mein brave young man!" cried Pappelmeister, choked with emotion and patting him on the back.

"But before I accept Mr. Davenport's kindness, I must know to whom I am indebted." His voice grew suddenly stern and he looked Quincy full in the eyes. "Is it true that you live in America only two months of the year and then only to entertain Europeans who wander to these wild parts?"

"Lucky for you, young man," said Quincy, toying with his eye-glass. "You'll have an Italian prince and a British duke to hear your scribblings."

"And the palace where they will hear my scribblings. Is it true that—?"

"Mr. Quixano," interrupted Vera on pins and needles lest he spoil his chance—"what possible—?" but David entreatingly held up his hand for silence and went on with an increase of firm self-command:

"Is this palace the same whose grounds were turned into Venetian canals where the guests ate in gondolas, gondolas that were draped with the most wonderful trailing silks in imitation of the Venetian nobility in their great winter fêtes?"

"Ah, Miss Revendal," Quincy turned to Vera. "What a pity you refused that invitation. It was a fairy scene of twinkling lights and delicious darkness. Each couple supped in their own gondola—"

"And the same night men and women died of hunger in New York!" David delivered his words with stinging directness, like a blow that came straight from the shoulder.

"What!" Quincy was so startled he dropped his eye-glass.

"And this is the sort of people you would invite to hear my symphony—these gondola-guzzlers!"

"Mr. Quixano!" cried Vera.

"David!" cried Mendel.

"You low down ungrateful—!" yelled Quincy.

"Not for you and such as you have I sat here writing and dreaming,—not for you shall my music sing of the true America, you who are killing my America."

"*Your* America! You Jew immigrant." Quincy had grown furious.

"Jew immigrant, yes." David's eyes flashed and he held his head high. "But a Jew who knows that your Pilgrim fathers came straight out of his Old Testament, pure and consecrated of spirit, like Abraham led out of a land of oppression to seek a land of promise. It is you, freak fashionables seeking only your own selfish pleasures, blind and deaf to the meaning of America, using her only as a money bag to be squeezed for her dollars,—you who are undoing the work of Washington and Lincoln, vulgarizing your high heritage, and turning the last and noblest hope of humanity into a caricature."

"Ha! Ha! Ha! Ho! Ho! Ho!" laughed Quincy. "You never told me your Jew scribbler was a socialist."

"I am nothing but a simple artist." David's manner grew once more unassuming and boyish, but his tone thrilled through and through with the tensity of his earnestness. "But I came from Europe one of her victims, and I know that she is a failure, that her palaces and peerages are outworn toys of the human spirit, and that the only hope of humanity lies in a new world. And here in the land of tomorrow, you are trying to bring back Europe."

"I wish we could," interjected Quincy.

FROM THE TOWER WINDOW

"Europe with her comic opera coronets and her worm-eaten stage decorations and her pomp and chivalry built on a morass of crime and misery. But you shall not kill my dream. There shall come a fire round the crucible that will melt you—you and your breed—like wax in a blow pipe. America *shall* make good!" The restrained certainty of his quiet words cut like a knife.

Quincy was so angry that he could only clench his fist and stand speechless.

At that Herr Pappelmeister, who had sat imperturbable throughout this remarkable scene, sprang up and began to wave his umbrella frantically.

"*Hoch* Quixano! Long live Quixano! *Hoch! Hoch!*" he cried.

"Poppy, you're dismissed," shouted Quincy and left the house at white heat. Mendel followed him hot on his heels in the vain hope of smoothing his ruffled feathers.

What on earth could his crazy David mean throwing such a chance away? thought Mendel.

"Oh, Herr Pappelmeister," said David, "you have lost your place!"

"And saved my soul!" cried Pappelmeister. "Dollars are de devil. I blay me now good music and no more cheap stuff by command of Quincy Davenport!" And off he went, his very umbrella bristling with newly found self respect.

Vera and David were left alone. David feared lest Vera would leave him now in anger at what he had done, and never see him again, but Vera glowed with admiration at the courage of his stand. Vanished from her heart was all her old prejudice against the Jew, vanished from David's all instinct against the Gentile. And in that moment of uplifted feeling they both discovered they loved one another.

Some time later when Vera was gone and Mendel once more came dejectedly home, David threw his arms boyishly around his uncle's neck.

"I am so happy, uncle," he said. "Vera will be my wife."

"Miss Revendal!" Mendel threw his nephew off as though he had struck him. "Have you lost your wits? Remember you are a Jew."

"Yes, and just think," said David, "she was bred up to despise Jews. Her father was a Russian baron."

"If she was the daughter of fifty barons, you could not marry her."

"Uncle," cried David in pained amaze. "You cling to old prejudice still? You who have come to the heart of the Crucible where the roaring fires of God are fusing our race with all the others."

"Not *our* race!" cried Mendel passionately. "Not your race and mine. The Jew has been tried in a thousand fires and only grown harder for them all."

"Fires of hate," answered David, "not fires of love. That is what melts. Here in this new republic we must look forward—"

"We must look backward too," interrupted Mendel.

"Backward—to what?" cried David. "To Kishineff and that butcher's face?"

"Hush!" Mendel was alarmed. "Calm yourself."

David struggled. "Yes, I will calm myself, but how else shall I do so, save by holding out my hands with prayer and music towards America, the Republic of Man and the Kingdom of God? The past I cannot mend. Take away the hope that I can mend the future and you make me mad."

"You are mad already—your dreams are mad. The Jew is hated here as elsewhere. You are false to your race."

"I keep faith with America. I have faith that America will keep faith with me."

"Go then," cried Mendel. "Marry your Gentile and be happy!"

"You turn me out?" asked David.

"You would not stay and break my mother's heart. You

know she would mourn at your marrying a Gentile with the rending of garments and the seven days' sitting on the floor. Go! You have cast off the God of our Fathers."

"And the God of our *children*!" thundered David, "Does *He* demand no service?" But he had scarcely spoken so stormily when he grew suddenly quiet. Touching his uncle affectionately on the shoulder, he said slowly, "You are right, I must go."

"I will hide the truth," said Mendel. "Mother must never suspect."

Just at that moment Frau Quixano was heard laughing uproariously with Kathleen in the kitchen.

"Ah!" said Mendel bitterly, "you have made this a merry Purim."

In rushed Frau Quixano with David's violin, begging him to play.

Mendel put out a protesting hand. "No, no, David, don't play now. I couldn't bear it."

"But I must," answered David. "You said she must never suspect, and it may be the last time I shall ever play for her." And he looked at the old woman lovingly as he took the fiddle and started the same old Slavic dance. Frau Quixano took a grotesque false nose from her pocket and clapped it on, laughing in childish glee. Torn between laughter and tears David laughed also.

"*Mutter!*" cried Mendel, shocked, but Frau Quixano's only answer to his dignified expostulation was to force a false nose on him also, unwilling though he was, and she and Kathleen danced to David's music till they both fell breathless into a chair. Then with a sad and affectionate farewell glance at his grandmother David took his hat, his coat and his violin and slipped quietly out of the house that had sheltered him so long.

It was only a two dollar a month garret, six feet square, that he could afford henceforth, but then that was as large as a first class cabin on board a boat, so David had only to pretend he had a state room on the top deck of one of the great ocean liners, and it seemed quite luxurious and himself a millionaire at least! He and Vera were very happy though he was not earning nearly enough so they could even dream of marrying and setting up housekeeping yet.

When Quincy Davenport discovered that Vera had chosen to marry David, he made haste to send off at once to Europe for the Baron Revendal as the only means he could think of to prevent her wedding another. Now the Baron had never ceased to love and long for his daughter, and when he learned that she was on the point of marrying a Jew, he set out at once for America with his second wife, the Baroness, to try to prevent such an insult to the blood of the Revendals.

A tall, stern, grizzled man of military bearing was the Baron, with a narrow, fanatical forehead, yet of honest, even distinguished appearance. He had the nervous suspicious manner of a Russian official, who pays the penalty for his tyranny by constant terror of a revolutionist's bomb, and in self defence he always carried a pistol. The Baroness was a pretty but showy creature ablaze with barbaric jewels, and she was determined to have Vera marry Quincy for the sake of his heaps of good American dollars.

Ere the Baron had seen his daughter he regarded the Jews as the dirt beneath his feet and could talk of slaughtering Jews as impassively as of slaughtering swine.

"Shooting is too good for the enemies of Christ," he said to Quincy, devoutly crossing himself. "At Kishineff we stick the swine."

"Ah! I read about that. Did you see the massacre?" Quincy's attempt to appear unconcerned at this careless mention of such an atrocity was not altogether successful.

"Ah yes," answered the Baron. "I had charge of the whole district and I hurried a regiment up to teach the blaspheming brutes manners."

"My husband was decorated for it," said the Baroness, "he has the order of St. Vladimir."

And yet in Vera's hands when he found her once again after all their years of estrangement, the Baron was as wax.

"Christ save us!" he said at first when he heard her speak of her love for David. "You have become a Jewess."

"No more than David has become a Christian," answered Vera. "We were already at one. All honest people are. Surely, father, all religions must serve the same God since there is only one God to serve."

Never could the Baron forget that Vera was the same little motherless girl who had nestled against his breast in all her childish troubles and whom he had tenderly comforted. Almost before he knew it and in spite of the vehement expostulations of his wife, the Baron had promised Vera that he would see her young Jew whom she called such a talented musician, and Vera had great hopes that her father's love of music would melt all his prejudice when once he heard David play. The Baroness was incensed that her husband should even dream of agreeing to such a proposal and insisted on his taking her at once to her hotel since under no circumstances would she consent to be introduced to a Jew.

While the Baron was gone with the Baroness, Herr Pappelmeister turned up at the Settlement in search of David. Since he had left Quincy, Herr Pappelmeister had created an orchestra of his own and he came now to offer David a fine position as one of the first violins. It was joyous news to Vera, joyous news to David, for it meant that now at last they could really afford to marry.

"Oh, Herr Pappelmeister," cried Vera in delight, **"you are an angel!"**

"No, no, my dear child," laughed Pappelmeister, roguishly twirling himself round about to display his ample waist-line.

"I fear dat I haf not de correct shape for an angel."

Nevertheless his goodness did not end even with his offer of the position to David. He had come furthermore to arrange with the young musician for the production of his symphony on the roof garden of the Settlement before all the immigrants there on the Fourth of July,—such a setting for his music as of all that were possible, David would most have desired.

"Played to the people! Under God's sky! On Independence Day! That will be perfect! It was always my dream to play it first to new immigrants, those who have known the pain of the old world and the hope of the new."

And when Herr Pappelmeister had left, David took up his fiddle and dashed into jubilant music.

"I will make my old fiddle strings burst with joy!" he cried.

"And nothing now shall part us!" cried Vera.

"Not all the Seven Seas could part you and me!" said David.

Just then came a knock at the door. They paid no heed, their happy faces showing no signs of hearing; then the door slightly opened and Baron Revendal looked hesitatingly in. As David perceived that face, his features worked convulsively, and the string of his violin broke with a tragic snap.

"The face! the face!" he muttered hoarsely and tottered backward into Vera's arms.

"David, what is it?" Vera steadied him in alarm.

"What is the matter with him?" harshly demanded the Baron.

David's violin and bow dropped from his grasp to the table.

"The voice!" he cried and struggling out of Vera's clasp he moved like one walking in his sleep toward the Baron. Putting out his hand, he testingly touched his face.

"Hands off!" commanded the Baron, shuddering back at the touch of a Jew.

"A-ah!" David raised his voice in a mighty cry. "It is no

vision! It is flesh and blood. No! it is stone, the man of stone. Monster!" And he raised one hand in a frenzy.

"Back, dog!" the Baron whipped out his pistol, but Vera with a shriek, darted in between the two.

Frozen again, David surveyed the pistol stonily. "Ho! You want my life too. Is the cry not yet loud enough?"

"The cry! What cry?" asked the Baron.

"The voice of the blood of my brothers crying out against you from the ground. Oh, how can you bear not to turn that pistol against yourself and execute upon yourself the justice which Russia denies you?"

"Tush!" said the Baron, a little shamefaced as he pocketed his pistol.

"Justice on himself!" cried Vera, "justice for what?"

"For crimes beyond human penalty!"

"David, you are raving. This is my father!"

"Your father!"—David staggered back as if struck in the face. "O God!"

The Baron tried to draw Vera toward him. "Come to me, Vera," he said.

"Don't touch me!" Vera shrunk frantically away from his hand. "Say it is not true. It was the mob that massacred— *you* had no hand in it."

"I was there with my soldiers," the Baron answered sullenly.

"And you looked on with that cold face of hate!" hissed David, "while my mother—my sister—. Now and again you ordered your soldiers to fire!"

"Ah!" cried Vera in joyous relief. "Then he did check the mob. He did tell his soldiers to fire!"

"At any Jew who tried to defend himself!"

"Great God!" Vera fell on the sofa and buried her face in the cushions.

"It was the people avenging itself, Vera," the Baron explained.

"But you could have stopped them," she moaned.

"Who can stop a flood? I did my duty by Christ," he crossed himself, "and the Tsar."

"But you could have stopped them!"

"Silence!" The Baron's patience was gone. "You talk like an ignorant girl blinded by passion. Look up, little Vera." His voice grew suddenly tender. "You saw how papasha loves you, how he was ready to hold out his hand and how this cur tried to bite it! Be calm! Tell him a daughter of Russia cannot mate with dirt!"

"Father, I will be calm," Vera rose to her full height. "I will tell David the truth. I was never absolutely sure of my love for him before—"

"Hah!" cried the Baron exultant, "she is a true Revendal!"

"But now—" she walked firmly toward the young Jew, "now David, I come to you and I say in the words of Ruth, thy people shall be my people and thy God my God."

"You shameless!" cried the Baron, but he stopped as he saw that David made no move to take Vera's outstretched hand.

"You cannot come to me," David's voice was low and icy. "There is a river of blood between us."

"Were it seven seas, love must cross them all," said Vera.

"Easy words to you. You never saw that red flood. Oh!" David covered his eyes with his hands while the Baron turned away in gloomy impotence. Then the young man sank into a chair and began to speak, quietly, almost dreamily.

"It was your Easter, and the air was full of holy bells and the streets of holy processions—priests in black and girls in white, waving palms and crucifixes, and everybody exchanging Easter eggs and kissing one another three times on the mouth in token of peace and good will, and even the Jew boy felt the spirit of love brooding over the earth. And what added to the peace and holy joy was that our own Passover was shining before us. My mother had

FROM THE TOWER WINDOW

already made the raisin wine, and my greedy little brother Solomon had sipped it on the sly that very morning. We were all at home—all except my father—he was away in the little synagogue where he was cantor. Ah! such a voice he had, and how we were looking forward to his hymns at the Passover table." David's voice broke for a moment and the Baron turned slowly toward him as if compelled against his will to listen to his story. "I was playing my cracked little fiddle. Little Miriam was making her doll dance to it. Ah, that decrepit old China doll, the only one the poor child had ever had—I can see it now—one eye, no nose, half an arm. We were all laughing to see it caper to my music. Suddenly my father flies in at the door, desperately clasping to his breast the Holy Scroll. We cry out to him to explain, and then we see that in that beloved mouth of song there is no longer a tongue! He tries to bar the door, a mob breaks in—we dash out through the back into the street. There are the soldiers—and the face—" Vera's eyes involuntarily sought the face of her father and he shrunk away from her glance. "When I came to myself, with a curious aching in my left shoulder, I saw lying beside me—Ah! by the crimson doll in the hand, I knew it must be little Miriam. The doll was a dream of perfection and beauty beside all that remained of my sister, my mother, of greedy little Solomon—" He broke down in ironic laughter. "Hush, David," cried Vera. "Your laughter hurts more than tears. Let me comfort you."

But he pushed her forcibly from him. "For you I gave up my people. I darkened the home that sheltered me. There was always a still small voice calling me back, but I heeded nothing only the voice of the butcher's daughter. Let me go home— go home." And he turned unsteadily away. Perceiving how useless now was aught that could be said or done, Vera slipped like a shadow out of the room before him. To David the Baron cried suddenly, "Halt!" Whipping out his pistol once more,

209

he advanced slowly toward the young man who stood still, expecting to be shot. But the Baron did not fire. He handed the pistol instead to David.

"You were right," he said, then he stepped back swiftly with a touch of stern heroism, in the attitude of a culprit at a military execution. "Shoot me."

David fingered the pistol and looked at it long and pensively as if with the sense of how little such a thing could accomplish in setting matters right. Then gradually his arm dropped and he let the pistol fall to the table. As he did so, his hand touched the string of his violin which yielded a little note. Thus reminded of his beloved fiddle, he picked it up and drew his fingers across the broken string.

"I must get a new string," he murmured and slowly dragged out of the room. "I must get a new string."

And so the Baron and Baroness were forced to go back to Russia without Vera, and Quincy was forced to give her up altogether. Vera kept on with her work at the Settlement though all the joy was gone out of it, and David went back to his people. But ah! for him, too, life was joyless after what he had done.

"You are stone all over, ever since you came back home," said Mendel. "Turned into a pillar of salt, Mother says, like Lot's wife!"

"That was the punishment for looking backward. Ah, uncle, there's more sense in that old Bible than the Rabbis suspect. Perhaps that is the secret of our people's suffering. We are always looking backward."

"I thought it was your Jewish heart that drove you back home to us, but if you are still hankering after Miss Revendal, I'd rather see you marry her than go about like this and so, I believe, would mother. You couldn't make the house any gloomier."

But in truth what troubled David most was the sense of his own defeat. He had preached of America as the great crucible

FROM THE TOWER WINDOW

wherein must be thrown all the old world hatreds to be melted by the fires of love, mutual forbearance, forgiveness and understanding, into a higher unity, and when the test had come home to him, when he had been asked to cast therein his long cherished and violent enmity that it too might be purged away, he had refused. His own hatred, the hatred of Russian Jew for Russian Christian, deep grained though it had been and with good reason all down through the tragic years, was but a type of all the old world feuds that must here be yielded up to make the true American. And he had clung to his animosity, hugged it tight. He who had talked always of looking away from the past and the God of our fathers toward the future and the God of our children, when the test had come to him, had clung to the past and let it ruin the future. He had pushed away from him one whom he loved and who loved him because he still clung to his hatreds, his hatreds and the past. Ah, he knew he was false, false to his vision, false to America, false to his music.

So came the evening of the eventful Fourth of July. At the Settlement House it seemed that David's life-long ambition had been fulfilled at last. His symphony was played by Herr Pappelmeister's orchestra before all that crowd of wanderers from the old world, and they had understood his music with their hearts and souls, and applauded and applauded, and cried out again and again for the composer to show himself before them. It seemed a remarkable triumph. Yet up on the roof garden of the Settlement House, refusing to come down and take to himself the plaudits, sat David all alone. From the depths of his soul he knew it had not been a triumph.

The sun was setting and below him stretched out a beautiful far-reaching panorama of New York. Irregular rose the sky line of that mighty city and off to the right lay the harbor with its gilded Statue of Liberty. Everything was wet and gleaming, for the sun had come out after rain. In the sky hung heavy clouds through which thin golden lines of sunset were just beginning to labor. David, hugging tight his violin case, sat on a bench and gazed moodily at the sky, while the enormous sounds of applause, muffled by the distance, rose up to him from below. Thither came Mendel and Herr Pappelmeister to congratulate him on his success. They roused no joy in his soul. He knew he had been a failure. Thither came Kathleen and Frau Quixano, also, on the same errand bent. It was Shabbos and Frau Quixano had climbed wearily puffing and panting up flight after flight of stairs rather than use the elevator and fail to keep her Shabbos. And lo! Kathleen, late bitter foe of all things Jewish, was escorting the old lady in her slow tottering course toward David with the air of a guardian angel, and lo! the old lady herself, lately cursing all things American, was wearing a tiny American flag in honor of the day. Ah! that was what David's America did to all races who came to her shore, each one giving to and accepting from the others, each melting into the whole, transforming and being transformed, till at last shall come the real American to embody all the best in the world.

"When you take your mistress down again, Kathleen, please don't let her walk," said David sweetly, after the old lady had satisfied herself by laughing and crying over him.

"But Shabbos isn't out yet!"

David smiled, "There's no harm, Kathleen, in going *down* in the elevator."

"Troth, I'll egshplain to her that droppin' down isn't ridin'," chuckled Kathleen.

"Tell her dropping down is natural not *work* like flying up."

But when Kathleen turned to look for Frau Quixano, she had wandered off over the rooftop in the wrong direction entirely.

"*Wu geht Ihr, bedad?*" Kathleen called after her in a ridiculous mixture of Irish and Yiddish. "*Houly Moses, komm' zurick!*" And as she took Frau Quixano by the arm and led her carefully off toward the elevator, she added over her shoulder, *"Begorra! we Jews never know our way!"*

Scarcely had David been left alone, when Vera came to the rooftop to convey to him from Miss Andrews the heartfelt thanks and congratulations of the Settlement. It was two months since they had seen each other.

"Please don't *you* congratulate me too," said David. "That would be too ironical. How can I endure all these congratulations when I know what a terrible failure I have made?"

"Failure!" cried Vera. "You have produced something real and new, a most wonderful success."

"Failure! Failure!" cried David. "Every bar of my music cried, 'Failure'. It shrieked from the violins, blared from the trombones, thundered from the drums. It was written on all the faces—"

"O no! no!" Vera spoke vehemently. "I watched the faces, those faces of toil and sorrow, those faces from many lands. They were fired by your vision of their coming brotherhood, lulled by your dream of their land of rest. And I could see you were right in speaking to the people. In some strange beautiful way the inner meaning of your music stole into all those simple souls—"

"And my soul, my soul!" cried David springing up. "What of my soul? False to its own music, its own mission, its own dream. That is what I mean by failure, Vera. I preached of God's crucible, this great new continent that could melt up all race differences and vendettas, that could purge and re-create and make anew. And God tried me with his supremest test. He gave me a heritage from the old world, hate and vengeance and blood, and said, 'Cast it all into my crucible.' And I said, 'Even thy crucible cannot melt this hate!' And so I sat crooning over the dead past, gloating over the old blood-stains, I, the apostle of America, the prophet of the God of our children. Oh, how my music mocked me! And you, so fearless, so high above all that has come to pass, how you must despise me, despise me!"

"I?" cried Vera. "Ah no!"

"You must! You do. Your words still sting. 'Were it seven seas between us,' you said, 'love must cross them.' And I—I who had prated of seven seas—"

"Not seas of blood," cried Vera. "I spoke selfishly, thoughtlessly. I had not realized what that sea had meant for you. Now I see it day and night."

"There lies my failure," said David. "To have brought it to your eyes instead of blotting it from my own."

"No man could have blotted it out." Vera shuddered.

"Yes," cried David, "by faith in the crucible. But in the supreme moment, my faith was found wanting. You came to me and I thrust you away. Ah! you can never forgive me."

"Forgive!" cried Vera. "It is I that should go down on my knees to you for my father's sin."

"No," David's voice rang strong with conviction. "The sins of the fathers shall *not* be visited upon the children. You owe me nothing." He suddenly stretched out both hands. "Come to me, Vera! Cling to me!"

"Shall I come to you and let the shadows of Kishineff hang over all your years to come?"

"Yes." He took both her hands in a firm, strong clasp as though he would never again let her go. "Cling to me despite it all, cling to me till all those ugly memories vanish, cling to me till love shall triumph over death."

"I dare not," Vera still drew back. "It will make you remember."

"It will make me forget."

There was a pause of hesitation, then Vera said very slowly:

"I yield. I will kiss you as we Russians kiss at Easter, the three kisses of peace." And she kissed him solemnly three times on the mouth as in a ritual ceremony.

FROM THE TOWER WINDOW

"See," said David calmly. "Easter was the date of the massacre, yet now when you speak of it I am disturbed no more. I am altogether at peace."

Vera spoke fervently. "God grant that peace may endure."

For a moment they stood hand in hand by the parapet overlooking the mighty city below, then Vera said softly, "Look how beautiful is the sunset after the storm." The sunset had indeed reached its most magnificent moment. Low on the horizon lay narrow lines of saffron and gold, but above, the whole sky was a glory of burning flame.

"It is the fires of God round his crucible," said David pointing downward. "There she lies, the great melting pot. Listen—can't you hear the roaring and the bubbling? There gapes her mouth,—" he pointed toward the east— "the harbor where a thousand mammoth feeders come from the ends of the world to pour in their human freight. Ah, what a stirring and a seething! Celt and Latin, Slav and Teuton, Greek and Syrian—black and yellow—"

"Jew and Gentile," added Vera drawing closer to him.

"Yes, east and west, and north and south, the palm and the pine, the pole and the equator, the crescent and the cross—how the great Alchemist melts and fuses them with his purging flame! Here shall they all unite to build the Republic of Man and the Kingdom of God. Ah, Vera, what is the glory of Rome and Jerusalem where all nations and races come to worship and look back compared to the glory of America where all races and nations come to *labor* and *look forward?*"

There was an instant's solemn pause. The sunset faded swiftly and the whole vast panorama below was suffused with a restful twilight, while the lights of the town, gleaming out through the dusk, added to all the tender scene, the poetry of the night. Far back over the darkening water, like a lonely guiding star, twinkled the torch of the Statue of Liberty. From below somewhere came up the softened sound of instruments and voices joining in the national anthem.

"My country, 'tis of thee,
Sweet land of Liberty
Of thee I sing."

David stood with Vera close by his side, his heart purified at last of the hideous stains of the past, his shining face turned transfigured toward the future alone, the future with all its glorious possibilities of working for the fulfillment of his dream, for the revelation in the hearts of men of that true America of liberty, humanity, brotherhood and justice. Slowly he raised his hands as in benediction over the shining city below.

"Peace, peace," he said, "to all ye unborn millions, fated to fill this giant continent. The God of our *children* give you peace."

STANZAS ON FREEDOM
James Russell Lowell

Is true Freedom but to break
Fetters for our own dear sake,
And, with leathern hearts, forget
That we owe mankind a debt?
No! true freedom is to share
All the chains our brothers wear,
And, with heart and hand, to be
Earnest to make others free!
They are slaves who fear to speak
For the fallen and the weak;
They are slaves who will not choose
Hatred, scoffing, and abuse,
Rather than in silence shrink
From the truth they needs must think;
They are slaves who dare not be
In the right with two or three.

FROM THE TOWER WINDOW

An Address to New-Made Citizens
WOODROW WILSON

You have just taken an oath of allegiance to the United States. Of allegiance to whom? Of allegiance to no one, unless it be to God.

You have taken an oath of allegiance to a great ideal, to a great body of principles, to a great hope of the human race. You have said, "We are going to America not only to earn a living, not only to seek the things which it was more difficult to obtain where we were born, but to help forward the great enterprises of the human spirit—to let men know that everywhere in the world there are men who will cross strange oceans and go where a speech is spoken which is alien to them, knowing that whatever the speech, there is but one longing and utterance of the human heart, and that is for liberty and justice."

And while you bring all countries with you, you come with a purpose of leaving all other countries behind you—bringing what is best of their spirit, but not looking over your shoulders and seeking to perpetuate what you intended to leave in them.

You cannot dedicate yourself to America unless you become in every respect and with every purpose of your will thorough Americans. You cannot become thorough Americans if you think of yourselves in groups. America does not consist of groups. A man who thinks of himself as belonging to a particular national group in America has not yet become an American.

My urgent advice to you would be not only always to think first of America, but always also to think first of humanity. You do not love humanity if you seek to divide humanity into jealous camps. Humanity can be welded together only by love, by sympathy, by justice, not by jealousy and hatred.

We came to America, either ourselves or in the persons of our ancestors, to better the ideals of men, to make them see finer things than they had seen before, to get rid of things that divide, and to make sure of the things that unite.

It was but an historical accident, no doubt, that this great country was called 'The United States,' and yet I am thankful that it has the word 'United' in its title; and the man who seeks to divide, man from man, group from group, interest from interest in the United States, is striking at its heart.

It is an interesting circumstance to me in thinking of those of you who have just sworn allegiance to this great government that you were drawn across the ocean by some beckoning finger of hope, by some belief, by some vision of a new kind of justice, by some expectation of a better kind of life.

No doubt you have been disappointed in some of us. Some of us are disappointing. No doubt you have found that justice in the United States goes only with a pure heart and a right purpose as it does everywhere else in the world. No doubt what you found here did not seem touched for you, after all, with the complete beauty of the ideal which you had conceived beforehand.

But remember this, if some of us have forgotten what America believed in, you, at any rate, imported in your own hearts a renewal of the belief.

I was born in America. You dreamed dreams of what America was to be, and I hope you brought the dreams with you. No man that does not see visions will ever realize any high hope or undertake any high enterprise. Just because you brought dreams with you, America is more likely to realize the dreams such as you brought. You are enriching us if you came expecting us to be better than we are.

We cannot exempt you from work. No man is exempt from work anywhere in the world. We cannot exempt you from the loads that you must carry—we can only make them light by the spirit in which they are carried.

That is the spirit of hope, it is the spirit of liberty, it is the spirit of justice.

I like to come and stand in the presence of a great body of my fellow citizens, and drink, as it were, out of the common fountain with them and go back feeling that you have so generously given me the sense of your support and of the living vitality in your hearts, of its great ideals which made America the hope of the world.

COALY-BAY, THE OUTLAW HORSE*
Ernest Thompson Seton

FIVE years ago in the Bitterroot mountains of Idaho there was a beautiful little foal. His coat was bright bay; his legs, mane, and tail were glossy black—coal black and bright bay—so they named him Coaly-bay.

"Coaly-bay" sounds like "Kolibey," which is an Arab title of nobility, and those who saw the handsome colt, and did not know how he came by the name, thought he must be of Arab blood. No doubt he was, in a faraway sense; just as all our best horses have Arab blood, and once in a while it seems to come out strong and show in every part of the creature, in his frame, his power, and his wild, free, roving spirit.

Coaly-bay loved to race like the wind, he gloried in his speed, his tireless legs, and when careering with the herd of colts he met a fence or ditch, it was as natural to Coaly-bay to overleap it, as it was for the others to sheer off.

So he grew up strong of limb, restless of spirit, and rebellious at any thought of restraint. Even the kindly curb of the hay-yard or the stable was unwelcome, and he soon showed that he would rather stand out all night in a driving storm than be locked in a comfortable stall where he had no vestige of the liberty he loved so well.

He became very clever at dodging the horse wrangler whose job it was to bring the horseherd to the corral. The very sight of that man set Coaly-bay a-going. He became what is known as a "Quit-the-bunch"—that is a horse of such independent mind that he will go his own way the moment he does not like the way of the herd. So each month the colt became more set on living free, and more cunning in the means he took to win his way.

When he was three years of age, just in the perfection of his young strength and beauty, his real troubles began, for now his owner undertook to break him to ride. He was as tricky and

*Used by permission of the publishers, Doubleday, Page & Co.

vicious as he was handsome, and the first day's experience was a terrible battle between the horse-trainer and the beautiful colt.

But the man was skillful. He knew how to apply his power, and all the wild plunging, bucking, rearing, and rolling of the wild one had no desirable result. With all his strength the horse was hopelessly helpless in the hands of the skilful horseman, and Coaly-bay was so far mastered at length that a good rider could use him. But each time the saddle went on, he made a new fight. After a few months of this the colt seemed to realize that it was useless to resist; it simply won for him lashings and spur-rings, so he pretended to reform. For a week he was ridden each day and not once did he buck, but on the last day he came home lame.

His owner turned him out to pasture. Three days later he seemed all right; he was caught and saddled. He did not buck, but within five minutes he went lame as before. Again he was turned out to pasture, and after a week, saddled, only to go lame again.

His owner did not know what to think, whether the horse really had a lame leg or was only shamming, but he took the first chance to get rid of him, and though Coaly-bay was easily worth fifty dollars, he sold him for twenty-five. The new owner felt he had a bargain, but after being ridden half a mile Coaly-bay went lame. The rider got off to examine the foot, whereupon Coaly-bay broke away and galloped back to his old pasture. Here he was caught, and the new owner, being neither gentle nor sweet, applied spur without mercy, so that the next twenty miles was covered in less than two hours and no sign of lameness appeared.

Now they were at the ranch of this new owner. Coaly-bay was led from the door of the house to the pasture, limping all the way, and then turned out. He limped over to the other horses. On one side of the pasture was the garden of a neighbor. This man was very proud of his fine vegetables and had put a six-foot fence around the place. Yet the very night after Coaly-bay arrived, certain of the horses got into the garden somehow and did a great deal of damage. But they leaped out before daylight and no one saw them.

The gardener was furious, but the ranchman stoutly maintained that it must have been some other horses, since his were behind a six-foot fence.

Next night it happened again. The ranchman went out very early and saw all his horses in the pasture, with Coaly-bay behind them. His lameness seemed worse now instead of better. In a few days, however, the horse was seen walking all right, so the ranchman's son caught him and tried to ride him. But this seemed too good a chance to lose; all his old wickedness returned to the horse; the boy was bucked off at once. The ranchman himself now leaped into the saddle; Coaly-bay bucked for ten minutes, but finding he could not throw the man, he tried to crush his leg against a post, but the rider guarded himself well. Coaly-bay reared and threw himself backward; the rider slipped off, the horse fell, jarring heavily, and before he could rise the man was in the saddle again. The horse now ran away, plunging and bucking; he stopped short, but the rider did not go over his head, so Coaly-bay turned, and seized the man's foot in his teeth. It was quite clear now that Coaly-bay was an "outlaw"—that is an incurably vicious horse.

The saddle was jerked off, and he was driven, limping, into the pasture.

The raids on the garden continued, and the two men began to quarrel over it. But to prove that his horses were not guilty the ranchman asked the gardener to sit up with him and watch. That night as the moon was brightly shining they saw, not all the horses, but Coaly-bay, walk straight up to the garden fence— no sign of a limp now—easily leap over it, and proceed to gobble the finest things he could find. After they had made sure of his identity, the men ran forward. Coaly-bay cleared the fence like a deer, lightly raced over the pasture to mix with the horseherd, and when the men came near him he had—oh, such an awful limp.

"That settles it," said the rancher. "He's a fraud, but he's a beauty, and good stuff, too."

"Yes, but it settles who took my garden truck," said the other.

"Wall, I suppose so," was the answer; "but luk a here, neighbor, you ain't lost more'n ten dollars in truck. That horse is easily worth—a hundred. Give me twenty-five dollars, take the horse, an' call it square."

"Not much I will," said the gardener. "I'm out twenty-five dollars' worth of truck; the horse ain't worth a cent more. I take him and call it even."

And so the thing was settled. The ranchman said nothing about Coaly-bay being vicious as well as cunning, but the gardener found out, the very first time he tried to ride him, that the horse was as bad as he was beautiful.

Next day a sign appeared on the gardener's gate:

FOR SALE
First class Horse, sound & Gentle
$10.⁰⁰

Now at this time a band of hunters came riding by. There were three mountaineers, two men from the city, and the writer of this story. The city men were going to hunt bear. They had guns and everything needed for bear-hunting, except bait. It is usual to buy some worthless horse or cow, drive it into the mountains where the bears are, and kill it there. So seeing the sign up, the hunters called to the gardener: "Haven't you got a cheaper horse?"

The gardener replied: "Look at him there, ain't he a beauty? You won't find a cheaper horse if you travel a thousand miles."

"We are looking for an old bear-bait, and five dollars is our limit," replied the hunter.

Horses are cheap and plentiful in that country; buyers were scarce. The gardener feared that Coaly-bay would escape. "Wall, if that's the best you can do, he's yourn."

The hunter handed him five dollars, then said: "Now, stranger, the bargain's settled. Will you tell me why you sell this fine horse for five dollars?"

"Mighty simple. He can't be rode. He's dead lame when he's going your way and sound as a dollar going his own; no fence in the country can hold him; he's a dangerous outlaw. He's wickeder nor old Nick."

"Well, he's an almighty handsome bear-bait," and the hunters rode on.

Coaly-bay was driven with the packhorses, and limped dreadfully on the trail. Once or twice he tried to go back, but he was easily turned by the men behind him. His limp grew worse, and toward night it was painful to see him.

The leading guide remarked: "That thar limp ain't no fake. He's got some deep-seated trouble."

Day after day the hunters rode farther into the mountains, driving the horses along and hobbling them at night. Coaly-bay went with the rest, limping along, tossing his head and his long splendid mane at every step. One of the hunters tried to ride him and nearly lost his life, for the horse seemed possessed of a demon as soon as the man was on his back.

The road grew harder as it rose. A very bad bog had to be crossed one day. Several horses were mired in it, and as the men rushed to the rescue, Coaly-bay saw his chance of escape. He wheeled in a moment and turned himself from a limping low-headed, sorry, bad-eyed creature into a high-spirited horse. Head and tail aloft now, shaking their black streamers in the wind, he gave a joyous neigh, and, without a trace of lameness, dashed for his home one hundred miles away, threading each narrow trail with perfect certainty, though he had seen them but once before. In a few minutes he had steamed away from their sight.

The men were furious, but one of them, saying not a word, leaped on his horse—to do what? Follow that free ranging racer? Sheer folly. Oh, no!—he knew a better plan. He knew the country. Two miles around by the trail, half a mile by the rough cut-off that he took, was Panther Gap. The runaway must pass through that, and Coaly-bay raced down the trail to find the guide below awaiting him. Tossing his head with anger, he wheeled on up the trail again, and within a few yards recovered his monotonous limp and his evil expression. So he was driven into camp.

This was Bear country, and the hunters resolved to end his dangerous pranks and make him useful for once. They dared not catch him, it was not really safe to go near him, but two of the guides drove him to a distant glade where bears abounded. A thrill of pity came over me as I saw that beautiful untamable creature going away with his imitation limp.

"Ain't you coming along?" called the guide.

"No, I don't want to see him die," was the answer.

Fifteen minutes later a distant rifle crack was heard, and in my mind's eye I saw that proud head and those superb limbs, robbed of their sustaining indomitable spirit, falling flat and limp— to suffer the unsightly end of fleshly things. Poor Coaly-bay; he would not bear the yoke. Rebellious to the end, he had fought against the fate of all his kind. It seemed to me the spirit of an Eagle or a Wolf it was that dwelt behind those full bright eyes— that ordered all his wayward life.

I tried to put the tragic finish out of mind, and had not long to battle with the thought; not even one short hour, for the men came back.

Down the long trail to the west they had driven him; there was no chance for him to turn aside. He must go on, and the men behind felt safe in that.

Farther away from his old home on the Bitterroot River he had gone each time he journeyed. And now he had passed the high divide and was keeping the narrow trail that leads to the valley of bears and on to Salmon River, and still away to the open wild Columbian Plains, limping sadly as though he knew. His glossy hide flashed back the golden sunlight, still richer than it fell, and the men behind followed like hangmen in the death train of a nobleman condemned—down the narrow trail till it opened into a little beaver meadow, with rank rich grass, a lovely mountain stream and winding bear paths up and down the waterside.

"Guess this'll do," said the older man. "Well, here goes for a sure death or a clean miss," said the other confidently, and, waiting till the limper was out in the middle of the meadow, he gave a short, sharp whistle. Instantly Coaly-bay was alert. He swung and faced his tormentors, his noble head erect, his nostrils flaring; a picture of horse beauty—yes, of horse perfection.

The rifle was levelled, the very brain its mark, just on the cross line of the eyes and ears, that meant sure—sudden, painless death. It was sudden death or miss—and the marksman missed.

Away went the wild horse at his famous best, not for his eastern home, but down the unknown western trail, away and away; the pine woods hid him from the view, and left behind was the rifleman vainly trying to force the empty cartridge from his gun.

Down that trail with an inborn certainty he went, and on through the pines, then leaped a great bog, and splashed an hour later through the limpid Clearwater and on, responsive to some unknown guide that subtly called him from the farther west. And so he went till the dwindling pines gave place to scrubby cedars and these in turn were mixed with sage, and onward still, till the far-away flat plains of Salmon River were about him, and ever on, tireless as it seemed, he went, and crossed the canyon of the mighty Snake, and up again to the high wild plains where

224

the wire fence still is not, and on, beyond the Buffalo Hump, till moving specks on the far horizon caught his eager eyes, and coming on and near, they moved and rushed aside to wheel and face about. He lifted up his voice and called to them, the long shrill neigh of his kindred when they bugled to each other on the far Chaldean plain; and back their answer came. This way and that they wheeled and sped and caracoled, and Coaly-bay drew nearer, called and gave the countersigns his kindred know, till this they were assured—he was their kind, he was of the wild free blood that man had never tamed. And when the night came down on the purpling plain his place was in the herd as one who after many a long hard journey in the dark had found his home.

There you may see him yet, for still his strength endures, and his beauty is not less. The riders tell me they have seen him many times by Cedra. He is swift and strong among the swift ones, but it is that flowing mane and tail that mark him chiefly from afar.

There on the wild free plains of sage he lives: the stormwind smites his glossy coat at night and the winter snows are driven hard on him at times; the wolves are there to harry all the weak ones of the herd, and in the spring the mighty Grizzly, too, may come to claim his toll. There are no luscious pastures made by man, no grain-foods; nothing but the wild hard hay, the wind and the open plains, but here at last he found the thing he craved —the one worth all the rest. Long may he roam—this is my wish, and this—that I may see him once again in all the glory of his speed with his black mane on the wind, the spur-galls gone from his flanks, and in his eye the blazing light that grew in his far-off forebears' eyes as they spurned Arabian plains to leave behind the racing wild beast and the fleet gazelle—yes, too, the driving sandstorm that overwhelmed the rest, but strove in vain on the dusty wake of the Desert's highest born.

The story of Coaly-bay is in the main true, and a recent

FROM THE TOWER WINDOW

letter from the West gives me new light on the history of the wild horse. The letter runs as follows:

"January 26, 1916. I, too, knew Coaly-bay, the glorious creature. He began his struggles in the Bitterroot Mountains of Idaho, left through the Salmon River country straggling tales of his fierce resentment under the yoke, and escaped triumphantly at last to the plains in the south.

"I was sixteen then and it is six years ago.

"Something, however, you failed to record. It is this: that before he escaped from the world of spur and lash, the world of compulsion, the world that denies to a horse an end in himself, he came to love one person—me, the woman who petted instead of saddled him, who gave him sugar instead of spurring him, who gloried in him because he dared assert that he belonged to himself.

"When I wandered joyfully through the evergreen labyrinths of the Florence Basin, sniffing like a hare or fox the damp spring smell of the earth, going far down the narrow, rock-walled canyons for the first wild orchids, Coaly-bay came, too. I did not ride or drive him. He trotted beside me as might a dog. We were pals, equals. I went with him where he could find the first young meadow grass, and he went with me where grew the first wild strawberries. As together we glimpsed, far below, the green ribbon that was the Salmon River, or saw, far off, the snow attempting to cover the sinister blackness of the Buffalo Hump,

we laughed at the stu- pidity of the world of man, who sought to drive things, to com- pel things, to master things, breeding hate and viciousness there- by; the stupidity of the world of men who never dreamed of the marvellous power of love! Yes, always I shall love the mem- ory of Coaly-bay. He was a symbol of the eternal spirit of Re- volt against the Spur of Oppression."

RICHARD FEVEREL AND THE HAY-RICK*
George Meredith

OCTOBER shone royally on Richard's fourteenth birthday. The brown beech woods and golden birches glowed to a brilliant sun. Banks of moveless clouds hung about the horizon, mounded to the west where slept the wind,—promise of a great day for Raynham Abbey to celebrate the birthday of Sir Austin Feverel's son and heir. Already archery booths and cricketing tents were rising on the lower grounds towards the river, whither the lads of Bursley and Lobourne, in boats and in carts, came merrily jogging to match themselves anew. The whole park was beginning to be astir and resound with holiday cries. For Sir Austin could be a popular man when he chose. Half the village of Lobourne was seen trooping through the avenues of the park. Fiddlers and gypsies clamored at the gates for admission. White smocks and gray, surmounted by hats of serious brim, and now and then a scarlet cloak, dotted the grassy sweeps to the levels.

And all the time the hero of these festivities, Richard Feverel himself, was flying farther and farther away from Raynham, losing himself from the sight of men in company with his reluctant friend and obedient serf, Ripton Thompson, who kept asking what they were to do and where they were going, and suggesting that the lads of Lobourne would be calling them to join in the sports, and Sir Austin would be requiring their presence. Richard paid no attention to Ripton's remonstrances. For

*Arranged from *The Ordeal of Richard Feverel*

FROM THE TOWER WINDOW

Richard had been requested by his father to submit to medical examination like a boor enlisting for a soldier, and he was in great wrath. He was flying as though he would have flown from the shameful thought of what had been asked of him. The two boys had the dog with them and had borrowed a couple of guns at the bailiff's farm. Off they trotted through the depths of the wood, Ripton following wherever his friend chose to lead. They were beating about for birds, but the birds on the Raynham estate were found singularly cunning, and repeatedly eluded the aim of these prime shots, so they pushed their expedition into the lands of their neighbors, happily oblivious that the law forbids as a criminal trespass, the shooting of game on another's land, unconscious too that they were poaching on the demesne of the notorious Farmer Blaize. Farmer Blaize hated poachers, and especially young chaps poaching who did it mostly from impudence. He heard the audacious shots popping right and left, and going forth to have a glimpse at the intruders, swore he would teach my gentlemen a thing, lords or no lords. Richard had brought down a beautiful cock-pheasant, and was exulting over it, when the farmer's portentous figure burst upon them cracking an avenging horse-whip. His salute was ironical.

"Havin' good sport, gentlemen, are ye?"

"Just bagged a splendid bird!" radiant Richard informed him.

"Oh!" Farmer Blaize gave an admonitory flick of the whip. "Tell ye what 'tis!" He changed his banter to business. "That bird's mine! Now you jest hand him over, and sheer off, you damn young scoundrels! I know ye!"

Richard opened his eyes.

"If you wants to be horsewhipped, you'll stay where you are!" continued the farmer.

"Then we'll stay," quoth Richard.

"Good! so be't! If you will have it, have it, my men!" And sweetch went the mighty whip, well swayed. The boys tried to close with him. He kept his distance and lashed without mercy. Black blood was made by Farmer Blaize that day! The boys wriggled in spite of themselves. It was like a relentless serpent coiling and biting and stinging their young veins to madness. Probably they felt the disgrace of the contortions they were made to go through more than the pain, but the pain was fierce, for the farmer laid about from a practiced arm and did not consider that he had done enough till he was well breathed and his ruddy jowl inflamed. He paused to receive the cock-pheasant full in his face. "Take your beastly bird," cried Richard.

Shameful as it was to retreat, there was but that course open to the boys. They decided to surrender the field.

"Look! you big brute," Richard shook his gun, hoarse with passion, "I'd have shot you if I'd been loaded."

This threat exasperated Farmer Blaize and he pressed the pursuit in time to bestow a few farewell stripes. At the hedge they parleyed a minute, the farmer to inquire if they had had a mortal good tanning and were satisfied, for when they wanted a further instalment of the same they were to come for it to Belthorpe Farm, and there it was kept in pickle! The boys meantime exploded in menaces and threats of vengeance, on which the farmer contemptuously turned his back. Ripton had already stocked an armful of stones for the enjoyment of a little skirmishing. Richard however knocked them all out, saying, "No! Gentlemen don't fling stones. Leave that to the blackguards!"

"Just one shy at him," pleaded Ripton.

"No," said Richard imperatively, "no stones," and marched briskly away. Ripton followed with a sigh. But Richard's blood was poisoned. A sweeping and consummate vengeance for the indignity alone should satisfy him. Something tremendous must be done and done without delay. At one moment he thought of killing all the farmer's cattle; next of killing him; challenging him to single combat with the arms, and according to the fashion of gentlemen. But the farmer was a coward; he would refuse. Then he, Richard Feverel, would stand by the farmer's bedside, and rouse him, rouse him to fight with powder and ball in his own chamber, in the cowardly midnight, where he might tremble, but dare not refuse.

"Lord!" cried simple Ripton, while these hopeful plots were raging in his comrade's brain. "How I wish you'd have let me shy one at him, Ricky! I'd feel quite jolly if I'd spanked him once."

To these exclamations Richard was deaf, and he trudged steadily forward facing but one object. After tearing through innumerable hedges, leaping fences, jumping dykes, penetrating brambly copses, and getting dirty, ragged and tired, Ripton awoke from his dream of Farmer Blaize to the vivid consciousness of hunger; and this grew with the rapidity of light upon him, till in the course of another minute he was enduring the extremes of famine, and ventured to question his leader whither he was being conducted. Raynham was now out of sight. They were a long way down the valley, miles from Lobourne, in a country of sour pools, yellow brooks, rank pasturage, desolate heath. Solitary cows were seen; the smoke of a mud cottage; a cart piled with peat; a donkey grazing at leisure; geese gabbling by a horse-pond; uncooked things that a famishing boy cannot possibly care for. Ripton was in despair—

"Where are you going to?" he inquired and halted resolutely. Richard now broke his silence to reply, "Anywhere."

"Anywhere!" Ripton repeated, "but aren't you awful hungry?"

"No," was Richard's brief response.

"Not hungry!" Ripton's amazement lent him increased

vehemence. "Why you haven't had anything to eat since break-fast! I declare I'm starving. Come, tell us where you're going."

Richard lifted his head, surveyed the position, and exclaim-ing "Here!" dropped down on a withered bank, leaving Ripton to contemplate him as a puzzle whose every new move was a worse perplexity. But Master Ripton Thompson was naturally loyal. The idea of turning off and forsaking his friend never once crossed his mind, though his condition was desperate, and his friend's behavior that of a Bedlamite. He announced several times impatiently that they would be too late for dinner. His friend did not budge. Dinner seemed nothing to him. There he sat plucking grass and patting the old dog's nose as if incapable of conceiving what a thing hunger was. Ripton at last flung himself down beside the silent boy, accepting his fate.

Now it chanced just then that a smart shower fell with the sinking sun, and the wet sent two strangers for shelter into the lane behind the hedge where the boys reclined. One was a travel-ling tinker, who lit a pipe and spread a tawny umbrella. The other was a burly young countryman, pipeless and tentless. They saluted with a nod, and began recounting for each other's benefit the day-long doings of the weather.

Ripton solaced his wretchedness by watching them through the briar hedge. He saw the tinker stroking a white cat, and appealing to her every now and then, as his missus, and he thought that a curious sight. Speed-the-plough was stretched at full length with his boots in the rain and his head amidst the tinker's pots, smoking, profoundly thinking.

Said the tinker, "Times is bad!"

His companion assented, "Sure-ly!"

"But everything somehow comes round right," resumed the tinker. "Where's the good o' moping? I sees it all come right and tight. T'other day I was as nigh ship-wrecked as the prophet Paul. We pitched and tossed. I thinks, down we're a-going.

But God's above the devil, and here I am, ye see."

Speed-the-plough lurched round on his elbow and regarded him indifferently. "God ben't al'ays above the devil, or I shoo'n't be scrapin' my heels wi' nothin' to do, and, what's warse, nothin' to eat. Why, look heer. Heer's a darned bad case. I threshed for Varmer Blaize—Blaize o' Belthorpe. Varmer Blaize misses pilkins. He swears our chaps steal pilkins. 'Twarn't me steals 'em. What do he take and go and do? He takes and turns us off, me and another, neck and crop, to scuffle about and starve, for all he keers. God warn't above the devil then, I thinks. Not nohow as I can see!"

The tinker shook his head and said that was a bad case.

"And you can't mend it," added Speed-the-plough. "It's bad, and there it be. But I'll tell ye what, master. Bad wants payin' for." He nodded and winked mysteriously. "Bad has its wages as well as honest work, I'm thinkin'. Varmer Blaize I owes a grudge to. And I shud like to stick a match in his hay-rick some dry, windy night." Speed-the-Plough screwed up an eye villainously. "He wants hittin' jest where the pocket is, do Varmer Blaize, and he'll cry out, 'O Lor,' Varmer Blaize will, if ye hit him jest there."

The tinker sent a rapid succession of white clouds from his mouth and said that firing Farmer Blaize's rick would be taking the devil's side of a bad case. Speed-the-Plough observed energetically that if Farmer Blaize was on the other side, he preferred to be on the devil's side.

There was a young gentleman close by who thought with him. The hope of Raynham had lent a careless, half-compelled attention to the foregoing conversation. He now started to his feet and came tearing through the briar hedge, calling out for the men to direct him the nearest road to Bursley. The tinker was kindling preparations for his tea under the tawny umbrella. A loaf was set forth, on which Ripton's eyes fastened ravenously. Speed-the-Plow volunteered the information that Bursley was a good three miles from where they stood.

"I'll give you a half-crown for that loaf, my good fellow," said Richard to the tinker.

"It's a bargain," quoth the tinker, "eh, missus?"

His cat replied by humping her back at the dog.

The half-crown was tossed down, and Ripton collared the loaf.

In a short time Speed-the-Plough and the tinker were following the two lads on the road to Bursley, while a horizontal blaze shot across the autumn land from the western edge of the rain-cloud. And more there was that passed between the boys and Speed-the-Plough on the road of a nature extremely interesting.

Search for the missing boys had been made everywhere over Raynham, and Sir Austin was in grievous discontent. No one had seen them. All the sports of the day,—cricket, bowling, archery contests on the green, all without him whom the festival had been designed to honor. At dinner in the evening, the company of honored friends, aunts, uncles, cousins, sat all about the great table and naught there was but a vacant chair and napkin in place of Richard. By ten at night the poor show ended, the rooms were dark and the guests departed.

It was late when old Benson the butler tolled out intelligence to Sir Austin, "Master Richard has returned."

"Well?" said the baronet.

"He complains of being hungry," the butler hesitated with a look of solemn disgust.

"Let him eat."

The boys were in the vortex of a partridge pie when Adrian Harley strolled in upon them. Adrian was Richard's cousin, a youth wise in the ways of the world, though perhaps not too scrupulous in his moral tone. He had been chosen by Sir Austin to superintend the education of his motherless son. Adrian found Richard uproarious, his cheeks flushed and his eyes brilliant, while Ripton looked very much like a rogue on the tremble lest he be detected in some crime.

"Good sport, gentlemen, I trust to hear?" began Adrian in his quiet banter.

"Ha, ha! I say, Rip: 'Havin' good sport, gentlemen, are ye?' You remember the farmer! We're going to have some first rate sport. Oh well! we haven't much show of birds. We shot for pleasure and returned them to the proprietors. But Rip and I have had a beautiful day. We've made new acquaintances. We've seen the world. First there's a farmer who warns everybody, gentleman and beggar, off his premises. Next there's a tinker and a ploughman who think that God is always fighting with the devil which shall command the kingdoms of the earth—"

Here a hideous and silencing frown from Ripton interrupted Richard's words. Adrian watched the innocent youths and knew that there was talking under the table. Soon Uncle Algernon, the one-legged veteran, shambled in to see his nephew, and his genial presence brought out a little more of the plot.

"Look here, uncle," said Richard. "Would you let a churlish old brute of a farmer strike you without making him suffer for it?"

"I fancy I should return the compliment," replied his uncle.

"Of course you would. So would I. And he shall suffer for it!"

But in the midst of all this riot there was one subject at Richard's heart about which he was reserved. Too proud to inquire how his father had taken his absence, he burned to hear whether he was in disgrace. At last when the boy declared a desire to wish his father good-night, Adrian had to tell him that he was to go straight to bed from the supper table. Young Richard's face fell at that and his gaiety forsook him, for he had a deep and reverent affection for his father. He marched to his room without another word.

At midnight the house breathed sleep. Sir Austin put on his cloak and cap and took the lamp as he always did to make his rounds of the place. He ascended the stairs and bent his steps leisurely toward the chamber where his son was lying in the left wing of the Abbey. At the end of the gallery which led to it, he discovered a dim light. Doubting it an illusion, Sir Austin accelerated his pace. A slight descent brought the baronet into the passage and he beheld a candle standing outside his son's chamber. At the same moment a door closed hastily. He entered Richard's room. The boy was absent. The bed was unpressed, nothing to show that he had been there that night. Sir Austin felt vaguely apprehensive. He determined to go and ask the boy Thompson, as he called Ripton, what was known to him.

The chamber assigned to Master Ripton overlooked the valley toward Belthorpe farm. Sir Austin found the door ajar and the interior dark. To his surprise Ripton's couch as revealed by the rays of his lamp was likewise vacant. He was turning back when he fancied he heard whispering in the room. Sir Austin cloaked the lamp and trod silently toward the window. The heads of his son Richard and the boy Thompson were seen crouched against the glass holding excited converse together. Sir Austin listened, but he listened to a language of which he possessed not the key. Their talk was of fire and of delay, of a farmer's huge wrath, of violence exercised upon gentlemen, and of vengeance. Over Lobourne and the valley lay black night and innumerable stars.

"How jolly I feel!" exclaimed Ripton. "But I think that

fellow has pocketed his guinea and jumped his job."

"If he has," said Richard slowly, "I'll go and I'll do it myself."

"You would?" returned Master Ripton. "Well I'm hanged! But I say, do you think we shall ever be found out?"

"I don't think about it," said Richard, all his faculties bent on signs from Lobourne.

"Well but," Ripton persisted, "suppose we are found out?"

"If we are, I must pay for it."

Sir Austin breathed the better for this reply. He was beginning to gather a clue to the dialogue. His son was engaged in a plot, and was, moreover, the leader in the plot.

"What was the fellow's name?" inquired Ripton.

His companion answered, "Tom Bakewell."

"I tell you what," continued Ripton, "you let it all out to your cousin and uncle at supper. Didn't you see me frown?"

"Yes, and felt your kick under the table. But it doesn't matter. Rady's safe and Uncle never blabs. Besides, you've got nothing to do with it if we are found out."

"Haven't I though? I didn't stick in the box of matches, but I'm an accomplice, that's clear. Besides, do you think I should leave you to bear it all on your own shoulders? I'm not that sort of a chap, Ricky."

A sensation of infinite melancholy overcame the poor father. This motherless child, for whom he had prayed nightly in such a fervor and humbleness to God, the dangers were about him, the temptations thick upon him. He was half disposed to arrest the two conspirators on the spot, and make them confess and absolve themselves, but it seemed to him better to leave his son to work out the matter himself, as was his custom, trusting all to the victory of the good he had been so earnestly implanting in the boy from his infancy.

The valley still lay black beneath the large autumnal stars and the exclamations of the boys were becoming fevered and impatient. By-and-by one insisted that he had seen a twinkle in the right direction. Both boys started to their feet.

"He's done it!" cried Richard in great heat. "Now you may say old Blaize'll soon be old Blazes, Rip. I hope he's asleep."

"I'm sure he's snoring! Look there! He's alight fast enough. He's dry! He'll burn! Lord! Isn't it just beginning to flare up?"

The farmer's grounds were indeed gradually standing out in sombre shadows.

"I'll fetch my telescope," said Richard. Ripton, somehow not liking to be left alone caught, hold of him.

"No! Don't go and lose the best of it. Here, I'll throw open the window and we can see."

The window was flung open and the boys stretched half their bodies out of it, Ripton appearing to devour the rising flames with his mouth, Richard with his eyes.

Opaque and statuesque stood the figure of the baronet behind them. The wind was low. Dense masses of smoke hung amid the darting snakes of fire, and a red, malign, light was on the neighboring leafage. No figures could be seen. Apparently the flames had nothing to contend against, for they were making terrible strides into the darkness.

"Oh!" shouted Richard, overcome by excitement. "If I had my telescope! We must have it! Let me go and fetch it! I will!"

The boys struggled together, and Sir Austin left them.

In the morning that followed this night great gossip was interchanged between Raynham and Lobourne. The village told how Farmer Blaize of Belthorpe Farm had his rick villainously set fire to; his stables had caught fire, himself had been all but roasted alive in the attempt to rescue his cattle, of which numbers had perished in the flames. A formal report of the catastrophe went on to tell of certain ludicrous damage done to the farmer's breeches and the necessity for applying certain cooling applications to a part of the farmer's person. Sir Austin read the report without a smile. The two boys listened very demurely as to an ordinary newspaper incident; only when the report particularized just what garments were damaged, and the unwonted distressing position Farmer Blaize was reduced to in bed, a fit of sneezing laid hold of Master Ripton, and Richard bit his lip and burst into loud laughter, Ripton joining him lost to consequences.

"I trust you feel for this poor man," said Sir Austin to his son somewhat sternly. He saw no sign of feeling.

At every minute of the day Ripton was thrown into sweats of suspicion that discovery was imminent by some stray remark of Adrian's. Adrian played with the boys as though they had been fish caught on his hook.

"By the way, my friends," he observed once, "you met two gentlemen of the road in your explorations yesterday, didn't you? A tinker and a ploughman, I think you said. Now if I were a magistrate of the county, like Sir Miles Papworth, my suspicions would light upon those gentlemen."

The boys tried to evade discussion but the hook was in their gills, and Adrian always drew them skilfully back to the subject.

"Transportation is the punishment for rick-burning," he said solemnly. "They shave your head. You are manacled. Your diet is sour bread and cheese-parings. You work in strings of twenties and thirties. Arson is branded on your back in an enormous A."

The boys, after deep consultation agreed upon a course of conduct which was loudly to express their sympathy for Farmer Blaize. Adrian relished their novel tactics sharply and led them to lengths of lamentation for the farmer. Ripton was fast becoming a coward and Richard a liar when next morning there came to Raynham Abbey, Austin Wentworth, another cousin, a young man who was greatly loved and respected there, but of straightforward, honest disposition, quite different from Adrian's. He brought news that one, Mr. Thomas Bakewell, had been arrested on suspicion of the crime of arson and lodged in jail awaiting the magisterial pleasure of Sir Miles Papworth. Austin's eye rested on Richard as he spoke these terrible tidings.

As soon as they could escape the boys got away together to an obscure corner of the park and there took counsel.

"Whatever shall we do now?" asked Ripton of his leader.

Scorpion girt with fire was never in a more terrible prison than poor Ripton, around whom the raging element he had assisted to create seemed to be drawing momentarily narrower circles.

"There's only one chance," said Richard folding his arms resolutely. "We must rescue that fellow from jail. We must manage to get a file in to him and a rope."

Austin Wentworth had the reputation of being the poor man's friend. He went straight to Tom Bakewell in jail and engaged in man-to-man conversation with him like a gentleman and a Christian. When he rose to go, Tom begged permission to shake his hand and said, "Take and tell young master up at the abbey that I ain't the chap to peach. He'll understand. He's a young gentleman as 'll make any man do as he wants 'em. But I ain't a blackguard. Tell him that, sir."

Austin was not clever like Adrian; he always went the direct road to his object, so instead of beating about the bush with the boys and setting them on the alert, crammed to the muzzle with lies, he came straight out and said, "Tom Bakewell told me to let you know he does not intend to peach on you," and left them.

Richard repeated the intelligence to Ripton, who cried aloud that Tom was a brick.

"He sha'n't suffer for it," said Richard.

The boys had examined the outer walls of the jail and arrived at the conclusion that Tom's escape might be managed if Tom had spirit and the rope and file could by any means be got to him. But to do this somebody must gain admittance to his cell. The boys decided to ask Austin Wentworth to do this. Ripton procured the file at one shop in Bursley and Richard the rope at another, with such masterly cunning did they lay their measures for the avoidance of every possible chance of detection. And better to assure this, in a wood outside Bursley, Richard stripped to his shirt and wound the rope round his body. It was a severe stroke when after all their stratagem and trouble, Austin Wentworth refused the office the boys had designed for him. Time pressed. In a few days poor Tom would have to face the redoubtable Sir Miles, and get committed, for there were rumors of overwhelming evidence to convict him, and Farmer Blaize's wrath was unappeasable. Again and again Richard begged his cousin to help him in this extremity. Austin smiled on him.

"My dear Ricky," said he, "there are two ways of getting out of a scrape,—a long way and a short way. When you've tried the roundabout method and failed come to me and I'll show you the straight route."

Richard was too entirely bent upon the roundabout method to consider the advice more than empty words, and only ground his teeth at Austin's refusal. He told Ripton that they must do it themselves to which Ripton heavily assented.

On the day preceding poor Tom's doomed appearance before the magistrate, the two boys entered the small shop of Dame Bakewell, Tom's mother. There they desperately purchased tea, sugar, candles and comfits of every description, as an excuse for their presence until the shop was empty of customers. They then hurried Dame Bakewell into her little back parlor, where Richard tore open his shirt and revealed the coils of rope and Ripton displayed the file. They told the astonished woman that the rope and the file were instruments to free her son and that there existed no other means on earth to save him. Richard with the utmost earnestness tried to persuade Dame Bakewell to disrobe and wind the rope around her own person, and Ripton sought eloquently to induce her to secrete the file. Dame Bakewell resolutely objected to the rope, but she was at length persuaded, though much against her will, to accept the file. This she carried secretly to her son. Tom however turned up his nose at the file and refused to try to make an escape. At this news, Richard was in despair. Moreover, just now Ripton was sent for to go home to London and Richard was left to face the whole matter alone.

When affairs were at this pass, Austin Wentworth went to consult with Adrian. But Adrian was little concerned about how the course Richard was pursuing would work out for good or evil in the boy's own mind and heart. He was anxious only to keep them all free from the action of the law. And he threw out the hint to Austin that he had already fixed matters up by means of a little secret dealing with the farmer's chief witness, so that there was no danger of anyone's being punished for the crime. This by no means satisfied Austin. His concern was less that Richard should escape punishment, than that he should act like a man.

A little laurel-shaded temple of white marble looked out on the river from a knoll bordering the Raynham beechwoods and was dubbed by Adrian, Daphne's Bower. To this spot Richard had retired and there Austin found him with his head buried in his hands, a picture of desperation whose last shift has been defeated.

"Well, Ricky, have you tried your own way of rectifying this business?" asked Austin.

"I have done everything."

"And failed!"

There was a pause, then Richard tried to evade the responsibility.

"Failed because Tom Bakewell's a coward!"

"I suppose, poor fellow," said Austin in his kind way, "he doesn't want to get into a deeper mess. I don't think he's a coward."

"He is a coward," cried Richard. "Do you think if I had a file, I would stay in prison? I'd be out the first night. He's a coward and deserves his fate. I've no compassion for a coward."

"Nor I much," said Austin. "I never met a coward myself.

But I've heard of one or two. One let an innocent man die for a crime he himself had committed."

"How base!" exclaimed the boy.

"Yes, it was bad." Austin agreed. "I have read also in the confessions of a celebrated philosopher that in his youth he committed some petty theft and then accused a young servant-girl of his own crime, permitting her to be condemned and dismissed."

"What a coward!" shouted Richard. "And he confessed it?"

"You may read it yourself. Would you have done so much?"

Richard faltered. No! He admitted that he could never have told people.

"Then who is to call that man a coward?" said Austin. "He paid the penalty for the wrong he had done as all who give way in moments of weakness and are not cowards must do. The coward chooses to think 'God does not see. I shall escape.' He who is not a coward, but has done wrong, knows that God has seen all, and it is not so hard a task for him to make his heart bare to the world. Worse, I should fancy it, to know myself an impostor when men praised me."

Richard suddenly hung his head.

"So I think you're wrong, Ricky, in calling this poor fellow Tom a coward because he refuses to try your means of escape. He has not acted like a coward in refusing to tell on you."

Richard was dumb. If he avowed Tom's manly behavior, then he would have to see Richard Feverel in a new light. Whereas, by insisting that Tom was a coward Richard Feverel was the injured one and in no way to blame. Austin had but a blind notion of the fierceness with which the conflict raged in young Richard. But happily Richard's nature wanted little more than an indication of the proper track and then he said in a subdued voice, "Tell me what I can do, Austin."

Austin put his hand on the boy's shoulder.

"You must go down to Farmer Blaize. You will know

what to say to him when you're standing there before him."

The boy bit his lip and frowned. "Ask a favor of that big brute, Austin? I can't!"

"Just tell him the whole truth."

"But, Austin," the boy pleaded, "I shall have to ask a favor of him. I shall have to beg him to help off Tom Bakewell. How can I ask a favor of a brute I hate? I shall hardly be able to keep my hands off him."

"Surely you've punished him enough, boy," said Austin.

"He struck me!" Richard's lip quivered.

"But you poached on his grounds."

"I'll pay him for his loss, but I won't ask a favor of him."

Austin looked at the boy steadily. "You prefer to receive a favor from poor Tom Bakewell? To save yourself an unpleasantness you permit a country lad to sacrifice himself for you. I confess I should not have so much pride."

"Pride!" shouted Richard stung by the taunt, and set his sight hard at the blue ridges of the hills.

Not knowing for the moment what else to do, Austin drew a picture of Tom in prison. Visions of a grinning lout, unkempt, coarse, rose before Richard and afflicted him with the strangest sensations of disgust and comicality, mixed up with pity and remorse,—a sort of twisted pathos. There lay Tom, hobnail Tom! a bacon-munching, reckless, beer-swilling animal and yet a man, capable of devotion and unselfishness. The boy's better spirit was touched, and it kindled his imagination to realize the abject figure of poor clodpole Tom, and surround it with a halo of mournful light. His soul was alive. Feelings he had never known streamed in upon him, an unwonted tenderness, an embracing humor, a consciousness of some ineffable glory. Toward clodpole Tom he felt just then a loving kindness beyond what he felt for any living creature. He laughed at him and wept over him. He prized him while he shrank from him. It was a genial strife of the angel in him with constituents less divine. But the angel was uppermost and won the day.

Austin sat by the boy unaware of the tumult he had stirred. Little of it was perceptible in Richard's countenance. Finally he jumped up, saying: "I'll go at once to old Blaize and tell him."

Austin grasped his hand and together they issued out of Daphne's Bower.

Farmer Blaize was not so astonished at the visit of Richard Feverel as that young gentleman had expected him to be. The farmer seated in his easy chair in the little low-roofed parlor of an old-fashioned farm-house, with a long clay pipe on the table at his elbow and a veteran pointer at his feet, had already given audience to Sir Austin Feverel himself who came to him secretly and frankly confessed the whole matter. Thereupon Farmer Blaize had decided that he would only give up the prosecution in exchange for three hundred pounds compensation to his pocket, a spoken apology from the prime offender, Master Richard, and a solemn promise that no one should try to bribe his witnesses to change their testimony. Sir Austin had readily promised him full indemnity in money for his loss, a satisfactory apology from his son and the assurance that no one would tamper with his witnesses.

Richard was received by a pretty little girl with the roses of thirteen springs in her cheeks and abundant beautiful bright tresses. She tripped before the boy and led him to the parlor, loitering shyly by the farmer's arm chair to steal a look at the handsome new-comer. She was introduced to Richard as the farmer's niece, Lucy Desborough, and Farmer Blaize said much in her praise laughing and chuckling, perhaps intending thus to give his visitor time to recover his composure. His diversion only irritated and confused our shame-eaten youth. Richard's intention had been to come to the farmer's threshold, to summon the farmer thither and in a loud and haughty tone, then and there to take upon himself the whole burden of the charge against

245

Tom Bakewell. Farmer Blaize was quite at his ease, nowise in a hurry. He spoke of the weather and the harvest. Richard blinked hard. In a moment of silence he cried.

"Mr. Blaize, I have come to tell you that I am the person who set fire to your rick the other night."

An odd contraction formed about the farmer's mouth. He changed his posture and said, "Aye, that's what ye're come to tell me, sir! Then, my lad, ye've come to tell me a lie!"

"You dare to call me a liar!" cried Richard starting up with clenched fist. "You have twice insulted me. I would have apologized to have got off that fellow in prison. I would have degraded myself that another man should not suffer for my deed, and you take this opportunity of insulting me afresh. You're a coward, sir. Nobody but a coward would have insulted me in his own house."

"Sit ye down! Sit ye down, young master," said the farmer. "Don't ye be hasty. If ye hadn't been hasty t' other day we should a been friends. I should be sorry to reckon you out a liar. What I say is that as you say an't the truth."

Richard angrily reseated himself. The farmer spoke sense, and the boy after his late interview with Austin had become capable of perceiving vaguely that a towering passion

246

hardly justifies one in pursuing a wrong course of conduct.

"Come," continued the farmer not unkindly, "what else have you to say?"

The boy blinked. This was a bitter cup for him to drink.

"I came to say that I regretted the revenge I had taken on you for you striking me. You shall be repaid for your loss, and I should be very much obliged, very much obliged," he stammered, "if you would be so kind (fancy a Feverel asking this big brute to be so kind), so kind as to do me the favor,—to exert yourself—to endeavor to—hem! (there's no saying it!) What I want to ask is whether you would have the kindness,—Well then I want you, Mr. Blaize, if you don't mind, will you help me to get this man Bakewell off his punishment?"

To do Farmer Blaize justice, he waited very patiently for the boy.

"Hum," said he. "But if you did it you know, and Tom's innocent, we sha'n't make him out guilty. Do you still hold to it, you set fire to the rick?"

"The blame is mine," quoth Richard with the loftiness of a patriot of old Rome.

"Na, na!" the straightforward farmer put him aside. "Ye did do it or ye didn't do it,—yes or no."

Thrust into a corner, Richard said, "I did it."

Farmer Blaize reached his hand to the bell. It was answered in an instant by little Lucy, who received orders to fetch in a dependent at Belthorpe going by the name of the Bantam.

"Now," said the farmer, "these be my principles. I'm a plain man, Mr. Feverel. Be above board with me and you'll find me handsome. Be underhanded and I'm a ugly customer. I'll show you I've no animosity. Your father pays, you apologize. That's enough for me. But the Bantam saw what happened t'other night. It's no use your denyin' that evidence."

Just then Miss Lucy ushered in the Bantam. In build of body, gait and stature, Giles Jinkson, the Bantam, was a tolerably fair representative of the elephant. He had been the first to give the clue at Belthorpe on the night of the conflagration and he may, therefore, have seen poor Tom retreating stealthily from the scene as he said he did. Leastwise, he was the farmer's principal witness. There he stood and tugged his forelocks to the company.

"Now," said the farmer, with the utmost confidence. "Tell this young gentleman what ye saw on the night of the fire, Bantam."

The Bantam jerked a bit of a bow to his patron, and then swung around, fully shutting off all view of the farmer from Richard. Richard fixed his eyes on the floor while the Bantam told his story. But when the recital reached the point where the Bantam affirmed he had seen Tom Bakewell with his own eyes, Richard was amazed to find himself being mutely addressed by a series of intensely significant grimaces, signs and winks.

"What do you mean? Why are you making those faces at me?" cried the boy indignantly.

"Bain't makin' no faces at nobody," growled the sulky elephant.

"You never saw Tom Bakewell set fire to that rick! How could you see who it was on a pitch-dark night?"

The suborned elephant was staggered. He had meant to telegraph to the young gentleman that he was loyal and true to certain gold pieces that had been given him and that in the right place and at the right time he should prove so.

"A thowt I seen 'un then," muttered the Bantam.

"Thought!" the farmer bellowed. "Thought! Devil take ye. Ye took yer oath on it! Say what ye saw and none o' your thoughts! Thinkin' an't evidence! Ye saw Tom Bakewell fire that there rick. You're a witness. Damn your thoughts!"

Thus adjured, the Bantam hitched his breeches. What on earth the young gentleman meant by making public his private signals he was at a loss to speculate. He determined at length after much ploughing and harrowing through obstinate shocks of hair, to be not altogether positive as to the person he had seen.

FROM THE TOWER WINDOW

It is possible that he became thereby more truthful than he had previously been, for the night had been so dark that you could not see your hand before your face. The party he had taken for Tom Bakewell, he said, might have been the young gentleman present. He could not swear which it was.

"But you swore to't, 'twas Tom Bakewell!" the farmer roared.

"No," said the Bantam, with a twitch of the shoulder and an angular jerk of the elbow. "Not upon oath!" A cunning. distinction, that between swearing and not swearing upon oath! No sooner had the Bantam ceased than Farmer Blaize jumped up from his chair and made a fine effort to lift him out of the room from the point of his toe. Richard would have preferred not to laugh but his dignity gave way and he let fly a shout.

"They're liars, every one!" cried the farmer. "Now look ye here, Mr. Feverel! You've been a-tampering with my witness! It's no use denyin'! I say ye have, sir! The Bantam's been bribed!" and he shivered his pipe with an energetic thump on the table. "He's been corrupted, my principal witness. Oh it's damn cunning but it won't do the trick. I'll transport Tom Bakewell now sure as a gun. Sorry you haven't seen how to treat me square and honest! I'd ha' 'scused you, sir. You're a boy and 'll learn better. But you've bribed my witness. Now you must stand yer luck, all o' ye. I will have the truth!"

Richard stood up and replied, "Very well, Mr. Blaize."

"I believe yer father," went on the farmer,—

"What!" cried Richard, with astonishment. "You have seen my father! My father knows of this?"

Farmer Blaize pulled the bell. " 'Comp'ny the young gentleman out, Lucy," he waved to the little damsel in the doorway. "And, Mr. Richard, ye might have made a friend o' me, sir, and it's not too late so to do. I'm not cruel, but I hate lies. Now if ye'll come down to me and speak truth before the trial—if it's only five minutes before, or if Sir Austin, who's a gentleman, 'll say there's been no bribin' my witnesses, if he'll give his word for it,— well and good, I'll do my best to help off Tom Bakewell. If not I'll see the fellow transported. Good afternoon, sir."

Richard marched hastily out of the room and through the garden, never so much as deigning a glance at his wistful little guide, who hung at the garden gate to watch him up the lane, wondering a world of fancies about the handsome, proud boy.

To have determined upon an act something akin to heroism, and to have fulfilled it by lying heartily, seems a sad downfall. But good seed is long ripening, a good boy is not made in a minute. Enough that the seed was in him.

Richard chafed on his road to Raynham at the scene he had just endured, and the figure of Belthorpe's fat tenant burnt like hot copper on the tablet of his brain, insufferably condescending and what was worse, in the right.

After dinner that evening Richard and his father were alone for the first time. It was a strange meeting. They seemed to have been separated so long. The father took his son's hand; they sat without a word passing between them. Silence said most. That pressure of his father's hand was eloquent to the boy of how warmly he was beloved. He tried once or twice to steal his hand away, conscious it was melting him. The spirit of his pride and old rebellion whispered him to be hard, unbending, resolute. Hard he had entered his father's study, hard he had met his father's eyes. He could not meet them now.

By degrees an emotion awoke in the boy's bosom. Love is that blessed wand which wins the waters from the hardness of the heart. Richard fought against it for the dignity of old rebellion. The tears would come, hot and struggling over the dams of pride. Shamefully fast they began to fall. He could no longer conceal them or check the sobs. Sir Austin drew him nearer and nearer till the beloved head was on his breast.

An hour afterwards, Adrian Harley, Austin Wentworth and

FROM THE TOWER WINDOW

Algernon Feverel were summoned to the baronet's study. Young Richard's red eyes and the baronet's ruffled demeanor told them that an explanation had taken place and a reconciliation. That was well. A general council was held. Slowly there was drawn from Richard the tale of his recent visit to the farmer and the ridiculous collapse of the Bantam's testimony, which part of the story caused Adrian to choke with laughter. But Richard also told of the farmer's belief that the Bantam had been bribed and the sudden return of his vindictive determination to have Tom transported. Adrian made a very persuasive plea that the Feverel family should now drop the whole matter. Tom Bakewell would not peach on Richard and it was most unlikely that the boy would be drawn into the affair. He argued well, but the basis of his plea being to do the expedient thing, the thing that was easiest regardless of what was right, Sir Austin answered him:

"Expediency is man's wisdom, Adrian. Doing right is God's."

And he rose and left the room saying that he would pay a second visit to Belthorpe, and attempt to straighten out the matter.

Richard saw his father go forth. Then he said slowly:

"Blaize told me that if my father would give his word there had been no tampering with his witnesses, he would believe him and drop the whole matter. My father will give his word."

Adrian was ill at ease. "Then you had better stop him from going," he said.

A moment Richard lingered. In his heart he knew that Adrian had bribed the Bantam to change his testimony. He knew his father never even dreamed of such a thing. If he let him go, his father who was honor's self, would all-unknowingly swear to a lie. It would be easy, so easy. His father would simply give his word, and then Farmer Blaize would drop the whole matter. He, Richard, would never have to swallow his pride again and tell the whole truth. But—his father would swear to a lie!

Sir Austin was in the lane leading to the farm when he heard

251

steps of some one running behind him. It was dark and he shook off the hand that laid hold of his coat, not recognizing his son.

"It's I, sir," said Richard panting. "You mustn't go in there."

"Why not?" said the baronet putting his arm about him.

"Not now," continued the boy. "I will tell you all tonight. I must see the farmer myself. It was my fault, sir; I—lied to him—the liar must eat his lie. Oh, forgive me for disgracing you, sir. I did it—I hope I did it to save Tom Bakewell. Let me go in alone and speak the truth."

"Go, and I will wait for you here," said his father.

The wind that bowed the old elms and shivered the dead leaves in the air, had a voice and a meaning for the baronet during that half hour's lonely pacing up and down under the darkness awaiting his boy's return. The solemn gladness of his heart gave nature a tongue. Through the desolation flying over head, his heart was newly confirmed in its belief in the ultimate victory of good within us.

And so after all his twistings and turnings, Richard took the one straight course and told the truth. The upshot of the whole matter was that Tom was not convicted. He was set free and Sir Austin took him into his own employ where Richard had plenty of opportunity to urge him on to better things than burning ricks. As to Richard himself he felt that he had had a sorry enough experience of what comes from giving way to passion. He wrote his thoughts on that matter to his old friend and accomplice, Rip, who had been paying the penalty for his share of the crime by suffering the gravest mental terrors, living in constant fear lest he should be found out and have to flee to America as the only means of starting life afresh as an innocent gentleman.

And it was necessary for Richard to order Adrian not to call him by his old nickname Ricky any more, for that redoubtable tease took to stopping short at the word Rick which, needless to say, was not a word with which Richard chose to be associated.

FROM THE TOWER WINDOW

SNOW-BOUND*
John Greenleaf Whittier

The sun that brief December day
Rose cheerless over hills of gray,
And, darkly circled, gave at noon
A sadder light than waning moon.
Meanwhile we did our nightly chores,—
Brought in the wood from out of doors,
Littered the stalls, and from the mows
Raked down the herd's grass for the cows:
Heard the horse whinnying for his corn;
And, sharply clashing horn on horn,
Impatient down the stanchion rows
The cattle shake their walnut bows;
While, peering from his early perch
Upon the scaffold's pole of birch,
The cock his crested helmet bent
And down his querulous challenge sent.

Unwarmed by any sunset light
The gray day darkened into night,
A night made hoary with the swarm
And whirl-dance of the blinding storm,
As zig-zag, wavering to and fro,
Crossed and recrossed the winged snow:
And ere the early bedtime came
The white drift piled the window-frame,
And through the glass the clothes-line posts
Looked in like tall and sheeted ghosts.

The old familiar sights of ours
Took marvellous shapes; strange domes and
    towers
Rose up where sty or corn-crib stood,
Or garden wall, or belt of wood;
A fenceless drift what once was road;
The bridle-post an old man sat

* Used by permission of Houghton Mifflin Company.

With loose-flung coat and high cocked hat;
The well-curb had a Chinese roof;
And even the long sweep, high aloof,
In its slant splendor, seemed to tell
Of Pisa's leaning miracle.

Shut in from all the world without,
We sat the clean-winged hearth about,
Content to let the north-wind roar
In baffled rage at pane and door,
While the red logs before us beat
The frost-line back with tropic heat;
And ever, when a louder blast
Shook beam and rafter as it passed,
The merrier up its roaring draught
The great throat of the chimney laughed;
The house-dog on his paws outspread
Laid to the fire his drowsy head,
The cat's dark silhouette on the wall
A couchant tiger's seemed to fall;
And, for the winter fireside meet,
Between the andirons' straddling feet,
The mug of cider simmered slow,
The apples sputtered in a row,
And, close at hand, the basket stood,
With nuts from brown October's wood.

WINTER NEIGHBORS*
John Burroughs

THE country is more of a wilderness, more of a wild solitude, in the winter than in the summer. You shall hardly know a good field from a poor, a meadow from a pasture, a park from a forest. The best-kept grounds relapse to a state of nature. Under the pressure of the cold all the wild creatures become outlaws, and roam abroad beyond their usual haunts. The partridge comes to the orchard for buds; the rabbit comes to the garden and lawn; the crows and jays come to the ash-heap and corn-crib, the snow-buntings to the stack and to the barn-yard; the sparrows pilfer from the domestic fowls; the pine grosbeak comes down from the north and shears your maples of their buds; the fox prowls about your premises at night, and the red squirrels find your grain in the barn or steal the butternuts from your attic. Winter, like poverty, makes us acquainted with strange bedfellows.

For my part, my nearest approach to a strange bedfellow is the little gray rabbit that has taken up her abode under my study floor. As she spends the day here and is out larking at night, she is not much of a bedfellow after all. It is probable that I disturb her slumbers more than she does mine. I think she is

 some support to me under there— a silent wild-eyed witness and backer; a type of the gentle and harmless in savage nature. She has no sagac· ity to give me or lend me, but that

✱ From *Birds and Bees.* Used by permission of, and by special arrangement with, Houghton Mifflin Company, the publishers.

soft, nimble foot of hers, and that touch as of cotton wherever she goes, are worthy of emulation. I think I can feel her good-will through the floor, and I hope she can mine. When I have a happy thought I imagine her ears twitch, especially when I think of the sweet apple I will place by her doorway at night. I wonder if that fox chanced to catch a glimpse of her the other night when he stealthily leaped over the fence near by and walked along between the study and the house? How clearly one could read that it was not a little dog that had passed there. There was something furtive in the track; it shied off away from the house and around it, as if eying it suspiciously; and then it had the caution and deliberation of the fox—bold, bold, but not too bold; wariness was in every footprint. If it had been a little dog that had chanced to wander that way, when he crossed my path he would have followed it up to the barn and have gone smelling around for a bone; but this sharp, cautious track held straight across all others, keeping five or six rods from the house, up the hill, across the highway towards a neighborhood farmstead, with its nose in the air and its eye and ear alert, so to speak.

A winter neighbor of mine in whom I am interested, is a little red owl, whose retreat is in the heart of an old apple-tree just over the fence. Where he keeps himself in spring and summer I do not know, but late every fall, and at intervals all winter, his hiding-place is discovered by the jays and nut-hatches, and proclaimed from the tree-tops for the space of half an hour or so, with all the powers of voice they can command. Four times during one winter they called me out to behold this little ogre feigning sleep in his den, sometimes in one apple-tree, sometimes in another. Whenever I heard their cries, I knew my neighbor was being berated. The birds would take turns at looking in upon him and uttering their alarm-notes. Every jay within hearing would come to the spot and at once approach the hole in the trunk or limb, and with a kind of breathless eagerness and excitement take a peep at the owl, and then join the outcry. When I approached they would hastily take a final look and then withdraw and regard my movements intently. After accustoming my eye to the faint light of the cavity for a few moments, I could usually make out the owl at the bottom feigning sleep. Feigning, I say, because this is what he really did, as I first discovered one day when I cut into his retreat with the axe. The loud blows and the falling chips did not disturb him at all. When I reached in a stick and pulled him over on his side, leaving one of his wings spread out, he made no attempt to recover himself, but lay among the chips and fragments of decayed wood, like a part of themselves. Indeed, it took a sharp eye to distinguish him. Nor till I had pulled him forth by one wing, rather rudely, did he abandon the trick of simulated sleep or death. Then, like a detected pickpocket, he was suddenly transformed into another creature. His eyes flew wide open, his talons clutched my finger, his ears were depressed, and every motion and look said, "Hands off, at your peril." Finding this game did not work, he soon began to "play 'possum" again.

Just at dusk in the winter nights, I often hear his soft *bur*-r-r-r, very pleasing and bell-like. What a furtive, woody sound it is in the winter stillness, so unlike the harsh scream of the hawk. But all the ways of the owl are ways of softness and duskiness. His wings are shod with silence, his plumage is edged with down.

Another owl neighbor of mine, with whom I pass the time of day more frequently than with the last, lives farther away. I pass his castle every night on my way to the post-office, and in winter, if the hour is late enough, am pretty sure to see him standing in his doorway, surveying the passers-by and the landscape through narrow slits in his eyes. As the twilight begins to deepen he rises out of his cavity in the apple-tree, scarcely faster than the moon rises from behind the hill, and sits in the opening, completely framed by its outlines of gray bark and dead wood, and by his protective coloring virtually invisible to every eye that does not know he is there. Dozens of teams and foot-passengers pass him late in the day, but he regards them not, nor they him. When I come alone and pause to salute him, he opens his eyes a little wider, and, appearing to recognize me, quickly shrinks and fades into the background of his door in a very weird and curious manner. When he is not at his outlook, or when he is, it requires the best powers of the eye to decide the point, as the empty cavity itself is almost an exact image of him. If the whole thing had been carefully studied it could not have answered its purpose better. The owl stands quite perpendicular, presenting a front of light mottled gray; the eyes are closed to a mere slit, the ear-feathers depressed, plumage, and the whole motionless waiting and ob- should be seen crossing the over any exposed part of twilight, the owl would upon it. Whether bluebirds,  the beak buried in the attitude is one of silent, servation. If a mouse highway, or scudding the snowy surface in the doubtless swoop down nut-hatches, and chicka- dees—birds that pass the night in cavities of trees—ever run into the clutches of the dozing owl, I should be glad to know. My impression is, however, that they seek out smaller cavities. An old willow by the roadside blew down one summer, and a decayed branch broke open, revealing a brood of half-fledged owls, and many feathers and quills of bluebirds, orioles, and other songsters, showing plainly enough why all birds fear and berate the owl.

The English house sparrows, that are so rapidly increasing among us, and that must add greatly to the food supply of the owls and other birds of prey, seek to baffle their enemies by roosting in the densest evergreens they can find, in the arbor-vitæ, and in hemlock hedges. Soft-winged as the owl is, he cannot steal in upon such a retreat without giving them warning.

These sparrows are becoming about the most noticeable of my

winter neighbors, and a troop of them every morning watch me put out the hens' feed, and soon claim their share. I rather encouraged them in their neighborliness, till one day I discovered the snow under a favorite plum-tree where they most frequently perched covered with the scales of the fruit-buds. On investigating I found that the tree had been nearly stripped of its buds— a very neighborly act on the part of the sparrows, considering, too, all the cracked corn I had scattered for them. So I at once served notice on them that our good understanding was at an end. And a hint is as good as a kick with this bird. The stone I hurled among them, and the one with which I followed them up, may have been taken as a kick. The sparrows left in high dudgeon, and were not back again in some days, and were then very shy. Our native birds are much different, less prolific, less shrewd, less aggressive and persistent, less quick-witted and able to read the note of danger or hostility,—in short, less sophisticated. Most of our birds are yet essentially wild, that is, little changed by civilization. In winter, especially, they sweep by me and around me in flocks,—the Canada sparrow, the snow-bunting, the shore-lark, the pine grosbeak, the red-poll, the cedar-bird,— feeding upon frozen apples in the orchard, upon cedar-berries, upon maple-buds, and the berries of the mountain ash, upon the seeds of the weeds that rise above the snow in the field, or upon the hay-seed dropped where the cattle have been foddered in the barn-yard or about the distant stack; but yet taking no heed of man, in no way changing their habits so as to take advantage of his presence in nature. The pine grosbeaks will come in numbers upon your porch to get the black drupes of the honey-suckle and the woodbine, or within reach of your windows to get the berries of the mountain-ash, but they know you not; they look at you as innocently and unconcernedly as at a bear or moose in their native north, and your house is no more to them than a ledge of rocks.

The only ones of my winter neighbors that actually rap at my door are the nut-hatches and woodpeckers, and these do not know that it is my door. My retreat is covered with the bark of young chestnut-trees, and the birds, I suspect, mistake it for a huge stump that ought to hold fat grubs (there is not even a book-worm inside of it), and their loud rapping often makes me think I have a caller indeed. I place fragments of hickory-nuts in the interstices of the bark, and thus attract the nut-hatches; a bone upon my window-sill attracts both nut-hatches and the downy woodpecker. They peep in curiously through the window upon me, pecking away at my bone, too often a very poor one. Even the slate-colored snow-bird, a seed-eater, comes and nibbles it occasionally.

The bird that seems to consider he has the best right to the bone is the downy woodpecker, my favorite neighbor among the winter birds. His retreat is but a few paces from my own, in the decayed limb of an apple-tree which he excavated several autumns ago. I say "he" because the red plume on the top of his head proclaims the sex. It seems not to be generally known that certain of our woodpeckers—probably all the winter residents—each fall excavate a limb or the trunk of a tree in which to pass the winter, and that the cavity is abandoned in the spring, prob-ably for a new one. So far as I have observed, these cavities are drilled out only by the males. Where the females take up their quarters I am not so well informed, though I suspect that they use the abandoned holes of the males of the previous year.

The particular woodpecker to which I refer drilled his first hole in my apple-tree one fall four or five years ago. It is a satis-faction during the cold and stormy winter nights to know he is warm and cosy there in his retreat. When the day is bad and unfit to be abroad in, he is there too. When I wish to know if he is at home, I go and rap upon his tree, and, if he is not too lazy or indifferent, after some delay he shows his head in his round doorway about ten feet above, and looks down inquiringly upon me—sometimes latterly I think half resentfully, as much as to say, "I would thank you not to disturb me so often."

Such a cavity makes a snug, warm home, and when the entrance is on the under side of the limb, as is usual, the wind and snow cannot reach the occupant. In digging out these retreats the woodpeckers prefer a dry, brittle trunk, not too soft. They go in horizontally to the centre and then turn downward, enlarging the tunnel as they go, till when finished it is the shape of a long, deep pear.

Another trait our woodpeckers have that endears them to me, is their habit of drumming in the spring. They are songless birds, and yet all are musicians; they make the dry limbs eloquent of the coming change. Did you think that loud, sonorous hammering which proceeded from the orchard or from the near woods on that still March or April morning was only some bird getting its breakfast? It is downy, but he is not rapping at the door of a grub; he is rapping at the door of spring, and the dry limb thrills beneath the ardor of his blows. Or, later in the season, in the dense forest or by some remote mountain lake, does that measured rhythmic beat that breaks upon the silence, first three strokes following each other rapidly, succeeded by two louder ones with longer intervals between them, and that has an effect upon the alert ear as if the solitude itself had at last found a voice— does that suggest anything less than a deliberate musical performance? In fact, our woodpeckers are just as characteristically drummers as is the ruffled grouse, and they have their particular limbs and stubs to which they resort for that purpose. Their need of expression is apparently just as great as that of the song-birds, and it is not surprising that they should have found out that there is music in a dry, seasoned limb which can be evoked beneath their beaks.

A few seasons ago a downy woodpecker began to drum early

in March in a partly decayed apple-tree that stands in the edge of a narrow strip of woodland near me. The bird would keep his position there for an hour at a time. Between his drummings he would preen his plumage and listen as if for the response of the female, or for the drum of some rival. How swift his head would go when he was delivering his blows upon the limb! After some weeks the female appeared; he had literally drummed up a mate; his urgent and oft-repeated advertisement was answered. Still the drumming did not cease, but was quite as fervent as before. If a mate could be won by drumming she could be kept and entertained by more drumming; courtship should not end with marriage. If the bird felt musical before, of course he felt much more so now.

The woodpeckers do not each have a particular dry limb to which they resort at all times to drum, like the one I have described. The woods are full of suitable branches, and they drum more or less here and there as they are in quest of food; yet I am convinced each one has its favorite spot, like the grouse, to which it resorts, especially in the morning. The sugar-maker in the maple-woods may notice that this sound proceeds from the same tree or trees about his camp with great regularity. A woodpecker in my vicinity has drummed for two seasons on a telegraph-pole, and he makes the wires and glass insulators ring. Another drums on a thin board on the end of a long grape-arbor, and on still mornings can be heard a long distance.

The high-hole appears to drum more promiscuously than does the downy. He utters his long, loud spring call, whick—whick—whick, and then begins to rap with his beak upon his perch before the last note has reached your ear. I have seen him drum sitting upon the ridge of a barn.

Our smaller woodpeckers are sometimes accused of injuring the apple and other fruit trees, but the depredator is probably the larger and rarer yellow-bellied species. One autumn I caught one of these fellows in the act of sinking long rows of his little wells in the limb of an apple-tree.

In the following winter the same bird (probably) tapped a maple-tree in front of my window in fifty-six places; and when the day was sunny, and the sap oozed out, he spent most of his time there. He knew the good sap-days, and was on hand promptly for his tipple; cold and cloudy days he did not appear. He knew which side of the tree to tap, too, and avoided the sunless northern exposure. When one series of well-holes failed to supply him, he would sink another, drilling through the bark with great ease and quickness. Then, when the day was warm, and the sap ran freely, he would have a regular sugar-maple debauch, sitting there by his wells hour after hour, and as fast as they became filled sipping out the sap. He made a row of wells near the foot of the tree, and other rows higher up, and he would hop up and down the trunk as these became filled. He would hop down the tree backward with the utmost ease, throwing his tail outward and his head inward at each hop. When the wells would freeze or his thirst became slaked, he would ruffle his feathers, draw himself together, and sit and doze in the sun on the side of the tree. This woodpecker does not breed or abound in my vicinity; only stray specimens are now and then to be met in the colder months. As spring approached, the one I refer to took his departure.

—Abridged

TREES*
Joyce Kilmer

I think that I shall never see
  A poem lovely as a tree.

A tree whose hungry mouth is prest
  Against the earth's sweet flowing breast.

A tree that looks to God all day,
  And lifts her leafy arms to pray.

A tree that may in summer wear
  A nest of robins in her hair;

Upon whose bosom snow has lain;
  Who intimately lives with rain.

Poems are made by fools like me,
  But only God can make a tree.

* From *Poems, Essays and Letters*, edited by R. C. Holliday, copyright 1918. George H. Doran Co., publishers.

263

MY BOOK HOUSE

MR. HAMPDEN'S SHIPWRECK*
John Masefield

WHEN I was a youngster of about eighteen or nineteen I was stranded with a ship's company in a lonely reach of the Magellan Straits. The ship lost her way in a fog, and went on the rocks. We got ashore in a ship's boat, which was so dry from standing on deck that the seams all ran little rills. It is a gloomy part of the world. It is all rocky hills, frosted with snow, and torn with glaciers. Here and there was a colony of birds, all so tame that we could catch them. It was very bleak and grim, living there. We rigged up a shelter out of a sail. We used to sit and shiver, while the wind howled over us. I can tell you, the wind there takes the heart out of you. It comes up straight from the Pole, with a kind of yell which scares you. We had nothing much to drink, either, except melted snow. As for food, we had the birds, a few shellfish, and a few very precious sodden biscuits, which had been left long before in the boat's locker. They were in a horrible state, but they were great dainties to us. We had no other breadstuffs. Well, there we were, in a part of the world where no ships ever came. We didn't even know the name of the reach or bay into which we had come. There we were, so lost that sometimes a man would go out of the hut and wander up among the rocks, and stare at the loneliness, and then come back and cry. Lonely? You don't know what loneliness is till you look out of a hut in the morning and see an iron-grey sea sulky with frost, and the masts of your ship sticking out above the water. She had been a two-masted ship. Her name was the *Inesita*. There she was, deep in the sea, with the fish flipping in her hold, and those two iron fingers raised. We couldn't stand the sight of those two masts. In the end we rowed out with one of the boat flags, and a sailor named Jim Dane swarmed up and made it fast, so that she might cut a better figure.

There was a hill at the back of our camp. At least, when I

*From the *Book of Discoveries* by John Masefield.

call it a hill, I insult hills in general. It wasn't a hill. It was a rock from which all the earth had been washed away by the weather. It was an extinct volcano, about three thousand feet high. There was no grain of earth upon it, only shale and rock, which had been frozen and buffeted till they were rotten. It was like a black cake dusted with snow instead of sugar. We called it Mount Misery. We went up it soon after we landed, hoping that it would give us our bearings. We hoped to see the channel from it, or the smoke of some steamer in the channel, or at the worst the smoke of some Indian's fire. But nothing of the kind. One could see the Sound curving and winding, and hills like Mount Misery shutting out the view, and crags, and ghastly great boulders, and never a green thing. There were always clouds, too, not very far away. We would see them banked all round us, but always thicker to the south—always rather reddish, I remember. They gave one a feeling of being shut in. Yet, though they were never far off, they looked in a way like distant land—as though they were a kind of ghost-land which the landscape turned. The worst of it was that they were always shutting down and blotting everything. They closed in twenty times a day. It would come on a thick whitish-yellow fog, wet as rain, and raw with cold—horrible!—and whenever this fog came down we couldn't see our hands in front of us.

Once we tried to get away, but first we had to caulk our boat with seaweeds, since she leaked like a sieve, and then we had to provision her. We killed a lot of stupid sea-birds. That was horrible, too, for I have always loved wild creatures. When we had provisioned the boat we had to water her.

Then the question came: Who should go in the boat? We couldn't all go. There were over thirty of us. The boat would only hold a dozen with any comfort, and I think everybody there was more than eager to be one of the first away. We spent a whole evening arguing about it, and then put it to the lot.

We drew matches out of the Captain's cap, and those who got
the unburned matches were to go. The second mate and ten
others were the lucky ones. They were the gladdest men in
camp that night. They were in great spirits. They made sure
that they had only to get out of the Sound to run into the main
channel where the steamers pass two or three a day. To leave
that camp was only a step to getting home. I thought of buying
or, rather, of trying to buy the place of one of the lucky men, but
then I felt that I ought not to do so. We were all equal there,
and the Fates, or Providence, had chosen to give him this chance
in preference to myself. I decided that I would bear what was
coming to me like the rest, so I said nothing.

After the drawing of the lots, the second mate and the other
officers argued and wrangled with the Captain about the course
the boat should steer. They could not agree about it. They
were not sure within twenty or thirty miles of where we could
be. The Sound spread out its arms like a great grey octopus.
It was heart-breaking to see it. How were we to know which
arm led to the channel? We tramped along arm after arm over
those miles of rotten rock. We would see the bends on ahead
curving round the hills, and each bend led, as we thought, into
the channel, but none did. You cannot think how cruel that
branching water seemed. We called each arm by a bad name—
Misery Harbour, Skunk's Delight, Disappointment, Old Footsore,
etc. Well, it was decided at last. They gave the second mate a
course, and when day dawned he sailed with his ten hands. We
lined up on the beach, and gave them three cheers, and they
gave us one cheer back; then we sang a sea-song called "Rolling
Home," which sailors are very fond of singing. After that they
cheered us again in the sea-fashion, with just one cheer. We
saw them get smaller and smaller as they sailed away over the
reach in the very light wind. It was a still morning, with a sort
of hard grey rawness on it which made all things grim. The last

face I saw of them was the second mate's face. He was standing up in the stern-sheets steering the boat with an oar.

We never saw them again. Whether they were drowned, or starved, or run down, or wrecked, we never heard. They just sailed away into—who knows what? Perhaps the natives killed them. Natives were a bad lot in those days. They cut off many poor fellows who were wrecked there. I like to think that they are all alive somewhere, though I'm afraid they were all dead before we left Port Misery. I like to think of them getting into the interior, to the settlements, to some good place or another, mining or ranching—not much chance of it, of course.

We were very melancholy after they had gone, but by the end of the day we had begun to be the brighter for it. We were so sure that they would get to the channel and be picked up by some ship. I remember that we talked among ourselves about the probable length of our stay there. The boat had sailed on Wednesday morning. She would be in the channel at latest, we thought, by Thursday noon, allowing for some delay in finding the way out of the pocket where we were. Thursday, at 3 p.m., as we reckoned, would be about the time for the Pacific liner from Punta Arenas to Chile. And if the Pacific liner passed the boat in a fog or snow-squall, as she well might, there would still be the Coronel Line's boat going the other way with the Chile mail. We reckoned to be out of the place aboard a good big liner within forty-eight hours. We waited three solid weeks there.

At first we were on tenterhooks all day long. Friday was a bad day. We were up betimes to make a smoke on Mount Misery as a sailing-mark. Most of us stayed on the Mount all the morning, going down in relays to get stuff for the fire—a kind of dry moss, a kind of peat. Towards noon we began to get anxious lest the boat or ship should come in a fog. I think all of us were a little afraid lest by some accident we should get left there. It was absurd, of course; but misfortune often makes people childish. Soldiers often cry when they have to fall back from a position. I've seen men cry because there was no water in the waterpan after a day in the desert. Cry? I've cried myself. One only grows up in certain things. A man's a great baby in most things till the end. Women have more sense.

By the early afternoon we had all left the mountain for the beach. We stood about on the beach looking out up and down the Sound, but there came no trace of any ship, not even the sound of a siren. We kept talking among ourselves, saying that it wouldn't be long before she came, or making excuses for her.

But in our hearts we thought all the time that the boat had come to grief somewhere. At dark we built up a good fire on the beach to guide them to us if they should come in the night. A good roaring blaze ought to show for five or six miles or more. We all worked hard gathering fuel for it. We still hoped, of course, for the steamer, but by dark we felt that something had gone wrong. None of us said so, only nobody protested when the Captain put us back to our allowance of salted bird. Ever since the boat sailed we had been eating as much as we pleased, thinking it foolish to stint ourselves when our misery was so nearly over. Now the Captain served out the allowance twice a day. It was roughly-salted sea-bird, tasting of fish, bad oil, and salt. Sometimes we had soup of it. What made it so horrible was its sameness.

Well, we picked watches that night. Some of us kept a bright look-out by the fire till Saturday morning. We saw nothing of any ship. Once we had a great start, thinking we heard the wash of a steamer's screws somewhere far off in the night; but it was nothing. Two of us said definitely that they had heard a ship; a third thought that it was like a ship's screws, but that it came from somewhere in the land. We listened with our ears close to the water's edge, but no sound came along the water. Our friends had been mistaken. Perhaps they heard a little fall of shale from one of the cliffs, or perhaps a big sea-bird or flock of birds swooped into the sea with that rushing scutter which sends them sliding twenty yards along the surface. Anyhow, it was not a ship's screws which they heard. That was not the only start we had during those watches. A shooting-star fell low down, and close to us (as it seemed)—so near to the water that those who saw it mistook it for a rocket. That was a lively alarm while it lasted, but it did not last long, of course. We very soon saw that we were wrong. After that nothing happened till daylight left us all free to turn in.

Saturday was not so hard to bear as Friday. The first disappointment and the keeping awake all night left us all a little dull and stupid. It was on Sunday that the real hardships began, for then we began to look at each other to see if anyone were going to be brave enough to say what all felt—that we were in a tight fix, without much chance of getting out of it. The Captain was a good man. He called us all up to him after mid-day dinner. He was an elderly man—sixty-five or so—married, with a family. He gave us a lecture on the situation which did him credit. He had lost his ship; he was hardly likely to get another at his age, even if we ever reached home; he had more home ties to brood over, and a harder future to look forward to, than any of us. But he was Captain still; he was responsible for us. I can't remember that he ever showed by any sign that the cards were against us. He told us that, although the boat had not returned, we were not to give up hope on that account. We were to pluck up heart, and cross no rivers till we came to the water. All the same, he said, we were beginning to be melancholy, which was a sign that we hadn't enough to do. He had been wrecked before, he said (on the coast of Hayti). I remember he made us all laugh here during his account of the wreck by telling us how the Captain of his ship had come ashore without his trousers. He said that on that occasion want of work had made the crew very melancholy, so that there had been a lot of trouble—"men drown-

ing themselves, and silliness of that sort." He wasn't going to
have anything of that kind while he commanded, so in future we
were to work. The usual work of the camp—getting fuel, killing
birds, keeping the fire going, and cooking—was not enough for
us. He was going to set us a new task, which he meant us to do.
We were to explore along the shore of the Sound till we found
out where we were. We were to split up into parties of explora-
tion. One-third of the company was to stay in camp in case the
boat should return, one-third was to go up, the other third to
go down, the Sound. Each exploring party was to travel for
three days in its particular direction before returning to camp
to report. So let us all cheer up, he said, and never mind the
rotten rock, but step out boldly and find the channel. We cheered
him when he finished. Afterwards we drew lots to decide which
of us should go. I was drawn for the party of camp-keepers,
unfortunately for myself. The Captain was quite right. Want
of work does make shipwrecked people melancholy. Those black
crags, and the water like steel, and the flurries of snow always
blowing past—never enough to lie more than an inch, if as much,
but always dusting down, fine and dry, on that dry cold wind from
the Pole. Ugh! that was a horrid place! It lowered at one,
and almost every day it started to blow a short, howling south-
wester which loosened your joints. A whirl of snow driving
everywhere in a yell of wind which was like death. And nothing
very much to do except to sit still to watch the snow coming.

Well, I learned then that I had wasted my time from my
youth up. I had been to school—to an English school, that is—
where I had learned to play cricket and to write very bad Latin
verses; and now, for the first time, I was face to face with something which really taxed my mind, and showed me where I was
empty. Some of my education had given me a tough, active
body; another part of it had made me cheerful, and able to take
whatever came without grumbling and troubling; but when I

came to overhaul my mind for something to amuse me and take me out of myself, I found that I had very little — less even than the sailors. The sailors knew how to make things with their hands; they knew how to sing, how to dance step-dance, and how to endure. Whatever they knew, they knew thoroughly. It was a part of their lives. Whatever I knew, I knew partially. It was something I had read in a book. You must remember, too that I was a landsman—the only landsman there.

Well, I had to find my amusement in myself, or go melancholy mad, like the men in the Captain's story. I set to work to imagine my home in the country. Whenever I was not working at my share of the camp duty, I was imagining the country which I knew as a boy. It was nothing very wonderful, of course. It was a little piece of Shropshire with a radius of about three miles, more of less. But it was England and home and whatever was dear to me. I went over every little bit of it time and time again. I tried to reconstruct that countryside in every detail, to make it real to my mind, so that I might, as it were, live there, or imagine myself living there, whenever the horror of Camp Misery became too great. I had lived in that little bit of the world for all the years of my boyhood; but when I came to build it up in my mind, so as to rest in it, there was so much that I had to write down as unexplored. There were so many blank spaces, fields which I had never entered, fields with shapes which I had forgotten, brooks with rapids and shallows which I could not place correctly, hedges into which I had never looked, animals and birds which I had shot at, perhaps, but never really known about. That seemed so strange to me, when I thought of it in Camp Misery—that I should have taken those creatures' lives without knowing what life meant to them, without ever having tried, or thought of trying, to know each strange little atom of life, so different, yet so alike. I made up my mind then and there that if I ever got back to England I would not waste my time again. I would look at the world with very different eyes; I would never forget, as I walked about, that the world is a continual miracle to be looked at earnestly, and remembered and read. Each little bit of the world is beautiful and interesting unspeakably. The more closely you look at a thing the more interesting it will become. All wisdom and all progress come from just that faculty of looking so closely at a thing that one can see its meaning as well as its appearance.

When I realized that I had wasted my time, and that I must never do so again, I realized, of course, that in a little while, perhaps, I should be away from that place for ever. Yet it might be that in England or elsewhere, in a fit of loneliness, I might long for that place, and wish myself back there among the rocks. I said to myself that a man's moods are very fickle. Hate is only love turned upside down. I might love my memory of this place within the year. I felt that it was my duty to take an exact record of it, so that in after years I might never feel that I had failed to get out of it all that it had to teach me; so that I might not rebuke myself when a few comfortable weeks at home had turned my present hate of it the right way up. And when I came to examine it, and to look into it closely, there was an infinity of beauty and interest in it. I began to puzzle out to myself how it was that the plants and creatures had adapted themselves to the natural conditions there; why the moss was as it was; why the seaweeds were as they were; why some of the birds had longer bills than others; and what the rocks had been long ago, before the wear of the weather ground them down.

I went out on the next search expedition. We went about twenty miles along a never-ending wilderness of inlets. We didn't find anything, except on the last day one thing—a little cairn of stones with an iron bar sticking out of it, and a tin box tied to the end of the bar. Some of the sailors thought that it was the mark of some shipwrecked crew, but it was really a surveyor's mark. It had been there for years and years evidently.

FROM THE TOWER WINDOW

We opened the tin box, hoping to find in it some writing from civilized people. You cannot imagine how eagerly we broke it open. We felt like people rifling the tomb of a King of Egypt. We did not know what secret might be hidden inside. There was nothing much inside except scraps of what had once been writing paper smeared with what had once been ink. All quite illegible. There wasn't even enough writing left to let us guess the date of the writer.

We couldn't make out from the position of the cairn whereabouts the open sea or the channel ought to be, for the very good reason that we were still on the wrong side of the Sound, and we found afterwards that the Sound reached on inland thirty miles from the farthest point reached by our explorers, so that it would have taken us a good five or six days farther tramp to get round it to the side from which we could see the channel. We had been wrecked most miraculously in the most awkward possible place the ship could have chosen for us. If we had not been picked up by another miraculous chance we should have left our bones there.

The day before we went ashore, one of the hands had been set to put new life-lines on the life-buoys, of which, of course, we carried several. Well, as he worked upon them he managed to knock one overboard. He took a glance up and down to make sure that the loss had not been seen, and then went on with another

life-buoy as though nothing had happened. As a matter of fact, a great deal had happened, for he had saved all our lives merely by knocking that life-buoy overboard. The life-buoy had the name of the ship *Inesita* painted upon it. While it floated it was a sort of advertisement of us. Anybody who found that life-buoy would say to himself: "Yes; the ship *Inesita* has passed this way, and something strange has happened on board her."

The *Inesita* ran ashore the day after leaving Punta Arenas. She was bound through the Straits to a place called Coronel, in Southern Chile. While at Punta Arenas she lay at moorings near a ship called the *Chiloe*, which was about to sail through the Straits for the same place when we left the port. I suppose she started some twelve hours after us. Quite by chance her look-out man saw our lost life-buoy bobbing in the sea. He reported it to the officer of the watch, who had it fished on board. When the officer saw that it was the *Inesita's* buoy he reported it to his Captain, who came on deck at once. It had been very blind, squally weather. It was a very blind, bad part of the Straits. Anyone finding a buoy in such circumstances would have jumped to the conclusion that something was seriously wrong. A few minutes later it happened that the Captain of the *Chiloe* saw what he took to be drifting wreckage—a cask, and a half-submerged case or two, which looked like a water-logged boat or floating hen-coop. His mate said that it was undoubtedly ship's wreckage, and added that "it looked like the smash-up of the *Inesita*." They agreed that they had better poke about a bit to see what evidence they could find. They sent a man aloft to the crow's nest to look out for boats and survivors.

And then down came one of the bad Straits squalls, yelling like a battle. It gave them plenty to think of for the next hour or two. As for seeing through it, that was impossible. One couldn't see ten yards from the ship, nor hear a hail nor a signal. What with the wind blowing the snow into their eyes, and tearing off the tops of the waves to fling them, as they froze, over their heads, and the worst bit of the Straits ahead, those officers had no time to think of the *Inesita*. They had to use all their wits to make a head against the storm, and to win through to safety. When the squall blew over there was no trace of the *Inesita's*

FROM THE TOWER WINDOW

wreckage. What had been mistaken for it lay ten miles astern.

The *Chiloe* continued her passage westward. When she reached Coronel she reported the finding of the buoy, and the sighting of floating wreckage. People concluded that "something had happened," and that we were all drowned. Somebody cabled it to England, and a distorted line about it got into the papers.

But an elderly lady—a very good, energetic soul—a great friend of mine, saw the announcement, and wondered if I had got ashore by any chance. She felt quite sure at last that I was alive there somewhere, living on shell-fish, watching for a ship. She cabled to the British Consul at Punta Concha, but the Consul could tell her nothing further. In his opinion, the *Inesita* had sunk with all hands. We were "posted as missing," and my relatives ordered mourning.

But not my good friend. She was quite certain that I was alive somewhere. She came up to London, and set to work on the charts of the Straits to see where I might have got to. A nephew of hers, a young naval officer, helped her with them. They had the position of the *Chiloe* when she found the life-buoy, the set of the current, and that was all they had to go upon. Or not quite all. An eastward-bound steamer, which ought to have passed the *Inesita* near the mouth of the Straits, reported that she had seen no sign of us. So that put the scene of the disaster, if there had been one, between the mouth of the Straits and the place where the life-buoy had been found. They reckoned that the exact spot would be about twelve miles west of the spot where the life-buoy had been found. The young Lieutenant said: "Cable to the Consul at Punta Concha. Tell him to send out a tug to explore."

But for some reason this lady had taken a prejudice against the Consul. Something in his former cable made her suspect that he was not seriously interested. She had had some experience of the ways of Embassies years before, when anxious about a friend in Paris during the Revolution of the Commune. She decided that nothing could be done through them in this case. She was quite certain that I was alive there, with other men, and the feeling that she could do nothing to help me, and that if she did nothing it might soon be too late, was more than she could bear.

Early in the afternoon she made up her mind that she would come herself to find me. She obtained a sum of money, found out that she could catch the Liverpool mail-boat when it called at Plymouth for the London passengers, telegraphed for a berth in it, raked together what warm clothes she could buy in the time, and started directly. At Plymouth the agents of the steamship company told her that the ship was full. Those were the days of the great South American boom. The ships went out from England crammed with people bound for the Argentine, Chile, and Peru. This particular ship, the *Las Casas*, was full to the hatches; there was no room even in the steerage. Not a berth in her was to be had for money. However, my friend was not easily daunted. She hired a boat, piled her trunks aboard it, and put out to meet the steamer, which was due to arrive there to pick up the London passengers about midnight. It was blowing pretty fresh, with a good deal of rain, but she was determined not to put back till something had been done. A man would have gone to a hotel and smoked by the fire, but my friend was not

like that.   She knew that the ship might only stay an hour there, or less even if there were no hitch.   She was going to run no risks.

Presently the *Las Casas* came into the harbour.   My friend ran alongside as she came to moorings, and they lowered a gangway for her and picked her up.   She said that she wanted to see the Captain.   The Captain was very busy, but it is the custom of this world to let the people who really want a thing with their might and main have what they want, if only they keep on long enough.   Presently the Captain came along fuming at being disturbed, and very well inclined to be rude.   She told him her story there and then, and asked him to take her on board, offering to pay almost any sum for a berth if one could be found—any berth, a stewardess berth or one of the officers' cabins.   But no.   It could not be done, he said.   Money was no object; the ship was full.   He wouldn't take another soul aboard if the Queen herself wanted a passage.   That was his last word, he said, and he was a busy man.   He couldn't stay there talking; he had a lot to see to. So away he went, grumbling about a lot of silly women wanting to throw the ship overboard.   He left my friend aghast.   She sat down, not knowing what to do, for the boats in those days only ran once a week, and a week's delay might be the end of everything.   Presently her boatman came up grumbling to ask if she were soon coming to tell him what to do with her trunks.   He wanted to be gone from that.   He was wet through, and the boat was taking in water, for out there at the moorings it was bad weather for any boat.   So she told him to bring her trunks on board and go.   She gave him a sovereign for his trouble.   I don't know why they let her trunks come on board, but in the confusion they did.   The boatman left them and went.   When he had gone she realized that she would be in a tight place if the Captain should prove a tartar.   She saw herself being flung out of the ship into the tug which had brought the London passengers alongside.

Presently an elderly stewardess came past.   My friend says

that the instant that stewardess appeared she knew that she had come to get her out of her trouble. She just rose up and said, "Stewardess, might I speak to you for a minute?" and the thing was done. I am ashamed to think how much it may have cost her, but she bribed that stewardess to give up her post. Within the next quarter of an hour they had settled everything. They had changed clothes. The stewardess had told her of her duties and shown her roughly the map of the ship, and where things could be found. She had introduced her to a friend (another stewardess), who promised to help in every way she could, and she had talked it over with the head-steward, to whom my friend promised five pounds if he would help her. The real stewardess had only just time to get off the ship before the bell rang for the tug to leave. Five minutes later the *Las Casas* was out of the harbour, butting into the heart of the channel, with spray coming over her in sheets. My friend was running about from passenger to passenger with tea and lemonade and ice. She had practically no rest until the ship left Lisbon. After the ship left Lisbon, when my friend knew that she could not be put ashore, she went boldly up and told the Captain what she had done. There was a scene. At first he vowed that he would make her work the full passage to Valparaiso. He was not going to be cheated out of a stewardess in that way. She was there on false pretenses; she was a stowaway; she was this, that, and the other. At last my friend told him frankly that, among other things, she was a lady, and meant to be treated as one. Soon after that the Captain was her very devoted humble servant, laughing with her at the trick she had played him, and admiring her pluck and energy. He offered her a berth, for one was now vacant, but she refused to take it. She would be a stewardess, she said, as far as the River Plate. At Monte Video, at the mouth of that river, she hoped to get some good Welsh or English woman to take her place.

She did her work very honestly. She was considered a model

FROM THE TOWER WINDOW

stewardess. At Monte Video she engaged a substitute, but she would not leave her work till the day she left the ship at Punta Concha. Only thirty-four days after the *Inesita* went ashore, she landed alone in a little gloomy Magellan port, where a prison and a Consul's office stood out big above a lot of shanties and dock-side clutter.

Well, there is no need to make a longer tale of it. She learned that a sailing-cutter out in the harbour was bound through the Straits in two days. She went aboard her, and paid the Captain to sail two days earlier than he had planned. In three days from then the cutter discovered the inlet into which the *Inesita* had found her way.

When we really saw the cutter coming up to us, we were not much excited—not so much as I had thought we should be. We were a little dazed, perhaps, and in our hearts I think we were one and all a little sore about it. That place had been home to us for all those days. The first person whom I met when I got on board was my friend. She was leaning over the bulwarks, watching the boat come alongside. She was wearing a kind of sea-helmet or woolen face-protector which covers the cheeks. I didn't recognize her at first. When I did recognize her, I had no words with which to thank her. She discovered me, and I discovered what her friendship was worth.

A CHRISTMAS SONG AT SEA★

Alfred Noyes

In Devonshire, now, the Christmas chime
        Is carolling over the lea;
And the sexton shovels away the snow
        From the old church porch, maybe;
And the waits with their lanthorns and noses a-glow
        Come round for their Christmas fee;
But, as in old England it's Christmas-time,
        Why, so is it here at sea,
            My lads,
        Why, so is it here at sea!

★From *Collected Poems*. Used by permission of Frederick A. Stokes Company.

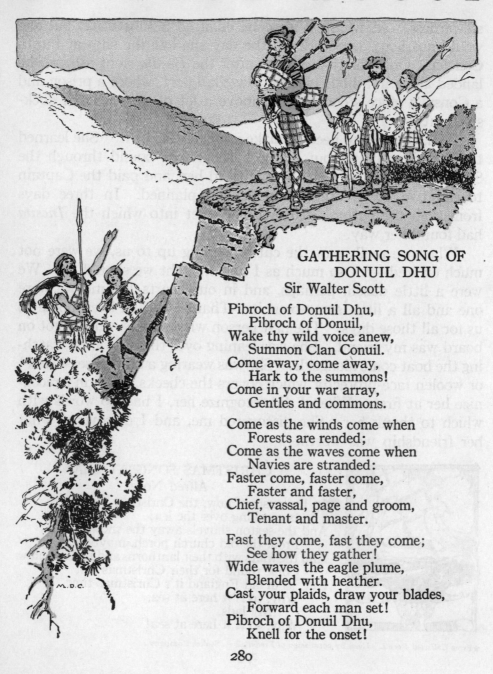

GATHERING SONG OF
DONUIL DHU
Sir Walter Scott

Pibroch of Donuil Dhu,
    Pibroch of Donuil,
Wake thy wild voice anew,
    Summon Clan Conuil.
Come away, come away,
    Hark to the summons!
Come in your war array,
    Gentles and commons.

Come as the winds come when
    Forests are rended;
Come as the waves come when
    Navies are stranded:
Faster come, faster come,
    Faster and faster,
Chief, vassal, page and groom,
    Tenant and master.

Fast they come, fast they come;
    See how they gather!
Wide waves the eagle plume,
    Blended with heather.
Cast your plaids, draw your blades,
    Forward each man set!
Pibroch of Donuil Dhu,
    Knell for the onset!

FROM THE TOWER WINDOW

ROBERT BRUCE, SCOTLAND'S HERO

MONG the wild highlands of Scotland, by her plunging mountain torrents, and emerald mountain lakes, on her bonnie lowland meadows and heath-covered moors, have dwelt always a people sturdy and independent, staunchly upholding their liberties with a spirit as keen and vigorous as the breath of their mountain air.

In the thirteenth century, King Edward I of England, better known as Edward Longshanks from the prodigious length of his legs, possessed himself by force and cunning of the Kingdom of Scotland and proceeded to govern it with the most oppressive tyranny. For some twenty years the Scottish people suffered all manner of injustice at the hands of the English king, all manner of insults and injuries at the hands of the English soldiery. Then awoke in the heart of one loyal Scotsman, Robert Bruce, a descendant of the ancient line of Scottish kings, the determination to rise up against the English, claim the throne of Scotland, and lead his down-trodden countrymen to battle for their freedom.

He galloped first to the border to meet Sir John, the Red Comyn, a strong and forceful baron who had been his rival in pretensions to the throne. Eagerly he desired to prevail on the Red Comyn to join with him, that they might by their common efforts expel the foreign foe. They met before the high altar of a church in Dumfries, but during the course of that consultation the two began to quarrel and came to high and abusive words. Then Bruce, so wise and courageous, so generous and courteous by nature, lost all control of himself, and in a moment of blind ungoverned passion, struck Comyn down with his dagger. Having done this rash deed, he instantly took to his horse and fled away.

For a time now he was desperate and consumed with remorse. To have set out to free his country and to have begun by clouding his soul with such a crime! To have cut off from himself irrevocably all the followers of the Red Comyn when Scotland had such need of unity and the unqualified support of all her sons! Alas! that one cruel deed of passion caused him endless miseries and misfortunes and a lifelong regret.

Hastily he summoned to meet him those few barons who still had hopes for the freedom of Scotland. In the Abbey of Scone where the Kings of Scotland always assumed their authority, he was crowned on the twenty-ninth of March, 1306. The rich light from the stained-glass windows streamed down on a slender gathering for such an affair of state, and everything relating to the ceremony was performed with the utmost haste. Longshanks had carried off to England the ancient crown of Scotland and a small circle of gold was hurriedly made to take its place. The Earl of Fife, whose duty it was to have placed the crown on the head of the king, refused to attend, so the ceremonial was performed without his consent, by his sister, the Countess of Buchan.

Edward was greatly incensed when he heard what had taken place and set out at once for Scotland at the head of a powerful army. Then followed defeat after defeat for Bruce, till he was driven with his wife, the Countess of Buchan and a few faithful followers, including young James of Douglas, to seek refuge in the mountainous recesses of the Highlands. Here they were chased from one place of refuge to another, often in great danger, half-starving and suffering many hardships. Everywhere Bruce found enemies. Sometimes they attacked him openly, sometimes with the most despicable stealth. Yet through it all he still kept up his own spirits and those of his followers; nor would he ever give up hope that they should yet set Scotland free. On the beautiful shores of Loch Lomond, girt by wild green mountains, amid the majestic grandeur of nature's most royal halls, Bruce and his queen held court with a band of ragged followers. The men hunted deer in the forest and fished in the streams for a bare subsistence, while the Queen and her ladies minded the cooking like the meanest of kitchen knaves. At last as winter drew near with the hint of snow in the air to come storming down on the mountains, living in such rude and unsheltered fashion became impossible for the ladies, so Bruce was obliged to separate from his wife, leave her in the only castle which remained to him, Kildrummie in Aberdeenshire, under the protection of his brother, young Nigel Bruce, and himself seek a winter refuge on the lonely island of Rachrin off the coast of Ireland.

Scarcely were the women established in Kildrummie when the English marched down on the castle and took it. They put the brave and beautiful youth, Nigel Bruce, to death, and threw the women into the strictest confinement, treating them with the utmost severity. The Countess of Buchan who had greatly offended Edward by placing the crown on the head of Bruce, was imprisoned in the castle of Berwick in an iron cage, like some wild beast.

News of the taking of Kildrummie, the captivity of his wife and the execution of Nigel reached Bruce in his miserable cabin at Rachrin and reduced him almost to despair. His crime in the church at Dumfries still weighed heavily on his soul and as he lay one morning on his wretched bed, he began to debate whether he had not better resign all thoughts of again attempting to make good his claim to the throne of Scotland, and redeem his great sin by going to the Holy Land to fight against the foes of Christianity. But then it seemed both criminal and cowardly to give up his attempts to restore freedom to Scotland while there yet remained the smallest chance of success. As he lay there, divided betwixt these two courses of action, his eye was suddenly attracted by a spider which was hanging at the end of a long thread from one of the beams above him and endeavoring to swing itself to another beam for the purpose of fixing the line on which it meant to stretch its web. The insect made the attempt again and again without success. Six times Bruce counted that it tried to carry its point and failed, and it came into his head that he had fought just six battles against the English, and that the poor persevering spider was in exactly the same situation as himself, having made as many trials and been as often disappointed.

"Now," thought Bruce, "I will be guided by this spider. If the insect shall make another effort to fix its thread and be successful, I will venture a seventh time to try my fortunes in Scotland, but if it shall fail I will give up hope and go to the Holy Land."

At that the spider swung itself again with all the force it could muster, and lo! the seventh time it succeeded and fastened its thread to the distant beam! At once Bruce determined, notwithstanding the smallness of the means at his command, to set out for Scotland.

On the mainland he was joined again by Douglas and others of his faithful followers, and they began to skirmish so successfully with the English as to force Lord Percy to retire from the province of Carrick. Bruce then dispersed his men upon various adventures against the enemy, but by thus doing, he left himself with such a small body of attendants that he often ran great risk of his life.

Once as he lay concealed in his own earldom of Carrick, certain men from the neighboring county of Galloway heard that Bruce was in hiding near, having no more than sixty men with him. So they resolved to attack him by surprise, and for this purpose got together two hundred men and two or three bloodhounds. Bruce who was always watchful and vigilant, had received information that this party intended to come on him suddenly and by night. Accordingly he quartered his little troop of sixty men on the side of a deep and swift-running river that had very steep rocky banks. There was but one ford by which this river could be crossed in that neighborhood, and that ford was so deep and narrow that two men could scarcely get through abreast. The ground on which they would land was steep and the path which led upwards from the water's edge was extremely narrow and difficult. Bruce caused his men to lie down to sleep at a place

about a half a mile distant from the river while he himself with two attendants went down to watch the ford. As he stood by the rushing river, he soon heard in the distance the baying of a hound. At first he thought of going back to awaken his men, but then he reflected that it might be only some shepherd's dog.

"My men," he said, "are sorely tired. I will not disturb their sleep for the yelping of a cur till I know more of the matter."

Slowly the cry of the hound came nearer, then Bruce began to hear a trampling of horses, the voices of men, and the ring and clatter of armor.

"If I go back now to give my men the alarm," thought Bruce, "those Galloway men will get through the ford without opposition, and that would be a pity since it is so advantageous a place."

He therefore sent his followers to awaken his men and remained altogether alone by the bank of the stream. The noise and the trampling of horses increased and soon, emerging from the black shadows of the distant forest into the bright moonlight that streamed across the river, he saw two hundred men with gleaming arms. The men of Galloway on their part, beheld but a single figure looming beside the ford, and the foremost of the party plunged confidently into the water. But as they could pass the stream only one at a time, Bruce met them with his spear when they landed and in such stout fashion that none climbed the bank alive. Soon the Galloway men began to fall back in terror, but perceiving that it was only one man who had checked their two hundred, they plunged forward with furious rage to assault him. By this time, however, the King's soldiers had come hurrying to assist him, and the Galloway men at sight of them beat a hasty and inglorious retreat.

Many an adventure of the same type befell the Bruce, yet he began to win some small successes against the English and these successes gradually grew larger and more important, till one by one the great Scottish nobles seeing him doggedly persistent, unfailingly courageous, and wondrously wary and intelligent, began to give up their grudges against him and rally to his standard, thus placing at last beneath his command a large and powerful army. In all parts of Scotland deeds of daring were done to drive the English out of their strongholds and this not only by the Douglas and other great nobles but also by the stout yeomanry and bold peasants of the land, who were as anxious to possess their small cottages in honorable independence as the nobles to reclaim their castles. Everywhere throughout Scotland, the determination to fight for their liberties was at last, by one man's persistent effort, fired into living flame.

But now Edward Longshanks was dead and his son, Edward II assembled one of the greatest armies which a king of England ever commanded, for the purpose of subduing Scotland. King Robert's army was scarcely a third as large and in matter of arms far more poorly provided. But during his eight long years of preparation for this great final test, King Robert had proved himself well able to make up by intelligent disposal of his troops what he lacked in arms and numbers. And his men had grown accustomed to fighting and gaining victories against every disadvantage.

Knowing that the superiority of the English lay in their splendid heavy armed cavalry and in their archers, which were better trained than any in the world, King Robert laid his plans carefully to overcome these odds. He led his army down into a plain near Stirling, where the English host must needs pass through a boggy country to reach them, while the Scots stood on hard, dry ground. He then caused all the ground on the front of his line where cavalry were likely to act to be dug full of holes about as deep as a man's knee. These were filled with brushwood, and the turf was replaced on the top so that no sign of them appeared.

When the Scottish army was drawn up, the line stretched on the south to the banks of the brook called Bannockburn, which are so rocky that no troops could attack them there, and on the north almost to the town of Stirling. Bruce reviewed his troops very carefully; all the useless servants, drivers of carts, and such he ordered to go behind a height, afterwards called in memory of the event, the Gillies' Hill, that is the servant's hill. He then made a stirring address to his soldiers, expressing his determination to gain the victory or lose his life on the field of battle and urging all who were not like-minded to leave ere the battle began.

Soon from the heights could be seen the approach of the vast English host, a beautiful and terrible sight, for the whole country seemed covered with men at arms on horse and foot, and above them waved a gallant show of standards, banners and pennons. As the van drew near, one among the English knights, Sir Henry de Bohun, saw King Robert, mounted not on his great war horse but on a little pony, riding up and down the ranks of his army, putting his men in order and carrying no spear, since he had no thought that there would be fighting that evening. Thinking to take him unawares and so easily bear him to the ground, de Bohun galloped upon him. Robert saw the danger but stood perfectly still till de Bohun drew very near, then he suddenly swerved his pony just a little to one side. So Sir Henry missed him with his lance point and was in the act of being carried past him by the career of his horse when King Robert rose up in his stirrups and struck him a blow with his battle axe that hurled him lifeless from his saddle.

On the morrow, June 24th, 1314, the battle began in earnest. The English archers started the fray by sending a hail of arrows into the Scottish ranks. But King Robert had in readiness a body of men-at-arms who rode at full gallop among the archers and as the latter had no weapons save their bows and arrows which they could not use when attacked hand to hand, they were cut down in great numbers by the Scottish horsemen and thrown into total confusion. The splendid English cavalry advanced at high speed to support the archers, but as they came dashing over the ground which was dug full of pits the horses fell into these holes, and the riders lay tumbling about without any means of defence, unable to rise from the weight of their armor. Then the English began to fall into general disorder and the Scottish king bringing up more forces, vigorously pressed his advantage. On a sudden while the battle was still obstinately maintained on both sides, the servants and attendants on the Scottish camp, seeing their masters were likely to gain the day, and wishing to share in the victory, ran forth from their concealment behind the Gillies' Hill. Seeing them come suddenly over the ridge the English mistook the rabble for another army come to sustain the Scots, and losing all heart they broke ranks and fled.

Thus by the victory of Bannockburn, Robert Bruce, so long an exile, at last won the freedom of Scotland, and he is universally held to have been one of Scotland's strongest and wisest kings.

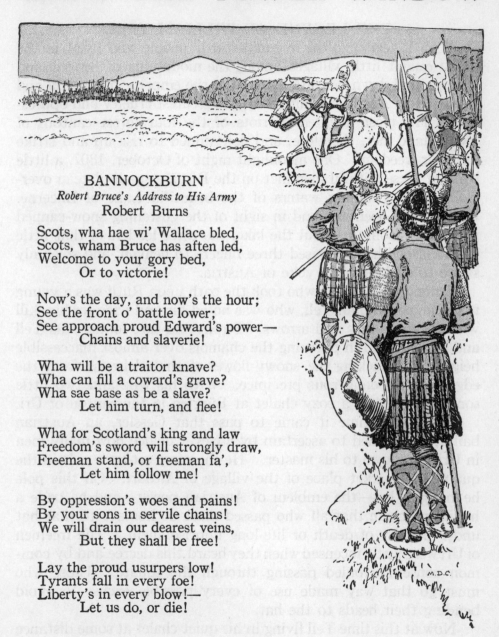

BANNOCKBURN
Robert Bruce's Address to His Army
Robert Burns

Scots, wha hae wi' Wallace bled,
Scots, wham Bruce has aften led,
Welcome to your gory bed,
    Or to victorie!

Now's the day, and now's the hour;
See the front o' battle lower;
See approach proud Edward's power—
    Chains and slaverie!

Wha will be a traitor knave?
Wha can fill a coward's grave?
Wha sae base as be a slave?
    Let him turn, and flee!

Wha for Scotland's king and law
Freedom's sword will strongly draw,
Freeman stand, or freeman fa',
    Let him follow me!

By oppression's woes and pains!
By your sons in servile chains!
We will drain our dearest veins,
    But they shall be free!

Lay the proud usurpers low!
Tyrants fall in every foe!
Liberty's in every blow!—
    Let us do, or die!

THE LEGEND OF WILLIAM TELL

MANY years ago the free and sturdy people who lived in the quaint little villages among the mountains of Switzerland were ground down beneath the heel of the emperor of Austria and governed by Austrian bailiffs with the greatest cruelty and oppression. The most devoted patriots of the four forest cantons of Switzerland met, therefore, and determined to rise up and strike for their freedom. One moonlight night of October, 1307, a little band of these faithful men met on the Rütli, a small plateau overlooking the gleaming waters of the beautiful Lake of Lucerne. Beneath the open sky and in sight of the glistening snow-capped peaks that loom up about the lake, the three leaders of that little band clasped hands, raised three fingers to heaven, and solemnly swore to shake off the yoke of Austria.

Among the patriots who took the oath upon Rütli was a young man named William Tell, who was noted far and wide for his skill with the cross-bow and arrows. Strong and sure-footed was Tell and he delighted in pursuing the chamois over almost inaccessible heights, or plucking the snowy flower of the edelweiss from the edge of some dangerous precipice. With his wife and two little sons Tell lived in a cozy chalet at Bürglen in the canton of Uri.

About this time it came to pass that Gessler, an Austrian bailiff, determined to ascertain by a clever device how many men in Uri were loyal to his master. He therefore set up a pole in the quaint old market place of the village of Altdorf. On this pole he hung a hat—the emblem of Austrian power—and he bade a herald proclaim that all who passed must do homage to that hat under penalty of death or life-long imprisonment. The freemen of Uri were justly incensed when they heard this decree and by common consent avoided passing through the square. Those who must go that way made use of every possible excuse to avoid bending their heads to the hat.

Now at this time Tell living in his quiet chalet at some distance

FROM THE TOWER WINDOW

from Altdorf, was ignorant of all that had recently happened there. One day he came down to the village bearing his cross-bow over his shoulder and holding his little son by his hand. Unconscious alike of pole, hat and guards he strolled across the square and was greatly surprised when suddenly a throng of soldiers surrounded him and placed him under arrest, crying out that he had defied the orders of Gessler. While Tell was protesting his innocence and striving to make the guards release him, he saw Gessler himself approaching on horseback around one of the quaintly painted houses that bordered on the square. Going at once to the bailiff, Tell loudly demanded justice. In the midst of a gathering crowd, the bailiff listened, sneering.

It happened, however, that Gessler had often heard men praise the remarkable skill of Tell as a marksman and he had long desired to see how well the man could shoot. Moreover, he wished to punish Tell in as cruel a way as he could devise for his neglect of the cap in order to make him an example to the other rebellious inhabitants of Altdorf. Therefore he thundered forth: "You shall be free on one condition only—if you shoot an apple from the head of your son at a distance of one hundred and fifty paces!"

The people who stood about gasped, and a murmur of indignation went up from all the crowd, but so great was the fear that Gessler had inspired in them all that no one dared interfere. Tell himself, a moment before so confident and self possessed, seemed suddenly to collapse at hearing the bailiff's words. Gessler could have thought of nothing more cruel than thus to insist that the father must shoot at his own little son.

"Place any other punishment upon me!" cried Tell. "What if the boy should move? What if my hand should tremble?"

"Say no more!" cried Gessler. "Shoot!"

Tell was in despair, but the little lad, his face bright with perfect trust, ran and stood against a linden tree at one end of the square.

"Shoot, father!" he cried. "Shoot! I know you can hit the apple!"

The boy's absolute and fearless confidence determined Tell. Yet he still trembled as he selected two arrows from his quiver, while a soldier took an apple from a fruit vendor who stood near and placed it on the boy's head. One arrow Tell thrust hastily into his belt, the other he carefully adjusted in his cross-bow. For a moment his eyes followed the distant line of the snow-capped mountains, resting to gather strength on their calm and quiet peaks. Then his hand grew steady and he took aim.

Twang! went the bow. The arrow whistled through the air. All noise in the square was stilled and everyone held his breath. But lo! the arrow struck the apple squarely in the center, split it, and carried it away! The boy had not moved a hairsbreadth! A mighty shout went up from the crowd! But as Tell was turning away, Gessler pointed to the second arrow which the marksman had stuck in his belt.

"Fellow," cried he, "what did you mean to do with that arrow?"

"Tyrant," was Tell's proud answer, "that second arrow was for you if I had struck my child."

Beside himself with rage at these bold words, Gessler angrily bade his guards to bind Tell fast and convey him down to his waiting boat at Flühlen, whence he should be carried across the lake and cast into the foulest of dungeons. Friends led the little boy away, but in the train of the tyrant, Tell was marched in chains down to the edge of the Lake of Lucerne. Placed in the boat with fast bound hands and feet, his useless weapons beside him, Tell despairingly watched the bailiff embark and the shore near Altdorf slowly recede. Soon, however, clouds began to hide the sun and roll down over the pure white peaks. The ripples in the water grew into waves, the sky grew darker and darker. At last there broke a mighty storm on the little boat. Thunder crashed, the water heaved and dashed in angry foam and lightning streaked from shore to shore. In vain did the Austrians try to guide the boat through the tempest. They were not well enough acquainted with the lake. Then the boatsmen, knowing well that Tell was the most clever steersman in the canton of Uri, began to implore Gessler to let him be unbound in order to help them. In a voice that could scarcely be heard above the shriek of the storm, Gessler cried: "Unloose the prisoner's chains. Let him take the helm!"

Accordingly, Tell was unbound. He seized the helm and the boat went plunging forward. With a strong arm and fearless gaze he directed it straight toward a narrow ledge of rock which forms a natural landing place in the mighty cliffs that at this point rise up sheer from the lake. The water there is seven hundred feet deep, but as the boat drew near and a sudden flash of lightning revealed the spot, Tell suddenly let go of the rudder and with one mighty leap sprang from the pitching boat across the seething waves to the shore. There were angry cries from the lake, but Gessler's boat went drifting off into the darkness again, hurled back, wildly tossing among the waves.

Tell made his way straight around the lake to a spot that Gessler would have to pass on his way home after his landing. There, crouching in the bushes on the steep bank, he waited patiently to see whether the tyrant would escape the storm. At length the bailiff appeared, riding proudly at the head of his troops. Then Tell took his second arrow, the arrow that he had meant should wipe out tyranny from Switzerland. As Gessler passed by, he let the arrow fly, and true to its mark it sped. Gessler fell and with him Austria's reign of tyranny. For the Swiss people, encouraged at hearing what Tell had done, threw off the fear that had bound them, rose up and made Switzerland once more free.

JOSEPH AND HIS BRETHREN

NOW Israel loved Joseph more than all his children, because he was the son of his old age, and he made him a coat of many colours. And when his brethren saw that their father loved him more than all his brethren, they hated him and could not speak peaceably unto him. And his brethren went to feed his father's flock in Shechem. And Israel said unto Joseph, "Do not thy brethren feed the flock in Shechem? Go, I pray thee, see whether it be well with them."

And when Joseph's brethren saw him afar off, even before he came near unto them, they conspired against him to slay him.

And his brother Reuben heard it and said, "Let us not kill him, but cast him into this pit," for he intended secretly to save him.

And it came to pass when Joseph was come unto his brethren, that they stript Joseph of his coat, his coat of many colours, and they took him and cast him into a pit. And they lifted up their eyes and looked, and, behold, a company of Ishmaelites came from Gilead with their camels bearing spicery and balm and myrrh, going to carry it down to Egypt. And they drew up Joseph out of the pit, and sold Joseph to the Ishmaelites for twenty pieces of silver. And they took Joseph's coat, and killed a kid of the goats, and dipped the coat in the blood; and they brought the coat to their father, and said, "This have we found." And he knew it, and said, "It is my son's coat! An evil beast hath devoured him." And Jacob rent his clothes, and put sackcloth upon his loins, and mourned for his son many days.

And the Midianites sold Joseph into Egypt unto Pot'i-phar, the Captain of Pharaoh's guard. And the Lord was with Joseph and he was a prosperous man and when his master saw that the Lord was with him and made all that he did to prosper, he made him overseer over his house. But the wife of Potiphar accused Joseph falsely of a crime, and the wrath of Joseph's master was kindled and he put Joseph into prison.

FROM THE TOWER WINDOW

And it came to pass that the butler of the King of Egypt and his baker had offended their lord. And he put them in ward in the house where Joseph was bound. And they dreamed a dream both of them, and, behold, they were sad. And they said unto Joseph, "We have dreamed a dream, and there is no interpreter of it."

And Joseph said unto them, "Do not interpretations belong to God? Tell me them, I pray you." And the chief butler told his dream to Joseph. And Joseph said unto him, "This is the interpretation of it: Yet within three days shall Pharaoh restore thee unto thy place: and thou shalt deliver Pharaoh's cup after the former manner into his hand. But when it shall be well with thee, I pray thee, make mention of me unto Pharaoh, for indeed I have done nothing that they should put me into the dungeon."

When the chief baker saw that the interpretation was good, he likewise told his dream unto Joseph. And Joseph answered and said, "This is the interpretation thereof: Yet within three days will Pharaoh lift up thine head from off thee, and shall hang thee on a tree." And it came to pass the third day, which was Pharaoh's birthday, that he made a feast unto all his servants. And he restored the chief butler unto his butlership again; but he hanged the chief baker as Joseph had interpreted to him. Yet did not the chief butler remember Joseph, but forgat him.

And it came to pass at the end of two full years, that Pharaoh dreamed and behold he stood by the river. And, behold, there came up out of the river seven well-favoured kine and fat-fleshed; and they fed in a meadow. And behold, seven other kine came up after them out of the river, ill-favoured and lean-fleshed; and stood by the other kine. And the ill-favoured and lean-fleshed kine did eat up the well-favoured and fat kine. So Pharaoh awoke.

And he slept and dreamed the second time And it came to pass in the morning that his spirit was troubled; and he sent for all the magicians of Egypt, and all the wise men thereof, but there was none that could interpret the dreams unto Pharaoh.

Then spake the chief butler unto Pharaoh, saying: "Pharaoh was wroth with his servants, and put me in prison, both me and the chief baker: and we dreamed a dream in one night, I and he; and there was with us a young man, an Hebrew, and he interpreted to us our dreams. And it came to pass, as he interpreted to us."

Then Pharaoh sent and called Joseph, and they brought him hastily out of the dungeon: and he shaved himself, and changed his raiment, and came in unto Pharaoh. And Pharaoh said unto Joseph, "I have dreamed a dream, and there is none that can interpret it: and I have heard say of thee, that thou canst understand a dream to interpret it." And Joseph answered, saying, "It is not in me: God shall give Pharaoh an answer of peace."

And when Pharaoh had told Joseph his dream, Joseph said unto Pharaoh, "The seven good kine are seven years. Behold there come seven years of great plenty throughout all the land of Egypt: and the seven thin and ill-favoured kine that came up after them are seven years of famine, and the famine shall consume the land. Now, therefore, let Pharaoh look out a man discreet and wise, and set him over the land of Egypt. And let him appoint officers over the land, and let them gather all the food of those good years that come. And that food shall be as a store to the land against the seven years of famine."

And the thing was good in the eyes of Pharaoh. And Pharaoh said unto his servants, "Can we find such a one as this, a man in whom the Spirit of God is?" And Pharaoh said unto Joseph, "For as much as God hath shewed thee all this, there is none so discreet and wise as thou art. Thou shalt be over my house."

And Pharaoh took off his ring from his hand, and put it on Joseph's hand, and arrayed him in vestures of fine linen, and put a gold chain about his neck; and he made him to ride in his second chariot which he had; and they cried before him, "Bow the knee," and he made him ruler over all the land of Egypt.

And in the seven plenteous years the earth brought forth by

handfuls. And he laid up all the food in the cities. And seven years of dearth began to come, according as Joseph had said: and the dearth was in all lands; but in Egypt there was bread. And all countries came unto Joseph for to buy corn. And when Jacob saw that there was corn in Egypt, Jacob said unto his  sons: "Get you down thither, and buy for us from thence." And Joseph's ten brethren went down to buy corn in Egypt. But Benjamin, Joseph's brother, Jacob sent not with his brethren; for he said, "Lest peradventure, mischief befall him."

And Joseph's brethren came, and bowed down themselves before him with their faces to the earth. And Joseph saw his brethren, and he knew them, but made himself strange unto them, and spake roughly unto them, "Whence come ye?" And they said, "From the land of Canaan to buy food."

And Joseph said unto them, "Ye are spies. Hereby ye shall be proved. If ye be true men, let one of your brethren be bound in the house of your prison. Go ye, carry corn for the famine of your houses, but bring your youngest brother unto me."

And they said one to another, "We are verily guilty concerning our brother, Joseph, in that we saw his anguish when he besought us, and we would not hear; therefore is this distress come upon us."

And they knew not that Joseph understood them; for he spoke unto them by an interpreter. And he turned himself about from them and wept. Then he took from them Simeon, and bound him before their eyes and he commanded to fill their sacks with corn. And they laded their asses with the corn, and departed thence.

And they came unto Jacob their father and told him all that befell unto them. And he said, "My son Benjamin shall not go down with you; for his brother Joseph is dead, and he is left alone."

And famine was sore in the land. And it came to pass that when they had eaten up the corn which they had brought out of

Egypt, their father said, "Go again, buy us a little food, take also your brother, and God Almighty give you mercy before the man."

And the men took a present and they took double money, and Benjamin; and rose up, and went down to Egypt, and stood before Joseph. And he asked them of their welfare, and said, "Is your father well, the old man of whom ye spake? Is he yet alive?" And they answered, "Our father is in good health, he is yet alive." And they bowed down their heads, and made obeisance.

And he lifted up his eyes, and saw his brother Benjamin, his mother's son, and said, "Is this your younger brother, of whom ye spake unto me?" And Joseph made haste for his bowels did yearn upon his brother: and he sought where to weep; and he entered into his chamber and wept there.

And he washed his face and went out, and said, "Set on bread." And they set on for him by himself, and for them by themselves, and for the Egyptians, which did eat with him, by themselves.

And he took and sent messes unto them from before him, but Benjamin's mess was five times as much as any of theirs.

And Joseph commanded the steward of his house, saying, "Fill the men's sacks with food, and put every man's money in his sack's mouth, and put my silver cup in the sack of the youngest."

As soon as the morning was light, the men were sent away, they and their asses. Joseph said unto his steward, "Up, follow after them and say, 'Wherefore have ye rewarded evil for good? Wherefore have ye taken the money and my lord's silver cup?'"

And he overtook them, and he spake unto them these same words. And they said unto him, "God forbid that thy servants should do according to this thing! With whomsoever the cup be found, both let him die, and we also will be my lord's bondmen."

Then they speedily took ever man his sack to the ground, and the steward searched, and the cup was found in Benjamin's sack.

Then they rent their clothes and returned to the city.

And Judah said unto Joseph, "What shall we say unto our

lord? or how shall we clear ourselves? We have a father, an old man, and Benjamin is the child of his old age, a little one; and his brother is dead, and he alone is left of his mother, and his father loveth him. Now therefore when I come to thy servant my father, and the lad be not with us, seeing that his life is bound up in the lad's life, it shall come to pass that he will die. Now therefore, I pray thee, let thy servant abide instead of the lad a bondman to my lord; and let the lad go up with his brethren."

And Joseph could not refrain himself, and he cried, "Cause every man to go out from me." And there stood no man with him, while Joseph came himself down unto his brethren.

And Joseph said unto his brethren, "I am Joseph; come near to me, I pray you." And they came near. And he said, "I am Joseph your brother, whom you sold into Egypt. Now therefore be not grieved, nor angry with yourselves, that ye sold me hither: for God did send me before you to preserve life. So now it was not you that sent me hither, but God: and he hath made me a father to Pharaoh, and lord of all his house. Haste ye, and go up to my father, and say, 'Thus saith thy son Joseph, God hath made me Lord of all Egypt: come down unto me, and thou shalt dwell in the land of Goshen, and thou shalt be near unto me, thou, and thy children, and thy children's children, and thy flocks, and thy herds, and all that thou hast: and there will I nourish thee; for yet there are five years of famine'." And he fell upon his brother Benjamin's neck. Moreover he kissed all his brethren, and wept upon them.

So his brethren departed: and came unto Jacob, saying, "Joseph is yet alive, and he is governor over all the land of Egypt."

And Israel said, "It is enough: Joseph my son is yet alive: I will go and see him before I die."

And the sons of Israel carried Jacob their father, and their little ones, and their wives, and they took their cattle and their goods, and came into Egypt. And Joseph made ready his chariot, and went up to meet his father, and he fell on his neck, and wept.

THE STORY OF ROLAND, A SONG OF DEEDS
From the French Chanson de Roland

DAYS were when the great emperor Charlemagne, crossing the snow-capped Pyrenees with his mighty host of warriors, conquered all Spain from the Saracen infidels from the highlands to the sea. Castle and keep went down before him and no city could withstand him save only Sar-a-gos'sa, the s t r o n g walled mountain town. In Saragossa, Marsile, the Saracen king held council and wailed his lot, that he had no more men to stand against the Franks. Then came crafty counsellors and argued in his ear, "Use trickery. Send gifts to Charlemagne and promise him submission. Thereat he will depart. Then we will break our oath, rise up and win back Spain!"

In Marsile's ear the words of craft were good. He sent ambassadors with gifts and olive branches to Charlemagne.

Now Charlemagne at Cordova, sat on a golden throne in the midst of a blossoming orchard, imperial in his majesty, with flowing beard and flowing robes. Around him stood his peers watching the martial games of fifty thousand warriors. Thither came the messengers of Marsile, humbly offering him submission. Then up spake Roland, Charlemagne's sister's son, bravest and best-beloved of all the emperor's paladins: "Marsile hath tricked us once. Why should we trust his promises again?"

But Ganelon, Roland's step-father stood by and in his heart was gnawing hatred of the splendid youth. "Rash fool!" he cried, "thou dost prize thine own glory more than the lives of thy fellows!"

And many another warrior argued likewise for peace until the emperor cried, "Enough! We will accept the offer of Marsile!"

Then Roland and Oliver, Roland's dearest friend, pressed forward suing eagerly to be given the dangerous task of bearing Charlemagne's answer to Marsile. The emperor would not spare his peers but bade them name some baron in their stead. Quoth Roland: "Ganelon was full anxious for the peace! Why not send Ganelon?"

Thereat the cowardly Ganelon was wroth, for in his heart he deemed the expedition so hazardous that he who went might nevermore return, and darkly he vowed vengeance on the youth for naming him. But Charlemagne, in his imperial dignity, silenced Ganelon, and delivered to him his glove as emblem of the office he bestowed, entrusting to him the message to Marsile. Trembling with rage and fear Ganelon reached out to take the glove, but in his haste he let it fall. Then great dismay and fear fell over all. "That bodeth little good," men whispered.

So went Ganelon and on the way fell into converse with the Saracen escort. In bitter terms he spoke of Roland crying, "While he lives, will fighting never cease. True, Charlemagne is old but Roland is old Charlemagne's right arm."

And, noting well his bitter tone the Saracens made answer: "We could rid thee easily of this Roland if thou wilt but arrange that he command the rear guard when Charlemagne leaves Spain."

And so while they rode thus, the dark-browed traitor, Ganelon devised with those false Saracens a plot to lead the hero Roland into ambush in the Pass of Roncesvalles and there to slay him. And when Marsile had heard the plan, far from slaying Ganelon, he loaded him with gifts and sent him safely back to Charlemagne.

In his camp at the foot of the mountain, Ganelon delivered unto the emperor the keys of Saragossa and reported that the infidels made complete submission to his will. So Charlemagne believed that now at last his task was done. Gratefully he offered thanks to God and made all ready for returning home. Yet on the night before he was to leave, his rest was sorely troubled with dreams, through which the gloomy face of Ganelon passed omi-

nously.   When he awoke the emperor was still haunted by these
dreams, yet he prepared his army for departure and commanded
that a guard of twenty thousand men should follow him some
distance in the rear to guard against surprise.

"Who will command my rear guard?" Charlemagne cried.

Then Ganelon answered eagerly, "Who so brave as Roland?"

But all could see that Ganelon but proposed the name of
Roland out of spite and Charlemagne answered with some heat,
"Nay! Roland shall remain with me!"   Yet did Roland himself
so earnestly entreat to be entrusted with the dangerous post that
Charlemagne at last gave his consent.

Reluctantly, with strange forebodings, Charlemagne bade his
nephew a sad farewell. Fully armed and mounted on his steed,
Roland stood upon a lofty cliff and watched the vanguard of the
Franks defiling through the narrow gorges far below.   "Farewell!"
he cried, "soon will we meet again in France!"

Mile after mile the vanguard marched, the traitor Ganelon in
their midst, but a nameless sense of evil filled them all and their
hearts were back with Roland on the treacherous soil of Spain.

> *High were the peaks and the valleys deep,*
> *The mountains wondrous dark and steep;*
> *Sadly the Franks through the passes wound;*
> *Fully fifteen leagues did their tread resound.*
> *To their own great land they are drawing nigh,*
> *And they look on the fields of Gascony.*
> *They think of their homes and manors there,*
> *Their gentle spouses and damsels fair.*
> *Is none but for pity the tear lets fall,*
> *But the anguish of Karl is beyond them all.*
> *His sister's son at the gates of Spain*
> *Smites on his heart and he weeps amain.*

Meantime, Roland, after waiting for the vanguard to gain some
advance, ordered his men likewise forward.   His dear friend Oliver,
his best loved comrade from his boyhood, rode beside him and

they held joyous converse as they rode, until they passed at last out of the sunlight into the dark and narrow pass of Roncesvalles, shut in by gloomy walls of rock. Then suddenly Oliver reined in his horse, shaded his face with his hand and looked ahead. "Behold!" he cried and his voice was hoarse, "the work of Ganelon."

Roland halted likewise and looked forward. There he saw advancing, an army, a multitude, a host of Saracens. And so he knew that he had been betrayed, yet he set his men in order, took his stand and staunchly cried, "Cursed be he who flees!"

"But Roland, Roland," Oliver urged, "these men outnumber us five to one! Wind one good blast on Ol'i-phant, thy horn. The Emperor will hear and turn him back to succor us."

Roland only answered, "Nay! Never will I for heathen felons blow one blast!" Thrice Oliver besought him; thrice Roland answered, "Nay!"

Then good Archbishop Turpin bade the Franks to kneel and pray preparing solemnly their hearts for battle. Thus refreshed the twenty thousand rose and took their stand. First of all came boldly rushing on, a nephew of Marsile's who loudly boasted. "Today we lop off Charlemagne's right arm!" Roland, spurring forward, pierced him at one onset with his lance. Then did each man in that small Frankish host do wondrous deeds and Roland and Oliver were ever in the thickest of the fray. Marsile himself cried out to Roland, "Face me in single combat!" But Roland struck him such a blow that he must needs be borne from off the battle field, wounded unto death, and with him fled full many of his men. Yet, one by one, before the onrush of those pagan hordes the brave Franks fell,—one by one, one by one. All nature seemed to feel the terror of that battle, for over the sunny fields of France, there broke a hideous storm. The thunder rolled across the sky, the lightning flashed and all the earth shook as with mighty grief. Great dread came over Charlemagne and all his men. Then Roland far away, so worn that he could scarcely find the strength

to blow, wound one long mournful blast upon his horn. Charlemagne heard the sound and cried, "Our Roland is in danger!"

"Nay! nay!" said Ganelon, "belike he is but hunting."

A second time that mournful call came wailing from the distance. "Never would he call that way unless in direst peril!"

"Nay! nay! he is but coursing a hare!"

But still a third time came that blast so long now and despairing that none might mistake the meaning of its call. So Charlemagne halted, crying: "All is going ill. Roland is in extremity!" And in wrath he ordered Ganelon into chains. Then bidding all his trumpets sound as signal he was coming he turned back with his whole host and went to Roland's rescue.

Amidst a heap of slain Roland mourned his fallen comrades, yet he urged the faithful handful left to do their best and never to surrender. And the Saracens not daring to approach that doughty little band, attacked them from a distance with spear and arrow. Mortally wounded by one of these cowardly spears, Oliver called out to Roland to bid him a last farewell. Half blinded, Roland fought his way to his beloved comrade's side. At sight of him so sorely wounded he was well nigh overcome. But each laid his head to the other and in love like this was their parting made.

Then lo! Roland and the Archbishop were left the only living in all that vast field and the Archbishop too was dying. A last time Roland put his horn to his lips and drew from it one long, pitiful blast that fell on Charlemagne's ear so weak and faint, he cried, "My nephew must be dying!" And he urged his men to greater speed.

Hearing the sounds of Charlemagne's trumpets the Saracens dared no longer stay but fled, yet in fleeing they flung missiles back at Roland till his shield dropped from his hand and his steed sank under him. Wounded unto death Roland could not pursue the foe. Tenderly he turned back to Archbishop Turpin, removed the prelate's armor and placed him comfortably upon the ground. Then slowly and with mighty effort he collected from mountain and valley the bodies of his twelve peers and friends and dragged them to the Archbishop's feet for one last blessing. While laying Oliver there, Roland swooned for grief and the Archbishop, seizing his horn, painfully raised himself to fetch his friend some water. But in his act of mercy, he too fell dead, and Roland woke to find himself alone. Grasping his good sword Du-ren-dal' and Oliphant his horn, the hero slowly toiled his way to the top of a hill that he might die with his face toward the foe. There he tried to break good Durendal against the rocks that no enemy might ever wield his sword. But the blade was of such steel he could not even dent it. So he laid it under him with Oliphant, that he might guard it even in death, and there upon the height, his face toward Spain he lifted up his hands, committed his soul to God, and thus he died.

Scarcely had Roland breathed his last when Charlemagne arrived to find of all his twenty thousand not one left. Mournfully he called his peers by name. Not one there was to answer,— not a single one. And on the height, his face toward Spain, they found the hero Roland. Great was the grief of all. Great was the grief of Charlemagne. His host pursued the Saracens and by the river E'bro, the Moors paid to the full the penalty of their treachery. Then bearing the bodies of Roland and Oliver, Charlemagne returned to France. Laden with chains and tied to a stake like a wild beast Ganelon was led before his judges for trial. By his dark deed lay twenty thousand dead. He was condemned and suffered a shameful death. But in the hearts of Charlemagne and all the people of France remained undying love for Roland, for he took his stand, and held it, never yielding, unto death.

JOAN OF ARC

the year 1412, there was born in the village of Dom-re-my' in France, a little peasant girl called Joan of Arc. Her parents were honest laboring folk and they lived in a cottage that bordered directly on the churchyard. In the cool and peaceful shadow of the church with all its holy associations, Joan spent with her brothers and sisters a very happy childhood. She shared with unbounded energy all their joyous activity and sports, yet who so ready as she to perform her share of the household tasks or respond to any command of her parents with simple loving obedience? Beneath the stately trees of the splendid old forest of Domremy, she tended her father's sheep and she aided him too in many a rough man's task, yet in heart and soul she was every whit a woman, thoroughly skilled in fine needlework and all womanly household arts. Every one in the village loved Joan for the charm of her sweet simplicity and her wholly unselfish kindness. Deep in the heart of the girl was implanted an earnest love of God as well as a love of her fellow men, and as she grew somewhat older she often went apart from the boisterous play of the other children to pass many hours in quiet meditation and prayer, her thoughts sweeping out far beyond the little circle of daily concerns that occupied her playmates.

Now the affairs of France were at this time in a most unhappy state. For the English in league with the Burgundians, had conquered almost the whole of France, and the Dauphin Charles VII, having never the courage to get himself crowned, was looking on in lazy indolence without a thought of resistance, even meditating flight and the total abandonment of his kingdom,—a sorry king with no money, no army and, worst of all, no spirit and no purpose.

Over all these things Joan pondered with the most serious

concern, and her deep-rooted conviction of the goodness and power of God, her live consciousness of God as a very real presence, filled her with the most certain assurance that naught so unjust as the forceful conquest of France by alien invaders could ever be accomplished. All the power and strength and might of God were against such injustice. In her heart and soul strange stirrings and longings awoke till at length all her waking hours were spent in almost continuous prayer for her country's deliverance.

One summer's day when Joan was thirteen years old she was wandering alone in her father's garden at midday, her spirit more than ever astir within her, when she suddenly heard a voice call her. Instantly a great light shone upon her and she saw the archangel Michael before her. He bade her continue to be a good girl and made the solemn announcement that it was she and none other who should save the kingdom of France, who should go to the help of the Dauphin and bring him to Rheims to be crowned. The child, so young and weak before such a mighty task, fell on her knees overcome. "I am but a poor girl," she said.

"God will help thee," answered the angel.

From this day Joan's life became even more pure and sweet than before. She loved to go apart from her playmates and meditate, and now heavenly voices often spoke to her telling her of her mission. These she said were the voices of her saints. Sometimes the voices were accompanied by visions. St. Catherine and St. Margaret appeared to her. Thus the child grew to young maidenhood, her mind elevated by her visions.

At the beginning of the year 1428, when Joan was sixteen, the Voices told her that the time was now come when she could no longer delay. She must go at once to the Dauphin to save the kingdom. They commanded her first to seek out the Sire de Baudricourt (Bo'dri-coor) and ask of him an escort to conduct her to the Dauphin. Conscious that her parents, bound by their fearful human love for her, would never aid her in such an undertaking, Joan went to an uncle and begged him to accompany her to the Sire at Vaucouleurs (Vo-coo-leur'). Her ardent sincerity overcame the objections of the peasant and he went with her.

Baudricourt's reception of Joan was brutal. When the girl told him that she was destined of God to lead the Dauphin to his coronation, and begged him to send her to Charles, he cried: "The girl is crazy! Box her ears and take her back to her father."

Thus Joan was returned with scorn to Domremy. Another less earnest and consecrated, might have been shamed by such a reception into yielding up her purpose. But urged by her Voices, Joan persisted and went once more to Baudricourt. He received her with the same mocking disbelief as before.

Soon nothing was talked of at Vaucouleurs but the young girl who went about openly saying that God destined her to save the kingdom and some one must take her to Charles the Dauphin. At length while the Sire and his noble friends utterly scoffed at the idea that God should give a poor peasant girl power to save a kingdom where the most experienced generals had failed, the simple-hearted people, moved by her faith, began to believe in her mission. A certain young squire offered to take her to Chi-non' where Charles was then staying. The poor folk, heaping all their little savings together, raised money enough to clothe and arm her and buy her a horse. Thus with a small escort she set out for Chinon. Baudricourt still flung his jibes after her, but the multitude, many among them weeping to see the young thing go so bravely forth to face such fearful odds, cried from the very depths of their hearts, "God keep you!"

English and Burgundians held all the country over which the little party must pass and every bridge was occupied by the enemy. Thus Joan had to travel by night and hide by day. Her companions soon began to lose heart in the face of such dangers and urge a return to Vaucouleurs, but Joan's answer was resolute; "Fear nothing, for God is leading me."

FROM THE TOWER WINDOW

On the twelfth day after starting, the party arrived at Chinon. Now the courtiers of Charles VII were by no means agreed as to how this maiden who made such remarkable claims should be received. Some, jealous of their power over the mind of the Dauphin, urged him not to receive her at all. But just at that moment came news from Orleans, almost the last great French stronghold to hold out against the English, that it was like to fall, and those courtiers who favored Joan carried their point that the last chance of saving Orleans should not be neglected.

By the flaring light of torches, Joan was led one evening to the castle. She had never seen the King and the great hall was crowded with nobles. In order to test the truth of the girl's claim that she was inspired of God, the Dauphin had attired himself in a plain costume and stood in the midst of a throng of his nobles while one of his courtiers in the royal robes sat upon the throne. Joan however did not hesitate. She singled Charles out at a glance, came at once and knelt before him.

"I am not the King," he asserted. "Yonder is the King."

"You are he, gentle Prince and no other," the girl insisted.

And then she proceeded to tell the Dauphin of her mission, assuring him with all the fire of her high and noble purpose burning in her eyes, that God had sent her to have him crowned and save the kingdom of France. Still the young coward hesitated. He was afraid that the girl might be a sorceress, so he sent her off to be examined by a body of learned men and ecclesiastics. For three weeks these men tormented her with questions, but she answered them always straight to the point and in face of all their suspicions and efforts to entrap her, her inspiration and self-command never once flagged or failed.

"If it be God's intent to save France, He hath no need of men-at-arms to accomplish His purpose," objected the tribunal.

"The soldiers must do the fighting, but God will give the victory," Joan quietly made answer.

At length the common people once again declared in favor of the girl and the learned and powerful were forced to yield to the simple faith of the multitude. The troops gathered at Blois and Joan arrived there followed by the greatest nobles of France. She rode in armor and on horse-back, an appealing girlish figure of a natural grace and dignity that softened and subdued even the rudest of the soldiers. She bore a white banner of her own design which was intended to remind the army continually of the purity of their cause and the God who was their strength.

Dunois who was in command at Orleans, came to meet Joan. She said to him simply, "I bring you the best of help, that of the King of Heaven. It comes not from me but from God Himself."

At eight in the evening Joan entered Orleans. The people crowded to meet her. In the midst of a throng so dense that she could scarcely make her way, she passed by torchlight through the city. Men, women and children wished to get near her and even to touch her horse. Joan spoke to them with compassion and promised to deliver them. First of all she asked to be led to a church to offer thanks to God. As she passed along the way, an old man cried out to her, "My daughter, the English are strong and well intrenched. It will be difficult to get rid of them!" She answered confidently, "Nothing is impossible to God."

Her confidence infected everyone around her. The people of Orleans so lately timid and discouraged, wished now to throw themselves at once upon the enemy. But Dunois, fearful of defeat, decided to await reinforcements which Charles had promised to send to Joan from Blois. In the meantime from the walls of Orleans, Joan summoned the English to depart and return to their own country, but they answered her with insults. The reinforcements from Blois were so long in appearing that Dunois at length went himself to see what had become of them. He arrived just in time to discover that the weak and changeable Dauphin had been influenced by jealous courtiers to desert Joan

and send the troops not to her but back to their quarters. With difficulty Dunois prevailed on Charles to send the men to Orleans.

On the fourth of May the battle began. Everywhere, Joan was in the thick of the fight, urging on her men without a thought of herself. But never did she use her sword; her standard was her sole weapon. Once while she was taking a little rest, the commander, without her knowledge, ordered an attack on a certain bastion held by the English. Always the commanders were jealously attempting to gain the victory without Joan in order to take to themselves the credit. But their attack failed and the French were retreating in great disorder when Joan awakened suddenly from her sleep and rushed up to their assistance. She rallied them and led them once more against the foe. This time the English strove in vain to maintain their position. They were forced to surrender the bastion. Thus Joan was led in great glory back to Orleans, but as she crossed the battlefield where in the heat of contest her determined spirit had upheld them all, she gave way and wept like any woman for compassion of the wounds and suffering that had been caused by the battle.

It was now a question how to follow up against the English this attack so happily begun. The leaders, far from pleased to be led by a peasant girl and to share with her the victory, met in secret to discuss the plans to be adopted. Joan presented herself indignantly at the council, and as the chancellor of the Duke of Orleans tried to conceal the decisions which had been made, she cried, "Tell me what you have concluded. You have been at your council and I at mine!"—she meant that she had been earnestly at prayer,—"and believe me, the counsels of God shall be accomplished and stand while yours shall perish!"

Thereafter she did indeed lead the French to most brilliant victory. Often she angered the generals by not taking their advice and pursuing the most approved military tactics, but she lent to the men a spirited resolution and inspired them with boundless faith. Moreover she herself was so persuaded that victory was inevitable if she persevered unflinchingly in her efforts to obtain it, that nothing could stand before her. So in four days the English, who had been for eight months before Orleans, were forced to give up the siege.

News of the victory spread far and wide and attested in the sight of all the truth of Joan's assertion that she was led of God. The holy maid did not linger to be praised and thanked by the people of Orleans, but returned hastily to Chinon, desiring to take Charles at once to Rheims to be crowned. But the Dauphin though he received her with great honors, refused to follow her to Rheims, not intending that she should disturb the base indolence of his royal existence. Accordingly Joan proceeded against the English again, and won three more great battles, driving the foe beyond the Loire. Then at last, still reluctantly, Charles was induced to surrender his ease long enough to go to Rheims. On the sixteenth of July, he entered the city at the head of his troops and the next day the ceremony of coronation took place in the cathedral before a great concourse of people. When Charles had been crowned, Joan flung herself at his feet weeping hot tears.

"O Sire," she cried, "Now is accomplished the will of God!"

"All who saw her at the moment," says the old chronicle, "believed more than ever that it was a thing come from God," and the attachment of the common people to her was a touching sight. They contested among themselves to kiss her hands or her clothes or only to touch her. It was the moment of her supremest triumph. And now that Joan had fulfilled all her mission, obeyed all the commands that God had given her, she earnestly besought Charles to let her return to her home to the sweet simplicity of her early life, for in all she had done she had no smallest thought of reward or self-glorification, but only of simple devotion to God and to France. The Dauphin however would not now let her go. He commanded her to remain at the head of his army. At this a great indecision came upon Joan. Against her judgment she obeyed him, and from the moment of her yielding to his will, instead of to her own inner counsellors, her Voices deserted her; her inspiration fled. Her path from now on was the sad downward path of defeat.

Joan wished to proceed at once against Paris, but the King hesitated and so gave the English time to prepare their defense. When the assault at last was made, it was repulsed, and Joan was severely wounded. Yet they had to drag her away from the foot of the ramparts to make her abandon the conflict. The next day the King utterly refused to renew the attack though Joan answered for its success. He was not willing to exert himself any further; he must resume his indolent ease. Therefore he stubbornly insisted on a retreat. With a heart full of grief, Joan followed the King. It was her first defeat and it instantly dispelled the implicit faith of the people in her. One sent of God they argued could never be defeated. Little they knew that since the coronation at Rheims it had been the King's will and not the inspiration of God to which Joan had been obedient. Thinking there had been enough of fighting and wishing to put a stop to Joan's successes, the courtiers induced Charles to disband his army and give up all further activity against the invaders. A sad situation for Joan. Taking unceremonious leave of the King, she went to help the French wherever they were still fighting.

At length, after many adventures, Joan came to Compiègne to lead the garrison out against the Burgundians who pressed them hard, but the English came to the aid of the Burgundians and the French gave back, carrying Joan unwillingly with them in the midst of their retreat. When she and her party came under the walls of Compiègne, they found the gates closed. The commander of the city whom Joan had come to succor, had deliberately shut her out from the shelter of its walls. With her back against the bank of the moat, Joan still defended herself till a whole troop rushed upon her. Nor did she ever surrender but was dragged by her flowing garments from her horse and taken prisoner. From the walls of the city the governor saw her taken but raised not a finger to save her.

So Joan fell into the hands of her bitter enemies who hated her for her successes against them, and after a few months, the Burgundians sold her to the English. All this time, Charles whom she had made King of France, never offered to ransom her, nor

FROM THE TOWER WINDOW

from now on through her time of trial showed the slightest interest in her. Shut up in the dungeon of the Castle at Rouen, she was guarded day and night by soldiers whose brutality and insults she was forced to endure. But now to her joy her Voices came back to console and support her. Once more she had the unspeakable comfort of knowing that God was with her.

At length she was given over to the inquisition for trial. To the insidious questions of her judges the unhappy maiden had nothing to oppose but the uprightness and simplicity of her heart. "Take good heed what you do," she said, "for truly I am sent by God and you put yourselves in great peril."

She was nevertheless condemned as a heretic and sorceress and ordered to be burnt at the stake in the market place at Rouen. On the thirtieth of May, 1431, she was led to the place of execution. At the foot of the pile, she asked for a cross, and she died with the name of Jesus on her lips, her eyes bright as with triumph and her whole face transfigured with the consolation of hearkening to her Voices. All were weeping, even the executioners and judges, and a great fear came upon all.

A TALE OF THE CID AND HIS DAUGHTERS

Retold from Spanish Chronicles of the Cid

IN the days when throngs of black-skinned Moors, swarming across from the African shores, had overrun the fair lands of Spain, when the slender towers and minarets of many a graceful Moorish castle crowned heights that once had owned Spanish sway, then arose the most dearly loved of all Spanish heroes to fight against these intruders, Ruy Diaz, called Cid or Chief, and Cam-pe-a-dor' or Champion.

In the Cid was embodied all the peculiarly Spanish spirit, its faults and its noblest virtues. Faults in truth he had—many and ugly, but largely they were the faults of his time, results of the sadly mistaken standards held good in that long-vanished age. And in spite of his faults, he looms up head and shoulders above the men that surround him, a figure of courage and loyalty, so far as he understood those virtues in a century of darkness.

"I ask nothing but justice of heaven and of man only a fair field!" Such was the standard with which the Cid faced life and fared forth on his adventures. For long years there was no sword so ready and gallant as his in loyal defence of his king, no heart so staunch to maintain the best that it knew of honor. And so there rose those about the King, Don Alfonso, who grew jealous of the Cid and sought to find occasion to incense the King against him. The greater the number of victories won by the Cid against the Moors, the greater grew the number of foes who envied him his honors. At last these petty enemies poisoned Alfonso's mind and persuaded him that the Cid was in secret league with the Moors. In a fury Alfonso ordered his faithful servant at once into exile.

And so the day came when Ruy Diaz must leave his home and the country he had so earnestly aimed to serve. With eyes overflowing with tears he looked back and saw the hall deserted where he had lived so happily, household chests unfastened and empty and thrown about in confusion, doors left carelessly open, and balcony and garden all bare of their graceful seats. It was a sad and mournful sight. But as the Cid rode away there were many good men who went with him, among whom was none more beloved than Alvar Fañez, his cousin. News of the Campeador's banishment spread like wild fire over Castile. People were both indignant and dismayed for they loved their champion whole heartedly and trusted in him above all others to defend them from the Moors. Therefore many left homes and high offices to follow him into exile.

As he rode through the streets of Burgos, where he was born, the people stood weeping beside the road, yet not one of them dared to offer him even so much as a single night's lodging, for Alfonso in his anger had sent letters to the city forbidding the people to shelter the Cid under pain of the direst penalty. So they who loved him could only greet him with tears, nor had they the heart to tell him of the stern edict against him. At length a little maid summoned the courage to tell the great chief the truth. Sadly he turned away, outlawed from his best-beloved city.

Now the wife of Ruy Diaz, the lovely Xi-me'na, with her two little daughters, was at this time at the monastery of St. Peter's beyond Burgos, and thither the Cid made his way. In the gray light of dawn, while the inmates of the monastery were still at their prayers, he and his company appeared at the gates. In the courtyard, beneath the flaming smoky light of torches and tapers, the Cid caught his little girls up in his arms and embraced his beloved wife. The Abbot made a great feast for the Campeador that day, but on the following morning, after giving into the Abbot's hands a sum of money for the support of his wife and children, the Cid bade farewell to them all. He embraced and blessed Doña Ximena and the little girls and wept over them for he knew not how long they were to be parted, then he rode sadly away. But he looked back continually over his shoulder so long as his dear ones remained in sight.

Man of no country that the Cid was now, he must needs win himself a country. So he and his followers rode straight against the Moors. Battle after battle he fought with the intruders till the time of his exile had stretched into many years. Gradually eight towns owned his sway and at length, in the year 1094, he succeeded in capturing the great Moorish stronghold of Va-len'ci-a and restoring it to Christianity. Now that he had once more a fixed abiding place, there rose in his heart the deep longing to have his beloved wife and sweet daughters with him again. So he sent Alvar Fañez loaded with gifts to the King to pray him to allow Doña Ximena and her children to come to Valencia.

When Alvar Fañez delivered his message and gifts to the King reporting how Ruy Diaz had conquered Valencia and many other cities and castles in the name of the crown of Castile, Don Alfonso was greatly rejoiced. True, the Cid's old enemies began to murmur, "Any man could have done as much!" But the years that were past had enabled the King to estimate more justly the faith of his most loyal subject, and he cried to these petty foes, "Hold your peace! For in all things, Ruy Diaz the Cid serves me better than any among you!" He not only granted permission to Doña Ximena and her train to go to the Cid, but offered to send a guard with them to the border.

How joyously then Doña Ximena and her daughters, Elvira and Sol, set out from the monastery to rejoin the husband and father they had not seen for so many years. As the cavalcade drew near Valencia, the Cid came forth to meet them riding the beautiful horse Ba-bi-e'ca that he had won from the Moors. A venerable figure he was, for in the day of his exile he had vowed never to cut his beard until he should be recalled, and thus the hair on his chin had grown to such remarkable length that it had to be bound back out of his way by means of silken cords. The meeting of husband and wife, father and daughters was too full of joy for words. Smiles and tears alone could express what

was in their hearts. Then the Cid led Ximena and her daughters into Valencia and showed them over the whole great city which owned him lord. He showed them the shady gardens and the sea, and from the top of the Al-ca-zar', the highest tower of the town, he bade them look out over all the rich and far-reaching countryside that he had restored to Castile.

For many months thereafter, nothing disturbed the Cid's happy life with his family, but in the following spring, came King Yu-cef of Morocco with fifty thousand Moors to lay siege to Valencia. The Cid's own forces numbered no more than four thousand, yet he had no thought but of victory. Soon after the Moors had encamped he arranged that some of his troops should make their way secretly out of the town and attack the foe from behind while he pressed them in the front. The Moors, caught thus between two forces, and greatly over-estimating the numbers of their foe, fled in a panic, allowing the Cid an overwhelming victory, and leaving behind to fall into his hands, huge quantities of treasure. Among other things there was a splendid tent, supported by two pillars of gold, and this, with two hundred horses, Ruy Diaz ordered sent as a gift to the King. The horses, each with a sword at the saddle and led by a child, were presented to the King by Alvar Fañez along with the splendid tent of King Yucef. Alfonso was overcome and admitted that never before had a Spanish king received such a gift from a vassal.

Now there were present at this ceremony two worthless young men of noble family named Di-e'go and Fer-ran'do Gon-za'les, the In-fan'tes of Carrion. These young men stood high in the favor of Alfonso because of the importance of their family, but at heart they were selfish and vain, cowardly and cruel. Perceiving what rich gifts the Cid was able to send the King they schemed between them to possess themselves of some of his wealth by suing for the hands of his two daughters. The King leant a willing ear to their proposal, and he bade Alvar Fañez tell the Cid that he had promised the maids in marriage to the Infantes of Carrion.

Such was the message that Alvar Fañez bore back to the Cid and his wife. And sad were they to receive it. Their daughters were no more than thirteen or fourteen years old and though that was not unusually young in those days for maidens to wed, still they had thought to keep unbroken for some time to come their little family circle that had been for many long years so sadly separated. Moreover, their hearts much misgave them as to the nature of these two Infantes.

"And yet," sighed the good Doña Ximena, "if it be the King's will, what can we do to prevent it?"

And so the Cid bent to the wishes of the King, obedient as ever. Then there was much hurrying to and fro, both in the court of Castile and the city of Valencia. Clothes were furbished up, horses and mules were brought out, richly caparisoned, and the Infantes of Carrion devised for themselves the richest of toilets.

At length the Cid, leaving his wife and daughters, went to

320

FROM THE TOWER WINDOW

meet his future sons-in-law with a most magnificent retinue. The Infantes were escorted to the banks of the Tagus River by Don Alfonso himself. There for the first time in many years, the King and Ruy Diaz met. The King marveled much at the Cid's remarkable beard and was almost overawed by his dignity and the pomp with which he was surrounded. When the Cid entertained Don Alfonso and the Infantes at a banquet, the chief men were served from dishes of gold and no one was asked to eat from aught less precious than silver. The Infantes were quite dazzled by the sight of so much treasure and were more than ever anxious to wed the Campeador's daughters.

When the banquet was over, the King having assured himself that Ruy Diaz meant to obey him, returned to his home, while the Cid escorted the Infantes to Valencia. Doña Ximena and the two young girls received Diego and Ferrando with every grace, and all things were done to make them comfortable and happy. In due season the wedding took place and the festivities lasted for fifteen days. Gala arches were raised in the streets, rich tapestries and embroideries were hung out from the balconies, and ladies flung down garlands on the bridal couples as they passed.

After the wedding the Infantes still lingered with their brides in Valencia, and now, alas! the Cid could not but see with deep sorrow that his sons-in-law possessed neither courage nor nobility. One afternoon it happened while the Cid lay sleeping in the hall, that a huge lion, kept in a cage in the courtyard, escaped from its keepers. The Infantes and others were playing at chess in the room with the sleeping Cid when they were suddenly startled half out of their wits by seeing the lion glaring angrily just at their very elbows. All present, with the exception of the Infantes, thought first of the sleeping Cid, and rushed to his side to protect him. But Diego and Ferrando thought of naught but their own precious skins. Ferrando, the younger, scrambled under the bench where the Cid was lying and with such speed

 that he burst his doublet and tore his mantle, while Diego fled to a door which opened down into the courtyard, and blindly jumping out, fell among the lees of a wine press, thus making himself ridiculous and utterly spoiling his finery.

At the sound of the lion's roar the Cid awoke and seeing at a glance what had occurred, he sprang forward, laid one powerful hand on the lion's mane and led him back to his cage. It was some time before Ferrando, pale and trembling, crawled out from his retreat, and Diego, wet and dirty, came in from the courtyard, but when they did appear, the whole company set up a shout and spared no laughter at their expense. Stung by the ridicule, the two young cowards felt compelled when next the Moors threatened the city, to make a great show of bravery and they boasted loudly of the mighty deeds which they should do in the battle. This appearance of courage delighted the old hero, but when Diego saw a stout Moor bearing furiously down upon him in the midst of the encounter, he took to his heels and fled. Just then a Spanish soldier appearing on the scene, slew the Moor, and Diego stopped running long enough to purchase from the victor the horse of the fallen Moor. He then returned to the city and boasted of the horse as a trophy which he himself had won by his bravery in the battle. The Cid was again delighted, but in a few days the truth of the matter leaked out and the Infantes became the objects of still more ridicule than before.

At length Ferrando and Diego began to resent so deeply the mockery that met them, that, being altogether unwilling to admit themselves to blame, they argued by some round about method that the Cid was responsible for it all, and they planned to be revenged on him in the cruellest manner possible. They would strike at him through his daughters, his lovely and innocent daughters. So they went to the Cid and said: "We have lingered here for two years with you nor ever presented our brides to our parents. Pray let us take them back to Carrion."

The thought of losing his daughters tore at the Cid's tender heart. "When ye take away my daughters," he said, "ye take my very heart strings. Nevertheless it is fitting that you should present them to your parents."

Doña Ximena's consent to her daughters' going was not yielded so readily, but at length her judgment was overborne and she and the Cid regretfully bade their daughters farewell while the lovely young things wept bitter tears at leaving their dearly loved parents. As a token of affection at parting, the Cid bestowed on his sons his two most valuable swords, Ti-zo'na and Co-la'da, won in course of battles against the Moors, and he sent his nephew, Felez Muñoz, along as escort to his daughters.

Two days after leaving Valencia, the Infantes prepared to carry out their revenge. They came at sunset to a beautiful oak forest called the Oak-wood of Corpes and here they prepared to spend the night. The trees grew thickly about, and wild mountains shut in the spot, abounding in savage beasts, but there was a clear green glade in the midst of the forest with a cool fountain near by and for this reason it was chosen for the encampment. At sunrise next day the mules were loaded and the cavalcade arranged in marching order when the Infantes gave orders for all to move on without them, saying that they should follow later in company with their wives. Slowly and much against their will, the escort under Felez Muñoz passed on out of sight and hearing, and the four were left alone.

"Why are we left thus alone?" asked Doña Elvira trembling.

"You shall soon see," said Diego sternly.

Then these two infamous wretches seized the girls by their hair, beat them cruelly and kicked them with their spurs. After this they stripped them of their rich ermine furs and their mantles, and left them grievously wounded at the mercy of any wild beast.

Now, Felez Muñoz, though he had ridden on ahead, liked not the looks of things, and being full of the darkest misgivings, he left the escort at length and rode back at full speed to the fountain. There he found his cousins alone and in such pitiful plight that they could not even speak. Casting his own cloak about the nearly naked women he bore them tenderly to a neighboring thicket and there he watched over them all night for he dared not leave them to go in quest of aid lest some savage beast attack them. Strong man that he was, he wept pitying tears over those two innocent girls who had suffered so unspeakable an indignity.

At dawn he hurried off to a neighboring village and there found a husbandman who was deeply bound by a debt of gratitude to the Cid. With his help the two girls were brought to the village and tenderly cared for in the husbandman's cottage, while Felez Muñoz rode off to tell Ruy Diaz what had occurred. On his way to Valencia, Felez met Alvar Fañez proceeding with a gift of Moorish treasures from Ruy Diaz to the King. Hearing the sad tale of Felez, Alvar Fañez went on in great grief and repeated the news to the King. Furiously angry, and knowing himself to blame for the marriage, Alfonso promised to hold a Cor'tes[1] in three months at Toledo, and there force the infamous Infantes to answer for their deed.

As to the Cid, when he heard what had happened to his beloved daughters, he wept bitter tears, yet he cried sternly to those followers who urged him to take speedy vengeance on the criminals, "Nay! Justice shall come to me through the Cortes. Do not stir mine anger more. I wish not to commit a deed of violence. I will wait the course of the law!"

Alvar Fañez, in returning, stopped at the village where the two girls had found refuge, richly rewarded the faithful husbandman, and brought them under his protection back to Valencia. The Cid came out two leagues to meet them, but now he wept no more. He greeted them with cheerful smiles though all of

[1] *Legislative assembly*

his company wept, and he soothed them tenderly saying, "Ye are come home, my children, and God will heal you." Thus the girls were restored to the arms of their mother and father.

On the day appointed for the meeting of the Cortes, the Cid went with much magnificence to Toledo, and he was there honored with a splendid seat at the very side of the King. Then came the craven Infantes, most unwillingly, to answer before the assembly for the crime which they had committed. Quietly, with splendid dignity, the Cid arose from his ivory throne. First he but asked the return of his two good swords. Glad to get off so easily, the Infantes produced them at once. Then the Cid demanded the return of all the money he had given the youths at parting. This they were not so willing to yield, but to this request also they agreed, hoping again that no more would be demanded. A third time the Cid arose and now at last he thundered forth such a denunciation, described the dastardly crime in such burning words that all men shrank away from the shame-faced Infantes and the Cortes decreed as one man that the young cowards must answer for their crime by facing in the lists, any knights whom the Campeador might choose. This was a terrible decree to such cravens as Diego and Ferrando.

The day of combat came and they stood in the lists against the Cid's most powerful champions. In such cowardly wise did they acquit themselves, that they were most infamously defeated. Thereafter they were made to confess their crime publicly and ever more suffered the scorn and contempt of all good men.

As to the Cid, he returned home with honor to his wife and daughters and not long thereafter the Princes of Aragon and Navarre proposed for the hands of the lovely young damsels. These two youths proved most worthy husbands and the Doñas Elvira and Sol at length found a well-deserved happiness which brought joy to the hearts of their mother and that hale old hero, their father, Ruy Diaz, the Campeador and Cid.

A PERFECT KNIGHT
GEOFFREY CHAUCER

A knyght ther was, and that a worthy man,
That fro the tymé that he first bigan
To riden out, he lovéd chivalrie,
Trouthe and honour, fredom and curteisie.
Ful worthy was he in his lordés werre, [1]
And therto had he riden, no man ferre, [2]
As wel in cristendom as in hethenesse,
And ever honoured for his worthynesse—
And though that he were worthy, he was wys,
And of his porte as meeke as is a mayde.
He never yet no vileynye ne sayde
In al his lyf, unto no maner wight.
He was a verray parfit, gentil knyght.

[1] wars. [2] farther.

FROM THE TOWER WINDOW

SIR BEAUMAINS, THE KITCHEN KNIGHT

A Legend of the Round Table

The King will follow Christ, and we the King
In whom high God hath breathed a secret thing.
Fall, battle axe, and flash brand!   Let the King reign!

It befell in the days of King Arthur, that there dwelt in Orkney with the old King Lot and Bel'li-cent, his queen, one last tall son, young Ga'reth, his elder brothers being gone to serve the King at Cam'e-lot. And Bellicent, yearning in her heart to keep her last born by her side to cheer the empty loneliness of her vast reechoing halls, would never yield consent that Gareth should leave his father and herself to follow Arthur. Still, Gareth never ceased from longing that he too might go to Cam'e-lot to serve the king,—to ride abroad redressing human wrongs, and wiping all things base from out the world.

"Ah, mother," he would cry, "how can you hold me tethered to your side? Man am I grown, a man's work must I do. I must follow the Christ, the King,—live pure, speak true, right wrong, follow the King. Else wherefore was I born?"

So Gareth besought his mother continually until at last Queen Bellicent was wearied of his prayers and cried:

"Go, if thou wilt. But an thou goest I shall hold this one requirement fast. Thou shalt disguise thyself as a kitchen-knave and serve amongst the scullions, nor ever tell thine own right name for a twelvemonth and a day."

By this request the Queen thought secretly to keep her Gareth by her side, for never did she dream that he would still persist, and take his way to Arthur's service through such mean and lowly vassalage. A moment Gareth stood silent. Then he cried, "Though I be but a thrall in person, I shall still be free in soul! And I shall see the jousts." And so he went.

In company with two old servitors clad like tillers of the soil, he journeyed to Camelot. And there at last, upon the royal mount, he saw the city rising, her spires and turrets pricking through the silver mists and flashing in the sun. Beneath the splendid carven gate he entered in, and ever and anon a knight with flashing arms would pass him by. From bower and casement lovely ladies glanced and through the busy streets a healthful people went about the business of the day in such security as comes from sure protection of a strong and gracious king.

Thus Gareth passed on to King Arthur's hall and there beheld the great king seated on his throne in all the majesty of mighty manhood, his tall knights ranged about, their eyes clear shining with the light of honor and affection and of faith in their great king. Thither came many more to make requests or seek for justice of the king, but in his turn young Gareth stood before the throne and cried: "A boon, sir King! I beg thee that thou give me place to serve among thy kitchen knaves a twelvemonth and a day, nor ask my name."

"Fair son," said Arthur, "thou seemest a goodly youth and worth a goodlier boon. But if thou askest nothing more, then have this, thy request. Serve under my steward, Sir Kay."

Now Sir Kay was a surly man of sour and evil temper.

"I undertake this fellow is a villain born!" he cried. "Doubtless he hath broken from some abbey or castle where he had not beef and brewis enow! But an he do well his work for me, he shall be fed like any hog."

"Nay," cried Sir Lancelot. "Methinks thou dost not truly judge the lad. He looks like one of noble lineage who hides some secret in his scullion's clothes."

"Noble lineage!" scoffed Sir Kay. "An he were noble, he would ask for horse and armor. Noble, forsooth! Sir Beaumains, Sir Fair-hands! Since thou hast no other name, I dub thee Fair-hands. Off with thee to thy knightly post beside the spit, Sir Fair-hands!"

FROM THE TOWER WINDOW

Thus it was young Gareth came by the name of Beaumains, which meaneth Fair-hands. Obedient to Sir Kay, he served within the sooty kitchen, turning the spit, drawing water, hewing wood, washing the greasy pots and kettles, and sleeping at night midst grimy kitchen knaves. And ever Sir Kay would harry him and hustle him and mock him beyond all others of his fellows. Yet for a twelvemonth and a day Gareth endured in patience and without complaint, and sometimes when there were jousts, Sir Kay would nod him leave to go. Forgetful then of aught besides, he watched the combats eagerly, and ever Sir Lancelot and others of the courtliest knights bespoke him fair, reverencing in spite of all his kitchen clothes, the nobleness writ on his face.

So passed the time till Gareth had fulfilled in all good faith his vow unto his mother. Then he sought the King alone and told him all his tale.

"O King," he cried. "Make me thy knight in secret. Let no man know my name until I make a name. But give me the first quest!"

"Make thee my knight?" the King spake thoughtfully. "My knights are sworn to vows of utter hardihood, of utter purity and gentleness, of uttermost obedience to the King."

But Gareth in full fire of youthful spirits answered, "O my King, for hardiness I promise thee. For uttermost obedience make demand of Kay, no gentle master to have served."

Whereat the King, loving his lusty youthhood, yielded half unwillingly. "So be it! I will make thee my knight in secret."

That same day there came into the hall, attended by her page, a lovely damsel with a brow of may-blossom and a cheek of apple-blossom and a nose tip-tilted like the petal of a flower.

"O King," she cried, "Lynette's my name. I come of noble lineage. Pray give me succor for my sister, the lady Ly'o-nors' who by a savage tyrant is shut up within her castle. About her dwelling place a river runs in three great loops and at each pass

329

across the stream, three hideous brothers of the tyrant stand,—all men that ride abroad to do but what they will, nor make acknowledgment of any law or king, and hate the very name of Arthur. These three are horrible enough, but he, the fourth, who keeps the last ward by the castle itself, a huge man-beast is he of boundless savagery. He always rideth armed in black and bears a ghastly skeleton on his arms. Such are those four that hold my sister prisoner to force her, will or nill, to wed with one of them. So am I come to thee to beg the best of all thy knights, Sir Lancelot, to save her from the clutches of these beasts."

Hereat rose up the kitchen-knave, Beaumains, and called with kindling eyes, above the throng, "A boon, Sir King! Grant me the quest!"

Much wondered all in that vast hall to hear a wretched scullion speak like this, but Arthur mindful of his promise, said, "The quest is thine! I grant it to thee! Go!"

Then was the damsel wroth.

"Fie on thee, King," she cried. "I asked for thy chief knight and thou hast given me but a kitchen knave." And she in anger took her horse and fled away.

With that, came one and told Beaumains that horse and armor stood ready for him—the gift of Arthur. And when he was armed therein, there were but few so goodly men as he. The people marveled, and the kitchen thralls, pressing from out the kitchen to see one who had worked more lustily than any among them, mounted and in arms, threw up their caps and shouted loud. Through midst of all this shouting Gareth rode away.

As he drew near Lynette, he cried, "Damsel, the quest is mine. Lead and I follow."

But Lynette with petulant thumb and finger nipped her slender nose—"Away!" she shrilled. "Thou smellest all of kitchen grease! And look behind! There cometh he, Sir Kay, thy master, to reclaim his kitchen-knave!"

FROM THE TOWER WINDOW

For Kay, angered at seeing his underling thus sent on knightly quest, had come pursuing with hot haste, in confidence that he should prick the bubble of the young lad's pride by hurling him at once into the dust and so return him to his kitchen vassalage.

And as he rode, the steward bawled, "Ho, Sir Beaumains, Sir Fair-hands, wait. Know ye not me, your master?"

"Master no more!" quoth Gareth. "Thou art the most ungentle knight in Arthur's court!"

Therewith Sir Kay ran furiously upon him. Sir Gareth met the charge, but at the first shock of encounter, Sir Kay fell to the ground so stunned he could not rise. Then Gareth once again cried to the damsel, "Lead and I follow!"

Fast she fled away at full speed of her horse and when Sir Gareth won her side, she cried, "Weenest thou that I think the more of thee because through some mischance thou hast overthrown thy master? Nay, broach-turner and dish-washer, to me thou smellest all of kitchen as before."

"Damsel," said Sir Gareth, "say to me what ye list, I will not leave you whatsoever ye say, for I have undertaken of King Arthur for to achieve your adventure and I shall finish it unto the end."

Maddened at his good words, the damsel flashed away again down the long avenues of the boundless wood. So they rode on until the dusk when from a hill-top they espied below a gloomy hollow, in the deeps whereof a mere, red as the round eye of an owl, glared in the half dead sunset. And there came flying toward them from the wood a serving man in great affright.

"O my lord," he cried to Gareth, "help me! For hereby are six thieves that have taken my master and bound him fast. They hate him for that it hath been his work to keep this forest ever free from thieves, and even now they are about to slay him."

"Bring me thither," Sir Gareth said.

Into the darkening pines they plunged and there, amid black shadows, saw six tall men haling a seventh along with a stone about his neck to drown him in the mere. Sir Gareth rode full boldly on the thieves. One at his first stroke he struck to earth and then another and a third. Thereat the other three in terror, fled, and Gareth was left master of the field. Right courteously he loosed the prisoner's bonds and took the stone from off his neck. He proved to be a stalwart baron, Arthur's friend, who thanked Sir Gareth gratefully and prayed him to ride back unto his castle that he might there reward him for his deed.

"Sir," said Sir Gareth sharply. "I will have no reward. For the deed's sake only did I do the deed."

And with his lady he rode on again. But Lynette bespake him all as haughtily as before. "Scullion, think not that I accept thee aught the more for running down these craven fellows with thy spit! A thresher with his flail had scattered them as easily. Nay, for thou smellest of the kitchen still."

Sir Gareth only answered, "Say thy say, and I will do my deed!"

Thus they rode on, and ever the lady chid him as before. That night they rested in the wood and on the morrow rose and brake their fast, then took their horses and rode on their way. The sun was scarcely risen above the tree-tops when at length they reached the first pass of the stream that coiled about the castle. Beyond a bridge that spanned the river with a single arch there rose a silk pavilion, yellow in hue with yellow banner flying, and before it paced a knight of huge, gigantic mould in yellow armor. When the Yellow Knight espied the damsel he cried out, "Ho, Damsel, hast thou brought this knight from Arthur's court to be thy champion?"

"Nay! nay, Sir Knight," Lynette quoth shrilly. "This is but a kitchen knave sent by King Arthur in much scorn of thee!" And turning to Sir Gareth she said, "Sir Scullion, flee now while thou mayest. For here stands one thou wilt not dare to face. Flee down the valley ere he gets to horse and none will cry thee shame. For thou art not knight but knave!"

FROM THE TOWER WINDOW

Said Gareth, "Damsel, I had liefer fight a score of knights than bear the stinging wounds of words like thine!"

Then cried the Yellow Knight, "A kitchen knave and sent in scorn of me! With such I will not deign to fight! I will but hurl him from his horse then take his steed and arms, and so return him to his cursed king!"

"Dog!" cried Sir Gareth, " 'twere well to win my horse and arms ere making thus much talk of taking them!"

He spake and all at fiery speed the two shocked on the bridge. Their spears both bent but did not break and both knights shot from out their saddles to the ground. Full quickly they arose and drew their swords and Gareth lashed so fiercely with his brand he drave his enemy backward down the bridge, whereat the damsel cried, "Well stricken, kitchen-knave!" So fought they till Sir Gareth laid his enemy grovelling on the ground. Then cried the fallen, "Take not my life! I yield!" And Gareth said, "So this damsel ask it of me, good!—then will I spare thy life."

"Insolent scullion!" cried Lynette, and all her face flushed rosy red. "I ask of thee? I will be bound for nothing unto thee!"

"Then shall he die!" And Gareth there unlaced his helmet as to slay him, but she shrilled, "Be not so hard, Sir Scullion!"

"Damsel," Sir Gareth said, "thy charge to me is pleasure. At thy command his life is spared. Arise, Sir Knight, and pass to Arthur's hall! See that thou crave his pardon for thy crimes. Thy shield is mine! Farewell! And, damsel, lead and I follow!"

Fast away she fled. "Methought but now," she cried, "when I watched thee striking on the bridge, the savor of thy kitchen came upon me a little faintlier, but the wind hath changed. I scent it twenty fold!"

Sir Gareth answered laughingly, "The knave that doth thee full service of a knight is all as good, meseems, as any knight toward freeing of thy sister!"

"Sir Knave," she cried, "thou art peacocked up with thy

success! But at this next turning thou wilt meet thy match!"

So when they reached the second river loop, they saw across a shallow ford a second huge knight all in green armor. Beholding with Lynette one bearing his brother's shield, he cried, "Is that my brother there with thee?"

"Nay!" piped Lynette, "this is but a kitchen knave that hath overthrown thy brother and taken his arms."

"False traitor!" bawled the Green Knight, "thou shalt die!"

Therewith he blew a blast upon a horn all green. There came three damsels from a green pavilion and armed him with a shield and spear, both green. Astride a monstrous horse he rushed upon Sir Gareth. In mid stream they met. At the first shock they brake their spears, and then they drew their swords and each gave other battle. A long while they fought thus, but at the last Sir Gareth smote the Green Knight such a buffet on the helm, that he fell heavily on his knees and yielded him. "O pray thee, slay me not, Sir Knight!" he begged. And so Sir Gareth sent him likewise to the king. Once more he cried unto Lynette, "Lead and I follow!" Quietly she led.

Said Gareth, "Hath the wind not changed again?"

"Nay, not a point! Right soon thou shalt be overcome!"

So they rode on and by mid-afternoon came to the last loop of the river. Here on a grassy plain there rose a silk pavilion all blood red, and round about on dark and mournful elms were hanging by the neck nigh forty goodly knights,—a woful sight!

"These knights," the damsel said, "came hither to do battle for my sister. All these the Red Knight overcame and put to such a shameful death. In the same wise will he serve thee!"

"A shameful knight who useth shameful customs," Gareth cried. "I fear him not!"

And then they saw fast by the stream a sycamore tree and thereon hung an horn, the greatest that ever they saw, made all of an elephant's bone. Thereunto Sir Gareth spurred his horse

and blew the horn so eagerly that all the forest rang. The Red Knight issued forth completely armed—a huge and threatening figure looming up in sinister blood red.

"Beware, Sir Fool," he roared. "Hath not the sight of yonder knights taught thee thou shouldst beware?"

"Weenest thou that such a shameful sight should make me fear? Nay, truly, it but causes me to have more hardihood to meet with thee!"

And so the two knights shocked together on the bridge. Both fell from off their horses and addressed themselves to battle on foot. A fearful struggle followed, for this knight had thrice the strength and fierceness of the other two. Like boars they fought. They hewed great pieces from their harness and their shields. Oft Gareth brought the Red Knight to his knees, but ever he vaulted up again and smote the harder, till Sir Gareth panted with the long-drawn struggle. But now Lynette called out, "Well done, knave-knight! Well stricken, knight-knave! O knave as noble as any knight, strike! thou art worthy of the Table Round! Strike! Strike! The wind will never change again!"

When Sir Gareth heard her speaking thus, he doubled his pace, and smote his foe so thick he drave him to the bridge's edge, and there at last forced that foul slayer of men to lose his footing, so he fell head long to the stream. And then Sir Gareth cried again unto Lynette, "Lead and I follow!" But the damsel full gently said, "I lead no longer. Ride thou at my side. Thou art the kingliest of kitchen knaves! Shamed am I that I so reviled thee. But I am noble and did think the King had scorned me to give me but a kitchen knave, and now thy pardon, friend, for thou art wholly brave yet ever courteous and gentle withal."

"Damsel, thou art not all to blame," Sir Gareth said. "I should have small esteem for any knight who let a maiden's words arouse his anger!"

Then cried the damsel, "Now thou hast done enough! Wonders thou hast done. Miracles thou canst not! Turn back and fetch Sir Lancelot to meet this last gigantic knave. I dare not have thee face this hideous man-monster who guards my sister's castle. So terrible is he that he never shows his face by day. But I have watched him like a phantom glide about at night. Nor have I ever heard his voice. Always he hath made a mouthpiece of his page who still reported him as having in himself the strength of ten. He calleth himself Death! O I beg thee face him not!"

But Gareth only went more straightly forward. Thus they came in gloomy twilight dusk upon the castle and there before it rose a huge pavilion all in black beside which hung a long black horn. Sir Gareth grasped the horn and blew a mighty blast. Within the palace lights began to twinkle, and high up in the tower, at one bright window Lady Lyonors appeared. Below came sound of muffled voices through the gloom, and hollow tramplings up and down while weird, misshapen shadows flitted past. Three times Sir Gareth blew his eager blast. Then through the black pavilion's gloomy folds, high on a coal-black steed there issued slowly forth the monster-knight in coal black arms, whereon in white a ghastly skeleton gleamed and on his helm a grinning skull. In the half light he came advancing but he spake no word. Thereat in indignation Gareth called, "Fool! Canst

336

FROM THE TOWER WINDOW

thou not trust the strength thy God hath given thee, but to make the terror of thee more, must trick thyself out thus?"

Still the monster spake no word which made the horror of him all the more. His black horse bounded forward. Sir Gareth met him with a steady shock. Then lo! what wonder came to pass! He of that fearful aspect, fell at the first encounter easily to ground. He rose and with one stroke Sir Gareth clove the grinning skull and helmet underneath. And out from all that trickery of terror issued but the bright face of a blooming boy.

"O Knight!" he cried. "Slay me not! My brothers bade me do it to make a horror all about the place! They never dreamed their passes would be passed."

Thus was the Lady Lyonors set free and in the castle was high revel held that eventide, that after all their foolish fears he whom they had so dreaded, was proven but a blooming boy. And in good time, some say, Sir Gareth won Lynette to be his bride.

OPPORTUNITY*

Edward Rowland Sill

This I beheld, or dreamed it in a dream:
There spread a cloud of dust along a plain,
And underneath the cloud, or in it, raged
A furious battle, and men yelled, and swords
Shocked upon swords and shields.   A prince's banner
Wavered, then staggered backward, hemmed by foes.

A craven hung along the battle's edge,
And thought: "Had I a sword of keener steel—
That blue blade that the king's son bears,—but this
Blunt thing!" He snapped and flung it from his hand,
And lowering crept away and left the field.

Then came the king's son, wounded, sore bestead,
And weaponless, and saw the broken sword,
Hilt buried in the dry and trodden sand,
And ran and snatched it, and with battle shout
Lifted afresh, he hewed his enemy down,
And saved a great cause on that heroic day.

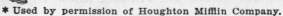

* Used by permission of Houghton Mifflin Company.

FRITHJOF, THE VIKING
Retold from the Norse Saga of Frithjof

IN THE royal halls King Be'le reigned. Power and might were his, and descent from a noble line of kings, yet his best beloved friend, his old brother-in-arms, closest of all to his heart, was none other than Thor'sten the Viking, born of no royal blood, but son of an humble yeoman. Staunch were the hearts of these two in devotion to one another. As the fast-passing winters silvered their heads, their friendship only grew deeper and stronger. Throughout all the Northern lands, in hall and bower, the skalds sang songs of that beautiful friendship.

Now King Be'le had two sons and one lovely daughter, Ing'-e-borg the Fair. But Thor'sten had one only son, the stalwart stripling Frith'jof. When Ingeborg and Frithjof were little more than smiling babes, their fathers committed them to the care of a third trusty friend, old Hil'ding, who dwelt at a distance from the court in a rich and handsome farm-house that rose from the midst of well-kept barns and blossoming fields and pastures. There in sturdy simplicity Ingeborg and Frithjof passed together a pure and joyous childhood,—she a soft-budding, sweet-blushing rose, and he an oak, straight and lordly. How happy was he when, as a mere boy, he took her first in his swift-skimming skiff out on the blue waters of the fjord, and she clapped her hands in childish glee as he set the snowy sail; how happy when he first lifted her up to peer at the eggs and little ones in the nests of the beautiful song-birds that lay hidden amongst the trees. No brook was ever so wide and angry that he did not carry Ingeborg across, her little white arms tight about his neck, her head against his breast. The first blossom in the woodland peeping up beneath the snow, the first luscious ripened strawberry glowing red from its tangle of leaves, the first golden ear of corn,—he carried them all to his little queen.

But ah! almost before old Hilding knew it, it was no more

these childish treasures, but a great bear, slain without a weapon in breast to breast struggle, that the young hero bore slung across his shoulder to lay at Ingeborg's feet. When winter came and the long home evenings, with all the housemates gathered together before the blazing hearth, young Frithjof read aloud the ancient lays of Odin, the All-father, and Valhalla's heavenly halls, but not one of all the goddesses, not even Freya the Fair, seemed to Frithjof more lovely than his own sweet playmate sitting there in the ruddy glow of the flaming logs, her hair in golden ringlets, her brow as white as the new-driven snow, her blue eyes soft and gentle as the tender sky in spring.

And Ingeborg herself, as she sat at her loom through the day, singing the deeds of heroes, and weaving into her tapestry with wool of many colors the figures of knights and soldiers and the heroes of her singing, began to make her hero more like in face and bearing to the stately Frithjof. Above all others on earth Ingeborg and Frithjof loved each other.

Then the heart of old Hilding misgave him.

"Beware my son," he said to his ward. "Let not this love of thine master thee. No good can come of it. Remember, Ingeborg is daughter of a King and thou art but son to a yeoman."

But Frithjof laughed the warning to scorn.

"The free-born man is second to none," he cried. "The world is the freeman's. I will do such deeds that the King himself will be proud to give me his daughter."

Now came the day when old Bele and Thorsten sitting side by side in the palace with faces lined and marked till they looked like ancient rocks deeply graven with runes, spake thus to one another: "Our day is done. For earthly sights our eyes grow dim. Ever nearer shines Valhalla. Ere the white-armed Valkyrs with flying hair bear us off to those heavenly halls, let us call our sons before us and give them good counsel. They should be ever knit firmly together as we have been in closest unity and love."

339

So came the sons—first Bele's eldest, dark and gloomy with stern and sullen brow, Hel'ge, heir to the throne, then Half'dan, Bele's younger lad, with sunny locks and noble features, yet too soft,—a maid almost, in warrior's guise. Last of all came Frithjof, by a head the tallest of the three, standing between the King's two sons like the full and radiant noon between shy dawn and lowering dusk.

"Sons," spake the King, "my day is sinking low and yours will soon be breaking. As you are brothers, so be friends and rule the land in harmony. Let Power stand guard at your borders, that no enemy enter in, but let Peace hold gentle sway within the land in your safe keeping. Your swords should never threaten, but protect. Guard well your people and act ever in unity with them, for a king is naught without the people. Be never hard when thou art King, O Helge,—only firm. Remember, gentleness alone leads a noble heart to right-doing, even as the Spring's mild breath opens the earth which wintry frosts but harden. And thou, Halfdan, be mindful that cheerfulness graces a wise man, yet do carelessness and frivolity ill beseem a King."

When the King had made an end of speaking Thorsten thus addressed his son:

"Honor the gods, O Frithjof, for reverence becomes a man. Obey the King and never envy him whose place is above thine own. Thou hast great bodily strength, but remember, such a gift is worthless unless joined with wisdom to direct it right. Turn thee from evil; bend thy will to what is good and noble, and do right. Thus wilt thou not have lived in vain."

Many more were the loving words spoken by the old warriors on that day. They told the youths of their long friendship and how through joy and sorrow, they had ever stood together, hand in hand, sharing alike the changeful gifts of life. And both bequeathed their friendship to their sons as a jewel of greatest price. Last of all, King Bele committed his beloved daughter,

FROM THE TOWER WINDOW

Ingeborg, with many tender words, to the care of his two sons. "When we are gone," he said, "old friend Thorsten and I, lay our bodies in two mounds, which you shall raise, one on each side of the blue bay. Its waves shall sing our dirge, but when the pale moon pours on the mountains her silver sheen, and the midnight dew lies cool upon the fields, then we two will still commune together in closest comradeship. And now, sons, fare ye well. Go back to your work and play. For us, our way lies to All-father's halls,—the place of rest, for which we long as long the weary rivers for the sea. Go, and the grace of Frey and Thor and Odin go with you."

Not many months thereafter, Bele and Thorsten had departed from this life for the glories of Valhalla, and their bodies, as directed, lay side by side in mounds on each side of the bay. Then went a herald riding through the land from farm to farm, from home to home, summoning all the people to the Ting, the general meeting of true-hearted free-men, in whose breasts is safely housed the honor of the nation. There Helge and Halfdan were elected joint-kings to rule the realm together.

Frithjof too, entered now into his inheritance—the homestead of his father at Framnäs, with hills and valleys and woods, three miles each way, and the sea as boundary on one side. The heights were crowned with birchwood, and many a shining lake mirrored mountains and forests where antlered elks stalked majestic. In the gently sloping fields the golden barley ripened in the sun, and rye so tall that a man might hide in it. The green and blooming pastures in the valleys were dotted with herds of kine and flocks of sheep as white and fleecy as the cloudlets in the sky. In the stables there stood in stately rows four and twenty fiery steeds, their manes braided with red ribbons, their hoofs glistening with polished shoes. But the wonder of the place was the banquet-hall, a palace in itself, built solidly of fir-trunks. So large it was, that six hundred guests hardly filled

it at the Yule-tide feast. The table of oak stretched the whole
length of the hall, and was waxed to a polish as bright as steel.
The raised platform at the host's end was adorned with two
statues of gods, Odin with royal mien, and Frey with the sun on
his brow. Between the two was the host's seat, covered with a
huge black bearskin, with scarlet mouth and silver-mounted claws.
It seemed but yesterday that Thorsten himself sat there, gravely
and yet genially entertaining his friends while the logs blazed high
on the deep stone hearth in the middle of the hall, stars peered
down through the smoke-escape in the roof, and the firelight
gleamed and glinted from the armor that hung on the walls.

But of all the family treasures which now fell to Frithjof,
the most dearly prized were the ancient and peerless sword,
Ang'ur-wa'del, and the great dragon-ship, El-lide'. Long stretched
as a sea serpent rose the prow of Ellide, the neck swung aloft in
graceful curves, the head with red mouth wide open. Her sides
were blue, with spots of gold; at the stern her mighty tail uncoiled
in rings, silver scaled; her sails were black tipped with scarlet,
and when she unfurled them she could fly like the storm-wind,
and far exceed in fleetness the eagle's flight. When filled with
men in armor she seemed like a floating castle. Great was the
fame of that ship. Far and wide was she known as peerless in
the North. Over all these treasures now was Frithjof master, and
he sat at the funeral feast a tearful host on his father's seat which
should henceforth be his own.

When the earth had donned once more her robe of green, few
dragon-ships still lingered in the harbors. Most of that bold
craft had sallied forth on foreign ventures as was the Norseman's
wont. But Frithjof's thoughts did not roam the seas these moonlit nights of lovely May. He sought the solitude of the woods.
While Ellide swung restlessly in the harbor tugging at her anchor,
his thoughts were full of Ingeborg alone. And so one day he
loosed the ship. She bounded from her moorings, and bore him

FROM THE TOWER WINDOW

with swelling sails across the bay to the spot where Helge and Halfdan sat, on King Bele's grave-mound, holding open court of justice. Proudly, yet respectfully, Frithjof spoke.

"O Kings, I love fair Ingeborg as mine own soul, and crave her at your hands to be my bride. Such, surely, was your father's wish, for it was by his will we two grew up together. True, my father was neither king nor earl, yet he did such deeds as give his name high place in all the songs of skalds. I, myself, could easily win a kingdom, yet would I liefer stay at home and guard your realm for you, protecting with my sword your royal castle and the poor man's hut alike. We are here on your father's mound. Hear ye, his sons, and do as he would have wished."

But King Helge started to his feet and spake in scornful tones.

"Our sister is not for the bonder's[1] son. Though thou shouldst by force of arms compel men to hail thee greatest of all Norseland's sons, never should maid of Odin's blood mate with a low-born adventurer! Nor is there any call for thee to take thought for my realm. I can hold it and care for it myself. If thou wouldst be my servant, there is a place for thee amongst my men-at-arms!"

At words so hateful, the warm-welling spring of friendship in Frithjof's heart closed tight. Fierce burning wrath sprang up instead. In clarion tones he cried, "Thy servant I will never be, black-hearted King. Take heed that thou keep well thy boast and find no need for my good sword. It is a trusty blade." And he clove with one furious stroke King Helge's golden shield that hung on the limb of a tree above him. As it fell with an ominous clang to the ground, Frithjof strode from the place, black-browed with that anger that consumes like fire and withers in the human heart all gently springing buds of great and good desires.

Meantime, in a nearby kingdom dwelt the old King Ring, a man of such piety and wisdom as were famed throughout the Northland. The verdant valleys and shady woods of his happy realm never resounded with the evil noise of war. Peacefully the

[1] yeoman's

crops ripened there and roses bloomed, for Justice sat enthroned, severe yet gracious, on the judgment seat, and Freedom dwelt with Peace in happy harmony. At the meetings of the Ting, every man was free to speak his mind without restraint or fear, and like a father was the King beloved by all his subjects.

But now King Ring's good wife was dead, and though he loved her with undying love, he saw necessity, for the sake of his country and his motherless babes, to choose himself another bride.

"My old time friend, King Bele, left a daughter," he said. "For her hand will I sue. True, she is but young, just budding into bloom, playmate of lilies and roses, while many a winter's snow lies on my scanty locks. Still, should she find in her heart some love to give an honest man, though he be old, and womanly care for tender motherless babes, then fain would my winter share with her spring this throne."

So he sent warriors and skalds with attendants many to bear gifts and honorable offers to King Bele's sons. Right royally was the train received, but when King Helge with his priests consulted at the altar to inquire the will of the gods concerning this marriage, the omens were so dark, portending such disaster, that Helge, ever a slave to dark and gloomy superstitions, rejected King Ring's wooing right curtly, while childish Halfdan with scant respect made an open joke at the old man's expense.

Bitterly angered, the envoys departed. All the story of their insulting dismissal they told to King Ring. The good old man, who would have accepted graciously a courteous refusal, answered little, but his words were grim. With his spear he struck the iron shield on the bough of an ancient linden tree, the signal that summoned all the people to arms. War heralds hurried right and left. Soon, in answer, the dragon-ships came crowding, with their blood-red crests, and helmets nodded in the breeze.

King Helge heard of this warlike array and was greatly perturbed in spirit, for though great pride of heart was his, he was utterly lacking in courage. Moreover, he knew that King Ring, although he loved not war, was all the more a powerful foe for the very reason that he never gave battle without just cause.

Knowing that King Ring's first attempt would doubtless be to carry Ingeborg away, Helge ordered his sister to retire into the enclosure of Balder's temple, thus placing her in the pure and gentle keeping of the best beloved among the gods. The temple of Balder was to all the peoples of the north the most sacred of all sanctuaries, and whatever woman or maid had taken refuge there was secure from the approach of any man. Death awaited him who should force a way into that holy place. There lovely Ingeborg sat day after day, sad and tearful, bending over her embroidery frame, plying her needle or sorting her silks and golden threads.

Frithjof, meantime, lived on, moody and moping in the seclusion of his freehold at Framnäs. He nursed his wrath and would not go to Helge's aid. All his thoughts centered instead on one fierce intent,—he would see Ingeborg once more, the sunshine of his life. No matter what the cost, he would enter the sacred enclosure of Balder. He sent secret word to Ingeborg that he was coming, and his good ship Ellide bore him by night to the unguarded shore of the temple grounds. There Ingeborg was waiting in the pale dusk of a northern night in spring. How joyous was their greeting, though likewise full of tears. True, Ingeborg was frightened at Frithjof's breaking thus into the sanctuary of

Balder, but he led her reverently to the carven statue of the gentle god and said: "Balder, the good, can never be angry at the innocent meeting of two lovers. We mean no disrespect to him. Before his altar we will ever bend the knee."

Thus many a happy meeting they two had in secret after that first daring step. But at length, with many prayers and tears and a thousand coaxing ways, Ingeborg won Frithjof's promise, when next the Ting should meet presided over by her brothers, to go before the people, once more ask her of the kings, and offer them his hand in friendship.

So came the day when free-men gathered to the Ting. On Bele's mound from top to bottom Norseland's free-men stood in ordered ranks, with hand on hilt, and shield to shield. On the stone judgment seat King Helge sat, dark as a thunder cloud, and by him Halfdan, a grown up boy, leaned carelessly on his sword. Suddenly Frithjof stood before them.

"King Helge," he said, "War stands at the borders. Thy realm is threatened. Give me thy sister and my arm is thine to fight thy battles loyally. Cast prejudice aside. Let all ill-feeling be forgotten. Here is my hand."

A murmur as of rising sea-waves, swept over the Ting. A thousand swords struck applause against a thousand shields, and voices here and there swelled into one mighty roar. "O give him Ingeborg. His is the best sword in all the land."

In vain. With cold contempt King Helge said:

"The bonder's son might even yet call Ingeborg bride. But never he who sacrilegiously broke into Balder's temple. Speak, Frithjof. Didst thou not commit that crime? Say—yes or no?"

A shout went up from the ring of men. "Say no, O Frithjof! We will believe thy word and woo for thee. Thorsten's son is the equal of Kings. Say no! and Ingeborg is thine."

But Frithjof answered: "The weal or woe of all my life hangs on my answer, yet would I never tell a lie to buy Valhalla's joys,

346

much less the joys of earth. I did in truth enter the sacred precincts of Balder's temple to speak with Ingeborg, but did not thereby disturb the peace of that holy place."

A groan of horror ran throughout the Ting. Those nearest Frithjof recoiled with blanching cheeks, as though his deed had been a crime unspeakable. In tones low and ominous Helge said:

"Our laws leave me free to order either death or exile for such a deed as thine. Yet will I be merciful. Far out on the western sea there lies a cluster of islands over which Earl An'gan-tyr rules. As long as Bele lived the earl sent yearly tribute, but not since Bele's death. Go! demand the tribute and bring it home. Thus and thus only mayest thou redeem thy life and honor."

Bitterly Frithjof sought once more Ingeborg in the temple. At first in his madness he urged her to flee with him, flee far away to the smiling blue seas of distant Greece, to that land of soft and balmy breezes, so different from the cold and hardy northland. But Ingeborg, though all her heart was longing, would not listen to his pleading. She would not flee away in lawlessness and let Frithjof taint his honor further still. By her gentle pleading she persuaded him to go and expiate his guilt by seeking Angantyr.

"Then," he cried, "when my task is performed, my honor cleared, and I am free from guilt, I will return and demand thee of the open Ting. That and not Helge is thy rightful guardian."

And he gave to Ingeborg, as pledge of his undying love, a wondrous golden armlet curiously wrought and adorned with a matchless ruby. So he went, and Ingeborg, from the mighty rocks on the shore, watched the dragon-ship Ellide make off to the distant sea. Long and wistfully she watched, her heart sad and full of forebodings.

Hard was Frithjof's journey westward and through terrific tempests, but at last, storm-battered and weary, he and his men arrived at the court of Earl Angantyr, Lord of the Orkneys.

Splendid indeed was the hall of the Earl, and far less crude than the halls of the Northland. Frithjof's walls had naught to cover the bare rough-hewn planks, but the Earl's were hung with gilt leather hangings stamped with many a cunning design. Instead of a hearth in the middle of the floor, Earl Angantyr's hall had marble mantles at both ends of the room with chimneys so well constructed that no smoke remained inside, and no soot blackened the walls. The windows had panes of glass, and for lighting at night there were silver sconces with waxen candles instead of the smoky but fragrant pine chip stuck in a chink of the planking to which Frithjof was accustomed. High on a dais in a chair of massive silver the Earl sat in state, his golden helmet and corselet flashing. He wore a rich purple mantle embroidered with stars and bordered with bands of ermine. Courteously he received Frithjof, for Thorsten had been his good friend.

When Frithjof had eaten and drunk, he frankly told Earl Angantyr that he had come for tribute. As he spoke thus boldly, a silence fell upon all in the hall, but at length Earl Angantyr said:

"Tribute I never paid. I held Bele in honor but never was vassal of his. As to his heirs, I know nothing of them. If they have any claim, let them be men and come and enforce it themselves. But Thorsten was my friend and this is my gift to my old friend's son—" So speaking he gave to Frithjof a belt-pouch worked in green with a clasp of rubies and a tassel of spun gold. The pouch was filled full of golden coins. "Do with this gift as pleases thee. If it be thy wish, give it over unto King Helge when thou returnest, but do thou and thy men stay with us the winter through, I pray thee."

So Frithjof remained in the Orkneys through the winter, but at the first breath of spring in the air, at the first touch of green in the thawing fields, he thanked his host and once again entrusted himself to the sea. Merrily Ellide drew the silver furrow over the dark blue plain.

What joy it is to the mariner to set the sails for home, to

watch for the smoke which rises from his own hearth, for the rock from which a faithful maid has daily looked for him out to sea. So watched Frithjof with beating heart and dimming eyes as he neared the rocky northern shore. This is his own land and those are his own woods. There is the temple of Balder where his beloved Ingeborg awaits him. And now he can hear the water-fall which rushes headlong down the rocks. He rounds the headland. A moment more and he will see the roof of his home-stead above the trees. He looks and rubs his eyes and looks again. There is no sign of his beloved Framnäs anywhere. Yet stay! A tall chimney stack, bare and black, rises from the midst of a heap of ruins. He looks and looks again. His heart stands still. Then he leaps ashore. Everywhere is a waste of cinders, ashes, charred and broken stones. Nowhere is there a sign of life. Only his faithful hound springs to him in wild glee and his favorite courser, milk-white with golden mane, comes bounding from the woods. A moment more and old Hilding stood suddenly by the side of the broken-hearted man.

"Alas, dear son!" he cried. "There was a battle with King Ring, just one, soon after thou didst go. Despite his boyishness, King Halfdan showed himself a man, but Helge lost heart and fled, and that was the end. As he passed thy homestead in flight he burned it to the ground. Then the brothers had no choice. King Ring would accept of no peace offering but their sister. Poor Ingeborg! How that brave and gentle spirit sorrowed! In these arms of mine, I lifted her from the saddle on her wedding day, slender and swaying as a lily stalk. King Helge caught sight of thy bracelet on her arm. Roughly he tore it off with a curse. Now by her wish thy last beloved gift is on Balder's arm, in his sacred keeping, but Ingeborg is the bride of King Ring."

Violently then Frithjof burst forth with words of madness in his mighty grief. "The coward! To rob the eagle's nest when the eagle was flown! I will repay him!"

349

It was Midsummer Night. Over the hills stood the midnight sun, blood-red and beamless. It was not day, it was not night— a something grey and weird between. On that night was held a yearly festival of sacrifice to Balder, and Frithjof knew full well that the priestly Helge would be found in Balder's Temple. Wild with grief and fury he rushed to the spot where Helge stood by the altar stone. At sight of him the blood left Helge's face. Frithjof spoke in a voice like the storm wind for fury.

"Here is thy tribute. Take it. Then here by Balder's pyre we fight for life or death."

As he spoke he took from his belt Earl Angantyr's heavy purse and hurled it straight at Helge's head. Blood spurted from the royal mouth and nose, Helge's knees gave way and senseless he sank to the ground.

"What!" mocked Frithjof. "Canst thou not stand the touch of thine own gold, thou most dastardly of Norseland's sons?"

Then he turned, scarce knowing what he said, to the statue of Balder. "And thou, pale Balder, check thine anger, for by thy leave, I must have that bracelet upon thine arm. It was never meant for thee."

He snatched at the bracelet to strip it off in his fury, but it seemed grown fast to the statue's arm. At last with a mighty wrench he jerked it free, but the statue swayed as he did so and fell headlong into the altar fire while the priests stood speechless with horror. In a twinkling the flames leapt upward and caught at the beams of the roof. At that awful sight, Frithjof awakened suddenly to the sacrilege of his deed. For a moment he stood transfixed. Then rushing to the doors he cried, "Open wide the doors. Get out the people. The temple burns. Water! Pour water! Pour the sea!"

From all directions men came running. A chain was quickly formed from the temple to the beach. Buckets ran from hand to hand and soon the water was hissing, sputtering on the heated wood. Frithjof climbed with frenzied bravery to the top of the threatened roof, and sitting there astride, midst the hideous flames and smoke, he flooded all with water as the buckets were passed up to him. His voice never ceased ringing out commands. He alone directed the work. But all was in vain. The flames he had started raged with the same relentless fury as those but now raging within his own breast. It was as though gentle Balder, roused to wrath, had meant to show him to the full the fierce destructive nature of that consuming fire he had nourished but now within his own heart. From the temple the flames spread to the trees of the surrounding grove, licking the curling shrivelling foliage up, sweeping with a roar like the tempest, challenging the very heavens. At last, from a sea of fire, the grove suddenly collapsed into a wilderness of glowing stumps, a vast heap of dead grey ashes and embers like angry red eyes. Early morning showed the night's awful work of destruction. Silently the people dispersed, and Frithjof went his way alone, filled full of the horror of his deed, made an outcast from among men by the frenzy of his fury, weeping the scalding tears of a strong man's despair.

For Frithjof now there seemed nothing to do but go to sea in his dragon-ship and lead the life of a Viking. Three years long he roamed the seas in his floating castle, the sore and restless spirit within driving him to many a wild adventure, till his name was named throughout the North for the crude bold courage of conquest. But in all this was nought to bring real content to the sorrowing soul of Frithjof. When he reached those softly smiling seas of sunny Greece, that once he had described to Ingeborg as a place of such delight, he was overcome with homesick longing for the rough and rugged Northland and for Ingeborg. And so he turned his dragon-ship at last to the realm of King Ring, with one thought only in his heart. He must see Ingeborg. He must.

It was Yule-tide. King Ring, serene and gracious, sat at the head of his own festive board with his queen fair and gentle beside him,—spring and autumn strangely mated. Suddenly a stranger stood in the doorway, an old man of enormous stature, wrapped in a bear skin, and leaning on a staff. At sight of him a company of youthful retainers by the door laughed and exchanged jeering glances. The stranger's eyes shot forth blue lightnings. With one hand he seized the nearest of the scoffers, a flippant beardless youth, and with no effort whatsoever stood him on his head. At that the others grew silent and King Ring called the man to him.

"What is thy name and whence camest thou?" he said.

"My name is nothing to thee," said the stranger. "Misery is my country, Want my patrimony. Yesternight I slept with a wolf. Tonight I come to thee!"

When the King had heard all this he said quietly:

"Come, sit thee down by me, but drop that clumsy disguise. I know thou art no old man and I like not deceit."

So the guest let the shaggy pelt fall back from his head, and there in the old man's place stood one in all the splendor of youth. From his brow long golden locks fell to his shoulders.

FROM THE TOWER WINDOW

A blue velvet mantle thrown back from his breast showed a broad silver belt on which was graven a hunt with flying hart and pursuing hounds. Broad bands of gold glittered on his arms. By his side hung his sword. Thus the hero stood revealed! Into the Queen's pale cheeks the blood shot quickly, even as a snow field flushes with reflection of the crimson Northern Lights.

"Thou art welcome," said the King, "to our Yule-tide feast."

Amid a profound and reverent silence the boar was brought in, the emblem of Frey, the sun god, who from this, the longest night of the year, begins to gather strength to overcome the evil brood of winter giants. The boar was a mighty forest beast, skilfully roasted whole with wreaths of evergreens around his neck and shoulders, and an apple in his mouth. As the bearer set the heavy burden down upon the table, the King and all his guests bent the knee. Then the feasting began.

"Come now, my queen," cried King Ring. "Serve our guest with mead."

Quietly Ingeborg took a horn mounted with hoops of gold that stood on bright silver feet upon the table before her, and filled it to the brim. Then she offered it with downcast eyes to Frithjof. Thereafter the skald took the harp and began to sing. High ran the harmless merriment. And ere the evening was done King Ring had invited his guest to stay with him all winter.

Frithjof made no promise, yet from day to day he lingered. Ingeborg gave no sign that she knew him, not even a glance, and a stern feeling of honor kept Frithjof from speaking save as an utter stranger to the Queen. Well he knew that King Ring regarded as his enemy that Frithjof whom he had never seen, but who once had wooed his wife. Yet now the old man seemed more and more to take delight in his unknown guest's companionship; he would hear of no excursion, no amusement without him. On a certain day the King and Queen and all their court went on a sleighing and skating expedition across the frozen waters of the fjord. King

Ring himself drove a famous Swedish trotter hitched to a swan-shaped sleigh, with Ingeborg in her nest of furs by his side. Frithjof on skates was racing the trotter to the court's amazement and delight. Suddenly there was a shriek of horror. Sleigh and horse had broken through a thin spot on the ice and almost disappeared. A moment more and they would be sucked by the current under the ice. But in that instant, Frithjof was on the spot. He grasped the horse's head at the bit, and with one pull had him out and on his feet. Then he helped him drag the sleigh with its precious human load beyond the line of danger.

"A good pull and a strong!" cried the King in admiration. "That wonder of strong men, mine enemy, Frithjof, could not have done better!" And now he pressed Frithjof so earnestly to remain until spring that at last the young man gave his promise.

In due time spring came with chirping of birds and woodland foliage and long, long days. Once more the rivers ran blithely singing, glad of their liberty, to the sea. A great hunt had long been planned to open the season. Bows creaked, arrows rattled, steeds pawed the ground, and at last she appeared for whom all were waiting—Ingeborg, the Lady of the Hunt, alas! so beautiful

that Frithjof must needs turn his eyes away. All was ready. Off they went. Horns blowing, falcons soaring, garments flying! Over hill and dale, heigho!

King Ring could not ride so fast as the others and he and Frithjof were thus left far behind, for Frithjof stayed ever courteously by the old man's side. Wearied out, the King at last dismounted from his horse to rest in a quiet grove midst ancient elms and birches. Frithjof took off his mantle and spread it on the ground. There King Ring stretched his weary limbs and soon fell asleep.

As he slumbered, hark! a blackbird sang into Frithjof's ear: "Haste, Frithjof, strike the old man while he slumbers and none are by to see. Then take the Queen, for rightfully she is thine!"

Frithjof listened, but hark! in the other ear a white bird sang.

"If no human eye can see, still All-father's eye is upon thee. Villain, the man is old and unarmed. Thou canst not kill him."

Thus by turns the two birds sang, till Frithjof drew his sword in horror, and to thrust temptation from him, flung the blade far off with violence. Then the blackbird flew away but the white bird soared on light pinions high up into the sunlight and its joyful carol was like the tone of a silver bell.

Abruptly the old King rose from his slumber.

"Where is thy sword?" he cried.

"It was not safe in my hand. I flung it far from me," Frithjof replied.

"Hear then, O youth," said King Ring. "I did not sleep as thou didst suppose but now. I only wished to test thee. Thou art Frithjof. I have known thee from the moment thou didst enter my hall, but well have I seen in these last moments that thou art a man to be trusted. I pity thee and forgive thine attempt to deceive me. I am an old man and soon will be rejoicing in Valhalla. When I am gone, take thou my queen—she is thine by right, and guard my realm for my infant son. But until I go, abide with me and be my son. There is no longer a feud between us."

Deeply Frithjof marveled at the old King's greatness of soul, humbly he acknowledged it, yet still in his heart burned the memory that he was an outcast from men by reason of his sin in Balder's temple, and for such as he there could be little hope of good. So he gloomily made up his mind to take his leave of the lovely Ingeborg.

On a certain day he came to say farewell, but in that very hour, King Ring departed this life to come into All-father's presence. What, then, could Frithjof do but linger?

In an open field under the blue canopy of heaven met the Ting. A new king must be chosen. There stood Frithjof straight and tall upon the judgment stone, and close to him the little gold-haired child of Ingeborg, King Ring's sole son. A murmur passed around the circle of men as they looked on Frithjof's stalwart form and coveted him for a leader.

"The child is too young to rule us," they said.

But Frithjof raised the little one upon his shield.

"Behold your King!" he cried, "the country's blooming hope! See how at ease he stands upon the unsteady shield. My sword shall guard his kingdom, and on his brow some day my hand shall place his father's crown."

Standing on the shield, the child looked up with eyes as bold as an eagle's, and when he had tired of this novel game, he sprang with a royal fearlessness from that great height to the ground. With a roar of delight the Ting greeted this daring feat and men cried out: "We choose thee king. Be as thy father great and good. And let Earl Frithjof rule in thy place until thou growest a man. Do thou, Earl Frithjof, take the mother of the boy to be thy wife!"

But Frithjof paid no heed. He only kissed the little king upon his brow in homage, and strode forth alone and silent, his grief for his mighty sin still keeping him from Ingeborg. Led by his deep repentance, he wandered back to that blackened grove and temple of his crime, longing, longing for forgiveness.

"Cannot repentance and a blameless life atone for a moment's madness?" he cried, and threw himself in mighty grief and sorrow on his father's mound, praying to know how he might redeem himself. As he lay there he slept and in his sleep saw a vision. A wonderful new temple he saw, a temple of marvellous beauty in place of the mass of ruins he had made, its dome of crystal pure and blue as virgin ice or the winter sky. Frithjof gazed in awe upon that structure, and then awaking, cried with joy, "The sign! I am to rebuild Balder's temple fairer than ever before. O joy that it is given me to atone!"

And so Frithjof set himself to work to redeem his sin of destructive fury by building anew the temple. More beautiful than ever, with a dignity more stately, a substance more enduring, it rose again, and when the work was done, the day of consecration came. Two by two twelve maidens entered the sacred place, robed richly in cloth of silver, the bloom of roses in their cheeks and in their innocent hearts. In graceful stately dance they moved around the altar as woodland fairies dance on the grassy mounds while morning dew yet sparkles on the grass. And as they danced they sang the sacred lay of Balder.

Frithjof stood leaning on his sword spellbound. It was as though his days of Viking life with all their lawlessness were passing from him altogether, while the joys and dreams of his boyhood came trooping around him, blue-eyed, flower-crowned, smiling, beckoning. Higher and higher his soul was lifted above the lowly haunts of human hatred, human vengeance. One by one the iron bands of dark enslaving human passions that had held his breast oppressed, fell off as winter's ice melts from some mighty rock. The sunshine of peace and love flooded his heart. He could have held the world in fond encircling arms.

Now entered Balder's high priest. tall and of commanding

presence, with silver beard flowing down to his girdle, and heaven's own graciousness in his mild and noble countenance. Frithjof's heart was thrilled with reverent awe as the old man spoke.

"Welcome, son Frithjof, I have looked for thee to return. For power misled into violence is sure to come to its senses at last and unite with gentleness, if the man's nature but be noble. Thou wouldst atone and be reconciled. Knowest thou the meaning of these words? To atone and be reconciled is to rise after a fall purer, better, than before. We offer sacrifices to the gods and call them atonement. But they are only signs, symbols, not the thing itself. No outward act can take the burden of guilt from thee. A man's atonement is within his own breast. I know of one sacrifice dearer to the gods than rarest incense. It is the surrender of thine own heart's hatred, thy thirst for vengeance. If thou canst not tame these, if thou canst not forgive, then hadst thou better stay away from Balder's fane. Then is thy building of this temple useless. Balder's forgiveness cannot be bought with a few blocks of stone. Thou hatest Bele's sons. Only now has there come news that Helge lies slain in Finnland. Halfdan rules alone. Offer him thine hand. Sacrifice to the gods thy wrath. Else is all thy building of the temple vain."

Here Halfdan stepped across the threshold and with timid look which well became his boyish beauty, stood waiting. Slowly Frithjof loosed from his belt the sword and dagger and laid them on the altar, then he approached Halfdan and held out his hand.

"I offer it thee in truest friendship," he said.

Flushing with joy King Halfdan laid his hand in Frithjof's and they two, long parted, joined in a new made bond as firm and strong as their native rocks. Even as they spoke Ingeborg entered in bridal robes. With happy tears she fell upon her brother's breast and he gently placed her in Frithjof's arms. Then was performed the wedding rite, and before Balder's face, now smiling once again, Ingeborg became the bride of the lover of her youth.

FROM THE TOWER WINDOW

KALEVALA, LAND OF HEROES
Retold from the Kalevala, the National Epic of Finland

COME and hearken to this story, caught from winds and waves and woodlands, from the pastures of the Northland, from the meads of Ka-le-va'la.

In the ancient times it happened in the shining Land of Heroes, that there dwelt an aged graybeard, Wai-na-moi'nen, famous minstrel,—in the vales and on the mountains, through the verdant fields and forests, in the ancient halls and dwellings, ever chanting tales of heroes, singing legends of his people. And so wondrous was his singing that it rippled like the rivers, easy-flowing like the waters, easy gliding as the snow-shoes, like the ship upon the ocean. Well beloved was Wai-na-moi'nen.

Now it chanced this ancient graybeard, sweetest, best of boasted singers, thought to take a wife unto him, from the dismal, darksome Northland, from the land of cruel winters, from the land of little sunshine, from the land of worthy women. So he ordered to be saddled his fleet-footed steed of magic, and astride that wondrous courser, he began his journey northward. O'er the plains of Ka-le-va'la, he went plunging onward, onward,—straight across the blue sea-waters, wetting not the hoofs in running.

But a minstrel less successful, evil-minded You-ka-hai'nen, nursed a grudge against the graybeard, in his heart the worm of envy. He prepared a cruel cross-bow, and at breaking of the day-dawn, turned his eyes upon the sunrise,—saw a black cloud on the ocean, something blue upon the waters. This he knew for Wai-na-moi'nen. Quickly now young You-ka-hai'nen, Lapland's vain and evil minstrel, aimed with steady care his crossbow, and with hatred pulled the trigger. Like the lightning flew the arrow, o'er the head of Wai-na-moi'nen, harmless to the upper heavens, scattered all the flock of lamb-clouds. Undiscouraged, You-ka-hai'nen shot again and yet a third time, striking then the graybeard's courser, that light-footed ocean-swimmer.

This story of the Kalevala is based on Crawford's translation and all the selections used are from that translation.

359

Thereupon wise Wai-na-moi'nen headlong fell upon the waters, plunged beneath the rolling billows, from the saddle of the courser. Then arose a mighty storm-wind, roaring wildly on the waters, bore away old Wai-na-moi'nen far from land upon the billows, washed him seaward on the surges, seaward, seaward, further, further.

Wai-na-moi'nen, old and truthful, swam through all the deep sea-waters, floating like a branch of aspen. Swam six days in summer weather, swam six nights in golden moonlight. Still before him rose the billows, and behind him sky and ocean. So at last he grew disheartened, sad and weary, hoping nothing. Then there came a bird, an eagle, sweeping downward from the heavens. He beheld brave Wai-na-moi'nen struggling there upon the ocean, and was moved with great compassion. Swift he flew unto his rescue. On his back he took the graybeard, bore him safely on his pinions, to the distant shore of Northland, to the dismal Sa-ri-o'la. There he left him, sad and weary, on a cheerless promontory, in his bitter accents weeping, longing for his home and kindred, for his home in Ka-le-va'la.

Now the fairest maid in Northland, young and slender Maid of Beauty, on the morning of the morrow, rose before the sun had risen, sheered her six, soft, gentle lambkins, scrubbed the smooth white birchen tables in her mother's low-ceiled dwelling, swept the ground-floor of the stable with a broom of birchen branches, carried in a copper shovel all the sweepings to the meadow. There she lingered by the surges, heard a weeping from the seashore, heard a hero-voice lamenting.

Thereupon she hastened homeward, hastened to her mother's dwelling, told to ancient, toothless Lou'hi, all the story of the wailing. And old Lou'hi hastening shoreward, pushed her boat into the waters, straightway rowed with lightning swiftness to the weeping Wai-na-moi'nen. Comfort gave she to the minstrel, wailing in a grove of willows. Then she took the hapless hero to her home in dark Poh-yo'la, where she

FROM THE TOWER WINDOW

fed him and revived him, gave him warmth and food and shelter.

And yet ever Wai-na-moi'nen, when his heart grew warm within him, still was longing for his homeland, for his native land and kindred. O, to hear the cuckoo singing, hear the sacred cuckoo calling!

Now the ancient toothless Lou'hi knew her guest for a magician, and she longed with great desiring to possess the magic grist-mill, that same magic grist-mill, Sampo, that could grind unmeasured treasures. So she cried to Wai-na-moi'nen, "I will give to thee my daughter, for thy bride the Maid of Beauty; I will send thee to thy homeland, to thy much-loved Ka-le-va'la, there to hear the cuckoo singing, hear the sacred cuckoo calling, if in turn thou forgest for me that same magic grist-mill, Sampo."

Wai-na-moi'nen, much regretting, answered that he could not forge it.

"How to forge the mill I know not. But," he said, "if thou wilt take me to my distant, much-loved homeland, I will send thee Il-ma-ri'nen. Worthy smith is Il-ma-ri'nen. He can forge for thee the Sampo."

So replied the hostess, Lou'hi. "If thou givest me thy promise, then to send me Il-ma-ri'nen, I will let thee leave Poh-yo'la for thy distant home and kindred."

Not delaying, much rejoicing, Wai-na-moi'nen gave his promise. Thereupon the hostess, Lou'hi, harnessed quick a faithful reindeer, hitched him to her sledge of birch-wood, placed within it Wai-na-moi'nen. But before her guest departed, she addressed him thus in warning.

"Do not raise thine eyes to heaven, look not upward on thy journey while the day-star lights thy pathway. If thine eyes be lifted upward ere the evening star has risen, dire misfortune will befall thee, some sad fate will overtake thee."

Thus advised, old Wai-na-moi'nen started fleetly on his journey, hastened homeward happy-hearted.

Fairest daughter of Poh-yo'la,
Glory of the land and water,
Sat upon the bow of heaven,
On its highest arch resplendent,
In a gown of richest fabric,
In a gold and silver air-gown,
Weaving webs of golden texture,
Interlacing threads of silver;
Weaving with a golden shuttle,
With a weaving-comb of silver.
Merry flies the golden shuttle,
From the maiden's nimble fingers.

Came the ancient Wai-na-moi'nen,
Rushing down the highway homeward,
Had not ridden long since starting,
Ridden but a little distance,
When he heard the sky-loom buzzing,
As the maiden plied the shuttle.
Quick the thoughtless Wai-na-moi'nen
Lifts his eyes aloft in wonder,
Looks upon the vault of heaven,
There beholds the bow of beauty,
On the bow the maiden seated,
Beauteous Maiden of the Rainbow,
Glory of the earth and ocean.

FROM THE TOWER WINDOW

Wai-na-moi'nen, ancient minstrel, quickly checked his fleet-foot reindeer, thus addressed the charming maiden:

"Come, fair maiden, to my snow-sledge. Come and seat thyself beside me. Let me take thee to my dwelling, to my home in Ka-le-va'la, there to be my queen and lady."

But the Maid of Beauty answered from her throne amid the heavens that she had no wish to wed him, had no wish to leave her homeland, had no wish to leave her mother, wished to stay a maiden always. All in vain the minstrel begged her. She but answered him with jeering. Could he now do this or that,—setting tasks that even magic scarce could hope to have accomplished, then she might consent to wed him. Nothing daunted, Wai-na-moi'nen, the most skilful of enchanters, every task she set, accomplished, crying always to her, "Maiden, I have done what thou desirest. Come thou then into my snow-sledge."

Lastly said the Maid of Beauty, casting down her magic spindle:

"I will go with that one only that will make me ship or shallop from the splinters of my spindle, from the fragments of my distaff."

Not delaying, Wai-na-moi'nen took at once the wooden splinters, set to work to make the vessel. Full of zeal he plied the hammer, swung the hammer and the hatchet,—till the power of evil, Hi'si, making use of that sharp hatchet, turned aside the axe in falling, cut the knee of Wai-na-moi'nen. From the veins that Hi'si severed, there came gushing forth a blood-stream, came a blood-stream, crimson-colored. Nor could then old Wai-na-moi'nen, for the whole of his great knowledge, stay the crimson stream from flowing. Truly, truly had old Lou'hi warned him never to gaze skyward till the evening star had risen, till he could not see the maiden.

Heavy hearted, full of weeping then he climbed into his snow-sledge, and went dashing down the highway seeking some one who could help him. Here and there he asked assistance. There

was no one who could heal him. But at last he found a graybeard dwelling in a little cottage. Wiser he than all the others.
When he heard the minstrel's story, from the hearth arose the
graybeard, crying thus, "O iron hatchet, tell who taught thee all
thy malice, tell who gave to thee thine evil?

> *"Ukko, God of love and mercy,*
> *God and master of the heavens,*
> *Come thou hither, thou art needed,*
> *Come thou quickly I beseech thee,*
> *Lend thy hand to aid thy children,*
> *Touch this wound with healing fingers,*
> *Stop this hero's streaming life-blood,*
> *Bind this wound with tender leaflets,*
> *Mingle with them healing flowers,*
> *Thus to check this crimson current,*
> *Thus to save this great magician.*
> *Save the life of Wai-na-moi'nen."*

Thus at last the blood-stream ended as the magic words were
spoken. Then the graybeard brewed a balsam, brewed a magic
healing ointment, touched the wounds of Wai-na-moi'nen with
the balm of many virtues, speaking words of ancient wisdom:

> *"Do not walk in thine own virtue,*
> *Do not work in thine own power,*
> *Walk in strength of thy Creator;*
> *Do not speak in thine own wisdom,*
> *Speak with tongue of mighty Ukko.*
> *In my mouth if there be sweetness,*
> *It has come from my Creator;*
> *If my hands are filled with beauty,*
> *All the beauty comes from Ukko."*

Wai-na-moi'nen, old and truthful, felt the help of gracious
Ukko, straightway stronger grew in body. Straightway were the
wounds united, straight he walked in perfect freedom. Then the
ancient Wai-na-moi'nen raised his eyes to high Ju-ma'la, looked
with gratitude to heaven, looked on high in joy and gladness,
thus addressed all-knowing Ukko:

FROM THE TOWER WINDOW

"O be praised, thou God of mercy,
Let me praise thee my Creator,
Since thou gavest me assistance,
And vouchsafed me thy protection,
Healed my wounds and stilled mine anguish.
God alone can work perfection,
Give to cause its perfect ending,
Never hand of man can find it.
Never can the hero give it.
Ukko is the only master."

Wai-na-moi'nen, the magician, quickly hitched his fleet-foot reindeer, put his racer to the snow-sledge, straightway sprang upon the cross-seat, snapped his whip adorned with jewels. Like the winds the steed flew onward, made the snow-sledge creak and rattle, made the highway quickly vanish. On he dashed through fen and forest, over marshes, over mountains, over fertile plains and meadows, till he came to Ka-le-va'la.

Then began old Wai-na-moi'nen in his secret heart to ponder: "It may now be far from easy to induce good Il-ma-ri'nen to go forth from home and kindred to the dismal darksome Northland. He may never be consenting to fulfill my given promise."

Long he spent in fear and doubting. So he called to aid his magic, and he sang aloft a pine tree, wondrous tall, with branches spreading in the ever-shining sunlight. And he sang again enchanting, sang the moon and Great Bear's starlets to come down from out the heavens, and to hide within the fir-tree, from its emerald branches shining. This accomplished, he went onward to the forge of Il-ma-ri'nen. There he found the mighty blacksmith, wielding his great copper hammer.

"Welcome home, good Wai-na-moi'nen," said the friendly Il-ma-ri'nen. "Where hast thou so long been hiding?"

Spake the minstrel, Wai-na-moi'nen: "I have much to tell thee, brother. I have spent my days in Lapland, all the days of my long absence. There I saw a lovely virgin, fairest maiden of the Northland.

"From her temples beams the moonlight
From her breast the gleam of sunshine,
From her forehead shines the rainbow.

Il-ma-ri'nen, worthy brother,
Thou the only skilful blacksmith,
Go and see her wondrous beauty,
See her gold and silver garments,
See her robed in finest raiment,
See her sitting on the rainbow,
Walking on the clouds of purple.

Forge for her the magic Sampo,
Forge the lid in many colors.
Thy reward shall be the virgin.
Thou shalt win this bride of beauty."

But the mighty smith suspected that already Wai-na-moi'nen had made promise in the Northland he should come to forge the Sampo. And he answered shortly, flatly, "I shall never visit Northland, go to dreary Sa-ri-o'la, not for all the maids in Lapland!"

Then alas! did Wai-na-moi'nen turn his wisdom into cunning, fearing lest good Il-ma-ri'nen never could be coaxed to going.

"If thou wilt not, then thou wilt not!" Thus he spake and seemed contented. "But I wish to tell thee, further, of a wonder seen but lately as I crossed the meadows homeward. In the branches of a fir tree I beheld the Great Bear shining, and the moon itself from heaven caught amongst those emerald branches."

"I shall not believe thy story," said the wary Il-ma-ri'nen, "till I see the blooming fir-tree, see the moon and Great Bear's starlets."

This was Wai-na-moi'nen's answer, "Come with me and I will show thee."

Quick they journey to behold it, haste to view the wondrous fir-tree. Il-ma-ri'nen in the tree-top spied the gleam of golden moonlight, spied the shining silver starlight.

FROM THE TOWER WINDOW

"Climb the tree," said Wai-na-moi'nen, "and bring down the moon and starlets."

Il-ma-ri'nen, struck with wonder, senseless, thoughtless, climbed the fir-tree, having neither wit nor judgment, thinking but to seize the treasures. Quick as thought old Wai-na-moi'nen sang again in magic accents, sang a storm wind in the heavens, sang the wild winds into fury.

Now the storm-wind quickly darkens,
Quickly piles the air together,
Makes of air a sailing vessel,
Takes the blacksmith, Il-ma-ri'nen,
Fleetly from the fir tree's branches,
Toward the never pleasant Northland,
Toward the dismal Sa-ri-o'la.
Through the air sailed Il-ma-ri'nen,
Fast and far the hero traveled,
Sweeping onward, sailing northward,
Riding in the track of storm-winds.

Lou'hi, hostess of Poh-yo'la, standing in the open courtyard, quickly spied the hero-stranger, coming thither on the storm-wind.

"Who art thou," she cried, "of heroes?"

Spake the hero then in answer, "Who am I but Il-ma-ri'nen,— I the skilful smith and artist."

"Il-ma-ri'nen!" cried old Lou'hi. "Long I've waited for thy coming!" And she turned into her dwelling, there to call the Maid of Beauty.

"Come thou fairest of my daughters. Dress thyself in finest raiment, deck thy hair with rarest jewels, for the artist Il-ma-ri'nen hither comes from Ka-le-va'la, here to forge for us the Sampo, magic mill of many treasures."

Now the daughter of the Northland straightway took her choicest raiment,—on her brow a band of copper, round her waist a golden girdle, in her hair the threads of silver. From her dressing room she hastened, full of beauty, full of joyance, there to greet the hero-stranger. Lou'hi, hostess of Poh-yo'la, led her guest unto her dwelling, seated him before her table, gave to him the choicest viands. Then she said to Il-ma-ri'nen:

"Can'st thou forge for me the Sampo, hammer out its lid in colors? If thou canst, then to reward thee, I will give to thee my daughter."

Il-ma-ri'nen looked about him, saw the maid of wondrous beauty, and he answered to old Lou'hi, "I will forge for thee the Sampo."

Thereupon he sought a workshop, sought to find the tools to work with. But he found no place for forging, found no tongs and found no hammer.

"Only knaves leave work unfinished, grow discouraged," said the artist, "never heroes, never brave men." And he went on seeking further. On the evening of the third day came a rock within his vision, came a rock of rainbow colors. There the blacksmith, Il-ma-ri'nen, set to work and built his smithy, forged the tools that he had need of, and began to forge the Sampo. First he mixed together metals, put the mixture in the caldron, laid it deep within the furnace, called the hirelings to the forging. Soon the fire leapt through the windows, through the door the sparks flew upward, clouds of smoke arose to heaven, clouds of black smoke, circling, rolling. On the third night Il-ma-ri'nen, bending low to view his metals, on the bottom of the furnace, saw the magic Sampo rising. Quick with tongs he seized the mixture, laid it down upon the anvil, beat it, skilful, with the hammer, forged at last the magic Sampo.

Wild rejoiced the old dame, Lou'hi, took from him the magic grist-mill, found it could in truth grind treasures. Then she bore it off in triumph, hid it in a place of safety.

But, full modest, Il-ma-ri'nen went to seek the Maid of Beauty. "Wilt thou come with me?" he asked her, "be my queen, O fairest maiden? I have forged for thee the Sampo, forged the lid in many colors."

Northland's fair and lovely daughter saw the artist stand before her, saw him young and strong and handsome. In her heart was secret liking, yet she answered shyly, coyly. "I shall never leave my mother, leave Poh-yo'la's fens and forests, leave my native fields and woodlands."

Il-ma-ri'nen, disappointed, yielded up his dearest wishes, turned away to leave the country, heavy-hearted, empty-handed. Lou'hi gave him every comfort, placed him in a boat of copper, made the North wind guide him homeward. Thus the skilful Il-ma-ri'nen reached again his native country.

Straightway Wai-na-moi'nen asked him, "Didst thou forge the magic Sampo?"

Spake the artist Il-ma-ri'nen, "Yea I forged the magic Sampo, forged the lid in many colors. Lou'hi has the wondrous Sampo. I have not the Bride of Beauty."

Then did ancient Wai-na-moi'nen think within him, "Now the

blacksmith has had every chance to win her, fairy maiden of the rainbow. And since he has failed to lead her to the halls of Ka-le-va'la, why may I not now attempt it, now attempt again to win her?" So he decked a magic vessel, painted it in blue and scarlet, trimmed in gold the ship's forecastle, decked the prow in molten silver, made the sails of finest linen,—sails of blue and white and scarlet. Wai-na-moi'nen the magician stepped aboard his magic vessel, steered the bark across the waters, sailing toward the dark Poh-yo'la.

But good Il-ma-ri'nen's sister saw the magic ship departing, hastened off and told her brother, told of Wai-na-moi'nen's going. Il-ma-ri'nen then, the blacksmith, bathed his head to flaxen whiteness, made his cheeks look fresh and ruddy, laved his eyes until they sparkled like the moonlight on the waters. Next he donned his finest raiment, donned his splendid silken stockings, and his shoes of marten-leather, donned a vest of sky-blue color, and his scarlet colored trousers, donned a coat with scarlet trimming and a red shawl trimmed in ermine. Then he wrapped about his body a great fur coat made of seal skin, fastened with a thousand buttons and adorned with countless jewels. On his hands he drew his gauntlets, with their splendid golden wristlets, on his head of many ringlets, put the finest cap in Northland.

Last he bade a trusty servant take the fleetest of his coursers, hitch him to his sledge of magic, place six cuckoos on the breakboard that should sit there, singing, calling,—on the cross bars seven blue-birds, richly colored, ever-singing. Straightway then the trusty servant did as he had been commanded, and the artist Il-ma-ri'nen stepped into his sledge of magic. O'er his knees he drew the bear-skin and the finest robes of marten, called then earnestly to Ukko, "God protect my magic snow sledge, be my safeguard on the journey."

Fast and faster flew the fleet-foot, down the curving snow-capped sea-coast, o'er the alder hills and mountains, through the sand and falling snow flakes, blue birds singing, cuckoos calling. Il-ma-ri'nen looked to seaward for old Wai-na-moi'nen's vessel. So at last he overtook it and thus hailed the ancient minstrel:

"O thou ancient Wai-na-moi'nen, let us woo in peace the maiden, fairest daughter of the Northland. Let each labor long to win her. Let her wed the one she chooses."

Wai-na-moi'nen then made answer: "I agree to thy proposal. Let us woo in peace the maiden, not by force or faithless measures. Let her follow him she chooses. Let the unsuccessful suitor harbor neither wrath nor envy."

Thus agreeing, on they journeyed.

Now the hostess of the Northland saw the splendid ship approaching, at the helm the ancient hero,—saw the sledge approaching likewise, cuckoos calling, blue-birds singing, in the sledge the proud young hero. And she hurried to her daughter, urging, "Hither come two suitors. One will offer countless treasure,—that the ancient Wai-na-moi'nen. He, the younger, Il-ma-ri'nen, cometh hither empty-handed. Choose thou then the man of treasures."

But the maiden made this answer, "I will wed no man for treasures. For his worth I'll choose a husband."

And when Wai-na-moi'nen landed, pulled his gaily colored vessel from the waves upon the sea-shore, hastened to the maiden, saying, "Be my bride and life companion," she made answer, shortly, surely, "I will never wed thee, greybeard!"

O, alas for Wai-na-moi'nen! Well for him had he not doubted, feared to trust the blacksmith's friendship, changed his wisdom into cunning, tricked his friend into the tree-top, raised the storm that sent him northward. For when Il-ma-ri'nen sought her, sought again the Rainbow Maiden, spite of Lou'hi's opposition, raising obstacles to hinder, it was he the Maid of Beauty chose at last to be her husband, yielding with her maiden sweetness to the strength of his bold manhood.

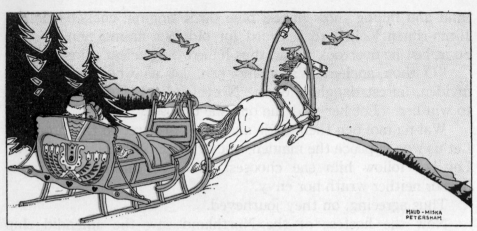

"Il-ma-ri′nen, I will wed thee."

So the ancient Wai-na-moi′nen lost the maiden he had sued for, and he knew, the wise and truthful, he had well deserved to lose her.

Long prepared they for the wedding in Poh-yo′la's halls and chambers,—finest linen on the tables, softest fur upon the benches, birchen flooring scrubbed to whiteness, all the rooms in perfect order. Then came young lads from the village, merry maidens from the hamlets. Thus the wedding guests assembled. Then the ancient Wai-na-moi′nen, keeping well his faithful promise, feeling neither wrath nor envy, sang the joy of all assembled, to the pleasure of the evening, to the merriment of maidens, to the happiness of heroes. Thus he sang, wise Wai-na-moi′nen:

"Grant, O Ukko, my Creator,
God of love and truth and justice,
Grant thy blessing on our feasting.
Bless this company assembled,
For the good of Sa-ri-o′la,
For the happiness of Northland,—
That we may recall with pleasure
Il-ma-ri′nen's magic marriage
To the Maiden of the Rainbow,
Snow-white virgin of the Northland."

FROM THE TOWER WINDOW

WHITE ASTER

Retold from a Romantic Chinese Poem

AUTUMN sunset glowing with gold, Mt. Aso's lofty summit looming dark against the sky, no sound save now and then the crinkling fall of withered leaves. List! from yonder distant grove, silver-toned through the stillness, the sound of a temple bell. From the last hut of frail bamboo on the edge of the little village comes a timid maiden weeping and lifting anxious eyes to the mighty mountain above her. Poor little White Aster! Three days ago her father left her and went hunting up the steep slopes of Mt. Aso—three days ago, and no sign since of his return. Has the great mountain some dread secret about him—does the mountain know why he lingers and leaves her thus alone?

Benign and majestic, Mt. Aso looked down upon her, but it did not tell her its secret. Sadly she turned—the little White Aster—and crept back into her lonely cottage. Then she set about kindling the fire and brewing the tea for supper, but if the oleander beside the door but swayed its branches lightly against her flimsy walls, if a rabbit leapt crackling through the bushes without, if the light breeze stirred the foliage somewhere near, each time she hoped it was sound of her father coming home at last.

The twilight slowly deepened. As it swallowed with its ashen gray the sunset's train of gold, White Aster stole out of doors once more to look anxiously about. Surely, it seemed, she must this time catch a glimpse of her father, climbing lightly down through the trees. Naught could she see anywhere save a flock of wild geese flying past, and purple rain clouds rising slowly, drifting across the heavens. Softly the little maiden shuddered, yet she felt in her heart the insistent longing to go in quest of her father. Returning to the hut, she donned a straw cloak and red bamboo hat, and, though night was already falling with threatened storm, she stole down the village street, crossed the swampy rice marsh, and began to climb the mountain.

The steep path wound with a swift ascent; the grass lay dry and dead beneath her feet; hushed were the voices of blithe insects. Only sable night yawned threatening from the vale, and soon the rain came pelting down. But still White Aster searched and called. No traces of her father could she find. At times the rain would cease, the clouds roll back, and pale white moonlight for a moment cleave the gloomy pines. Far did the maiden climb alone in the darkness, up and up and up, till she knew not where she was, and all about seemed only night. Then suddenly she spied through the trees a faint red gleam and heard low chanting of a priest, monotonous, at prayer. Welcome the sound of human voice to the maiden's lonely ears! Going in the direction of the light, White Aster passed through a grove of cypress and camphor trees, and came upon a ruined temple overhung by weeping willows that gleamed brightly beneath a sudden silvering of the fitful moon. Her light footfall on the broken stone approach fell upon the hermit's ears, and, all unused to hearing steps in his retreat, far distant from the haunts of men, he fancied some demon or evil spirit must be coming to tempt him. Seizing a light, he flashed it out through the door, and shouted forbiddingly:

"Begone! thou spirit of evil, begone!"

But when he caught a glimpse of little White Aster's lovely

face, so innocent and sweet, her eyebrows twin half-moons, her dark hair like a cloud upon her snowy temples, he changed his mind and all his heart went out to her in pity. Taking her gently by the hand, he led her inside the sanctuary, and up where a great stone Buddha stood, benign and placid and august. Then he seated her at Buddha's feet before he asked:

"Whence camest thou, little maid, and what art thou doing in this wilderness by night?"

White Aster saw that her host was a man still young, of kind and comely countenance. Timidly she answered him:

"White Aster is my name. I came but now from the village down below to seek my father, who has been for three days lost upon the mountain." Here tears stayed her from speaking further, but the hermit soothed her with his gentle voice and, warmed by his compassion, she burst forth with all her tale—"Ah me! the sadness of these later years. Ah me! Ah me! And yet my childhood was so happy with tenderest father and mother, a splendid home and many servitors in those fair southern islands far away. So happy was I there! And then there came a day when savage foes bore down on my beloved homeland. Fire, sword and ruin took the place of peace. My mother and I fled for our lives, and in our flight were separated from my father. All night and day we fled, and stopped at last for shelter in a ruined temple. There, when we had recovered ourselves by rest, we built a booth to shelter us. Though neither she nor I had ever before performed a hard or difficult task, so tenderly cared for had we been in that dear home of ours, we managed, day by day, to make provision for our own most pressing wants, but ever our hearts were longing, longing for news of my dear father. Two sorrows bore upon my mother's soul, the loss of him, her husband, and sorrow for her only son, a most beloved youth, who had been so wild and wayward that my father banished him from home or ever I was born. Such tender love for him, her little

A-ki-to'shi, my mother cherished in her heart, such grief for his unworthiness, such yearning once again to gaze upon his face, that what with dwelling ever on her sorrows, as weeks and months went by with no news of my father, she pined away and died. Ah!" cried White Aster, weeping, "Nature's self

*Seemed to be mourning with me, for the breeze
Of Autumn breathed its last, and as it died,
The vesper-bell from yonder village pealed
A requiem o'er my mother.   Thus she died,
But dead yet lives—for, ever, face and form,
She stands before my eyes; and in my ears
I ever seem to hear her loving voice
Speaking as in the days when, strict and kind,
She taught me household lore—in all a mother.*

"When she was gone, I lived alone in that rude shelter, till it chanced one day my father who had wandered everywhere in search of us, came on my place of refuge. His joy at finding me was great, but when he heard how my dear mother was gone, not all my tenderest love could soothe him or stay his soul from longing for her, and for that dear beloved son, the erring A-ki-to'shi. Oh me! Ah me! my father, my dear father!"

During all this artless tale, signs of deep emotion had possessed the hermit's features. Akitoshi—O alas! What sorrow he had caused!—the wayward Akitoshi! At hearing of him, the hermit hid his face within his hands that none might see him weeping. Yet he spoke no word till little White Aster had finished. Then he bade her tarry there within the temple until the sunrise, since the mountain at night was no fit place for such a tender little maid.

White Aster, therefore, slept at Buddha's feet, shivering with cold, for her garments were far too thin to protect her from the cutting keenness of frosty mountain air. As she slept, she dreamt that her father himself appeared to her and said: "Dear little maid, a false step on the mountain hurled me down a deep ravine. Thence for three days I have been vainly trying to escape."

At length the red dawn tipped the mountain tops, and birds,

FROM THE TOWER WINDOW

awakening one by one, peered from their nests to greet the day
with joyous matin songs. Their music roused the sleeping maid.

"Kind friend," she said to her gentle host, "farewell! I
dreamed a dream about my father, and must start without delay
once more upon my quest."

The hermit stood within his door and looked long after her
light form departing up the path. Skirting the trunks of mighty
trees, stealing beneath whispering pines, White Aster threaded
many a different part of that vast mountain solitude. Now a
timid deer fled from her path, and now some other woodland
creature, but nowhere were there any signs of her beloved father.
So intent was the little maiden on her quest that she never noticed
two dark forms, which shadowed her to rearward, and ever came
creeping nearer, nearer. At length there pounced upon her from
behind two robbers. Little heeding her prayers or tears, they
bore her away, and off, off to their rocky den. In vain she sent
her wailing cries abroad for help. Echo with its hollow voice
resounding from the lonely cliffs,—echo was her only answer.

The brigands' lair was in a dark and gloomy spot beneath an overhanging cliff. Here they had erected a miserable hut, with thatch so broken that it would have offered little shelter, save that dense foliage of a gingko tree, growing near, quite overshadowed it. In front a noisy stream went brawling by, while all the rocks about were hung with heavy curtains of ivy, which added to the gloom and dreariness of that dark place.

Having brought their prisoner safely to this den, where dwelt the others of their band, the robbers cast her roughly on the floor, and proceeded then to eat and drink, making no use of chopsticks, but snatching with their fingers at the food, so wolfish was their hunger. Helpless sat the little maid before them, tears streaming down her cheeks.

"We have plucked a pale-faced moon-flower!" jeered one among the band. "A tender blossom, to crush full easily beneath our feet if it smile not at our bidding."

And so the robbers taunted her while they were eating. When their meal was done, the captain took a koto or harp and thrust it into her hands, the while he cried with savage threats:

"Now let us hear thee play! If thou dost hesitate, I swear with my good sword to cut thee into bits!"

White Aster dried her tears and drew one slender finger tremblingly across the strings. But at the sound of that one single splendid chord, all terror left the maiden suddenly,—her heart was filled with confidence and power. Again and once again she swept the strings and drew from that small instrument such harmony of sound, such witchery of sweetness, such deep, soul-stirring melody, that, one by one, those robbers ceased all movement and listened, spell-bound and entranced.

So it chanced they failed to hear footsteps rapidly approaching their deeply hidden lair. Ere they suspected aught, the door flew open, and in burst one full armed with sword and spear. Sharp conflict followed, whereat the little maiden shrieked, and dropped her harp, and hid her face within her hands to shut out such a sight. The stranger bore himself right nobly. All that desperate robber band he stretched upon the ground before him, save only one who burst from out his grasp and fled into the forest.

At length came stillness in the room, and kind and tender arms lifted little White Aster. She dropped her hands that covered her face and saw the hermit before her.

"Ah, little one," he cried, "I could not let thee thread the wilderness alone, and so I followed thee. White Aster, I must tell thee something. I am thy long lost brother—I! I am that worthless Akitoshi, for whom our father and mother mourned. How my heart yearned to tell thee so when thou didst pour out all thy story in my hut, but false pride kept my lips tight closed, and so I let thee go alone forth into the forest."

"My brother, Akitoshi, thou! O thanks be to great Buddha!"

"Yea," said the hermit. "Long ago I sorrowed for my way-wardness, and for the grief that I had caused. But when at last I went to seek my parents out and beg for their forgiveness, O alas! I found our native village all in ruins, my father and mother gone, and no news of them anywhere. Now thou, White Aster, must be all in all to me. Together we will seek our father."

Trustingly, then, White Aster put her little hand within the hermit's greater palm, and they two fared forth from the robbers' lair, and passed on side by side through twilight dusk, where the deep stillness of the night had hushed the forest, save now and then, for some shrill cry of monkeys. They were at last on the very point of emerging from the dark ravine, when that one robber who had escaped the fray, fell suddenly upon the hermit. A desperate struggle followed. Little White Aster, in dismay, sought to flee to some safe distance. But in the darkness, she lost her way, nor when she sought to find her brother again, did she know how to retrace her steps. In vain she called: "O Akitoshi! Akitoshi! Brother!"

No answer came. All night again she wandered on the lonely mountain. Just as the sun was rising, she came out upon the summit of a cliff whence, looking down, she saw a tiny village nestling in the valley, and near it a wayside shrine. Making her way slowly thither, White Aster knelt in prayer.

"O Buddha, divine protector, save a little maid!" she cried.

Just then there passed an aged peasant of the place, and seeing her so weary, with pale face and drooping form, he invited her to go with him to his own cottage. So he led her to his rustic home and there gave her over to the care and comradeship of his young daughter, who received her kindly and with sweet compassion.

In this rude home White Aster dwelt for many a day, yet never once ceased longing for her father and Akitoshi. But so lovely grew the little maid, that fame of her soon traveled over all the land. At length the governor himself, in his great palace, heard tales of her surpassing beauty and determined to have her for his bride. Without delay he sent a matrimonial agent to bargain with the peasant for her hand. Now the peasant had been always kind to the little guest who thus had come beneath his guardianship, but the prospect of so brilliant an alliance turned his head, and he consented to the marriage on the spot, without consulting White Aster. When the agent in his glory had departed, the old man went unto White Aster and said:

"White Aster, I have promised thee today in marriage to the Governor. Thou art honored above women. Make thee ready."

Tears filled the little maiden's eyes.

"I do not wish to wed the Governor," she said.

"What matter thy wishes? Thou must," the peasant answered.

"But, in very truth, I cannot," the little maid replied with tears. "I am already promised to another. If I must tell thee all my secret, then know that I am not own daughter to that dear beloved mother who reared me from my childhood. She found

me couched amidst the white chrysanthemums within a temple
garden, when I was but a babe, and, deeming Buddha had sent
me as a gift to bless her, brought me up and loved me ever as a
daughter. But ere she died she made me vow full solemnly to
wed none other but her son, my foster-brother, Akitoshi."

Now as she pleaded, weeping, the old peasant, might, per-
chance, have heeded her, for in his heart he loved her, but
at that very moment came hurrying from the governor the agent
once again, bearing a chest full to overflowing of most magnificent presents. Acceptance of these on the guardian's part would
make the bargain for marriage binding. Making of all a great
display before the peasant's eyes, the agent so dazzled the poor
old man that he greedily accepted them, while wondering neighbors stood gaping by, admiring with huge amazement.

So little White Aster in despair perceived that, whether she
wished or no, she would be forced to wed the mighty Governor.
Stealing at midnight from the peasant's home, she made her way
across the rice fields to the rushing river. There she climbed up
the high, curved bridge that over-arched the stream, and thought
to cast herself into the plunging waters. No other way there
seemed to end her troubles. Closing her eyes she uttered a final

prayer and was about to spring, when a strong hand grasped her shoulder and a man's voice firmly cried: "Stay, White Aster! Stay!"

Looking up, White Aster saw her Akitoshi himself.

"So long have I sought thee, my little White Aster," he cried.

The maiden knew not what to say for very joy. Words failed her at so great a moment. Once more, as on that night long past, she put her little hand in his great palm and let him lead her tenderly away. Through the forest to his home they went.

But now in Akitoshi's hut another joy awaited White Aster,— a joy so great that her very soul went leaping up within her. For who sat there beside the fire, but her beloved father? Eagerly she sprang to meet him; solemnly he rose and blessed her.

"I found him many months ago, when I was seeking thee," said Akitoshi, "and he has granted me his most august forgiveness."

"Dear father," the little maiden cried, "why didst thou leave me so long alone? Didst thou, indeed, as I once dreamed, fall from the mountain side into a deep ravine?"

"Aye, little White Blossom," the father said. "I fell into a deep ravine, with sides so steep I tried in vain to scale them. For three long days I tried, then gave up in despair. There seemed no hope but that I must most surely perish, when suddenly appeared above, high on the summit of the cliff, a band of monkeys gibbering and grimacing. Swinging out on the hanging vines that overhung the rocks, the monkeys showed me how I, too, might climb up by that means. Seizing a vine, I scaled at last, though with the greatest difficulty, that perilous ascent. Then I remembered well that once not long ago when I was hunting on the mountain, I spared the lives of a mother monkey and her babe. So in my need those whom I blessed, blessed me with large return."

Thus little White Aster found her foster-father once again, and great was the rejoicing in that hut. In time she married Akitoshi, and they three dwelt in happiness together, beneath the protecting shadow of the calm, majestic mountain.

FROM THE TOWER WINDOW

THE EXILE OF RAMA

Retold from The Ramayana, the Sacred Poem of India

IN THE midst of the pleasant plain, above the waving green of mango trees, arose the walls and stately towers, the gilded turrets, battlements and spires of fair A-yod'hya, ancient capital of King Das-a-ra'tha and the children of the Sun. Now this great King had led a life of virtue and of valor; yet, though he had three Queens, he had no son to follow him on the throne. So when his years were many, he besought of Heaven a worthy heir to take his place, to rule his people wisely and guard them well. In answer to his prayer there came not one fine son, but four,—Ra'ma, eldest born, son of the Queen Kau-sal'ya, a babe as lovely as a star, so bright that every torch grew dim before him in the chamber of the Queen; Bha'rat, the second son, beautiful and meek and mild, child of the Queen Kai-key'i; and Laksh'-man and his twin brother, sons of the youngest Queen.

Nursed with care, these babes grew into fair, strong youths, filling their father's heart with joy, and he lived in such sweet comradeship with them that he seemed no father but an elder brother to them all. Modest were the princes and in them all the virtues blended. They loved each other as brothers ever should, and roamed the palace grounds together in sweet accord, Rama and Lakshman always side by side. Each prince rendered unto the other's mother such reverence and affection as to his own, and not one of all three Queens but loved the sons of her sister-consorts as dearly as her own.

So the father's bosom glowed with joy and pride for the rare virtues of his sons and the love they showed to one another. But best and noblest of the four, lord of all virtues, in whom all peerless graces dwelt, the King's chief glory was his eldest child, young Rama.

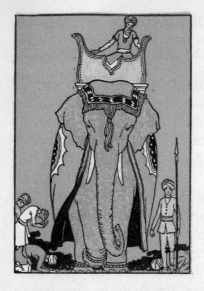

For he was gallant, beautiful and strong,*
Void of all envy and the thought of wrong.
With gentle grace to man and child he spoke,
Nor could the churl his harsh reply provoke.
He paid due honor to the good and sage,
Renowned for virtue and revered for age.
Just, pure, and prudent, full of tender ruth,
The foe of falsehood and the friend of truth;
Kind, slow to anger, prompt at misery's call,
He loved the people and was loved of all.

The years passed by for those four brothers and their father and mothers in joy and happiness, and Rama, through strong courage, won to wife the fairest maid beneath the heavens, sweet Si'ta, Rose of Women, with whom he lived in tenderest affection.

Then came a time when there arose in the monarch's breast a longing to lay aside the duties he had borne so long, and make his beloved Rama regent-heir, giving over to his hands the reins of government. When he made known his wish unto the people, there arose from all such shouts of loud acclaim as shook the very palace with a storm of sound. How often had Prince Rama, passing through the ample city streets upon his stately elephant or in his gold-decked chariot, bent to greet the townsmen as beloved friends, asking how each one fared, how thrived his wife and babes and servants. And so those townsmen loved him with exceeding great devotion. Joyous preparations were begun at once to consecrate Lord Rama regent in his father's stead.

But now, though Rama was his father's best beloved son, the lovely Queen Kai-key'i, mother of Bharat, was the King's most cherished wife. A princely palace he had built this favorite Queen, with many a little balcony that overhung fair gardens, where trees were ever glowing with fruit, where all was bright with vivid oriental flowers, and gay flamingoes stalked midst swans

* The selections from The Ramayana used in this story are from the translation by Ralph T. A. Griffith.

and cranes and peacocks spreading gorgeous jewelled trains. From the roof of this splendid palace, Kai-key'i's little hunchbacked maid looked out over all the town, and saw its temples gleaming white, its palaces and gay bazaars arrayed as if for holiday, with pennons flying in the scented air, and concert of glad music rising on the breeze. Learning that the cause of all this festive array was that Prince Rama, son of Queen Kau-sal'ya, was to be proclaimed the regent-heir, she ran in furious haste to where her mistress lay asleep.

"Up, up, my queen! Arise!" she cried. "Great peril threatens thee. Thy lord will make Prince Rama regent over all the land! Then will all wealth and honor be given to Queen Kau-sal'ya, and thou wilt be despised. All power will be Prince Rama's, and how sad will be the fate of thy dear son, Prince Bharat!"

But Kai-key'i only rose, delighted with the news.

"I rejoice that Rama shares his father's throne!" she cried. "Kau-sal'ya's son is even as dear to me as mine own child. He

hath been ever good and kind, meek to his mother and meeker still to me. What difference though he rule? There is no cause to fear. His brethren are as dear to him as his own soul."

But the crook-backed maid, burning with jealous envy, so urged her point that at the last she poisoned Queen Kai-key'i's mind, and there flamed within her but one single thought, to make the King, her husband, name her son, Prince Bharat, regent in the place of Rama, and send beloved Rama into exile in the woods. Then the evil-minded maid, eager to work her will, reminded the jealous Queen how she once tenderly nursed her husband of a wound received in battle and he, out of love and gratitude, had sworn to grant her any two requests. A vow so deeply sacred, no true Hindu would ever dare to break.

"Ask that he name thy Bharat regent," said the maid, "and send Rama into exile far within the woods."

Now Prince Bharat was from home just then, attending at an uncle's court, and his mother took upon herself alone the full responsibility for his fate. Casting aside her splendid robes and jewels, she dressed herself in mourning garments and threw herself upon the floor in a mean and wretched little chamber, there awaiting her husband in pretended agony and woe.

Slow and majestic as the moon gliding in glory across the calm fields of the autumn sky, passed King Das-a-ra'tha to his darling's palace. Not finding her awaiting him at the usual place, where she was wont to gladden his eyes by sight of her at that hour, he anxiously sought news of her from her maids. Being by them informed where she had taken herself, he passed on to the mean and wretched chamber, and there found her prostrate on the ground. Anxious to soothe her grief, he knelt beside her and tried many a kind caress, coaxing her to tell him what moved her to such sorrow. Seizing her chance, the Queen reminded him of his promise long since given when she had nursed him of his wound, and bade him now swear to grant her two

FROM THE TOWER WINDOW

requests. Betrayed by his great love, the King leapt like a deer into the snare she laid. With a fond smile, he placed his hand beneath his darling's head and raised her up, then solemnly swore to grant her any two requests, reminding her that no one on the earth was dearer to him than she, save only Rama.

"This solemn pomp that thou hast begun in Rama's honor," she cried, "give over to Bharat! Consecrate my son and send thy Rama, banished for fourteen years, into the distant forests."

Struck dumb with horror at her words, the King spoke not a word at first, the while there dawned upon him all the meaning of the boon she asked—the deep-laid scheme by which she had entrapped him. Then in his indignation he burst forth:

"The world may live without the sun as well as I without my Rama! Take Rama from me and what is life then worth to me? How couldst thou scheme so foul a plot? What has my Rama ever done to thee? Hast thou not often held him as a babe upon thy knee and when he smiled, sworn he was dear to thee as thine own son? Has he not ever shown thee sonlike love and sweet obedience? O wife, have mercy on my bitter cry. Take all my treasures but leave my Rama here with me!"

No thrill of pity stirred the soul of that envy-hardened queen. She still claimed stubbornly fulfilment of the oath. The whole long dreary night the unhappy King spent in entreaty, searching out the way to touch her heart. He could not move her from her purpose. So dawned the morning of the day that had been set aside for Rama's consecration, and that noble youth, summoned from his beloved Sita's side to seek his father, entered the chamber where the King and Queen Kai-key'i lingered. Reverently Rama bowed to greet his royal sire, and then as reverent, did obeisance at Kai-key'i's feet. The King with downcast eyes, that brimmed with tears, could only murmur, "Rama!" and then say no more. The youth beholding what a change the night had wrought in his dear father, and seeing him thus weeping and unstrung, was pierced with sorrow, and turning to Kai-key'i asked her courteously the cause for such a change. That greedy dame, lost now to shame, told the whole matter to the prince, how the King, his father, had taken most solemn oath to grant her two requests, yet now would shamefully refuse to keep his word because the boons she asked meant that her Bharat should be regent and he, Rama, sent off for fourteen years to exile.

No angry word, no sharp reproof passed Rama's gentle lips. At once he said:

"Fear not, O lady, my father's faith shall never be pledged in vain. If he hath promised I will go. Heralds shall summon Bharat home to take my place as regent, and I will don the hermit's garb and fare forth to the forest. One duty I hold above all others—that a son should ever serve and be obedient to his father."

Then he gently stooped to comfort his beloved father, who in speechless woe had heard his words. With reverent farewell he left the bower where Queen Kai-key'i sat exulting in her triumph, and went to pay one last sad visit to his own beloved mother. As he passed along the streets, he saw the signs of joy, no more for him, and all the sacred vessels arranged for that great day, the golden chalices, whose water poured upon his head would have ordained him lord. He saw and did not turn his eye away. His glance betrayed no anguish, his foot no haste. Still on his brow, though his high hopes were dead, shone that great glory that was all his own.

He found his mother in linen robes of purest white, intent on holy rites, for she was of more serious mood than lotus-eyed Kai-key'i. But when she heard his news, how hope of being regent was no more for him, but exile in the distant forest in its place, she wept in black despair and none could comfort her. Then came the faithful brother, Lakshman, devoted to Prince Rama, and in anger cried that he would set his Rama on the throne by force if Rama would permit, for what had come to pass was all unfair. With streaming eyes the mother too begged Rama to give heed to Lakshman's counsel.

"Forgive me, mother," said the hero gently. "I have no power to disobey my father. See me at thy honored feet and give me now thy blessing, for I needs must go."

So forced at last, Kau-sal'ya let him go.

"May virtue be thy sure defence!" she cried. "Thy tender love and meek obedience, like a mystic charm, will arm thy soul, my Rama! Go forth my son, my pride and glory, go!"

Then Rama fell upon his knees before her, pressed her dear feet and said his last farewell. With Lakshman still beside him, he turned his anxious steps toward his own home. The hardest trial of all remained before him still, to take his leave of his beloved Sita. As he passed through his stately halls, his eye was drooping and his brow was overcast. Wont as he was to curb each passion with a firm control, he yet could scarcely bear within his own strong bosom the load of anguish that was heavy there. Quick to trace the sorrow on his face, sweet Sita cried:

"What ails thee, O my lord?   This happy day
Should see thee joyful.   All but thou are gay.
Why does no royal canopy, like foam
For its white beauty, shade thee to thy home?
Where are the tuneful bards thy deeds to sing?
Where are the fans that wave before the king?
Why doth the city send no merry throng
To bring thee home with melody and song?
Why doth no gilded car thy triumph lead,
With four brave horses of the swiftest breed;
No favored elephant precede the crowd
Like a black mountain or a thunder-cloud;
No herald march in front of thee to hold
The precious burthen of thy throne of gold?
If thou be king, ordained this day, then why
This sorry plight, pale cheek and gloomy eye?"

Thus Sita questioned in her wild suspense and Rama told her gently all the tale, how there was no anointing now for him, how, forced by duty's higher law, he must go forth to exile, leaving her and all he loved behind.

"Be firm and strong, dear wife, when I am gone," he said, "and ever serve with tender care the King, my father. Be dutiful unto Bharat, too, since he will rule, and never vex him; cheer my beloved mother, and show love to all the consort-queens—they are my mothers even as mine own. Be ever gentle, humble and content."

But Sita answered, modest and yet firm, "The wife's fit place is by the husband's side. I spurn the terrace and the pleasant seat at ease in palaces when thou must face the hardships of the woods. If thou wilt go, then I go too. No heaven is anywhere for me, if thou art gone."

Lost in deep thought, the hero stood, yet still he feared to lead this tender flower into the rough and fearsome forest.

"Life in the woods is naught but grief and pain," he urged. "There the lion roars in his rocky cave, the tiger stalks abroad, and everywhere wild beasts in ambush lie. Within the streams ferocious crocodiles lie hid, and oft wild elephants rush forth, while on the gale comes borne the wolf's long howl. The homeless wretch, clad in a rough and untrimmed coat of bark, must wander through a wilderness of sand and thorn and sleep upon the ground. Enough, dear love. A life like that is not for thee. Stay home, my Sita, and be happy here."

But Sita spoke once more with weeping eyes: "The woe, the terror, all the toil and pain will but be joy to me, joined with thy love. O let me go! Whate'er I may endure, following thee, will only make my soul more pure. Fear not for me! O my Rama, let me go!"

And with a bitter cry she flung her arms round Rama's neck and clung there till he gave her leave to go.

"I knew not, love, the strength of thy fond heart," he said. "Naught now shall ever part me from my wife."

FROM THE TOWER WINDOW

Then Lakshman's eyes began to overflow with generous tears. Fondly caressing his brother's feet he said, "If thy purpose then is changeless, I too will follow thee nor ever leave thee."

Rama sought in vain to urge his brother to remain behind. That true and faithful friend would not yield his intent. So the royal three, Rama, and his true wife, Sita, and Lakshman, faithful to the end, walked for the last time to the palace, to see the aged King. Through crowds that filled each street and balcony, each portico and roof, they passed, and pity moved the hearts of all to see the highborn princess and the kingly youths so humbly walking in the way. Loud from their loving hearts the people called to Rama to remain and be their King. Firm in duty, he heeded not their words but passed on to the palace.

Surrounded by his queens and ladies of his court, the King stood waiting. When his two sons with Sita came within the hall, the wretched father fell prostrate to the ground, and all the mighty hall was rent by one great wail. Mid the silver sound of tinkling ornaments that bound their wrists, a thousand women in one wild lament, cried, "Rama! Rama!"

Still no complaint the noble Rama made. He comforted his father and spoke soothingly to all.

"Let chariots, elephants, horsemen, all my treasures follow in Lord Rama's train to ease his exile!" cried the King.

But Rama answered: "All that—the host, the riches, and the pomp would be quite useless to me, sire. For I have left the world and all its false desires, its pride and cares behind. I shall lead within the wilderness the hermit's life of sweet simplicity."

Then Queen Kai-key'i, with unblushing brow, handed out with her own hands the rough bark mantles to the three. Removing their fine garments, Rama and Lakshman donned at once the hermit's dress, but tender Sita in her flowing silks, eyed the strange garment trembling. Nestling closer to her Rama's side, she begged him in her soft, low, faltering accents to help her put it on. With

391

his own hands Lord Rama fastened it, but over her silks, not next
her tender skin. Then the Rose of Women took her seat in the
sun-bright car the King had waiting; Rama and Lakshman sprang
in by her side, and bearing with them naught save only a basket
bound in hide and a husbandman's hoe, they left the city, crowds
following their chariot, weeping and lamenting. Last sight of
all, Lord Rama saw his father, grief stricken, on the ground, and
with him his sad mother and her train, and his last look of love
and grief was in the eyes of that beloved mother.

Riding thus, the exiles came by night where the dark river
Jum'ne pours her tributary tide with kissing waves into the
Ganges' crystal flood. There beneath a spreading banyan tree
they spent the night and in the morning built a raft, by means
of which they crossed the sacred stream. From there Lord Rama
watched the faithful subjects who had followed him to Ganges,
sadly wending homeward on the far bank of the river. Then
with Sita bidden always to walk between him and his brother,
that they two might guard her from all harm, he plunged into
the forest. In single file they marched through the wonderful
tropical jungle, amidst a wealth of vivid flowers, beneath huge
trees where brilliant birds made music, and chattering monkeys
leapt from limb to limb. And so they came at last where that
vast mountain Chit-ra-ku'ta, tinged with a thousand dyes, lifts
his summit to the sky, while all about him higher peaks ascend.
So beautiful was that spot that, beholding it, Lord Rama's soul

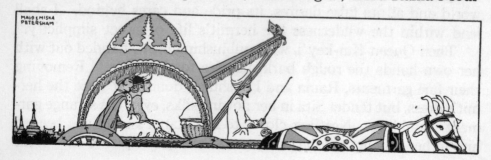

was filled with deep content and he cried unto his comrades:

"See waving in the western wind,
The light leaves of the tamarind;
And mark that giant peepul through
Those feathery clumps of tall bamboo.
That depth of shade, that open lawn
Allure the wood-nymph and the fawn;
And, where those grassy glades extend,
The spirits of the air descend,
To while the summer night away
With dalliance and mirth and play.
Look, from the mountain's woody head
Hangs many a stream like silver thread,
Till, gathering strength, each rapid rill
Leaps, lightly laughing, down the hill,
Then, bounding o'er the rocky wall,
Flashes the foamy water-fall."

Thrilled with the joy of that wonderful spot, the exiles went on a little further till below them they saw a beautiful river, a glorious limpid stream. On its shelving bank, their early bathing done, stood a company of hermits lifting reverent hands in prayer.

"There," said Lord Rama, "will we make our home."

So the exiles joined that colony of simple souls, whose days were passed in sacred study, who sought to work not, speak not, think not sin. There Rama and Prince Lakshman built a rustic bower for Sita, and in that spot they three dwelt long in mutual love and tenderness. In the gentle stream sweet Sita often bathed and plucked red lilies for her hair, then in some green and grassy glade she and Lord Rama took their fill of gazing on the landscape, watching now the bright flamingoes with their rosy wings, and now the swans and herons on the stream below, or troops of deer come gently to the banks to drink. Rama and Lakshman gathered fruit for food and brought in trophies of the chase, which Sita with gay cheerfulness prepared and cooked.

Thus in simple joy the time passed by until it chanced one day that one among the hermits brought disturbing news of a great multitude seen marching through the forest toward the hermitage. Climbing quickly to the tipmost top of a giant tree, Lakshman beheld a long procession winding through the woods. In great excitement he descended to the ground and cried:

"O Rama, I doubt not that this is Bharat come to finish his envious mother's work and put thee by force out of his way forever! Beware!"

Gently Lord Rama rebuked his brother, for it was not in his heart ever to think evil of another.

"Nay, my dear Lakshman," he replied. "That cannot be. If Bharat comes at all, he comes to do us good, with some most loving purpose in his heart."

And so when the long train drew near, Lord Rama greeted Bharat with the tenderest affection, while Lakshman stood half scowling and suspicious by. But Bharat flung himself before Lord Rama's feet with bitter tears.

"Dear brother," he said, "on my return from visiting our uncle, how shocked was I to hear what in my absence had been done, how my poor mother, deluded quite, had forced our father to name me regent in thy stead and drive thee into exile. And now, O Rama, out of grief for thee, our father, alas! is dead, thy mother his best comfort in his latest hours. And I, my lord and King, will never take thy place. Return, dear brother, to thy rights and reign in fair A-yod'hya!"

Overcome at first with grief at hearing of his father's death, Lord Rama made no answer, but at last he said:

"Nay, brother, what are pomp and wealth and pride of place? 'Tis virtue only marks the line between the great and good, the low and mean. I promised for full fourteen years to stay in exile. Shall I then break my oath and prove untrue unto my holy promise, when truth is root and spring of every virtue? Misled by false desire for power and might, shall I despise that holy gem of truth, attracted by an earthly prize? Nay, brother! Urge this plea no more. I still will keep my oath nor leave this forest till the fourteen years are past. Do thou return and act as regent of the realm, and this I promise thee—I will not live my years of banishment in idleness, but will spend them so that they shall shower rich blessings on my people."

In vain Bharat entreated. Rama stood steadfast in his purpose. Then Bharat, bending to embrace his brother's feet, besought of him his golden sandals, crying, "If thou thyself wilt not return and I must be the regent in thy stead, then will I never sit upon thy throne. Thy sandals only shall occupy that royal seat beneath the white umbrella of the King. Bharat will rule in Rama's name."

With utmost generosity and love those brothers said farewell, and the gorgeous train with Bharat at its head, slowly wended once again its way through the forest paths to fair A-yod'hya. And there for fourteen years by Bharat's will, the sandals of Lord Rama occupied the throne beneath the white umbrella, and all men did homage to those sandals, nor was Bharat tempted once within his soul to prove untrue unto his elder brother.

As to Rama in the forest,—he rose up in all the might of noble manhood and sought out, through toil and long and difficult adventure, the source and well spring of all evil in the world, that impious demon, Ravan, who defied the Lord of Lords, and all the Hosts of Heaven. Him Rama slew, and so indeed, through his long years of self-for-getful exile, brought deliverance to his people. But when the fourteen years were up, with Laksh-man and sweet Sita, Rose of Women, he returned once more unto A-yod'hya, and there midst loud re-joicings of his people, took at last his right-ful seat upon the golden throne beneath the regal white um-brella that served only for the King.

CUCHULAIN, THE IRISH HOUND
Retold from Songs of the Ancient Gaelic Bards

N DAYS when the world was young and men towered up in elemental hardihood and simple majesty, like wind blown oaks, there dwelt in Erin a race of giant heroes— the Red Branch Knights of Ulster. Mighty, exceedingly were these men and vast was the hall where they met together in the dun[1] of E'main Ma'cha, so vast that a man, as men are now, standing in the centre and shouting his loudest, would not be heard at the circumference, yet was the lowest laughter of the King sitting at one end, clearly audible to those who sat about the Champion at the other. The length of that great hall was a mile, nine furlongs and a cubit, and it was illumined by innumerable candles, tall as spears. The vast murmur of talk when all the Red Branch were assembled there, was like distant thunder, or the far off boom of stormy waters; the roar of their tremendous brazen chariots shook the very heavens, and their giant steeds drank rivers dry.

So, in their might and in their glory they rejoiced, yet more in that inviolable unity which bound them all together, a host of comrades, of heroic valor, but of heroic affection, too, which neither strength nor cunning, neither power, unseen nor seen, could ever destroy. Of these colossal heroes was Con'co-bar Mac Nes'sa, King, and Fer'gus MacRoy, Champion. Yet gigantic as they were, and gigantic as their deeds, they looked for one to come, a youth, in spirit more gigantic still, to lead them forth to mightier victories. So had the long beard, the Arch-Druid, foretold, high-priest of Erin's ancient gods and prophet of the clan.

"Yea, he is coming; he draweth nigh.
Verily it is he whom I behold—
The predicted one—the child of many prophecies—
Chief flower of the Branch that is over all,
The mainstay of E'main Ma'cha,
The torch of the valor and chivalry of the North,
The star that is to shine forever upon the forehead of the Gael."

[1] *Stronghold usually on a hill.*

396

FROM THE TOWER WINDOW

Now it chanced at this time that Su-al'tam of Dun Dal'gan on the Eastern Sea, King of a rugged, mountainous land, had taken to wife Dec-ter'a, sister of Con'co-bar Mac Nes'sa, and they two had one only son, Se-tan'ta. Se-tan'ta was a child of simple, hardy purity of mind who knew not guile or baseness. Along the sands and by the rolling waves he played. He had a ball and an ashen hurle shod with bronze. Joyfully he used to drive his ball along the sand, shouting among his playmates. The Captain of his father's guard gave him a sheaf of toy javelins, and taught him how to cast, and made for him a sword of lath and a painted shield. They made him a high-chair too, and in the great hall of the dun, when supper was served, he used to sit beside the Champion of that little realm, over against the King. Ever, as evening drew on and candles were lit so the dishes on the table, the armor and trophies hanging on the walls shone in the cheerful light, there among those dark-browed, bearded men appeared Setanta, very fair and pure, yellow haired, in his scarlet bratta,[1] fastened with a little brooch of silver, serene and grave beyond his years, shining like some bright star on the edge of a mighty thunder cloud.

As to the palace where he dwelt, it was of timber, staunched with clay and roofed with thatch of rushes. Without, it was washed white with lime, so that it shone and glistened from its height far, far out to sea. There was a rampart around the dun and a moat spanned by a drawbridge. Before it was a spacious lawn, down which there ran a stream of sparkling water. On this Setanta sailed his boats, now where it stayed in silent stillness, now where it hummed in hurrying rapids, now where it clothed itself in silver to

[1] *Mantle.*

397

make liquid music or blow its little trumpet as it leaped in cataracts.

But at length the quiet life in that remote dun no longer pleased Setanta, for the spirit awoke within him and drave him to be doing. Moreover, he longed for comrades, and his mother, who loved him dearly, would no more permit him to play with other children of that realm, whose rude behavior she misliked for her dear child. In summer he sat often with the ancient bard under the thatched eaves of the dun, while crying swallows came and went above, asking many questions concerning his illustrious forefathers of the line of Rury,—who had lived worthily and well? And ever he loved best to hear of deeds of that great champion Fergus MacRoy. Upon his seventh birthday, scarcely after dawn, Setanta ran to his mother, and cried:

"Mother, send me now to Emain Macha to my uncle!"

Dectera's face grew pale, her knees smote one against the other for loving fear. For answer she withdrew Setanta from society of men and kept him by herself within the women's quarter, from the upper story of which a door opened on a balcony just above the King's throne in the banquet hall. Thence Dectera was wont of mornings to direct the labors of the household thralls, and thence, ere he went to bed, Setanta was permitted to cry "Good night," to those good friends, whose company he once had shared in the hall below; and those great bearded heroes laughed much among themselves, for well they knew the cause of little Setanta's imprisonment.

Save for this, Setanta saw no more of men, and Dectera gave straight commandment to her women to speak no word to him concerning Emain Macha. The boy as yet knew not even where lay that wondrous city, whether in heaven or on earth or beyond the sea. To him it seemed a fairy city or one in the land of dreams. But still the strong spirit from within urged him on, irresistibly. He watched long lines of lowing kine and laden garrans[1] wending o'er the plain and wondered if their way led to the city. One day it chanced his mother let drop words that made Setanta know the road to Emain Macha went past the mountain, Slieve Fuad, and thenceforth when he gazed upon that purple mountain-top, he thought it nodded and beckoned to him. Next morning, after he had broken fast among the women, he donned his best attire, took his toy weapons, a new ball, and his best ashen hurle shod with red bronze, and when his mother had kissed him, went forth as at other times to play alone upon the lawn. Under the eaves his father sat sunning himself and gazing on the sea. The boy kneeled and kissed his father's hand. Sualtam stroked his head and said, "Win victory and blessings, dear Setanta!"

In the window of the upper chamber sat Dectera amongst her women, embroidering a little garment for her boy.

"Mother," he cried, "watch this stroke!" And he flung his ball into the air, then, leaning back, he met it with his hurle as it fell, striking it with such force that it flew high up into the clouds.

"Give me thy blessing, dear mother!" he cried, stopping beneath her window ere he ran to search for his ball.

"Win victory and blessings forever, dear Setanta," she answered. "Truly thou art an expert hurler!"

"These feats," he replied, "are nothing to what I shall do in needlework, O mother, when I am of age to be trusted with my first needle, knighted by thy hands and enrolled amongst the valiant company of thy sewing women!"

"What meaneth the boy?" said his mother, perceiving he spoke awry.

"That his childhood is ended, O Dectera," said one among the women.

The Queen's heart leaped, blood forsook her face, she bent her head over the little garment she was working and tears fell from her eyes. After a space she looked out again upon the

[1] *A breed of small horses used for rough work especially in Ireland and Scotland.*

399

lawn to see if her boy had returned. He was not there, so she bade her women go and fetch him. Everywhere they searched. They called aloud, "Setanta! O Setanta!" But there was no answer, only silence, and from the leaves of those tall sentinels, the watching trees, a sound like low and mocking laughter—for Setanta was far away!

The boy went swiftly for there was power upon him that day.

In his left hand was his sheaf of toy javelins, in his right the hurle; his little shield was strapped upon his back. With his hurle he ever urged his ball forward and followed running where it fell. At other times he would cast a javelin far westward and pursue its flight. Divers persons, noble and ignoble, passed him on the way, some riding in chariots, some going on foot, but they went as though they saw him not. In the evening he came to Slieve Fuad. Here he gathered a bed of moss, wrapped himself in his mantle and lay down to sleep, feeling neither cold nor hunger. Loud singing of birds awoke him, and, light of heart, he started from his couch, while dawning day still trembled through the half bare trees. Hastening to a brook nearby, he bathed in the clear pure water, then he put on his shirt of fine linen, and his woolen tunic of many pleats that reached to his knees, and his little woolen bratta of divers colors and went on his way. Reverently he laid a stone in tribute on the well-heaped cairn[1] sacred to the memory of the hero of the mountain, and so at last he came to the brow of the hill. Looking off to westward, he saw far away, all white and shining, the walls and low rambling buildings of the marvelous city, Emain Macha, whereat he trembled and rejoiced and wept. Then on he went more slowly till he drew near the great, painted, glowing palace. But here he was filled with awe and fear. Covering his face with his mantle, he wept aloud and said he would return to Dun Dalgan, for that he dared not set unworthy feet in such a holy place.

But as he wept, there fell upon his ear the cheerful voices of

[1] *A rounded or conical heap of stones erected as a memorial.*

FROM THE TOWER WINDOW

happy boys who brake from the palace and ran down the wide, smooth lawn to the hurling ground. At sight of them, his heart yearned for their companionship. He longed to go to them and say, "I am little Setanta. My uncle is the King and I would be your friend and playfellow!" But he knew not how they would receive him. Fear strove with hope and love within his heart. Yet he was urged forward—by what power he knew not. Reluctantly, with many pausings, he drew nigh the players, and stood solitary near the southern barrier, for the company that held that goal appeared the weaker. He hoped that some one among them all would call to him and bid him welcome, but none called or welcomed. Some looked at him, but with looks of cold surprise as though they said, "What does this stranger here?" Silently the child wept. He had thought he would be welcomed and made much of because of his skill in hurling, and because he was the nephew of the King, and because he himself longed so exceedingly for companions, and there was in him such a fountain of loving-kindness and affection. Many a time happy visions had passed before his eyes of his meeting with his future comrades, but now that he was with them, no one bade him welcome, or took him by the right hand and led him in; no one seemed glad of his coming and he was here of no account at all. Bitter were his tears. Soon the ball, struck sideways, bounded into a clear space near Setanta.

"Thou of the javelins!" cried the Captain of the distressed party, "the ball is with thee!"

On a sudden Setanta, filled with all the glow and ardor of the mimic battle, cast his javelins to the ground, slipped the strap of his shield over his head, flung the shield beside his javelins on the grass, and pursued the bounding ball. Outrunning all the rest, he took possession of it, and urged it forward, now to right and now to left. Deftly he played it before every opponent who sought to check him, carrying it swiftly and cunningly past each, till finally with one strong stroke he sent it straight through the middle of the north goal. Loudly the boys of his adopted party praised him. Setanta's eyes were sparkling and his face flushed with joy. But the Captain of the northern company came down across the lawn with his boys crowding around Setanta.

"Thou art a stranger here," he said, "and on sufferance, and we will permit thee to join our company only on condition that thou wilt acknowledge thyself subject unto us."

Setanta's brow fell and he answered, "Put not upon me, I pray you, these hard terms. I would be your friend and comrade. I cannot be your subject, being what I am."

And they said, "Who art thou?"

And he answered, "I am the son of King Sualtam and Queen Dectera of Dun Dalgan and nephew to thy King."

Then the boy who was Captain of the whole school and biggest and strongest of all stood over him and said:

"Thou, the King's nephew! And comest hither without chariots and horsemen, and a prince's retinue and guard! Nay, thou art a churl and a liar to boot. Hie thee hence with wings at thy heels, or verily with sore blows I shall beat thee off the lawn."

Thereat the blood forsook Setanta's face. He stood like a figure carved of white marble. And that other, angered to see him stand so still, and mistaking for fear the pallor of wounded tenderness, raised his hurle and struck at the boy with all his might. Setanta sprang back, avoiding the blow, and ere the other could recover himself, smote him, back-handed, over the right ear. The boy's knees suddenly relaxed; the useless weapon fell from his hands. Then some lads stood aside but the rest ran upon Setanta in a crowd to beat him off the lawn. Stoutly the stranger defended himself, for in his gentle heart awoke the spirit that brooks no injustice. Many a time he was overborne and flung to the ground, but again he arose, overthrowing others, never quitting hold of his hurle, and whenever he got a free space, wielding that weapon like a war-mace. The skirts of his mantle were torn; only a rag remained round his shoulders, fastened by the brooch. While his foes closed in upon him on each side, he beat his way to the grassy rampart where was the goal, and standing there, flung them a challenge.

"You have bade me proclaim myself your subject!" he cried, "and I would not, but now since you have fallen on me, many against one, I swear to you that you and I do not part this day till you have acknowledged yourselves subjects unto me!"

Then a boy stood out from the rest, freckled and red-headed.

"Henceforth thou shalt have a comrade in thy battle, O brave stranger," he cried, and running to Setanta, he knelt down and took his hand. "I am thy man from this day forward!"

And so he was, brave Laeg, Setanta's closest friend forever more. A few who loved the stalwart red-haired boy, came now over to Setanta's side, and though their numbers still were few, they drave the multitude before them over the whole playing-ground until they brake their ranks and fled. Of the fugitives, some ran round to that fair lawn before the palace, where beneath a spreading tree, Concobar, the King, and Fergus, the great

Champion, sat on three-legged stools before a table spread with brightly colored cloth, and played at chess with men of gold and silver. But Setanta, in hot pursuit, sprang lightly over the table. Then Concobar caught him by the wrist and brought him to a stand, panting and with dilated eyes.

"Who art thou," he cried, "who thus misusest my boys?"

"I am Setanta, son of Sualtam and of Dectera, thy sister, and it is not before mine own Uncle's palace that I should be dishonored."

Concobar smiled, well pleased with the behavior of the boy, but Fergus caught him up in his great arms and kissed him, offering to be his tutor. Thus Setanta came unto his uncle's court, and the reward of his first show of courage was that the boys elected him to be their Captain. A just and gentle Captain he made, a good playfellow and comrade. And ever his closest friend, who slept in the same bed with him, was Laeg, who came so nobly to assist him. In that great school for boys kept at the King of Ulster's Court, Setanta was taught to hurl spears at a mark, to train war-horses, and guide war-chariots, to use the sword, to run, to leap, to swim, to rear tents of turf and branches swiftly and to roof them with sedge and rushes, to speak and bear himself toward all in seemly fashion, to respect his plighted word and be ever loyal to his Captains, to reverence women, and in hearing tales of his illustrious ancestors to distinguish between those who had done well and those who had done ill. So much Setanta learned at court that his good mother could but be reconciled to their parting.

Now it happened when Setanta had reached his tenth year that there came unto Emain Macha a man, grim, huge, and swarthy, messenger from Chulain, the smith, mightiest craftsman of those days, who made weapons, armor and chariots for the Ultonians. Chulain dwelt with his industrious journeymen and apprentices in a huge and smoky dun, where the ringing of hammers and roaring of bellows seldom ceased. At night the sparks from his anvils and the red glare of his furnaces painted far and wide the sky above the barren moor—a fearful sight. This grim messenger, Chulain had sent to bid Concobar unto a feast with such of his followers as were not too hearty eaters, which prudent provision for the saving of his substance caused among Concobar's men much secret mirth.

As the King, with his followers, set forth, they passed the lawn where Setanta and his friends were playing and stopped for a moment to look on. The lad was straight and well-made, with sinews as hard as tempered steel. When he saw the company looking at him he blushed, and his blushing became him well.

"Chulain, the smith, hath invited us to a feast," said Concobar. "If it pleases thee, come too."

"It pleases me indeed," replied the boy, for he ardently desired to see the famous artificer, his furnaces and engines. "But let me first finish my game and then follow you."

So Concobar gave his permission and went on.

When Chulain saw far away the tall figures of the Ultonians against the sunset, and the flashing of their weapons and armor, he cried out with a loud voice to his people to stop working, wash from them the smoke and sweat of their labor, and put on clean clothes to receive the Red Branch. Then he sent those among his men who were best dressed and most comely to receive the High King of the Ultonians on the moor, but he himself stood looming in the great doorway, leaning upon a huge, long-handled sledge, his vast and hairy chest, half-covered by a leathern apron. As the King and all his knights filed by, he gave to each a grave and friendly welcome. When all had entered, dusk had fallen.

"Are all thy people arrived?" then asked the smith.

"They are," said Concobar.

So Chulain bade his people raise the drawbridge which spanned the deep black moat surrounding the dun, and after that, with

his own hands he unchained his one and only dog. This dog was of enormous size and fierceness. It was supposed that there was not a single man in Ireland whom he could not overpower. He had no other good quality than that he was faithful to his master and guarded his property at night. Being let loose, he sprang over the moat and careered three times around the city, baying fearfully. It was just then precisely that Setanta set forth from Emain Macha.

In the meantime the vast doors within the dun were shut, candles were lit and the feast began. Full bountiful it was, in spite of the great smith's request that no too-hearty eater should attend. On his high seat sat Chulain with his dusky sons and kinsmen round him, and opposite, contrasting strangely, sat the fair-haired Concobar, and all his bright and beautiful Ultonians. Many kindly speeches praising one another made the smiths and sons of Ulster, till, the evening being well advanced, there remained not one past hero of the Ultonians who had not been praised and pledged in mead. Then rose up Concobar MacNessa to speak of future heroes of his line and sang the praises of Setanta.

"Is he then a boy of such promise?" asked the smith.

"He is all that I say," answered Concobar, somewhat hotly. "And of that thou shalt thyself judge, for he is coming and I am momentarily expecting to hear the loud clamor of his brazen hurle upon the doors of the dun after his having leapt at a single bound both thy moat and thy rampart!"

At these words the smith started from his high seat, uttering a great oath, and sternly chid Concobar because he had said that all his men had arrived.

FROM THE TOWER WINDOW

"If the boy comes now," he cried, "ere I can chain the dog, verily he will be torn to pieces."

Just then they heard the baying of the hound sounding terribly in the hollow night and every face was blanched throughout that vast assembly. Then there followed, without, a noise of trampling feet, short, furious yells, and gaspings as of one exerting all his strength, and, last of all, a dull and heavy thud that shook the earth. Ere the people in the dun could do more than look at one another, speechless, they heard a clear, yet not clamorous, knocking at the door. Some of the smith's men shot back the bolt. In out of the night the boy Setanta stepped. He was very pale, and his linen tunic and scarlet mantle were in rags, but he made a courteous reverence, as he had been taught, to the man of the house and his people, then modestly withdrew toward the upper part of the chamber. Eagerly the Ultonians ran to meet him, but Fergus McRoy took the lad upon his mighty shoulder and set him down at table between himself and Concobar.

"Did the dog come against thee?" asked Chulain.

"Truly," answered the boy.

But at that moment, entered a party of the smith's people, bearing between them the body of the hound. Great silence fell upon the chamber. When Chulain spake at last his voice was charged with wrath and he thundered forth in sorrow. Loudly he demanded that Concobar make him payment of an enormous eric[1] to requite him for his faithful hound. Then answered Concobar in like fury that his nephew had been forced in self defense to slay the monster, and no eric, great or small, should ever be had of him. This speech the Ultonians applauded fiercely, whereat the smiths, in wrath, armed themselves with hammers, tongs, fire poles and mighty bars of unwrought brass, and the great Chulain himself seized a tremendous anvil to destroy the Red Branch. On their side, the Ultonians sprang to the walls where they had hung their arms, plucked down their spears and

[1] A form of blood fine in the primitive laws of Ireland.

shields from the pegs and drew their swords. The whole vast chamber glittered with shaking bronze, shone with the eyeballs of angry men, and rang with fierce shouts of defiance. The Red Branch embattled themselves on one side of the hall, the smiths upon the other, all burning with unquenchable wrath, earth-born. But ere the first missile was hurled on either side, the boy, Setanta, rushed into the middle space which separated the men and cried aloud in his clear, high voice that rang distinct above the tumult:

"O Chulain, and you, Ultonians, my kinsmen, restrain yourselves! Forbear to hurl! Unto thee, O Chief-smith, will I pay an eric not unworthy for the death of thy brave hound. For verily I myself will take thy dog's place and nightly guard thy property, sleepless, as was he. So will I continue to do until thou dost procure a hound as valiant and as trusty as the one I slew. Truly, I slew not thy dog in any wantonness of superior strength, but only in defense of my own life, which is not mine, but my King's. Three times he leapt upon me with white fangs bared and eyeballs red with murder. Three times I cast him off and hurt him not, but when the fourth time he rushed upon me like a storm, I seized him and flung him over against a pillar, meaning but to make him stupid, for I had no thought to kill him. And truly I am sorry that he is dead, seeing that he was brave and faithful and so dear to thee whom I have ever honored and desired to see. I thought our meeting, whensoever it might come about, would be other than this, and wholly friendly."

As he went on, the fierce brow of the smith relaxed. First, he regarded the lad with pity, being so young and fair, and then with admiration for his bravery. But at last, as he thought on his own boyish days, a torrent of kindly affection and love poured from his heart toward young Setanta.

"Thy proposal is pleasing to me," he said. "I will accept thy eric!" And he flung his mighty anvil over his left shoulder into the dark end of the vast chamber, while all the smiths with mighty clatter laid aside their weapons and their wrath, and the Ultonians, rejoicing, hanged their weapons once more on the walls. Feasting and pledging in friendly speeches were renewed, and there was no more anger anywhere. The harpers harped, the Ultonians sang their mighty gathering song, and the smiths sang one of their wild, rousing songs of labor to the tune of tripping hammers ringing upon anvils.

And so Setanta remained long with the smith, and Chulain and his people loved him greatly and taught him many things. It was thus he came by his second name, Cu-chu'lain, meaning Hound of Chulain. Under that name he wrought all his marvellous deeds.

On a solemn day when Cuchulain was seventeen, Concobar called him out from the ranks of his comrades, and, with due sense of the importance of his task, bade him take over the charge of keeping clean and bright the sacred Chariot of Macha[1], wherein that mighty lady of battles when she dwelt in visible form upon the earth, had ridden forth to conquer giants,—most holy relic in Emain Macha, entrusted to the care of Concobar, the King. The chariot was of enormous size and beauty, and by its side, within the building where it stood, were two horse stalls with racks of golden bronze and mangers of yellow brass, wherein once had been stabled Macha's weird gigantic horses. The room was without windows but was lit by nine great lamps.

Obediently, Cuchulain took the fawn-skin towel and polished the chariot, and mighty though it was, he lifted it with his strong arms and made the wheels spin round, then put fresh hay and barley in the stalls while Concobar was polishing the pole, the yoke and chains, and taking from the wall long shining reins of interwoven brass and the head-gear of the horses.

"Where are the horses, my uncle Concobar?" asked the boy.

"I know not," said the King. "But, verily, they are somewhere. Li'ath Ma'cha and Black Shangh'lan are their names,—

[1] *An ancient Irish goddess.*

for three hundred years they have not been seen in Erin, but they are to come again for the promised one who shall deliver Erin from her foes, and bear him to the conflict in this chariot."

"Mayhap that ancient hero, Kimbaoth, will return to earth to be the great deliverer," said Cuchulain.

"Nay," answered Concobar. "It hath not been so prophesied. Kimbaoth was great and stern and formidable. But our promised one is gentle exceedingly. There will be more of love in his heart than war, and he will not know his own greatness." So saying, Concobar looked steadfastly upon the youth, but Setanta had no thought whatever of himself. He only answered, "Mayhap, Conall Carnach is to be that hero."

On a certain night thereafter, Cuchulain entered the armory of the Red Branch and there suddenly appeared before him the majestic figure of a man with port and countenance of some ancient hero, save that his face was shining with unearthly light.

"Thou shalt go forth tonight, Setanta," said the man, "and take captive the Liath Macha and Black Shanghlan. Power will be given thee. Go boldly forth."

"I am not wont to go forth fearfully," the lad made answer. "If this task be for me, I will perform it."

Forth he went into the night, and, having got of Chulain two such bridles as the strongest steeds could never break, he sought the mountain Slieve Fuad, and came unto the great Gray Lake. The moon was shining and the lake gleamed everywhere like silver. A huge gray horse was feeding by the waters. He raised his head and neighed when he heard footsteps on the hill. Seeing Cuchulain, he rushed fiercely toward him. The boy had one bridle knotted round his waist, the other between his teeth. He leaped upon the steed and caught him by the forelock and his mouth. Mightily the huge horse reared, but great power was on Cuchulain and he held him fast. The weird gray steed grew greater and more terrible—so did Cuchulain likewise.

FROM THE TOWER WINDOW

"Thou hast met thy master, Liath Macha, this night!" he cried.

Long they reeled together, steed and hero, and that gigantic horse leapt like a thunderbolt from crag to crag and peak to peak thrice round the whole of Ireland. Cuchulain held fast to him, nor would let go, until he stood still, conquered. Then Cuchulain rode him forth unto the Dark Valley, past the

black phantom shapes that guard the entrance into the land of everlasting night, where was a roaring of unseen rivers in the darkness, and a rush of grim black cataracts. The Liath Macha here neighed mightily. A horse neighed joyfully in answer. There came a sound as of a door burst open and thunderous trampling on the hollow-sounding earth. A coal black steed came dashing toward the Liath Macha. In the dark, Cuchulain seized his head and bitted him and bridled him ere he was aware. The horse reared and struggled, but in vain. The Liath Macha dragged him down the valley.

"Struggle not, Black Shanghlan," said Cuchulain. "I have tamed thy better! Yield thee!"

Slowly the black horse ceased to struggle also, and betwixt the two Cuchulain rode to Emain Macha.

Thus came that momentous day when Concobar agreed to knight Cuchulain. Forth from the palace the young hero came, in all the glory of his regal manhood, yet with a beautiful shame-fastness, proud in his humility, and glittering like the morning star. His silken mantle was of many hues all playing into one another, and it was fastened at the breast with a brooch like a wheel of silver. The leathern belt that girt his linen tunic was stained in color like a wild briar rose, and on his feet were comely shoes sparkling with plates of bronze that took the color of what-soever they approached. The grown men held their breath as he drew nigh, moving white knee after white knee over the green and sparkling grass.

When all the other rites had been performed, Cuchulain put his right hand into the right hand of the King and so became his man. Then Concobar gave him a shield, two spears and a sword, the best in all the land, and from those lads who once had been his playmates Cuchulain chose the faithful Laeg to be his charioteer. Wild neighing of the immortal steeds was heard in that long silent stable, then thunderous rumbling of the great war chariot, and there it came to view, guided by Laeg, out of the darkened door-way, glorious green and gold in color, with twinkling wheels, the mantle of the charioteer streaming far outward in the wind, the while he labored to restrain the furious dashing of the steeds.

Like a hawk swooping along the face of a cliff when the wind is high was the rush of those horses. The earth shook and trembled with the velocity of their motion. But the charioteer drew rein until Cuchulain sprang into the car beside him, then once more the steeds went dashing on, and all that whole assembly lifted up their voices shouting for the new-made knight, for that Cuchulain, their long-promised hero.

And in very truth Cuchulain did fulfill the promise of the long-beard, the Arch-druid, for he proved to be the greatest champion of the Gaels, the pure-burning torch of the chivalry of Ulster, in whose soul burnt that divine and godlike fire by which are ever sustained the glory and prosperity of nations.

FROM THE TOWER WINDOW

HOW BEOWULF DELIVERED HEOROT
Retold from the Old English Epic, Beowulf

 O! We have heard tell of the might in days of old of the Danish folk-kings, how deeds of daring were done by their athelings. For long in the walled towns was Hroth'gar, the beloved folk-king of the Scyl'dings known to fame among the peoples. A great following of dear kinsfolk and young warriors dwelt in his hall and obeyed him gladly. Then it burned in his spirit to bid men build him a dwelling greater than children of men had ever heard tell of, and there within it to share with young and old the blessings that God had given him. On all his kindred, far and wide through the mid-earth, was the task laid of making fair the folk-hall. Speedily it befell that it was in every wise ready, the greatest of hall-houses, and he made for it the name of *He'o-rot*, that is to say *The Stag*. The hall rose lofty and broad gabled, made out of timber, its steep roof plated with gold that shone from far. The main pillar at each end rose high above the gable peak, carven and painted, bearing antlers of the stag. Spoils of the chase decked it without. Within, it was hung with hangings.

Then Hroth'gar belied not his pledge unto his kinsmen and retainers, but held a great feast when the hall was complete, dealing out generously unto them rings and plates of gold, brooches, collars, armlets, swords and treasures in abundance. Each day was heard loud rejoicing in the hall, with sound of harp and clear song of gleemen. So the warriors lived in joy and plenty, till a foul fiend, fell prowler about the borders of the homes of men, heard their rejoicing, and being enemy of all mankind, a lonely one, terrible, himself bereft of joy, could not abide that others should be happy. This grim demon who trod in man's shape the path of exile, save that he was greater in size than any man, held the moors, the fens and fastnesses, and was called Gren'del.

When night had come, Grendel came to spy about the house

413

and see how the Danes had left it after the feasting. There he found a company of athelings asleep. The baneful wight, grim and greedy, fierce and pitiless, man-devouring, slew where they rested, all those thirty thanes. Thence fared he back homeward exultant with his spoils.

At dawn, with break of day, came servants to the place. There was the mead-hall, that lordly dwelling, empty of athelings, with bench-boards over-turned and everywhere signs of struggle. The cry of those who saw, brought Hrothgar to the spot. He looked about and found gigantic footsteps leading from the hall to the sluggish waters of a mountain tarn, the dwelling place of Grendel. Then was weeping upraised in He'o-rot after all their glad feasting. Sorrow of soul was theirs and mood of mourning. The King himself sat joyless, sorrowing for his thanes. Nor was it longer than after one night that Grendel again wrought murderous destruction still more grievous. Too old was the white-haired Hroth'gar, friend of the people, to fare forth himself to meet Grendel. Full often boasted his warsmen that they would await in the mead-hall the monster. Whenever they did so, by just so many the less were the King's thanes numbered next day. At last could the athelings no more sleep in the hall, but must find a place of rest apart, till the fairest of dwellings stood idle and useless, so soon as the evening's light had faded from the heavens.

Thus had Grendel mastery and warred against the right, he alone against all. A great while it was, twelve winters that the King endured this woe. The grisly monster, the dark death-shadow, rested not in pursuit of young and old. Night after night he held the misty moors, and in this wise wrought many an outrage. So without ceasing, Hroth'gar brooded his season of sorrow, despairing of succor.

In due course it became known openly to the children of men, as gleemen sang the sorrowful song abroad, how Grendel strove against Hroth'gar. So it chanced that Be'o-wulf, the Geat, thane of Hy'ge-lac, King of the Geat-folk, heard tell of the tale when he was from home. Strongest in might of manhood was Beo-wulf, noble and powerful. Out of largeness of soul he bade be fitted for him a good sea-goer, and said he would fare over the whale-path, over the waters, to seek out Hroth'-gar, and aid him to master the foe. Then the valiant-minded hero took to himself picked warriors of the Geat-folk, the boldest he might find. They bare their bright trap-

pings, war-gear splendrous, into the vessel, and shoved out the well-joined wood on its willing journey over the swan-road. Sped by the wind, the foamy-necked ship glided the waters, likest a bird, till on the day following, the sea-farers saw the land, the shore-cliffs gleaming before them. Thereupon the Geat-folk sprang to the beach and fastened their vessel. God they thanked because the wave-paths had proved easy for them.

Then from the steep shore the warden of the Scyldings, whose duty it was to keep watch of the sea-cliffs, saw the warsmen bear over the bulwarks their shining shields and gear ready as for battle. Their burnies (hard, hand-linked armor of metal rings) gleamed from afar, and on their gold-decked helmets graven boars kept watch as if grimly warlike of temper. The warden was fretted in his mind's thought with the wish to know what men they were.

"What men are ye, having battle gear, clad in burnies," he shouted, "who thus come leading a deep ship hither over the sea-road, over the waters?"

"We have come with kind intent to seek thy lord," said Beowulf, and made known his race and errand to those shores.

"I gather that this fellowship is of true thought toward the lord of the Scyldings," spake the warden in answer and guided the Geat-folk till they saw before them, splendid and covered with gold, the timbered house where the King dwelt, that was among earth-dwellers famed beyond all others of halls under heaven,—the sheen of it flashed over many lands. A cobbled street led them further. Thus they came faring first to the hall, and were led by a warrior where Hroth'gar sat, old and with hair exceeding white, among his band of athelings. Then spake Beowulf:

"Refuse me not one boon, O Prince of the Bright Danes, guardian of warriors, beloved friend of the people,—that I alone with my band of earls may cleanse Heorot; by my single hand that I may bring Grendel, the demon, to judgment!"

So Hroth'gar bade Beowulf welcome, and told in sorrow of soul the story of Grendel, the horror that compassed him. A bench was set for the strong-hearted ones, the Geat-men, and all were bidden to feast together. The King sat on his high seat at the head of the hall, his retainers and guests at tables on a raised platform along the sides of the room, while a fire blazed red on the earthen floor in the centre of the chamber. A thane looked to the task set him, to bear in his hands the fretted ale-stoup, and pour out the shining mead. Now and again the glee-men sang clear. There was joy among the warriors and laughter of heroes.

Weal'theow, the Queen, in her deckings of gold, came forth, mindful of courtly custom, to pass the mead-cup. She greeted the men in the hall, and then, as wife free-born, gave the cup first to the King. He in gladness partook of the feast and the hall-cup. Then the proud-thoughted Queen, decked with her diadem, went about to old and young in every part, giving the gemmed beaker, till the time came that she should bring it to Beowulf. She greeted the lord of the Geats and thanked God for the coming of one to help in their trouble. Then answered Beowulf:

"Either I will do deeds that shall free your people wholly or fall in the fray, fast in the fiend's grip."

These words pleased the lady. In her deckings of gold, she passed on to sit, the free-born folk-queen, beside her lord. Then again, as erstwhile, was brave speech spoken in the hall. In gladness were the people till Hroth'gar had a mind suddenly to seek his evening's rest, for he knew that an onslaught was purposed on the high hall by the monster so soon as they might no more see the sun's light, when night should grow dusk over all, and creatures of the shadow-realm come stalking, dark, beneath the sky. Then Hroth'gar, lord of the Scyldings, and Weal'theow, his wife, went forth from the hall with their troop of warriors. Beowulf and his men were left alone in the place. Truly the Prince of the Geats put ready trust in his bold might and in the Lord's grace. He took off his iron burnie and all his war-gear he laid aside.

"With my hand-grip shall I join with the fiend!" he cried. "And at the end may the wise God, the Holy Lord, award the mastery on either hand as seemeth him meet."

Then the brave one in battle mounted his bed, and about him many a hardy sea-farer bowed him to his hall-rest. Not one of them thought that he, thereafter, should ever again seek his loved home, his people, or the free town where he was reared. But the Lord gave help and aid to the Geat-men, such that through one man's strength the foe was defeated. The truth is made known that the Mighty God ruleth mankind from everlasting.

In the dark night came striding the walker in shadow. From the moor, from under the misty fells, came Grendel, striding. Under the clouds he went till he might see without trouble the mead-hall, the treasure house of men, brave with gold. So came he, the warring one, severed from joy. The door fastened with bars, forged in the fire, soon gave way when he laid hold of it with his hands. Bent on evil, puffed up with wrath, he brake open the mouth of the hall. Quickly then the fiend trod in on the shining floor, strode on, fierce of mood. An unlovely light, likest to flame, stood in his eyes. He saw in the hall many warriors sleeping. Then his heart laughed within him. He thought, the grisly monster, to have a fill of feasting. But Beowulf, bold of heart, was watching intently. For a beginning Grendel seized quickly on a sleeping thane and devoured him, then he stretched out his claw to reach for the hero. With set purpose, Beowulf grasped that arm in a hand-grip that had the strength of thirty. Soon found that herder of evils that never in any other man had he met with a mightier hand-grip. Grendel was affrighted, mind and heart. His one thought was to get him gone; he was minded to flee into the darkness, away to his fen-lairs, to seek the drove of devils. But he could not get his arm free. Then the lordly hall grew clamorous with din of struggle. Mead-benches many, decked with gold, fell over on the floor. The thanes awoke and panic fell on all who heard the outcry,—God's foe yelling out his stave of terror, his song of defeat. Then found he that before in mirth of mood had wrought mankind many evils that his body would avail him not. Much too strongly that one held him who had of men the strongest might in this life's day. The grisly monster, struggling, wrenched his own arm at last clean from the socket. To the fen-fells he must flee away wounded unto death, but with the valorous one he left his arm and claw. So was fame of the battle given to Beowulf. So had the wise one and bold cleansed Heorot and saved it from peril.

FROM THE TOWER WINDOW

In the morning, from far and near, the leaders of the people fared through the wide ways to see the tracks of the foe, to scan the way he trod after his undoing, how, worsted in the fight, he bare himself away to die in the mere of the monsters. Back then from the mere on their joyful way went riding the old tried comrades, men of valor, on their dapple-grays, and many a youth, likewise, measuring the yellow road with his courser. The King himself also, walked in stately wise from the Queen's bower with a great company, and the Queen with her train of women paced up the path beside him to the mead-hall, where hung the claw of the fiend, the trophy of victory. Thus Hroth'gar spake:

"Now hath a man through the Lord's might done a deed we

might none of us compass aforetime for all our wisdom. Now will I love thee, Beowulf, best of men, as a son in mine own heart. May the Almighty requite thee with good, as till now He hath ever done!"

Forthwith Hroth'gar bade men deck Heorot and prepare a feast. Gleaming with gold shone the hangings on the wall. In reward for his victory, the King gave Beowulf a golden standard, a broidered war banner, a helmet and burnie and other mighty treasures. He bade eight steeds, their harness heavy with gold, to be led indoors on the floor of the hall. These, likewise, he gave to Beowulf. Nor were the earls who came with Beowulf over the swan-road unrewarded with gifts. Then came forth Wealtheow, the Queen, under her golden diadem, to give her gifts to the conqueror. Songs and sound of playing were heard in the hall. Again rose the revel, the clamor along the benches resounded clear.

When that even came, Hroth'gar led Beowulf and his men to sleep in a place of honor, apart from the hall, but there remained to keep watch in Heorot unnumbered Danish earls, for they thought that all danger was past. Through the length of the raised platform, they spread beds and pillows. Their weapons and armor they laid by their heads, then sank down to sleep.

But Grendel's mother kept thought of her sorrow, a she-one, a monster-wife, in form like a woman. She dwelt midst the water's terrors, in the cold tarn, an outcast filled with hatred. Greedy and dark of mood, she came to Heorot to avenge her son. Into the hall she came stalking and straightway was terror there as in the days of Grendel. Some of the earls seized their weapons, many in utmost confusion thought not of helmet or burnie. But the monster was in haste and in no mood to linger. Quickly she seized in her grip one of the athelings, dearest of all to Hroth'gar, then in her other hand she grasped Grendel's arm, the trophy of victory, and made off to the fens.

FROM THE TOWER WINDOW

Loud was the outcry in Heorot. Sorrow began anew and the old King was stricken in spirit. From his rest was Beowulf fetched, the warrior crowned with victory. A steed with plaited mane was bridled for Hroth'gar and forth he fared with Beowulf midst a foot-band of warriors. They followed the track of the monster over the murky moors, along the forest ways, over the steep stone fells, by beetling cliffs, and many a monster's lair, till they came to a mountain forest, dank and foul, the joyless wood, leaning over the hoar rock, and beneath it, a tarn of black and boiling waters. Above, hung dark mists, and over all played a weird and fearful light.

Here Beowulf bade farewell to his comrades and hasted, in his valor, to plunge down into the waters. It was a day's while that he swam about, encountering many a monster ere he fell in with her he sought. Then a great claw laid hold on him and dragged him down, down to a fearsome hall, a cavern at the tarn's bottom where no water entered. By the light of fire, a flashing flame, he saw it was Grendel's mother who held him. Then the lord of the Geats shrank not at all from the strife, but seized the fiend by the shoulder. Long they struggled together. Useless was Beowulf's sword against such a she-one. He cast it aside, the strong and steel-edged, set with jewels, and trusted once more to the might of his hand-grip. At last, spent in spirit, the fighter on foot, strongest of warriors, tripped so he fell. Then the water-wife threw herself on him and drew her dagger, broad and bright-edged. So had the hero, foremost of fighters, gone to his death, had not Holy God, the Wise Lord, held sway over the victory, awarding it aright. Among the war gear on the cave's walls the Ruler of men vouchsafed it to Beowulf to see of a sudden, a blade oft victorious, an old sword of the giants, doughty of edge, the glory of warriors. Choicest of weapons it was, save that it was greater than any man else might bear to the battle. Beowulf seized it and, smiting, slew Grendel's mother.

Steadfast of thought, the hero looked through the cavern, and finding where Grendel lay dead, bore off his head as token to Hroth'gar that there lived no more such a doer of evil. Soon was he swimming that had borne erstwhile the battle-shock of the foe. In his hand the war-brand, the sword, began to melt like an icicle, for foulness of the waters where demons had died, till naught remained but the hilt, decked with dragons. Up through the waters he dove. The safeguard of sea-farers, the strong of heart, came swimming safely to land. Then went to him his chosen band of thanes who alone had awaited his coming. God they thanked, for they had thought him dead, so long had he been in the water. Forth then they fared by the footpath, joyful of heart, bearing Grendel's head unto Hroth'gar. In the hall, brave with gold, thus spake Beowulf:

"Lo, with joy we have brought thee, lord of the Scyldings, in token of glory, the sea-spoil thou here beholdest. Not easily came I forth with my life. Almost had I been over-borne, save that God shielded me. Henceforth, I promise thee, thou mayest sleep in Heorot free from care with thy fellowship of warriors. Thou needest no longer, O lord of the Scyldings, have dread of death peril!"

Then the white-haired King kissed the best of thanes and clasped him about the neck, while his tears fell for heart-felt thanks.

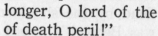

Now that Beowulf's work was done and Heorot cleansed of demons, the Geat-men were eager to fare once more to their people. So the hero, great of soul, went with his earls where his sea-goer rode at anchor. There they bade the Spear-Danes farewell and stepped into their vessel to fare forth over the swan-road, over the whale-path, home-ward to their Geat-land.

FROM THE TOWER WINDOW

THE HOME-COMING OF ULYSSES
Retold from the Odyssey of Homer

SING of U-lys'ses, the hero, who in manhood's prime fared forth with all the mighty men of Greece to conquer Troy. Ten long years he spent in labor to reduce that little-to-be-honored city that harbored thieving Paris, and when that work was done, still ten years more must wander o'er the deep, laboring to bring his comrades safely home, and longing ever in his heart of hearts for his own fireside, and Pe-nel'o-pe, his dear beloved wife, and sweet Te-lem'a-chus, his little son. Oft was he tempest-tossed and cast upon strange, savage shores where hideous monsters lurked, lured now by sweet-voiced Sirens to destruction on the rocks, tempted now by eaters of that sleepy lotus flower, to waste his days in lazy, idle dreams; and when he had o'erpassed these dangers and temptations all, shipwrecked at last through disobedient folly of his men, and borne, sole survivor of them all, clinging to a battered mast, up on the shores of fair Ca-lyp'so's isle.

Now the bright-haired nymph Calypso found the storm-worn hero half washed up upon the beach. She drew him in to safety and led him to the grotto where she dwelt. A lovely spot it was, hid far within a depth of greenery where birds were ever singing. A vine with glistening leaves and clustering purple grapes crept over all the cliff without. About grew alders, poplars prim and cypresses of resinous fragrance. Hard by, from out the rocks, four clear crystal springs gushed sparkling forth, and everywhere about, the meadows bloomed with fairest wildwood blossoms. Here in joy and plenty Calypso entertained Ulysses, and Ulysses was at first full grateful and content, but as the days passed by, within his heart awoke the longing to be once more on his way to Ith'a-ca, Penelope and home. Yet by this time Calypso of the amber hair had grown to love that wise, large-hearted hero, and had no mind ever to let him leave her more.

So she sought to charm his fancy and lull him to forgetfulness of home, nor would she lend her aid to find him any boat or craft wherein he might once more embark upon the deep. Then went Ulysses to the craggy rocks that edged the shore and there sat sorrowing all alone, gazing with tear-wet eyes far off across the sea, wishing for a well-oared galley to fly swift before the wind, longing, yearning to be home. And now for aught the bright-haired nymph might do she could not turn him from his purpose.

While thus Ulysses yearned and sorrowed on Calypso's isle, in high O-lym'pus met the gods who guide the affairs of men, and Pal'las A-the'ne, light of wisdom unto human-kind, and ever protectress of the sage Ulysses, mindful of all the hero's woes, pleaded his cause to that high-thundering Jove, her father, Ruler of Storms, and mighty King of Heaven. And father Jove, moved by her words, from his high throne of power, sent Her'mes, his dear son, and messenger of the gods, to that fair nymph, Calypso, to bid her, under pain of his severe displeasure, aid Ulysses in the building of a raft, and leave him free to start once more upon his journey home.

Hastily Hermes bound upon his feet his golden sandals that bore him over land and ocean like the wind, and down he plunged unto the deep, skimming its surface like a hovering seamew that often lightly dips her pinions in the brine. But when he reached Calypso's cave he found the nymph within.

> *A fire burned brightly on the hearth, and far★*
> *Was wafted o'er the isle the fragrant smoke*
> *Of cloven cedar burning in the flame,*
> *And cypress-wood. Meanwhile, in her recess,*
> *She sweetly sang, as busily she threw*
> *The golden shuttle through the web she wove.*

Perceiving Hermes coming, Calypso bade him welcome and placed him graciously upon the shining seat of state within her grotto. Then said Hermes:

"Nymph, Jove bids thee send Ulysses hence with speed; for here he must not perish, far from all he loves. Obey, for well

★ All the quotations from the Odyssey used in this story are from the translation by William Cullen Bryant.

thou knowest, neither god nor man hath power to withstand Jove."

Then with winged words Calypso wailed her lot, but since in truth none could withstand the purposes of Jove, at last she yielded up her will to his wise ordering and promised to obey. She sought Ulysses out and told him how she meant to give him means to build a raft, with bread and wine and water to provision it, that he might leave her happy isle, if so he chose. But ah! she cautioned him if he but knew through what great dangers he must pass, not all his longing for Penelope and home would ever lead him forth to face them all. But that great-hearted hero, not for an instant to be turned aside from his firm purpose, said, "Let come what will, I go,

> *for in my bosom dwells a mind*
> *Patient of suffering; much have I endured*
> *And much survived in tempests on the deep*
> *And in the battle; let this happen too."*

Now when the Child of Dawn, Aurora, rosy-fingered, looked abroad, Ulysses donned his mantle; and the nymph, robed all in delicate silver-white with a fair golden girdle at her waist, and on her head a filmy veil, made ready to aid the hero in his labors. She gave him first an axe and adze and led him to that corner of the woods where grew the tallest trees. Twenty tall trees Ulysses felled, and squared their trunks and smoothed their sides and wrought them by the line. Then he fitted these together and made them fast with nails and clamps. Upon the massy beams he reared a deck and floored it with long planks; on this he raised a mast and fitted to the mast a yard. He shaped a rudder next, and fenced the raft with woven work of willow boughs, to guard her sides against the dashings of the sea. Then Calypso brought him ropes and canvas wherewith he rigged a sail, and thus, his vessel all complete, he launched her in the deep. On the fifth day the nymph gave him, to put on board, a skin of dark red wine, and one of water, and a basket stored with choicest viands.

So Ulysses bade her graciously farewell, the nymph with

amber hair, and spread his canvas joyfully to catch the breeze. For seventeen days he fared in safety on his craft, till the Phae-a'ci-an shores came full in sight, where it had been foretold his sorrows should be ended. But now great Nep'tune, ruler of the sea, who held Ulysses ever in enmity, saw him at last about to escape the dangers of his realm, and, burning with fierce wrath, he urged his coursers with fair-flowing manes on through the deep to where Ulysses stood.

He spake, and round about him called the clouds,
And roused the ocean,—wielding in his hand
The trident,—summoned all the hurricanes
Of all the winds, and covered earth and sky
At once with mists, while from above, the night
Fell suddenly.

From on high a huge and frightful billow broke, whirling the raft around, and washing Ulysses from the deck. A fierce rush of all the winds together snapped the mast in twain; the yard and canvas flew far off into the deep. The billow held the hero long beneath the waters, but struggling through the waves at last, he reached his battered craft and sprang once more on board. As thus he clung in such a woeful case, a delicate-footed nymph beheld him, and filled with pity, rose up from the deep, perching on his raft, in form a great white bird.

"Let go thy raft," she cried. "Cast thyself into the sea and swim for the Phae-a'ci-an shore. Take this, my veil; bind it across thy breast and fear no danger. When thou hast reached the land, fling then my veil far out to sea."

The nymph, thus speaking, vanished and Ulysses bound the veil about his breast obediently, then plunged into the deep. Two days and nights among the stormy waves he floated, but on the third day reached a rocky shore beetling on high with crags and walls of rock. Against this he had been crushed to death, had not Pallas Athene ever informed his mind with wisdom how to save himself. So he came at last upon a smooth and quiet shore within a little cove and crept up on the beach, whence, when he had regained his breath from that long struggle, he flung the good nymph's veil as she had ordered, far, far out to sea. Then on a height above a little stream that poured its tranquil waters there into the mighty ocean, he found a pleasant wood wherein he entered, and heaping up a couch of leaves, flung down his wearied limbs, and slept.

Now while Ulysses thus found fitting rest, Pallas Athene, meaning that he should be found by those well able to save him, appeared within the gorgeous chamber where slept Nau-sic′a-a, fair daughter of the large-souled King, Al-cin′o-us, of Phae-a′-ci-a. Assuming the shape of one of this young virgin's maids, Ulysses' fair protectress said:

"Nau-sic′a-a, has then thy mother brought forth a careless housewife? Thy marriage day is not far off, and yet the garments thou hast all prepared have not been washed. Tomorrow with

the dawn, let us make suit to thine illustrious father that he bid his mules and car be harnessed to convey thy girdles, robes and mantles to the washing place, where we will wash them clean."

Nau-sic'a-a, thus prompted, arose with the bright morning light and went to seek her parents. She found her mother by the hearth, turning her distaff 'midst her maids, her father on the threshold going forth to meet his chiefs in council. Modestly the maiden proffered her request, and soon, obedient to the King's command, servitors made ready in the outer court the strong-wheeled chariot, and led the harnessed mules beneath the yoke. Into the polished car, Nau-sic'a-a and her maidens gaily piled the shining garments, while the good Queen mother filled a hamper full of pleasant meats and flavored morsels for the day's repast. Then Nau-sic'a-a lightly climbed into the car, seized the scourge and shining reins and urged the good mules forward, while her maidens trooped with merry laughter round the wain.

Now when they reached the river's pleasant brink where lavers had been hollowed out in which to do the washing, they loosed the mules to browse upon the grass, and took the garments out. Flinging these into the water, they trampled them with hasty feet in frolic rivalry as was the manner then of washing. And when the task was done, and all the garments cleansed, they spread them out along the beach to dry wherever the stream had washed the gravel cleanest. Then in sportive mood, they bathed themselves within the river, splashing sparkling jets of spray into one another's faces, mischievous in mimic battle. Once more clothed in their light robes, they spread their noonday meal upon the grass beside the river's brink, and ate of it with buzz of busy conversation. When thus they were refreshed, mistress and maids cast their veils aside and all began to play at ball. Now here, now there, the little ball went flying through the air, while all those lithe and graceful figures leapt and swayed and bounded, twinkling in the light.

FROM THE TOWER WINDOW

At length, white-armed Nau-sic'a-a cast her ball at one of her handmaidens, but the ball missed of its aim, went far beyond the maid and fell into a whirling eddy of the stream. Then all those pretty players shrieked aloud, and at that sound Ulysses was awakened from his sleep. Arising from his couch of leaves, he came forth from the thicket, and at unexpected sight of such a wild and uncouth stranger, the maidens fled, shrieking once again, to right and left. White-armed Nau-sic'a-a, only, kept her place, for Pallas gave her courage. Then Ulysses came no nearer lest he frighten her, but told her of his shipwreck and his woes, beseeching pity, and begging that she give him some old robe wherein to wrap himself, and lead him to the city. Much moved, Nau-sic'a-a bade her maids return and said:

> *"This man comes to us*
> *A wanderer and unhappy, and to him*
> *Our cares are due. The stranger and the poor*
> *Are sent by Jove, and slight regards to them*
> *Are grateful."*

Then she bade the maids bring him a cloak and tunic and a cruse of oil and leave him there to cleanse and clothe himself. And when Ulysses had washed the salt spray of ocean from his back, anointed all his limbs with oil, and donned the garments she had given, he appeared of such a stately size and such majestic mien that fair Nau-sic'a-a knew his tale could but be true. She bade him follow her until they came nigh unto the town, and then, lest men should jeer at seeing him, a man, amidst her crowd of maids, she bade him wait within a little poplar grove outside the walls till she should have had time to reach her home. Thereafter he should come alone unto her father's palace. Obedient to her wish, when she had mounted to her wain, that now was loaded with the good day's work, he followed with the maidens all on foot. But at the poplar grove he left the joyous crowd, nor took his own way forward till Nau-sic'a-a long had been at home, her mules unharnessed and her wain unladen.

At the city gate, as he approached alone, Pallas Athene met Ulysses in the guise of a young maiden with an urn, and led him to the palace, casting over him a cloud of darkness, so that no rude dwellers in the city should do him any harm. Now the Phae-a'-ci-ans were expert with oar and sail and loved naught so much as masts and shrouds, and as he went his way, Ulysses saw—

Wondering, the haven and the gallant ships,
The market place where heroes thronged the halls,
Long, lofty, and beset with palisades.

So he arrived at last before the splendid palace of Al-cin'o-us, and that friendly veil of darkness sheltered him from curious eyes, until he came where sat the royal pair, Al-cin'o-us and his Queen, and falling, clasped the good Queen's knees. Then only was the veil withdrawn and the great hero visible. He poured out once again all his sad tale. "O great Al-cin'o-us," he begged, "send me once more to Ithaca, my home!" A great-souled man Al-cin'o-us was; he raised the hero, promised him protection, and seating him upon a silver-studded throne, saw to it that he was most honorably entertained, the while the Queen, recognizing such garments as he wore, learned how he had come by them, and delighted in her daughter's goodness.

At daybreak, King Al-cin'o-us led Ulysses to the market place beside the harbor filled with ships. Thither came, too, all the Phae-a'ci-an chiefs, and when Al-cin'o-us had made known to them how that this nameless stranger sought their aid to take him to the home from which he had so long been absent, it was agreed that all should feast together in his honor that day; whereafter they would load the suppliant with gifts and in one of their own galleys send him home. There followed then within the palace a splendid feast, with singing of the blind De-mod'o-cus, bard of the silver tongue, and feats of wrestling, running, discus-throwing, wherein Ulysses much excelled, and graceful dancing of the lithe-limbed youths. When this was done, the good Phae-a'ci-ans loaded down their guest with gifts; he paid his grateful thanks

wife could scarce be credited, and going down to meet the stranger still in beggarly attire, she could not well believe that here her husband stood once more. Ulysses then, longing for sweet dawn of recognition in her eyes, proposed that all should purify themselves and sit to feast together. The while he cleansed and clothed himself, Pallas Athene once more returned him to his own fair form. And when Penelope beheld him thus, she fell upon his neck in deepest joy, and he—so long, lone wanderer o'er the earth, wept grateful tears, as in his arms once more he held his dearly loved and faithful wife.

And thus Ulysses came into his own again, to rule his people with that same benignity and wisdom that were his before, or ever he left the Ith'a-can shore to humble distant Troy.

A STORY OF RUSTEM, THE HERO OF PERSIA
Retold from the Shah—Nameh (Book of Kings) by Firdusi

N the days when the great Chieftain Saum ruled over the province of Seis-tan', there was born unto him a son named Zal, who had hair as white as a lily, as white as a goose's wing, as white as the snows on the mountain tops. For that reason, though the child's form was straight as a cypress tree, his face in beauty shining like the moon, men laughed at the Chieftain, Saum; and Saum, the hero of many battles, fell conquered as any coward weakling before the taunts and scorn of men. On a night of storm and thunder, he gave commands that his helpless babe should be left to perish on a mountain top. Now on the border of Seis-tan', far from the homes of men, stands the mountain called Elburz. Its lofty crest towers up to meet the stars; its sides are rocky cliffs so steep that mortal foot hath never scaled them. Here, far, far beyond the reach of men, the Si-murgh' has her nest, the giant bird, the bird of marvel. Of shining ebony, black as night and fragrant sandal-wood that nest was builded; around its base the cliffs were thickly veined with golden quartz, and gleamed with rubies, topaz, opals, brilliant stones of fire. From out the swirling banners of storm, a voice addressed the Bird of God and bade her save the babe. Sweeping down she took him gently in her talons and bore him to her nest, there to warm him with her own dear nestlings under her tender golden wings. In her lofty eyrie the Simurgh brought the babe to boyhood. Many a time, at her request he sprang upon her mighty back and was borne in free and glorious flight, up, up to the golden moon, in and out amongst the silvery stars, till he knew all the wonders of the heavens; then sweeping down, down over all the earth, till he knew all the wisdom of men.

But the time came when the lonely Saum repented sorely what he had done, so that even the remembrance of his deeds of valor was but as dust in his nostrils. Then he went to Mt. Elburz, found his son, now grown a youth, bowed his head to the earth before him, and besought him to return unto Seis-tan'. With grief and tenderness, the Silver-Crowned One bade his foster-mother farewell and went back home with Saum. A mighty hero he grew to be to gladden his father's heart, but the greatest moment in all his life was that wherein the Bird of Wisdom, the all-knowing Bird of God, brought unto him and his fair bride Ru-da-beh', a son, a splendid boy whom they called Rus'tem, which meaneth "delivered." "For," said the wise men, "while he liveth, will he ever stand between Persia and her foes."

Now the child was as fair as a nosegay of lilies and tulips and of marvelous strength. At news of his coming the whole land of I-ran' was given over to feasting and rejoicing. Everywhere flowers were flung into the streets, gay Persian carpets were hung from the balconies, and young and old came forth to sing and dance with mirth and music. But the great Saum himself was away at this time, fighting the Deevs of Maz-in'-de-ran, so his son sent swift messengers on wind-footed dromedaries bearing unto him a likeness of Rustem worked in silk, representing the babe on a horse, armed like a warrior and carrying a cow-headed mace. When the old champion beheld this image he was overwhelmed with delight and returned thanks at once unto Or'-muzd for this splendid gift to his house.

The boy waxed daily in strength and intelligence, but not until he was eight years old, might the eyes of Saum be gladdened by the sight of his wonderful grandson. Then, when Saum returned from his wars, Rustem went forth to meet him in the midst of a body-guard mounted on coal black steeds, with golden maces and battle-axes gleaming in the sun, while lords and nobles of the land with waving plumes and splendid banners followed in gaily decked howdahs borne on the backs of elephants, to the squealing of fifes, the blare of trumpets, clash of cym- bals and beating of drums.

When Rustem beheld his illustrious grandsire approaching, he dismounted as was meet, and humbly approached on foot, pausing before his elephant, and bowing reverently to the ground. Beholding the youth, Saum was struck dumb with wonder and joy, for he saw that not half had been told him as to the boy's stature and grace. Filled with delight, the old warrior blessed his grandson and bade him ascend into the howdah beside him. Thus the two rode together unto Za-bu'-li-stan'. And Rustem said unto Saum; "O, my grandsire, I rejoice to be grandson to such a doer of deeds as thou. For mine own desires are not after pleasure; neither do I think of play nor rest nor sleep, but ever and always I long to be a hero, performing deeds of valor, defeating those demons of darkness, the Deevs, saving Persia from her foes. And most of all now I crave a horse of mine own and a helmet and coat of mail."

Now Saum was delighted with these words, and ere he left the house of Zal again to go forth to battle he said:

"Remember, my silver-crowned son, when this child's stature equals thine, he is to have a horse of his own choosing, and all the trappings thereto. Honor this as my parting command."

Short and full were the days of Rustem's childhood, filled with many a deed of valor, and he was still but a lad in years, when the great day came whereon Saum decreed he had earned the right to choose his own horse, as had been promised. Accordingly, a proclamation was sent out to all the provinces of Persia, commanding that upon the first day of the approaching Festival

of Roses, all the choicest horses in the land should be brought to Zabulistan that Rustem might choose from among them. Soon the hills without the city grew white with the tents of traders from Ka-bul' and the Af'-ghan pasture-lands, while hordes of half-wild Tar'-tars in black sheepskin caps swarmed over the plains with their herds of dark-maned horses; low-browed men from the Cas'-pi-an, standing erect in their saddles, rode their clean-limbed animals at full speed beneath the city walls, and troops of high-spirited Arab coursers went prancing hither and yon in charge of a dignified Sheik of the desert.

On the morning of the Festival of Roses, when the meadows smiled with verdure, filling all the air with fragrance, Zal and Rustem took their seats on a beautiful golden throne just without the western gate midst a throng of people gathered together to see the splendid show. One by one, the mettlesome steeds were led for inspection before the seat of Rustem. Proudly each master approached, but though many a horse was swift and beautiful and gentle, Rustem, the powerful, bore down the weight of his hand on each and not one among them but sank to his haunches from force of that mighty pressure. Crestfallen, his master was forced to lead him away. Alas! so fared it with horse after horse, till keen disappointment filled the soul of Rustem and he knew not what he should do to find a steed to bear him. But, letting his eye rove over the field in one last muster, behold! he suddenly spied beyond the tents of Kabul, a a mare and her foal, feeding quietly on the hillside. The mare appeared strong as a lioness, but it was the colt that held Rustem's eye, for its color was that of rose-leaves, scattered on a saffron ground. It appeared as strong as an elephant, as tall as a camel, as vigorous as a lion, and its eyes fairly beamed with intelligence. Seeing this, Rustem cried:

"O sons of Kabul, unto whom belongeth yon splendid colt?"

The herdsmen shook their heads gravely and answered, "Most gracious Prince, we know not. All the way from the Afghan valleys the colt and his mother have followed us, and we could neither drive them back nor capture them. We have heard it said however that the name of the colt is Ra'-kush or Lightning because he is swift as a flash and his spirit is fire. Many have desired to possess him, but in vain. No man hath ever mounted him."

No sooner had Rustem heard this than he seized a lariat from the nearest herdsman, ran quickly forward, and threw the noose without warning over the head of the startled colt. Then followed a furious tussle, not so much with the colt as with the frenzied mother, but lo! the son of Zal strove with such mighty strength that he soon drove the mare from the field. Then he pressed his hand with all his weight down on the colt's back. But Rakush did not even bend under it! So Rustem gave a glad cry, and caressing the creature fondly, said:

"O Rakush! Rakush! verily thou shalt be my throne. Seated on thee I shall do great deeds, my beauty!"

So speaking, with a great bound the young prince leaped

upon his back and the rose colored steed bore him over the plain, with the speed of the wind. But at a single word from his master, Raskush turned and came quietly back to the city gates where the vast crowd was mightily cheering. Then Zal said unto the herdsmen:

"Good herdsmen, what wish ye in exchange for this steed?"

But the herdsmen, turning to Rustem made answer gravely:

"His price is the land of Persia. Mount him and give us in exchange I-ran' delivered from her foes!"

Thus it was that Rustem won his good horse, Rakush, and ever after they two were fast in devotion, loving one another.

Now the chief foes of Persia, in those days, were the Deevs, dark demons who dealt in sorcery. They walked upright like men but had horns, long ears, and tails like beasts and many were cat-headed. Some were small and black, but more were huge and gigantic, and ever the land where they dwelt was a place of illusions and magic. It took the heart of a hero to do battle with such as these.

The Shah over all Persia at that time was one, Kai'-kous, whose riches and power had so increased since he sat on the throne of Light, that he grew puffed up with self-admiration and pride, indulging more and more in the wine cup, until in the midst of his luxury and feasting, he beheld in all the world no man but himself! Then it came to pass one day as the vain Shah sat in his trellised bower in a garden of roses, that a Deev, disguised as a minstrel and playing sweetly upon his harp, presented himself to the King's chamberlain and with honeyed words sought entrance.

Beguiled by the charm of the youth the Chamberlain hastened at once to the King to beg an audience for him.

"O shelter of the Universe," he said, "at thy gate is a minstrel with his harp. And lo! in his throat he hides a flock of singing birds that will make thy bower a paradise. He hath come hither desiring to prostrate himself before the King of Kings, the most illustrious of all the Shahs of Iran, and he awaiteth thy commands, being naught but the dust beneath thy feet!"

The King, blinded by the flattery, so that he perceived no guile, commanded the musician to be brought before him, and the youth, having made obeisance, began to sing of the enchanted land of the genii:

"Now thus he warbled to the King*
Ma-zin'-de-ran is the bower of spring,
My native home; the balmy air
Diffuses health and fragrance there;
So tempered is the genial glow,
Nor heat, nor cold we ever know;
Tulips and hyacinths abound
On every lawn; and all around
Blooms like a garden in its prime,
Fostered by that delicious clime.

The Bulbul sits on every spray,
And pours his soft melodious lay;
Each rural spot its sweets discloses,
Each streamlet is the dew of roses;
The damsels, idols of the heart,
Sustain a most bewitching part.
And mark me, that untravelled man
Who never saw Ma-zin'-de-ran,
And all the charms its bowers possess
Has never tasted happiness!"

Now as the King's desire was to drain the cup of happiness to the dregs, no sooner had he heard the minstrel's lay of this enchanting land than straightway he became inflamed with the desire to possess it for his own, and declared unto his warriors that they must set forth to conquer it at once. Alas! the nobles when they heard these words of vanity and folly, grew pale with dread, for they had no desire to invade the country of the Deevs. But words were useless to restrain the Shah. Neither the wise counsel of the white-headed Zal would he heed, nor of any other

* The selections from the Shah-Nameh used in this story are from *Champeon's translation*.

noble. He boasted in answer that naught beneath the sun could withstand the prowess of Kaikous, the Mighty. Ere the week was out the great army of Iran was in motion, the vainglorious King at its head, his magnificent retinue of richly caparisoned horses, camels and elephants, making the earth tremble beneath their tread. So they marched, pitching their tents each night and passing the hours in revelry that ill became those about to do battle with evil. Then the King sent out his bravest warrior, Gew, while he himself remained encamped on the plain at a safe distance from the conflict and he bade Gew break down the gates of the first city in Mazinderan, sparing no man, woman nor child.

So Gew advanced, and when he was come unto the city he found it indeed arrayed in all the splendor of paradise, even as the minstrel had sung. Beauty, verdure, fragrance filled all the senses with delight while gold and jewels glittered everywhere. In the streets were beautiful maidens richly adorned, with faces as bright as the moon. But Gew knew that all this beauty was but the illusion of sorcery and that in truth the Deevs were ugly and foul. He was not, therefore, beguiled. Soon clubs rained down upon the Deevs like hail and ere night had fallen the city that had resembled a garden was become a heap of ruins.

Kaikous was wild with elation at news of the victory that he had done naught to win, and, more puffed up than ever with vanity, he gave command to plunder and pillage, taking thought of nothing at all, save only to slake his greed, and all unworthy the mighty victory over the powers of darkness, which he knew not how to turn to any good account. But over his foolish head hung the sword of vengeance. For the King of Mazinderan, hearing what had happened to one of his mighty cities, sent to the most dreaded and powerful magician in all the land, the Great White Deev, and bade him destroy the men of Iran. And the Great White Deev rose up in wrath and sent a heavy black cloud to envelope the drunken plunderers, causing stones and javelins to rain down on them out of the pitch black sky. All was terror and confusion, nor could any man protect himself. By morning, who was not fled or dead, was stricken stone-blind, and among these latter Kaikous himself. Then came twelve thousand Genii to thrust the blind men into prison. And a voice called out mocking unto Kaikous:

"Verily, O, Shah, thou hast attained Mazinderan which was thy heart's desire, wherefore be now content!"

Thus Kaikous dwelt in the land after which his heart had yearned until, the eyes of his soul being opened in genuine repentance, he bowed himself in the dust, casting black earth upon his head, and acknowledged his fault. Then, and then only, means appeared whereby he might send a messenger unto Zal.

When the Silver-Crowned One heard the sorrowful news, he delayed not, but sent Rustem at once to the rescue. Clad in his tiger-skin and iron helmet, with only his faithful steed for company, the young hero set forth on the perilous journey. Long and difficult was the way, and in many a sore extremity Rakush succored his master, saving him now from a lion, now from a dragon, keeping watch and ward over him while he slept and cheering him ever with faithful comradeship and affection.

So Rustem came at last out of a desert into the land of enchantment, and as everything here was illusion, everything seemed to the eye most beautiful. Feathered palms lazily nodded their heads, bananas flaunted their ribbon-like leaves over clusters of ripened fruit, and on the ground in rich profusion temptingly lay pomegranates, apricots, citrons. In the leaves overhead the nightingale sang, and lo! there suddenly appeared to the astonished sight of the hungry hero a table daintly spread with viands. Unsaddling Rakush and bidding him graze, Rustem sat down to break a long fast, but he ate full temperately and sang as he ate:

> *"Oh, the scourge of the wicked am I;*
> *And my days still in battle go by;*
> *Not for me is the red wine that flows*
> *In the reveller's cup, nor the rose*
> *That blooms in the land of delight,*
> *But with monsters and demons to fight!"*

As Rustem sang, his voice reached the ears of the wicked enchantress who had delayed him with the table, and changing herself into a beautiful maiden with a face of spring she appeared unto him. Her skin was like shell-tinted ivory, her lips and cheeks like the pomegranate, her soft dark eyes curtained with long, sweeping lashes, and her misty garments gave forth such a fragrance that they perfumed all the air. At her approach Rustem was enraptured. She seemed like an houri from paradise, but minding the duties of hospitality he extended to her a goblet, saying, "Drink in the name of Ormuzd[1]."

No sooner had he named the name of God than lo! that wicked sorceress changed color becoming in a twinkling black as coal. Then Rustem knew her for no houri but a witch and he snared her in his lasso crying, "Wicked creature, show thyself in thy true shape!" Whereon he held in his grasp naught but a leering, decrepit, old woman. He smote at her with his sword, but she

[1] *The Persian name for God.*

slipped from his hand and vanished with mocking, fiendish laughter. Vanished, too, were the table and viands, and Rustem lingered no more, but saddled Rakush and went on his journey.

Now he passed through a land of pitch black darkness and inpenetrable gloom, where he knew not what dangers might lurk on either hand. But, lifting up his heart unto Ormuzd for protection and guidance, he gave unto Rakush the rein and plunged boldly forward, emerging at length, thanks to the All-merciful One, into a most beautiful country where the sun was shining. Herein he found one Au'-lad, a chief, and pressed him into his service as guide, by whose aid he came at length to the fateful spot where Kaikous fell into the hands of the enemy. There he beheld the great camp of Ar'-zang, mightiest of all the White Deev's chiefs, and Arzang came boastfully forth to meet him. But in Rustem's heart was neither boasting nor vanity—only sure confidence of the hero, who forgetteth himself and knoweth his cause is just, and he seized the mighty sorcerer like a puny worm in his grasp and slew him and hurled him headlong into the ranks of his own shuddering Deevs, who beholding the fate of their chief, fled, one and all, terror-stricken before the conqueror.

Then Rustem paused not for a moment, but guided by Aulad, pressed on at once to the prison of Kaikous. Great was the joy of Kaikous and his comrades at their deliverance. They offered up thanks to Ormuzd and showered upon Rustem their gratitude. But Kaikous counseled the young hero to proceed at once and slay the Great White Deev in his lair in the Seven Mountains, ere that sorcerer learned of his coming and brought against him such a multitude of Evil ones, that not even Rustem could withstand him. And he told him that three drops of the White Deev's blood in their blinded eyes would recover sight to himself and his miserable companions.

Thus exhorted, the son of Zal vaulted into his saddle and Rakush bore him off like the wind. So they sped till they came